Praise for *Te1...*

"Prepare to be swept away by a unique and captivating fated mates romance that will enthrall you from start to finish. A fresh and imaginative take on the genre that is sure to leave you spellbound."

Judy Corry, USA Today
Bestselling Author
of Sweet Contemporary Romances

"With a Twilight feel, readers looking for a young adult urban fantasy will enjoy the hidden Elemental world of Terra. Excellent series for teen and up."

Morgan L. Busse, award-winning
author of the Ravenwood Saga,
Skyworld series, and the Nordic Wars

"Terra was a delightful surprise and kept me hungry for more. Weaving a tale of intrigue, romance, and danger, Sofia Simpson masterfully tugs on the heartstrings and crafts a tale of hope and redemption. A story to savor and an author to watch!"

Tara Johnson, Author of
To Speak His Name

Tidal

Also by Sofia

Dream Weaver

An Elemental Series
Terra
Torch
Tempest
Tidal

Operation Kane Novella Bk 2.5

AN ELEMENTAL SERIES

BOOK 4

Tidal

SOFIA SIMPSON

TIDAL

Published by Starlight Books

First Edition

ISBN: 979-8-9993845-0-8 (ebook)

ISBN: 979-8-9993845-1-5 (paperback)

Cover by: EAH Creative

Editing by: Jessica Gwyn

Illustrations by:
Damian in the Den (Vela and Linc)
Joanna Hadzhieva (Rayne)

Maps by: Sofia Simpson

To my dear, sweet husband, Matt.
This book, this series, would not be
possible without you and your love.

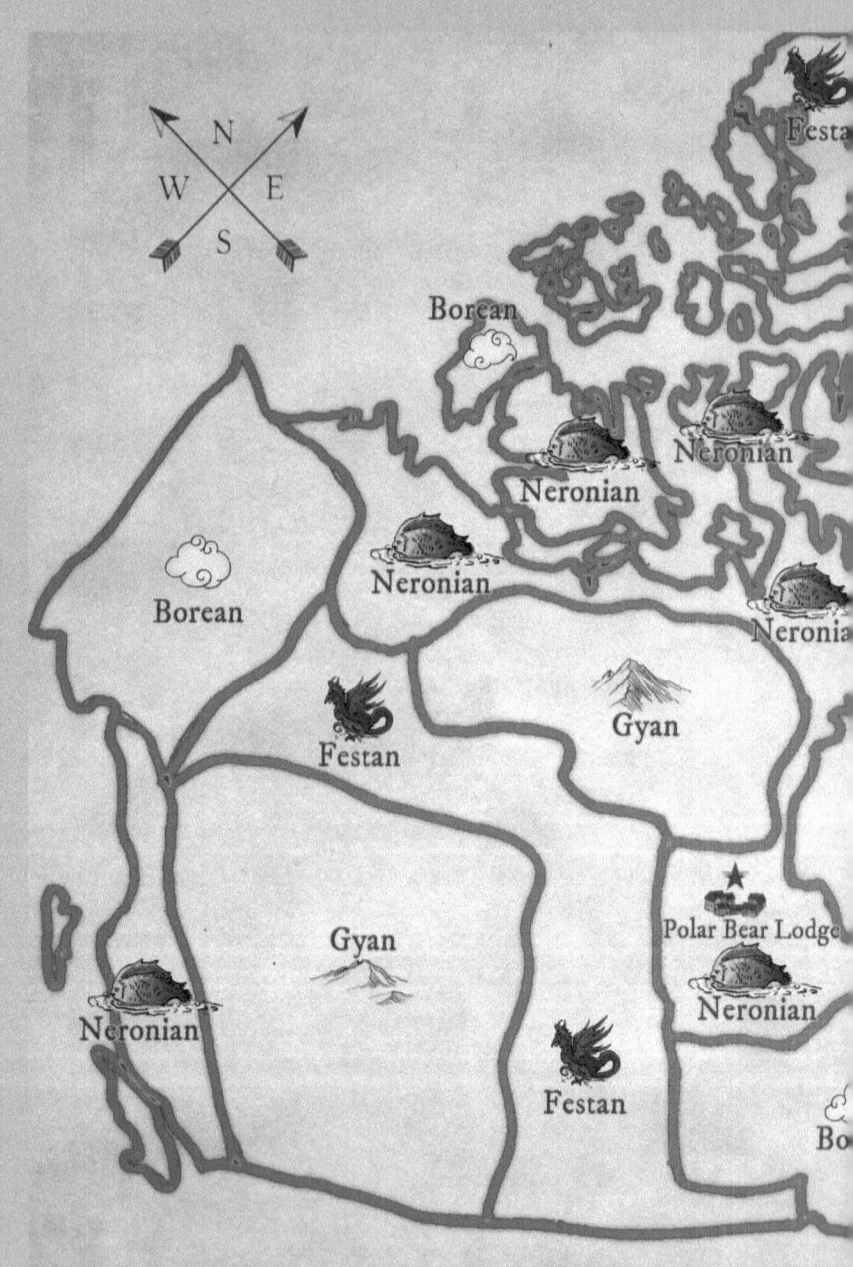

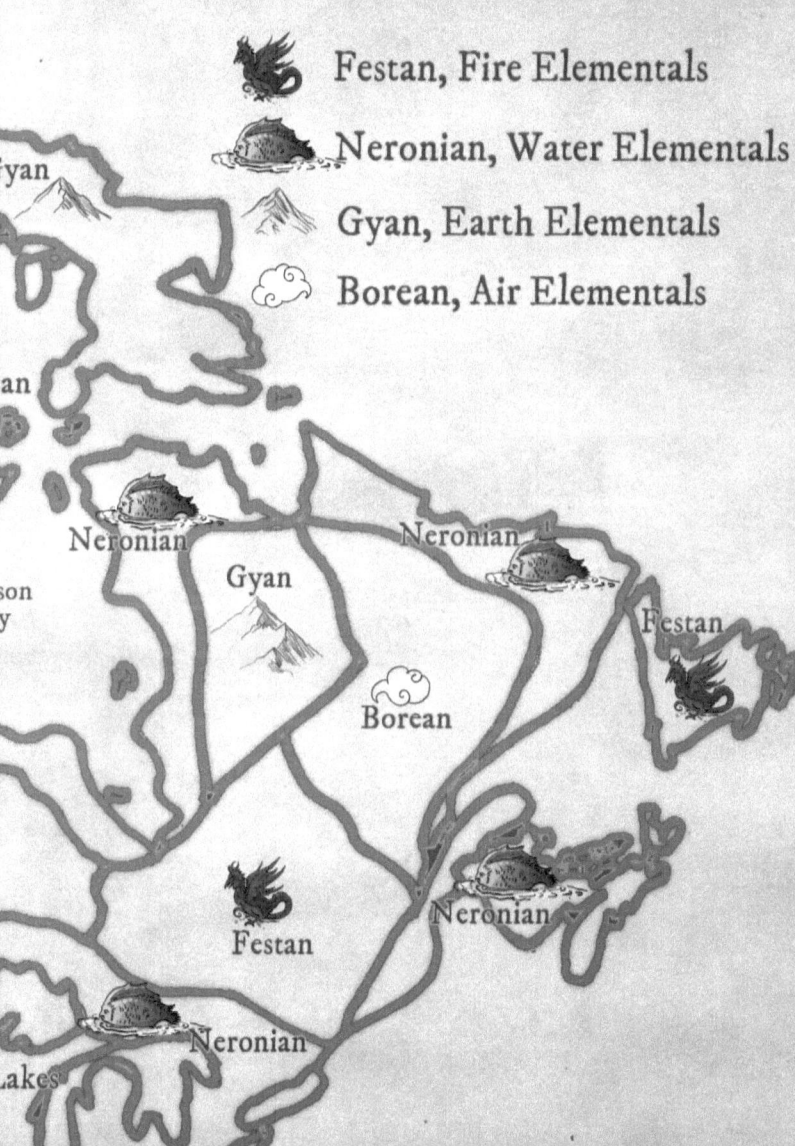

Canada
Clan Territories

Festan, Fire Elementals

Neronian, Water Elementals

Gyan, Earth Elementals

Borean, Air Elementals

As of 7/7/25

UNITED STATES

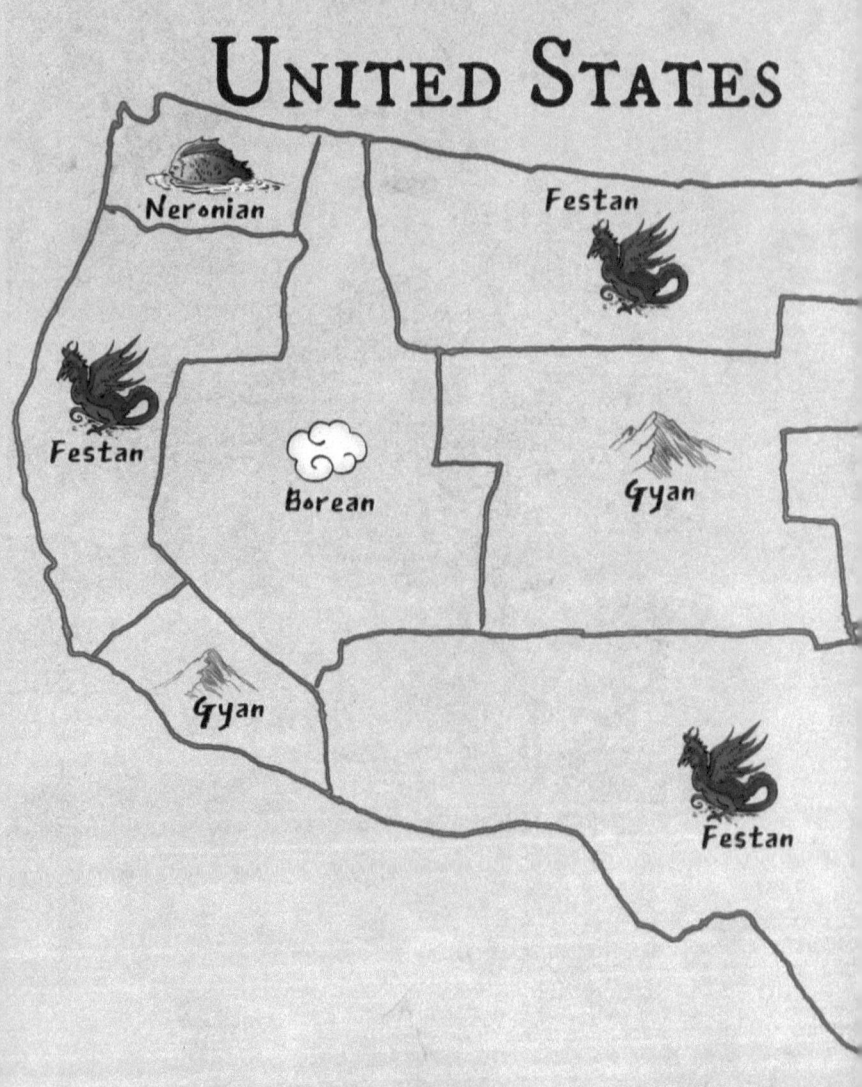

FESTAN-FIRE ELEMENTALS
BOREAN-WIND ELEMENTALS
GYAN-EARTH ELEMENTALS
NERONIAN-WATER ELEMENTALS

CLAN TERRITORIES

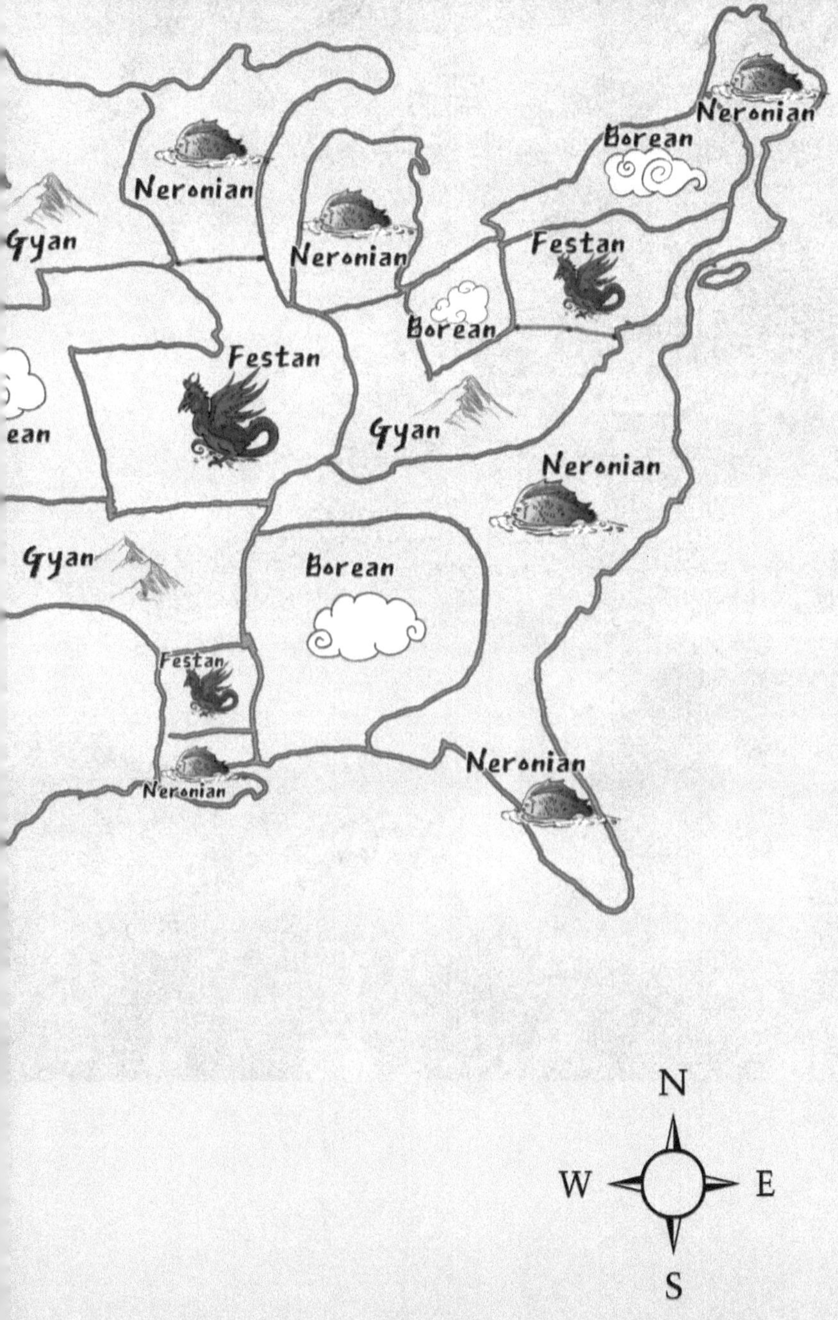

Neronian

Gyan

Neronian

Borean

Neronian

Festan

Festan

Borean

Gyan

Gyan

Neronian

Borean

Festan

Neronian

Neronian

Rayne

When the day and night are of equal length, a
warrior star who will bear the child will rise.
Under the Winter Solstice, the Hunter will emerge.
He will capture the Goat under the Northern sky
and they will produce the one who unifies.
Though their elements are diverse, through them
the Child will command them all.

Unknown
Around 1600 AD

Prologue

I f I don't protect my wife and unborn child from these Extremists, they will die. I have to do something.

My wife whimpers as I floor the gas pedal in a last-ditch effort to shake off our relentless pursuers. She groans and pulls in a long breath after a painful contraction. "The baby's coming soon. I don't have much time left."

I scour the countryside for anywhere I could lose the car tailing us. The rain will help. I decide to aid its efforts in hiding our tracks.

Reaching deep within myself, I spin the air behind us into a cyclone of water, wind, and ice. Freezing the rain isn't hard, but maintaining the force of the winds I'm creating is much more taxing. I ignore the headache pounding in my forehead and keep an eye on the road ahead of me, which is blessedly empty of cars. I'm sure to keep the new tornado far enough from us so that the winds don't drag our car in.

Praying the ones following us don't have an Air Elemental like me with them, I put all my efforts into making it impossible to follow us.

I watch grimly as the spinning storm rages. When I see the tornado following us, I stop the car and use my waning strength to push the tornado toward our attackers. They'll need to back-track quickly to avoid being sucked into the violent vortex.

Gritting my teeth, I strain as I push the tornado further. Knowing I need to save some of my strength to find a place to birth our baby. I feed my energy into the tornado until I'm sure we're safe, holding on for as long as I can.

I drop my hold on the violent storm, and without my powers it dissipates into nothing. I'm enormously relieved when I see the car that followed us is gone.

Panting, I lean over the steering wheel, gathering as much strength as I can before I turn my attention to our location.

As if God Himself placed us here, I see a farmhouse two-hundred feet away with its porch light on. Knowing it's our only chance to have this child in a safe, warm place, I steer the car in that direction.

"We're here, love. Get ready. I've found us somewhere to have this baby."

1

Vela

I'm facing a mob of thoroughly incensed Elementals. Shock roars through me when they advance. I back up, my heart beating painfully. My hands are clammy as I fist them at my sides, wondering if I'll need to use my gifts on these angry people.

"You aren't the Chosen Child, there's no way!" one woman yells with her fist raised in the air.

"You're nothing but a fake!" someone else in the mob shouts.

"The Chosen Child is meant to be a guy, not a girl!" one man screams at me, spit flying from his lips, his eyes angry with unrighteous judgment.

My mouth drops open to refute that last one, but a part of me agrees. Wouldn't it just make sense for a strong male child to take on the role of Chosen One? Doubt creeps into my thoughts, snaking through the tenuous confidence I had felt, stealing any assurance I had that I'm right where I should be. I mean, I'm one person. Can I really do this? With all the force I can, I shove that feeling down. I start to say something, but Linc beats me to it.

"Quiet!" he roars. He advances toward the mob and raises both hands.

The crowd, drawn to his magnetism, quiets to listen. The air is tight with tension but is finally free of insults.

After traveling with Jack, Linc, and our guide for two days to reach the Saddleback community in upper Manitoba, Canada, I expected a warm welcome. I mistakenly thought they would easily accept me as the Chosen Child, much like the Polar Bear Lodge did.

The Polar Bear accepted me with huge open arms, but the only arms I'm facing now are ones that are about to swing...into my face.

Jack growls, his hair sticking up on the back of his neck. I hold his collar to keep my loyal guard dog firmly by my side. We showed up an hour ago, and I've faced nothing but hostility. When they discovered why I'm here, to announce my new position, I was met with angry people wearing looks of distrust and unbelief.

I swallow convulsively to help my poor, dry throat. I desperately look around, searching for those I believe to be my biological parents. Surely, they will support my claim. But I don't see any version of me in the faces of this mob.

Linc gives me a look to boost my confidence, but then he turns to face the crowd, and his expression changes to one of fury. He's ready to take on about thirty Elementals all on his own. He allows the charged air to cool, staring the crowd down as if daring them to continue speaking.

Maybe God didn't grant me the gift of persuasion, but gave it to Linc, my Intended, instead. Makes sense. He's my soulmate, my other half. I hold my breath as he steps back and grabs my hand, raising it high.

"This young woman is Vela Ashcroft. She has been gifted by God to master *all* four elements. He's even given her the ability to take elements and bestow them on someone else. Who can deny this is irrefutable proof that she's the Chosen One?"

He takes a hard look around. When the man who screamed that I should be a guy opens his mouth, Linc puts his hand out to stop him.

"If you say she should be a guy one more time, you're going to meet my fist," he warns in a deep voice. The man scowls but wisely keeps quiet.

My heart swells at the fierce protectiveness Linc has for me. And his unwavering *belief.* He's convinced I can do this awesome and impossible act of bringing our Elemental world under one banner, not the four that represent separate clans like it is now. I desperately cling to his belief and will it to reach the deepest parts of myself so I can believe it, too.

Linc continues, "I know we've all had our own ideas about the identity of the Chosen One. But make no mistake. Vela *is* our Chosen Child. I have every confidence that this young woman will do the job. But she needs to start here. Support her like the Polar Bear has. Put your trust in this woman, who, for all intents and purposes is our savior. She will do away with the violent boundaries, the need for secrecy if you have parents with different elements. She will stop the lies the Extremists has spread about mixed Elementals. That you're evil and unnatural. Give Vela a chance to speak. Give her the courtesy of your attention as she explains the mission God has given her."

At that, Linc steps back and leaves me to speak to these people alone. He's right about me. I need to believe his assertions as much as he does. I feel his presence calming me even now.

Taking my cue from him, I inhale deeply and square my shoulders. I can do this. I face my people, my chin held high. Because they are mine. I'm the Chosen One, the one who is meant to unify our race.

Surely God wouldn't have given me this momentous task and left my fear of public speaking intact. I must trust God to provide me with the ability to share His message just as He gave me the three extra gifts: my original element, earth, my second gift, wind, and now most recently, water and fire.

Taking a quiet breath, I begin by saying, "I know I'm not who you pictured as The Chosen One. Believe me, I was as shocked as you are."

Grumbling starts, but I hold up my hand.

"Wait. Before you start voicing your very loud opinions again, just listen. I have had the enormous honor of getting to know mixed Elementals from the Polar Bear Lodge. I've seen how you've had to live, how you've had to scrape together a life for you and your families in this secret, backwoods place. All because the Extremists hunt you down for either falling in love with a different Elemental, or because you're a child of two elements. I'm prepared to right that wrong," I say in a strong, clear voice.

"What could you possibly do to make any of this right?" a man in the back of the crowd sneers and gestures all around him.

Looking intently at him, I call out firmly, "I'm going to announce my God-given purpose as The Chosen Child. I'm also going to help teach Elementals that those with two elements are not bad."

A woman gasps. "You're going to expose us?" She pulls a small child toward her protectively.

Looking at her with sympathy, I understand her fear. The Extremists have forever silenced any couple that consists of more than one element. And their children meet the same fate.

"No. I'm going to introduce all of you to our world. I'm going to elicit such awe that no Extremist would dare harm you, because I'm going to do it in a way where every Elemental will protect you."

"How?" she croaks, the color draining from her face.

"I'm inviting any mixed Elementals to travel with me and join my supporters and protection team. As a benefit to protecting me, you all can abandon your secret world and come into the spotlight with me. Join my team, and we can show the world what I can do."

At that, I nod for Linc to take Jack's collar, raise my hands, and with one grand sweep, I bring forth three elements at once. Fire bursts out of one hand and water, the other. Wind wraps around the fire and water and spins them into two tall cyclones of spiraling magnificence.

I hold my hands high, bringing my creations with me as I walk toward the shocked crowd who collectively backs away. With barely a thought, I reach for earth and create pillars of dirt to hold the two creations. I lower my hands, settling the cyclones of spinning water and fire, watching with satisfaction as they continue to rotate on their own, becoming living statues of elements.

Previously angry faces now show a combination of shock and wonder. Joy creeps into some of their expressions and my heart lifts. I don't know if it's what I promised them, or what I can do with only a thought that changed their minds, but it's working.

I'm winning them over.

A child walks toward the pillar of fire, reaching his hand out. My heart leaps in fear that he might hurt himself, but when he gets close enough for me to sense he's a Festan, I relax. He hovers his hand over the fire, his fingers trailing it and looks at the spinning flame in wonder. Then he turns to the water cyclone and laughs in delight.

He looks at me, his gap-toothed mouth stretched in a wide grin. "You did all of this? By yourself?" He looks behind me at Linc, who is grinning with his arms crossed over his chest, looking supremely pleased with my efforts. Then the boy points at Linc. "Did he help you do this? He's a Festan, I can tell."

Linc's smile drops at the question as he looks sternly at the boy. "Just like you can sense I'm a Festan, you should also feel all the elements in her." He points at me. "Go on, close your eyes if you need to."

The boy obeys and closes his eyes as he steps toward me. After a quiet moment of concentration, his eyes pop open and his mouth gapes. "It's true!" He spins around and turns to point at me. "She has all of them. She can control all the elements!"

With that announcement, the crowd starts to move like a wave. Disbelief tapers, and a sense of wonder enters into every eye. They approach to sense what I am.

With a wave of my hand, I drop my hold on the show of elements, so more can reach me. The earth absorbs the dirt from the pillars, but water from the funnel splashes on the ground, leaving a puddle. The fire collapses into a smoky cloud.

I stand still, and I'm soon surrounded by the entire crowd of once angry Elementals. Linc steps close to me, standing at my back. I hold my breath as Elementals come close, some even going so far as touching me. Gasps soon fill the air when, one by one, they all realize what Linc and I have claimed is true. They can feel the sensations of all four elements in me. Shocked faces turn in every direction as they look at each other in disbelief.

"Is she the One?"

"Can it really be her?"

"How else would she have all the elements?"

"Is there a way she inherited all the gifts?"

Linc scoffs at that statement, but I keep my mouth firmly closed. I know we need to let them come to this decision themselves.

"No! You idiot," one voice says, "you can't inherit *four* gifts, just two."

"What if two Elementals who each have two gifts have a child?"

Someone scoffs. "Even then, everyone maxes out at two gifts."

"She's got four. I can't believe it."

"Is this real?"

I almost smile at that comment. I ask myself the same thing all the time. The fact that I've been so blessed to have this great and monumental gift bestowed on me still makes my heart squeeze. But I've finally grown to accept it. If God chose me to have this position, this awesome, impossible power, I'm going to do my best to fulfill His mission.

"I need your attention." Holding Linc's hand, I step back with him until we're standing in front of everyone again. I gather comfort at having Linc always at my side, my protector.

"I have a very special message I want to share with you." When the space quiets, I say in a loud voice. "Linc has already mentioned it, but God told me He is sending me out to accomplish His will to unite the clans."

When the crowd murmurs, I hold my hands out and silence reigns again. "He also told me to take elements when necessary and gift them to others. I've already started this mission."

The voices start up again.

"Is she going to take our gifts?"

"Is that why she's here?"

"Why would she take our gifts?"

Linc comes forward at these outrageous statements. His loud, commanding voice overcomes the crowd's voices. "Listen to me. That is not what she means. Give her a chance to explain. Stop jumping to stupid conclusions."

Once the people quiet, I step forward and join Linc. "You might not have heard yet, but the Polar Bear was attacked." At the crowd's shocked gasps, I quickly say, "We overcame the intruders, but you can guess that they were Extremists. We captured the ones who weren't killed in the battle. I began God's mission by taking the Extremists' gifts and bestowing them on Polar Bear members who volunteered to take a second element."

Excited conversations burst out, filling the air with celebration. I look at Linc, relief washing over me. His eyes hold understanding and pride.

That did it. We won them over. My first job is finished. The rest should be easy.

Just when I think that the hardest part is over, my mind stops when I see a couple run into the community. They skid to a stop in front of me, their mouths open and tears already filling their eyes.

The woman has long blonde hair braided and hanging in one plait over her shoulder. Her eyes, *my eyes*, are cornflower blue and look at me with such love my knees almost buckle. I stumble back into Linc, who puts his arms around me in silent support.

I turn to the man. His eyes are green, but I hungrily look over his other features. I see my nose, mouth, and chin have come from his kind face. Because he's looking at me so tenderly, I can easily see kindness emanating from him. But there's more to his expression. He clearly recognizes me and hasn't seen me for years.

There's no doubt. These are my biological parents. James and Sandy. The ones I've been trying to find.

We're all frozen, each in our own state of shock, but Sandy comes alive first. With a cry, she rushes at me and wraps her arms around me, her sobs joining mine as she squeezes me tight. "Oh, my baby, my beautiful baby."

James laughs and embraces both of us. He rocks us, and his sobs join ours. "I can't believe we've finally found you," he cries into my hair.

Distantly, I realize Linc's arms haven't left my waist, so he's included in this group hug. It's only right that he's with us. He's as much their son as I'm their daughter.

"Mama and Papa, I'm so glad I've found you," I say with choked tears. Instinctively, I give them different names than my adopted parents. They are just as important to me as the ones who raised me, and they deserve their own distinction.

After a long moment of crying, laughing follows, and Sandy leans back to cup my face in her hands. "Darling girl, we've been looking so long for you."

James leans back but keeps his arms around us. "You don't have any idea what happened, but we can explain everything. We didn't want to give you up. It was the only way to protect you."

Sandy gives him a pained look but then nods vigorously. "We were watched for too long. We just found this place a few years ago. Before that, we had to live on the run." She sniffs as tears fall down her cheeks. Her face contorts in a painful grimace. "We never meant to lose you."

Confused at her meaning, I still don't hesitate to say, "It's okay. We'll talk about what happened later. But did you know? That I'm the Chosen Child?"

James's smile turns blinding as he and Sandy nod in unison. "We did. Too many things lined up with the prophecies that we knew on the day of your birth. When Sandy went into labor the day of the prophecy, we knew without a doubt you are the Chosen One. We've told everyone we've met about you so that they could help us find you."

I say in a rush, "Two men from here, Gene and Jerry, told us about you. They said you were looking for a daughter you had to give up. And that I looked just like you." I direct that at Sandy, and her eyes shine with tears. She turns to look over her shoulder, like she's searching for someone in the crowd.

James looks too, and when they only see the curious crowd, they look at each other with concern.

I step back from their loose embraces and lean into Linc's arms as he continues to hold my waist. "Are you looking for someone?" I ask, an ominous feeling coming over me because their expressions have changed from those of joy to suspended anxiety.

Sandy looks at me as James continues to scan the crowd. She bites her lip. "Yes, we're looking for your little sister, Adele."

My heart jumps at hearing that I have a sister. I've dreamed of such a gift for so long, but when I look again at their expressions, I ask warily, "What's wrong? Is she okay?"

"Oh, yes! She's great. She's just..." Sandy says, hesitating, looking to James for help.

He finishes, "Adele's just having a hard time with all of this. It's only been the three of us in our family for so long. She must not be ready to meet you."

Emotions crash in my chest as I hear his explanation for why Adele isn't here to greet me. Linc squeezes his arms around me, and I appreciate his show of love.

Nodding, I swallow. "Okay, well, when she's ready, I'll be happy to meet her."

At this point, the crowd is tired of being ignored. A woman approaches James and Sandy. "Do you know this young woman?" the older woman asks with a penetrating green gaze. Her voice has strength, like she's used to being in charge.

Sandy answers, "Well, yes. This is our long-lost daughter." She turns to me, her eyes soft. "I named you Evangaline. What did your new family name you?"

I croak, "Vela," my throat suddenly tight. Powerful emotions swamp me with memories of my family. I suddenly miss my mom, dad, and brothers very much. Blinking back tears, I say, "My name is Vela Ashcroft."

2

Linc

I have never been prouder of my Vela. *The Chosen One.* And I know she's mine because she promised herself to me. She agreed to be my *wife*. Pushing those amazing thoughts away, I focus on the conversation that has frozen my poor Intended in her steps. She's just found her biological parents and learned that her sister doesn't want anything to do with her in one fell swoop. Add to that a mob, and I'm surprised she hasn't melted into a puddle of tears and nerves. But she's slaying it, proving she is who she says she is.

I kiss her shoulder softly when she leans into me. A woman has just approached us and acts like the leader of this place. I'll reserve my judgement until I hear if she'll accept my girl or not.

"Where are Gene and Jerry?" the older woman turns and barks at a man behind her.

I study the woman with critical eyes. Her white and gray hair speak of experience, but it's her eyes that I notice first. The green orbs pierce everything and everyone. It's like she can see every truth or lie under your skin as easily as if you spoke them.

The man splutters, "They were here an hour ago. Where did they go?"

The woman scowls. "Find them. They were telling me of a young woman of this Vela's description. I need to know if she's the same girl."

I say in a firm voice, "She is. You can look for Gene and Jerry all you want, but I spoke to those men myself at the Polar Bear. They told me about James and Sandy, and we pieced together that Vela is the Chosen Child before she even knew it herself."

My Intended turns to look at me with surprise. I give her a reassuring look and move to stand by her side, my arm remaining around her waist. She doesn't know of my conversations with the two men because we weren't on speaking terms at the time. She needed some space after I took over the mind of her loyal sidekick and furry best friend, Jack. Jack, who has been surprisingly calm despite the tension flying through the air. Usually, when any aggression is shown toward Vela, he's the first to warn the potential threat to back off. Besides the one growl he warned the crowd with, he even allowed people to approach Vela to see for themselves that she has all four elements.

Vela hasn't let go of Jack's collar, though, except for her demonstration and joyful reunion with her biological parents. She has him back in her grip, though. Vela must have known she needed to keep Jack close as soon as she saw the angry crowd and now, too.

"Well, despite the opinion of someone I don't know or trust yet," the older woman tells me with narrowed eyes, "We will wait for Gene and Jerry."

Everyone goes quiet as if they've accepted the woman's decree, even Sandy and James. Vela, too, stays quiet. Her face is smooth and seemingly free of anxiety, but I know her well enough that the pinched skin by her eyes gives away the stress she's feeling. She's also stiff with tension.

My heart breaks for her that she's finally found the people who gave birth to her, but a sister wants nothing to do with her. It actually makes me angry, which I need to give to God right now, because I don't want to fall into that greedy pit again. I can't give into my anger like I used to. There must be a reason this Adele girl won't give Vela a chance. Maybe she will once she meets her.

I can only hope so, for Vela's sake. She has enough opposition ahead of her. Like my mother, for instance. At that, my chest heats up with anger again. I force it down and refuse to allow it to affect me.

My mother needs to accept that Vela will be my wife. *Soon.* That day can't come fast enough for me.

My heart swells at that thought. Vela has not only embraced the role of Elementals' uniter, but she took my near death and used it like a battle axe to take on two new elements added to her Borean and Gyan gifts and made them her own. All because she thought she had lost me. She's accepted God's will for her life so calmly. I'm amazed by her.

Watching her interact with and stand up to my indomitable and immovable mother just made me more in awe of my fiancée. She was fierce and so full of confidence I could only offer my silent support.

No one stands up to my mother and gets away with it.

That thought makes me nervous for my future bride. She's painted a large target on her back by crossing my mother and Vela has enough of those. In addition to the Elemental Extremists who will hunt her down to the ends of the earth, she has made an enemy of the Grand Elder of Festans.

My relationship with my famous mother has never been easy, but ever since the death of my little sister, she's been downright antagonistic. I'm more of a tool in her toolbox. She made sure I'm skilled with every kind of weapon, can dominate the art of politics, and that I am a masterful leader. She expects me to pick up her mantle.

Grand Elder positions are not inherited. This one will be, though, if my powerful mother has anything to say about it.

I don't know how I feel about that. With Vela as the Chosen Child, she'll need me more than ever. Our clans are spread out worldwide into separate entities, and we battle over boundaries daily. Vela will need my support in the massive undertaking of uniting our clans. Taking on the role of Grand Elder would allow me precious little time to devote to Vela's crusade.

But whatever God's will is, I will accept.

One thing I know for sure is that Vela will need an army of people around her to help her accomplish this monstrous goal. And this community and the Polar Bear are going to be her support.

But it looks like we'll have to get through Battle Axe Granny first. I hold in a chuckle at my name for this elderly woman who still hasn't introduced herself. We could use an indomitable presence in our camp, and it looks like this woman is one of those strong souls.

Gene and Jerry finally arrive, walking up to us at a brisk pace, looking rather harried. "Sorry Petra, we were in the middle of something and only just now heard you wanted us," Gene immediately apologizes to the older woman. Jerry's already noticed Vela and me, and he's sporting a big grin. Just then, Gene notices us when the leader, apparently named Petra, moves. "Oh, hey! You guys made it. That's great!"

Petra stares at Gene and Jerry then glances around with her hard eyes. Gene seems to understand the situation when he takes in the crowd, too. "I see you've met Vela...and Linc." He appears unsettled, and Jerry asks me, "Have you told Petra what we discussed?"

I look at Vela when I say, "We've announced to your whole community that Vela *is* the Chosen Child. God's granted her all the gifts, every element, plus more."

"More?" Gene blurts out. "She has another element?"

"No, well, kinda," Vela answers. "I have the ability to take an element and gift it to another."

Jerry laughs and holds his head in his hands. "Dad! We were right! She is the Chosen Child, and she's here! What's the problem?" he asks in a disbelieving voice. He looks at Petra's stern face. "Do you not believe her?"

Petra says in a cool voice, "It's clear she has all the elements, which is proof enough, I guess. But I want to know if she's ready for such a task."

Vela surprises me when she answers Ole Battle Axe herself. "If God thought to gift me with all the elements at 17-years-old, I guess he meant for a child to be as ready as she'll ever be. I plan on fulfilling my destiny, and I'd like your help to do that. Can I count on your support?"

At that direct question, Petra settles her cool green stare on Vela for several moments. Vela meets her gaze with one of her own.

Finally, Petra says, "Come, let's go in and discuss this further." She turns and walks into the community. They part for her like the Red Sea parted for Moses. James, Sandy, Gene, and Jerry all follow like they're used to such commands.

I hang back and wait until I know if Vela wants to follow this woman. It seems like she does when she sighs and looks at me with resignation.

"Are you sure you want to go?" I ask softly.

She nods. "We have to start somewhere. She's one of many I'll have to convince. We could use someone like her on our side."

I nod because I agree. Petra is perfect for bullying people into submission. We'll need every type of personality behind us, and her pushy ways could be quite useful.

With my sigh, Vela tugs on my hand, and we follow the team of people who will either help or hinder Vela's efforts to guide our world into unity.

The community is a blend of the Polar Bear and the First Nation one we visited. There isn't a big community building like the Polar Bear has, but then, they didn't have Andy to spearhead those efforts. Speaking of Andy, I wish he were here with us. It's just Vela and me, as our guide has already left, now that I know my way here. Since Andy won Hannah's heart, he's glued to her side. Not that I can blame him. He pined for her long enough. He deserves his time with the woman who stole his heart a year ago.

As we pass several homes, I admire the backdrop. Traveling here, we walked through red, yellow, and orange trees, but the way Saddleback has situated itself inside a haven of these brightly lit trees fills me with awe. It's like God used a fall paintbrush to decorate the edges of this community. The homes are spaced further apart than the ones in the Polar Bear, much like the First Nation settlement. Just then, I spot a blonde head pop out behind one of the houses ahead of us, but it disappears as soon as I notice. I wonder if that's the elusive Adele we've yet to meet. I glance at Vela, but she doesn't seem to have noticed anything.

Deciding to leave it alone and let things happen naturally, we arrive at the biggest home and follow Petra inside.

"Petra, is it all right if my Jack comes in with us?" Vela asks, her knuckles white on his collar. I wish she didn't feel anxious, but it's normal after the scene we just endured.

Petra frowns at Jack for a moment, then turns and waves us in.

I'm immediately hit with a sweet scent when we walk inside the cavernous space. One large room dominates the home, and I see doors that lead to other rooms and a kitchen off to one side. Vanilla and sweet fruit, like pears and apples, compete in my nostrils, and I hold my nose to keep from sneezing. I glance at Vela, and she's noticed the scent, too. Her cute nose wrinkles, and I almost laugh at the surprised look on her face.

Not that it's a big deal, but out here in the middle of nowhere, I didn't expect to come across a home fragrance. Petra's décor is also distinctly feminine, which contradicts her no-nonsense, rather gruff attitude.

Everything about this woman is a surprise.

Petra turns and once she watches me shut the door, she flicks her finger in a motion to lock it. With her wind gift, the lock engages. I also sense Neronian in her, so that's not her only trick. Everyone turns to her while an air of expectancy fills the room.

"Thank you for coming to my home. Everyone, make yourselves comfortable. If you need more chairs, you'll find some in the kitchen over there."

We make ourselves busy and once we're all seated, Petra in the biggest and most comfortable chair in the home, the leader holds court. Vela's newfound parents sit on one side of her, and I sit on the other with Jack at our feet. I'm happy Vela is at least surrounded by people who believe in her.

Petra folds her hands in her lap and begins, "I've been the leader here, as most of you know," she says, nodding her head at the residents, "for twenty years. There's not much I haven't seen, but I must admit that what you did back there, young lady," she narrows her eyes at Vela, "I have never laid eyes on. And I don't think I will again. It is truly a miracle. Now, here's what I need to decide. Is this a fluke of nature, or a miracle from God, meant to bring our clans together?"

She spears Vela with a look, and Vela's back straightens even further. "I think that I've stated my opinion on the subject already," she says firmly. "I shared what God told me Himself. The question is, what do you want to believe?"

"What I want to believe," Petra whips out, two gray lines drawn down over her eyes, "is that I have the true Chosen Child in my home. It's what all of us have wished for since we were children. My instinct tells me to be wary, however, and I always trust that feeling. It's never let me down before. Anyone here could attest to that," she says, waving her hand at the group.

I couldn't be prouder when Vela pipes up, "Could it be that you're looking for someone quite different than me? That your preconceived notions about what the Chosen Child would be like which gender, the qualities you've dreamed up, haven't been met, so you are more likely to doubt it's me than to accept the hard facts proving I am who I claim to be? You don't want to believe that God has granted these abilities to a young woman. Your Chosen Child is right here, sitting in your living room. The sooner you believe that the quicker we can start making plans to fulfill my destiny and accomplish God's mission."

Vela's words hit home with everyone seated here. I force myself to keep my hand from grasping hers in silent support. She needs to stand on her own two feet right now, and I won't distract her from that purpose. To convince these people of her true, God-given identity.

Petra digests Vela's words for a few moments. Then, inhaling deeply, she looks down at her hands clasped tightly in her lap. "You are perceptive. I'll grant you that. And eloquent," she says quietly. "Which I would imagine are abilities God would give to the one He's chosen to lead us. But I'm still not sure."

"Ask me anything. Ask me how I came to possess these gifts."

I keep my smile to myself. She'll get these people on board, I'm certain of it. I wait to see if she needs me to step in.

Petra smiles grimly. "Okay, I'll bite. How did you come by all four elements?"

Vela's voice is loud and clear as she tells the account of my near death and her grief for me, which God used to fuel her when He granted all the elements to her. "So, you see. I have a job to do. I was born with the Gyan gift, thanks to my parents here," she nods at James and Sandy, who beam proudly at her. "I was coming into the Wind element this past month, which I hear is normal for someone born of two different Elementals. But, after the battle with the E.E. at the Polar Bear, when I thought I had lost Linc..." her voice cracks and she clears her throat. "When I thought I'd lost Linc, I sank into a vision. That is when God spoke to me of a mission to take and give away the elements. No one, not even you, can convince me I imagined that conversation. I heard God's voice, and I'm ready to obey."

Petra leans back at this story of life and death. Something it seems she's familiar with, if the grief in her eyes is any indication. "You can take away the power in our veins? Just like that?" There's a warning in her voice, and I tense at the danger I suddenly see for Vela.

Vela nods, unaware of, or just ignoring, the change in the air, and says, "I can. I don't take this new gift lightly. I've only used it to administer justice to the Extremists who attacked the Polar Bear. The ones who were left alive, anyway."

Petra's voice gets harder. "You took their gifts? Permanently?"

She must know about the Neronian's secret gift of taking a gift away momentarily.

Vela nods. "As of the day we left the Polar Bear, the gifts I took remained with those I bestowed them upon. I don't know if I need to be present for them to continue to stay with the Elementals who volunteered for the task. We'll see when I return."

"What's your plan going forward?" Petra asks, a calculated look taking over her hard eyes.

Vela promptly responds, "Like I told your community, I would like to gather the support of mixed Elementals to travel with me and announce my identity and mission to the Elemental world. In so doing that, mixed Elementals will be seen in a positive light traveling with me, instead of as dangerous, the way the E.E. paints with their lies."

Petra's face twists in a scowl. "I agree that we need to right those wrongs of the vicious lies." Her eyes turn thoughtful. "I'm surprised you would take that job on."

Vela's voice is like steel as she says, "You are all stuck out here, hiding because the Extremists have hunted for me among your ranks. They've known the Chosen Child will have two different

Elemental parents for thousands of years. Your community, and others like it, have children like that in spades. It's only because I'm here that you can finally escape this hidden lifestyle."

Petra's look shifts. It's subtle, but I see it easily. I've had a lot of practice reading body language, and she looks like she's becoming more open.

She turns to James and Sandy. "This is your daughter? You're certain of it?"

James and Sandy both nod vigorously. "How could you deny she's ours? She looks just like her sister," James says in a gruff voice. He looks proudly at Vela, who smiles at him in response. "She has Sandy's Gyan gift and my Borean gift, well she started with those two. We proudly claim her as our long-lost daughter."

I turn when I hear the choked noise Vela makes.

This time, I don't hesitate. I reach and grab her hand.

3

Vela

I barely hold in my emotions at hearing my new Papa announce that I'm his daughter. I've been my adopted dad's daughter all along but knowing that James and Sandy have been searching for me for years and that we've finally found each other is about to overwhelm me. Jack whines as his nose nudges my knee. Petting his head, I rein in my feelings.

Linc grabs my hand, and his eyes search mine, his concern washing over me. I hold my breath, not allowing the overwhelming emotion of finally being reunited to take over. This is not the place. Not in front of Petra, who looks like she could chew nails and spit them out at my feet. I'm not sure she would suffer a breakdown from me and even less from the Chosen Child.

I squeeze my eyes shut, willing the tears to fade. *Don't let them see me go to pieces,* I tell myself over and over.

Petra's voice surprises me. It's filled with compassion. "Vela, you have every right to feel what you do. You've only just found your lost parents. You are allowed to feel emotional. There is no shame in that."

Tears slip down my cheeks at her permission, and I sink into my mom's side embrace. I sniff when I feel James come to us, too, wrapping his arms around the both of us.

One thing is for certain. Petra is a born leader. I have a strong feeling that if I could learn even a fraction of what she knows, I would be a very fortunate woman. Suddenly, I feel fiercely that I want her to leave this place with us. Respect for her swells inside me.

I let go of the steel grip I have on my emotions and give myself a minute to cry and hug my new parents. After several moments while Petra gives us time to be a new family, I inhale deeply, wipe my eyes, and lean back. James cups my face and smiles tenderly at me. He gives me an encouraging nod as he wipes his own face dry. Mama squeezes my hand, smiling at me through her tears. "You're doing great," she whispers.

A sense of love and relief helps all the anxiety pent up in me wash away like a flood. I didn't realize the stress I felt, not knowing who my biological parents were until this moment when I finally let it go. I squeeze my birth mother's fingers and relish the feeling of her hand in mine. Straightening up, I let go of her hand and reach for Linc's again..

He's my lifeline in this whole chaotic mess. He's my direct source of comfort and peace, and I need his love desperately.

I reach inside to gather my tangled feelings and put them back in some semblance of order. Looking at Petra, who's talking quietly to the man next to her, I clear my throat. I appreciate her giving my family and me our moment more than I can say.

Petra sits up in her seat and smiles at me. We've somehow turned a corner in our fragile and new relationship, but it seems like whatever she was looking for in me, she finally saw. Maybe one day she'll tell me what my small breakdown told her about me.

"Now I know what you can do and what your plans are, but I want to be sure I understand," she says formally.

I wait with bated breath.

Petra leans toward me, and she again spears me with an intense look. "You want my people, my community, to come with you to tour the world? To help protect you and free our mixed heritage from the lies the E.E. has told others about us?"

I nod. "Yes." I can't help but feel my hand sweat as I squeeze Linc's. Somehow, I know this moment is important. If I can get her on my side, others will follow. She wouldn't tolerate anything less.

At my answer, she nods briskly and leans back in her seat. Then she turns to look around the room. That's when I notice that Gene and Jerry are literally sitting on the edges of their seats. They look like they're ready to jump up and leave for our world tour right now.

Hope surges in my chest. Maybe, just maybe, I've said and done what I needed to gain this community's support.

Petra's voice commands the room, like before. "Gene and Jerry, we need to hold a council. I'm not going to force anyone to do something they don't want to do. We need to decide as a community if we're going to support this young woman. But I, for one, believe her."

At that, several people in the room inhale. I can't help but feel thrilled blood shooting through my veins. I turn my surprised face to Linc, who's smiling at me widely. He nods at me; his gaze loaded like he knew this would happen all along.

I turn to Petra and hold in my questions. What changed her mind? What did I say to convince her I am the Chosen One?

"Now, we have a lot to do. Everyone can leave here except for Gene and Jerry. James and Sandy, I'm sure you'd like to spend some time with your daughter, or both of them, I should say. Has Adele met Vela yet?"

Our faces fall, and she nods as if she understands. She knows Adele better than I do, so it's conceivable that Petra understands

Adele's reluctance to meet me. "Well," she says, "it looks like you have some things to sort out."

And just like that, we're dismissed. I stand up and Linc leads me, Jack, James, and Sandy outside.

I walk with numb legs as Linc pulls my hand. *What just happened?* First, the mob, then my parents and a sister who apparently hates me, then I somehow, someway, convinced Petra to accept me as the true Chosen Child.

I'm still not sure how that happened. But I'm not going to look a gift horse in the mouth. I'll take this as a huge win in my efforts to complete my mission.

Sandy turns and wraps her arm around my side. "Now, it's time to find that sister of yours. She owes you an apology."

I stop in my tracks. "No," I plead. "Don't make her feel bad for not wanting to meet me. She's entitled to her feelings and," I bite my lip, "I'd like to meet her on her terms, not ours."

Sandy studies my eyes and finally nods. However, it's James who says, "Well, be that is it may, we've raised her to have manners. Let's hope she remembers them. You're going to be a guest in our home. She can be civil. No reason for her not to be."

Once I think about it, there are a lot of reasons she might resent my presence. I'm sure James and Sandy have filled her head her whole life with their staunch belief that I'm the Chosen One. She has no reason to believe that I can be successful, neither do I, for that matter. But I'm going to try to convince her to help me. And she's had her parents' sole attention her whole life. I don't expect her to be happy about sharing it with a sister she's never met. I vow to do my best to win her over. She's my sister. Blood runs thick between us. I intend to treasure her, the sister I've always wanted.

James asks Sandy, "Where do you think she is?"

I'm surprised when Linc says, "I think I know."

Since we have barely stepped foot in this place, my mouth drops open at his statement. He smiles and puts his finger under my chin, closing my gaping lips. He says, "I've spotted her hiding around the buildings since we arrived. She isn't far. The last time I saw her, she was behind that house." He points two log houses down and sure enough, I see a blonde head pop out, and when the girl sees our attention on her, she quickly ducks behind the building again.

My heart squeezes at the one look I've gotten of my sister. She's younger than me by about two years, if I had to guess. But it was the look on her face. She's *worried*. I do not want to be the reason for her anxiety.

When James grunts and starts walking toward the house that conceals his other daughter, I pull on his arm to stop him.

"Wait. Let me talk to her. It's obvious she knows who I am. Let us meet alone the first time."

Sandy worries her lip with her teeth, and James gives me a doubtful look. "Are you sure?" he asks.

"She can be a lot," Sandy says. "And she's upset. Maybe we should be the ones to break it to her."

Linc laughs. "I don't think there's any doubt about who Vela is to you two. Anyone can see the resemblance. Maybe Vela's right. Maybe they need to meet just the two of them." He puts his hand on the small of my back, and I lean into it, needing his belief to leak into me.

Now that I've suggested it, I'm terrified I'm going to mess this up. What if I say something that Adele won't forgive? I push away those dispiriting thoughts and focus on James and Sandy. "Let me try, at least."

They both reluctantly nod. I inhale deeply, order Jack to stay behind, take one last look at Linc, who gives me a soft smile and takes over holding Jack's collar. Then I walk toward the building we last saw Adele hiding behind.

I make it to the back of the building, but she's gone. Looking around, I see a form dashing toward the woods.

Shaking my head, I take off at a run. This is my sister; I won't give up on her. Sprinting, I see the back of her head as she dodges trees, zigzagging around the clusters that surround the community.

I take a guess where she's going. There's an outcropping of rocks to the right with a dense amount of trees, somewhere she could more easily hide. I take a shortcut, spreading the bushes that stand in my way, so I have an easy path.

Coming out the other side, I skid to a stop and see I've popped up directly in front of her. She stops so suddenly, I'm afraid she's going to fall over, but she just pinwheels her arms and, with narrowed eyes, spins around to run in the other direction.

"Wait," I cry. "Give me a chance, just one! Please?"

She stops, her back to me. Her breath heaves in and out in the cool air, and I hold mine as I wait for her to decide whether she'll listen to me.

Heaviness in my chest lifts when she turns around slowly. Her hands are in fists at her sides, and I prepare myself for an attack. Just how angry is she at me? Will she attack?

I pray she doesn't.

I drink in her face. She's the spitting image of me, besides her hair. It's not quite as long as mine and has James's slight curl to it. I could be looking in a mirror from two years ago. I hold my hands up, asking her wordlessly to stay.

"Please, give me one chance to talk to you," I ask. Then I pray for the right words. I fist my hands, so I don't reach for her and pull her into a hug she clearly doesn't want. Her face is so distrustful, my heart pinches. "My name is Vela. You're Adele?"

She glares at me, her face a stony mask of anger.

"Okay, so it's pretty obvious we're sisters. I've always wanted a sister, have you?" I hold my heart, like I could stop it from squeezing with pain. She wants nothing to do with me.

Not yet, I tell myself firmly.

Her face gets even more angry, if that's possible.

"Look, I know you don't want me to be here. But I am here, and I'd very much like to get to know you. I'm sure there are so many things we can talk about."

Her lips thin in displeasure, and she remains silent. She turns her body like she's going to run again. I can sense it in her emotions. Wild fear laced with sorrow runs so strongly in her, I can taste it.

"Hey, don't go. I'm sorry for how I just came into your life without warning. But I want you to know I'm here for you, always. I've just met you, and I already love you. You're a part of me, as if we've always known each other. I don't want you to worry that I'm going to take your parents away from you. But I'd like them to be in my life, too, all of you, now that I've finally found you."

Her face crumples for a moment, then she sniffs, and it's back to a blank mask of fury.

I can't help it. A tear falls loose from my eyes. My emotions are all over the place, especially since I can feel hers beating against me so harshly. I meant every word I just said. How can I convince her I'm her friend, not an enemy? "I can sense that you're scared, angry, confused, and maybe a hint hopeful. Can you also sense my emotions, or is Gyan your primary element, too?"

At my words, she turns her body toward me, like she's willing to talk. When she sees my loss of control, her eyes track my tear and a crack in her harsh demeanor shows. She bites her lip and looks away. Then I realize she's crying, too. As the first few tears slip down her cheeks, she suddenly breaks out in a sob. She holds her face, and her shoulders slump as she crumples to the ground.

I couldn't stay still if my life depended on it. I run over to her, my knees skidding in the earth. I pull her into a hug, squeezing her tightly as my tears join hers.

Holding her head, I press my cheek to it and cry at all the opportunities we missed out on not growing up together. She's clearly suffering, and I hold her as she sobs. We sit there for what feels like an hour, but must only be a few minutes. I'm not exactly sure. I pray that God will soften her heart to me and that we can be loving sisters. I pray harder than I've ever prayed in my life.

Finally, her sobs quiet, and when I only hear sniffles, I lean back. She allowed me to hold her, but she hadn't held me back. Will she accept me in her life?

Wiping my eyes, I wait for her to look up. When she does, she takes one glance at me and gives a soft cry. She wraps her arms around my neck. I don't know what she saw on my face, but apparently it meant something to her, because her sobs are back. I hear her voice for the first time when she says, "Your name is Vela?"

I nod as I hold her back.

She leans back and studies my face with a look of wonder. I know what she sees: a picture of what she's going to look like in two years. "But my mom named you Evangaline," she says, hiccupping.

I laugh softly. "She should have put that on the note she left in my basket. My mom gave me a name when I didn't have one."

She nods as she studies my features. Her eyes still swim with tears and when one slips down her cheek, I brave the desire to wipe it away. She smiles when I do and puts her hand on mine against her cheek. "I'm sorry," she whispers. "I was so afraid."

"Afraid of what?" I ask softly and search her eyes that now look troubled again.

She shakes her head and looks away, dropping her hand. "I've imagined meeting you my whole life. I've thought of every scenario. You being nice, rude, bossy, everything. But," she twists her lips and looks back at me with a measure of remorse in her expression, "not once did I imagine you saying what you just did. I thought..." her face crumples and more tears fall. Sniffing, she wipes her tears away impatiently. "In every scene I imagined, you took my parents away from me. I was sure you'd want to change everything."

I smile sadly. "I would never come between your relationship with Mama and Papa."

At my names for our parents, her face brightens. "That's what I call them, too."

"Really?" I ask, smiling. "I call my adoptive parents Mom and Dad, so I gave our parents different names." I reach and hold her clenched hand. "I promise you, I might bring some changes in your life, but never will I ask our parents to love you any less. Just add me to your family. Please?"

She hesitates and then nods. "Where have you been? Mama and Papa have been looking all over for you."

"Well, I guess it was a good thing they had a hard time finding me." When her face transforms into hurt and confusion, I rush to say, "Only because if they couldn't find me, then the E.E. would have had a hard time as well." My mouth twists in a frown. "They still found me, though, despite our best efforts."

Her eyes lose their wariness. "Mama and Papa did everything they could to find you, but then the E.E. found us and we had to hide out here for the past few years." She looks around and sniffs, wiping her face clean of the last of her tears.

"I'm sorry," I say, squeezing her hand. "How has it been?"

She shrugs. "It's not bad. I miss having a computer, though. I'm a graphic designer, or at least, I enjoy the process. I'm okay at hand drawing, but my real love is creating graphics on the apps I had."

My heart lifts at hearing her share something about herself. Then it tightens again at all the time we've lost. I'm crying before I know it, and I let go of her hand to cover my eyes. "I'm sorry," I choke out. "There's just so much I don't know about you, so many years we've missed out on."

I feel tentative arms come around me. My heart swells painfully at the contact, and I take a minute to relish it. I hold her arms and cry at the pain of our missing past, but I have tears of joy, too. We have the rest of our lives to get to know each other.

I will take every moment God gives me with my long-lost sister and treasure her dearly.

After several minutes, I straighten, wiping my face with my shirtsleeve. Smiling, I cradle her face in hands and just look at her lovingly. She laughs and puts her hands on mine. Soon, we're both laughing.

After we bend over laughing for long blissful moments, we finally straighten.

She says, her nose scrunching, "It's weird. You look exactly like me."

I laugh again, holding my aching stomach. "I know." I shake my head. "I almost can't believe it."

She shakes her head, too. When I think of our parents who are probably worried for us, I hold out my hand. "What do you say we go back? I think we're probably giving our parents a heart attack, not knowing what's happening between us."

She nods, her eyes a little sad.

"What's the matter?" I ask, still kneeling.

"I'm sorry I worried them...and you," she says softly.

I hold her shoulders and give her a nudge to look at me. When she does, I say, "They understand. And I do, too. But let's not make them wait any longer."

We both rise to our feet. She holds out her hand and with a big smile, I grab it, holding it tightly. We start walking back and she snorts at the path I created to reach her. "I can't do that yet."

I look at her with surprise, then realize the sensation I'm getting from her is Borean. Her dominant gift is James's, not Sandy's. Interesting. Well, that's one difference between us.

I shake her hand. "You will. Give it time. I'll teach you how to do it myself when you're ready."

She smiles tentatively at me and then asks, "Who was that guy with you?"

I grin at her. "My Intended."

She gasps and almost stumbles. "You found your Intended? How?"

I happily tell her the story, and when she admonishes me for giving Linc a hard time when we first met, I accept her scolding. "I should never have rejected Linc. It's one of my biggest regrets," I say with a sad smile.

"As it should be," she says firmly. Then she adds wistfully, "If I ever find my Intended, I will never let him out of my sight."

My heart breaks at her words, because the chances are so slim she'll ever meet him. But maybe, just maybe, if I'm successful in bringing our world together, she'll have a better chance.

I have yet another reason to succeed in my mission.

4

Rayne

I'm sick and tired of hiding as I follow Vela and Linc around, but I have little choice. If I want to get my gifts back, Vela's the only one who can return them to me.

From what I've seen, she is facing a lot of pushback from the Saddleback people at her claim to be the Chosen Child. I wonder if she'll get this reaction in every Elemental community.

As I watch, I'm impressed at how she's standing up under their onslaught. Linc would never allow any harm to come to Vela, so I sit back and watch the show. If they need my help, I wouldn't hesitate. I would aid them.

Thinking of when Vela came into her power as the Chosen One makes me cringe. I've run the gamut of dark emotions, but the dominant one is guilt. I never should have tried to kill Linc, and I can't say how relieved I am that he's alive. Hannah is a truly gifted healer to heal him of my death blow.

I was just so angry and hurt that Vela and *my* community had accepted him so easily. It was so clear to me that he was the reason the Polar Bear was attacked. They should have held him accountable, not allowed him to lead the inquisition of the captured E.E.

They should have been *suspicious* of him, not so welcoming.

Anger still flows through my veins at that memory, but I shove it aside as I watch Vela put on a show of her gifts. Even I must admit, it's undeniable that she is who she claims to be.

I had a feeling Gene and Jerry were onto something when they talked about the couple looking for their lost daughter. What happened that they had to give her up?

I wonder if they knew she was the Chosen Child. If so, then they must have had to hide. I had no question before that Vela was the One, but now, it's cast in cement. Vela is who Gene, Jerry, her parents, and I thought. The fact that she stole my powers was just further proof. She's the Chosen One.

Even now, I deeply mourn the loss of my gifts. I can't believe she took them like that. She couldn't have a rational discussion with me first? Well, I guess after watching Linc drop when I sliced his throat open; she wasn't exactly thinking clearly.

Will she ever forgive me? I've abandoned all hope that she could ever care for me. When I watched her lose it over Linc, I knew I had no chance of winning her. It's funny. I thought I would always hold a torch for that girl, but that scene of Linc dying changed my feelings, too. I want someone to love me like Vela loves Linc. It was clear from the beginning how he felt about her. But I always wondered how much of that was their Intended bond and how much of it was them.

I scoff. It doesn't matter. They're together, and I wouldn't think of coming between them now. For the first time, I wonder what it would feel like to find my Intended. I know I have one somewhere. I just never gave myself any hope of finding her.

And now, I'm half a man. I'm not even an Elemental any-more. At that thought, my chest spears with pain. Would my Intended want me like I am?

Brushing that thought aside, I know the chance is so small I'll ever find her that it's not worth thinking about. Instead, I process what happened. After I nearly killed Vela's Intended, I guess it's fitting that she would punish me in the most terrible way she could. I'd rather she killed me than take away my wind and water, though.

I don't even recognize myself. She's stolen my entire identity, the very root of who I am.

Cursing quietly, I peer around the trees and see that Petra is leading Vela and Linc and a small group of people away. A couple in the group look like they could be Vela's biological parents. That must be them. The woman has long blonde hair and, from what I can see, looks a lot like Vela.

It seems Vela's gained the support of one of the toughest people I've ever met. Petra has that effect on people. I've never seen anyone question her judgement or decisions. If Vela gets that woman behind her, she's going to do just fine as the Chosen Child. I haven't been to Saddleback in a number of years, but time doesn't erase the impression that no one crosses Petra.

How am I going to get Vela to give me my gifts back? I lean against a tree and run that question through my mind again. I need to get her alone, for one. I'm sure I could convince her if she would just listen to me without Linc there to sway her mind.

Vela has not only my gifts, but my support as well. I believe that she can unite our world. I'll just have to help her behind-the-scenes until I can speak with her and convince her to return my gifts.

I'm no one without my gifts. No one.

I've followed Vela to Petra's house a short distance away and wait about thirty minutes for their meeting to be over. I straighten when I see Vela, the couple who looks like her, and Linc leave the house. They seem to be looking for someone. I duck behind a tree when they turn in my direction. But when I look again, I see Vela run off to the opposite side of the community. I don't hesitate to follow. Skirting trees, I give Saddleback a wide birth and make my way around the community, straining to hear voices.

If I remember correctly, she ran in the direction of the rock outcropping close to the homes. I take off in that direction, making sure my footfall is quiet as I run. I've had a lot of experience hunting, and I've learned how to run through the trees like a ghost.

When I reach the rocks, my gamble pays off because I see Vela talking to a teen girl who has long blonde hair, similar to Vela's. When I squint my eyes, they widen when I see how much the girl looks like Vela.

Something about this girl makes my heart beat faster, wilder. I hold my chest, wondering what is wrong with me? I can't tear my eyes away from the girl who appears to be Vela's sister, and when I realize I'm staring, I squeeze my eyes shut.

What am I doing?

Confusing feelings tear through me. I have an irrational desire to approach this girl. Blowing out a quiet breath, I steel my muscles, forcing myself to stay where I am. Fisting my hands, I try to get hold of my foreign emotions. I want to meet this girl. No, it's a *need.*

Flustered, I ask myself, *Why am I so drawn to this girl?*

Is it because she looks like Vela? I hate myself right now. I'm so disgusted that I open my eyes and force myself to watch the exchange between the two girls.

Vela is holding the young one now, as they kneel on the ground. When I see the teen girl's shoulders shaking, a hot, visceral reaction shocks me when I want to jump up and see what's wrong.

Blindly, I flee. I'm barely able to quiet my footfalls as I race away.

What is the matter with me?

I pump my arms and bury my thoughts deep inside. I do the only thing I can. Run and put distance between myself and the one who twisted my insides into a strange mess.

5

Linc

I'm not surprised when Vela emerges from the trees holding her little sister's hand. They walk toward us, swinging their arms and smiling widely. Jack tugs on his collar, trying to get to Vela, and I let him go, chuckling when he bounds over to her, his body wiggling in happiness.

Relief fills every part of me because Vela would have been devastated if she had failed in forming a relationship with her just-found little sister.

I'm shocked at how much the girl looks like my Intended. I try to keep my surprise to myself, but I must fail because James and Sandy laugh at my expression.

"We couldn't believe how much they look alike, either," James says as he proudly watches his girls approach.

"They're like mirror images of each other," I say in awe.

"I guess Vela won her over," he muses with a contented smile.

"I had no doubt she would. Vela would tolerate nothing less than a good relationship with her sister."

Sandy watches proudly, too, but her look is more emotional. She passes her hand under her eye, and I realize she's crying. James notices too and puts his arm around her shoulders. She sniffs. "Seeing them together is a dream come true, one I wasn't sure we'd ever see in real life." She wraps her arms around her middle, like she's holding herself still.

James puts both hands on her shoulders and gives her a slight push. "Go, baby. Go to your girls."

Without any further hesitation, she runs toward Vela and Adele, who match her movements, and the three of them meet in a tangle of arms. They all hug each other.

Glancing at James, I ask, "Don't you want to go join them?"

"More than anything," he says in a hoarse voice, his eyes reflecting a world of pain. "But it's my fault she had to give our child up. It's only fitting she enjoys this reunion first."

Puzzling over his guilt, I think I'll ask later what he means by that. It must have been an impossible choice to give up his child.

When the girls finally emerge from their embrace, they look at us and wave James over to join them. Jack barks, agreeing with them.

With a pained smile, James walks to them, his fists clenching, like he's trying to contain his gift.

I understand that feeling. When an Elemental's emotions are especially high, it's easy to lose control. I can imagine James is feeling powerful emotions right now. I notice the air whipping the tops of the trees, but I don't know if that's Vela's emotions getting away from her or James's.

I wait for Vela's family to spend some much-needed time together. I half think I should make myself scarce, but when Vela keeps looking my way, I know that wild horses couldn't drag me away. I'll be here for her in any capacity.

I pray we'll never be apart from each other again. Losing her in the woods was the most miserable experience of my life. Knowing she was completely under the spell and power of the enigmatic and handsome Rayne nearly drove me crazy.

The situation ended with me in the arms of my Jesus, though. I smile at the memory of giving my life back into the hands of the One who is in control of all things in this wild world. One that He's tasked Vela to fix by bringing the Elementals together. It's a seemingly impossible mission, but if He thinks Vela can handle such a job, who am I to argue?

I'll be her strongest support, her other half, whatever she needs me to be.

As if I've drawn her to me with my thoughts, the group walks back, and I realize I don't know James's and Sandy's last name. Will Vela keep her Ashcroft name or take theirs? Then my heart stills. *Wait, she's going to take my name.* That thought makes my lungs squeeze so tightly, I have to take a deep breath to bring air back into my chest.

I'm marrying this girl soon. I can't wait for her to truly be my other half, to share my name. I already feel like she's a part of me. And it's more than the bond. It's all her.

Vela asked for us to come here before we found a state where we can legally marry since she's still seventeen. I agreed because I knew how important it was for her to find her biological parents.

Now that she's found them, I chafe at waiting to embark on our next mission: our wedding. I force my impatience aside. Vela and her new family need time together, and I can wait a bit longer for her to be ready to tie her life with mine.

I smile at Vela, Adele, James, and Sandy talking together. I can only imagine having a child and being forced to give him or her up. If Vela and I have a child, which I dearly hope we do, it would take a cataclysmic force to tear that baby out of my arms. I'll have to get the whole story out of James and Sandy someday.

It's important to know all the details of Vela's birth and the necessary separation from her biological parents. I need to know my enemy backward and forward. The E.E. have hunted for Vela for thousands of years. They certainly won't stop trying to end her life after she announces her identity to the Elemental world.

The reunited family approaches in a line, arms entwined around waists. Vela's face is beaming, and I'm pleased she's so happy.

It's funny. I didn't ever think I would adopt another person's feelings like my own, but with Vela, I see that I do just that. I don't even care anymore about my happiness. It's hers that I strive to meet.

Adele breaks away first, striding up to me. She puts her hands on her hips. "Now, who might you be?" Her eyes drill into mine like I better have a good explanation for being here.

I try not to show how strange it is to be talking to someone who looks just like my Intended. "I'd be Linc, Vela's Intended," I say, fighting a smile.

Adele does not back down. "And how are you going to prove you're worthy of my sister's affections?"

My eyebrows have climbed into my hair, and I know I look as shocked as I feel. I turn to Vela, but she's no help. She's leaning over and giggling hysterically. James and Sandy chuckle, too.

"Because she's everything my heart could possibly ask for in a partner. She will be my wife, and I'm blessed enough to call her my Intended, too."

Adele's eyebrow rises slowly. "Prove it. Prove your gifts are amplified by Vela being your soulmate."

Shock makes me freeze, and my mouth moves in silent question. Vela and her parents watch our standoff in amusement.

"Well?" she asks, her foot tapping impatiently.

"You really want me to do this?" I ask Adele, giving her one last chance to stop what I'm about to do.

"Yep, I sure do," she says, her arms crossed. She smirks.

I'm nothing if not a sucker for a challenge, so I raise my arms and let an inferno blast, blowing a huge wave of fire into the air. I stand up under the forty-foot-tall furnace and hold it there for a good thirty seconds. When I'm sure that the little brat is properly convinced, I drop my arms, and the fire dissipates. A billowing cloud of dark smoke fills the air all around us and when we emerge from it, everyone's coughing.

It takes James, Vela and Adele working together to blow the smoke away and clear the air.

I fold my arms and look at Adele. "Does that satisfy you?"

"Yeah, you'll do," she says dismissively, like I didn't just do something pretty fantastic.

I huff and look at Vela, who's holding her stomach, trying to contain her giggles. I stride over to her and, unable to help myself, I pick her up and swing her around. "Enjoy that, did you?"

Her peals of laughter fill my ears as she clings to my neck. "Yes," she says in between laughs. "You've convinced me. You're worthy to be my Intended."

"Oh, did you need more proof?" I ask, putting her down and holding her shoulders to look her in the eyes.

She stands straight. "It's nice to see you showing off your rather impressive powers, so yes, I did need to see it. Thank you, Adele, for vetting him like that," she says over her shoulder to her little sister, who hides a smile behind her hand.

I squeeze Vela's shoulders. "I will get you back for this. Did you guys plan that?"

Her eyes glint in amusement. "We might have. What are you going to do about it?"

I have some really good ideas on how I could properly repay my Intended for making me the butt of her and her little sister's joke, but instead, I tweak her nose. "I'm going to get you back."

This time, Vela laughs. "I can't wait to see what you'll cook up."

Adele bursts out in laughter, and I spin around and rush her. I pick her up easily, putting her over my shoulder. I spin her around and she squeals, begging to be put down. After quite a few spins, I do as she asks. She stumbles a bit on her feet before she falls flat on the ground.

I point at her. "That's getting you back." I turn to face Vela, who's warding me off with her hands, so I won't do the same to her. "I have better plans for you. Prepare yourself."

"No," she says, laughing. "I'd rather know right now what you have planned."

"Nope. Yours is going to be a surprise. I will get you." I smile at her, and she folds down in a fit of giggles.

Happy to have been included in a family hazing, I cross my arms and watch Vela as she walks up to Adele and leans down to whisper in her ear.

"No," I shout, "No more ganging up on me!" I look at James and Sandy. "Can I get some help here?"

They're too busy laughing to say anything remotely helpful. I sigh and throw up my arms. I give up. I have no idea what those girls are planning to do to me next. I'll just have to just keep my eyes open.

Sandy walks over to Jack, who's jumping on Vela, wanting to be a part of her conversation with Adele. "Now, who is this sweet little baby?" Sandy asks, crouching to look Jack in his warm brown eyes.

He wiggles his body in happiness at finally getting some attention and licks Sandy's face. She laughs, rubbing his barrel chest.

Vela kneels and rubs Jack's smooth red head. "This is Jack, and where I go, he goes. We've only been separated once, and I hated it." Vela gives me a look, and I know she hated being away from me, too.

James and Adele bend down to pet Jack. He circles their legs, happy to have so much attention, his tongue hanging out his mouth as he pants.

"How about we go inside?" Sandy asks.

We all nod, and I follow the happy family into the community that not an hour ago almost attacked Vela full force. Now we pass curious faces, but nothing threatening. I'll have to keep my eyes and ears open for any kind of danger to Vela.

We stop at a charming log house that has pretty flowering bushes in front of it. It always amazes me to see what families can do with their homes in the middle of nowhere. Other houses have plants and bushes in front, too, and it's clear this community takes great pride in their homes.

When I see James and Sandy knocking the dirt off their shoes before entering, I do the same, then step into their small, but warm house.

My first impression is it reminds me of the coziness of Hannah's house. Like Petra's home, the large living area dominates the space, and a kitchen sits to the left near two doors that look like they lead to bedrooms. Crocheted blankets drape over the backs of large handmade sitting chairs and even one wood frame couch. James gets right to work, stirring up the embers in the fireplace. As he gets a fire going, I call Jack to me and lead him over to the couch.

Suddenly needing to be close to Vela, I choose the seat with room for two, and I'm happy when she settles next to me. I scoot until our legs touch, and she smiles warmly at me, reaching for my hand.

I lean in close, whispering, "Are you happy?"

Her eyes are bright as she looks lovingly over at her family members and nods. "I'm the happiest I've been since I left home. I can't wait for Mom, Dad, Drew, and Kane to meet my new Mama and Papa...and Adele."

"I love that you have different names for each of your parents," I say softly and look up when the room gets quiet. Everyone is seated and looking expectantly at Vela and me.

Taking a deep breath, I take this lull to dive into our most important topic. "As you all know, Vela has a very important job to do. We need to get started, but," I say with hesitation, because I'm not sure what their reaction will be, "first, Vela and I are getting married."

Vela squirms next to me, and when I look at her to corroborate my statement, she looks uncomfortable.

"Right?" I ask Vela. "That is the first step in our plan," I say carefully, my heart hitching.

"Yes, of course, it's just I wanted to break it to my parents a little more gently than that." She looks at the stunned faces of James and Sandy, and I realize she's probably right.

Clearing my throat, I glance at Adele, who looks so excited I wonder if she's going to bounce off her chair. It's such a change from the grilling she gave me earlier. I do a double take.

"A wedding?" she squeals. "I've always wanted to be in a wedding. I mean, I want to have my own wedding, of course, but until then, I'd love to be your bridesmaid." She gives Vela such a hopeful look, Vela laughs.

"Of course, it will be small, nothing extravagant, but it'll be ours," Vela says, reaching for my hand and looking at me softly. I notice the blush on her cheeks and my chest swells in manly pride that I put that adorable shade of red there.

"You're still a child!" Sandy cries, holding her hands to her chest. "We've only just gotten you back."

Vela quickly rises from her seat and goes to Sandy, kneeling in front of her. Jack, of course, follows, resting his head on Sandy's lap. I'm happy to see one member of our trio included in Vela's new family. I try not to be hurt that James and Sandy don't want me to be a part of their family yet.

James asks in a hard voice, "Do you feel this is your only option?"

"Yes. It is the only option," I say, my voice sounding a little more forceful than I intended. The frustration just slips out.

James looks at me, then at Vela and Sandy, who are now holding hands and speaking quietly. He shakes his head. "How old are you, Linc?"

"I'm eighteen," I say in a strong tone. I barely stop from mentioning I'm almost nineteen. It'll sound like I'm trying to force this on them. Which I am. This marriage is non-negotiable, and I'm suddenly fearful they'll convince Vela to see their way of things.

"Look, we know what it's like to be young and in love," James says. For the sake of being respectful, I allow him to finish. I clamp my lips shut. "But there's no reason to rush a wedding. Vela has enough on her plate without worrying about a wedding dress and bridesmaids," he says, waving his hand at Adele.

"I disagree," I say, looking over at Vela and wondering what her mom is saying to her. "We very much want to honor God in our relationship, and if we're going to be traveling together, which we are," I say, my eyes not leaving his, "we need to be married."

James frowns.

"Look, I know you've just been reunited with your long-lost daughter. I am totally on board with all of you coming with us and getting to know your new family dynamics. But what do you expect Vela and I to do while she's bringing our world together? To date? Won't it only help for people to see her in a strong relationship with her Intended?"

"A *strong* relationship? You're talking about marriage!" He huffs loudly. "They're going to think she's..." He waves his hand in the air. "You know."

Adele helpfully supplies, "Knocked up?"

James's face turns red as he splutters, "Well, wouldn't you think that of a friend getting married at seventeen years old?"

I half rise from my seat, anger surging through me. "People can think what they want to think. When we don't have a child right away, those suspicions will be laid to rest."

James stands up, his chest heaving, "I don't want those rumors floating around about my daughter! Now, this is ridiculous. She's not getting married, and that's that."

He takes a step toward me when Sandy's quiet voice stops him. "Yes, she is, James. Now sit down before you have a heart attack."

6

Vela

My heart is galloping like I've just run a mile. I look at my furious father with wide eyes, wondering how Sandy is going to calm him down.

She continues in a sure voice, "Vela explained to me how important this is to her, and we need to support, not hinder her." She gives a steady look to her furious husband.

He clenches his hand at his side, and he looks at Linc in frustration, like he wants him to change her mind. That's not happening. Linc's fully on board with what she's saying.

James's lips are in a white, thin line as he considers. "Am I going to be given any explanation? Or do you just want to force this marriage down my throat?"

I now see where I get my temper from. I slowly get up and resume my seat next to Linc, reaching for his clenched fist, unfolding his fingers to hold mine.

Sandy sighs and nods. "Of course you can have an explanation. From what I understand," she says, giving me a long look. I nod my head at her, encouraging her to continue. "These two have been forced into some compromising situations already and would very much like to honor God in regards to their physical relationship."

James's face gets redder. I expect that if he was a Festan, the house would erupt in flames. As it is, a wind stirs our hair.

"Now, before you explode, I want to remind you of what we went through when we first met. It wasn't too different from their experience. And, for the record, I agree with Linc that a marriage will only help Vela's image. To see her married to the Festan Grand Elder's son will be a strong influence for some to give Vela their support."

Linc looks like he's never been happier to be his mother's son.

James visibly calms and blows out a breath as he contemplates everything she just told him.

"Sir, if this is any help, I love your daughter," Linc says in a calm, sure voice. My heart swells in love for him as he utters some of the sweetest words I've heard him say. "I have more love for her than I have breath in my body. Besides who I am in Christ Jesus, I am her other half and happily so."

James stares at Linc intently. "Did you have as much firepower before you met Vela?"

I know what he's implying, he's wondering if our Intended bond is real. I watch as Linc gives him a steady look and says firmly, "Not even close. I couldn't do half of what I can now that Vela and I are together."

"You should see what he can do with a pack of wolves, too, Papa," I offer. "Or a huge grolar bear."

James looks impressed as he regards Linc with a new expression. Like he could be worthy of me.

I hold my breath and wait for his acceptance or rejection of Linc.

James looks like he's swallowed a sour lemon, but he says grudgingly, "It appears your bond is real. And if what my wife tells me is true," he looks pointedly at me. When I nod at him, he continues, "then maybe marriage is the best course for the both of you. But does it have to be so soon?" he asks gruffly.

Linc speaks up before I can. "Yes. We've waited long enough. Things will be easier if we can be married as soon as possible. And she'll have my protection in every room."

At the mention of a room, I immediately think of a bedroom and blush furiously. It's something on the forefront of my mind all the time, especially since our engagement. I can't wait to have that life with Linc, to share that side of myself with him. I'm suddenly as ready as Linc to get married and will do anything to make it happen as soon as possible.

His thigh is right next to mine, and I feel his tension as James considers Linc's insistence to marry quickly. I understand Linc's rush. The desire between us has reached volcanic proportions, and it's only a matter of time before we both combust or give in.

Marriage is our only option if we're going to spend any kind of time together alone.

James blows out a long breath. "I guess I'm outvoted. Adele can't wait to be in a wedding and Sandy is ready to plan one. Don't think I can't see the wheels turning in your mind," he tells Sandy with a soft smile.

Deliriously happy my family is on board with our plan, I turn when Linc speaks.

"There's something else we need to discuss," Linc says, his thumb stroking distracting lines down my hand. "After we get married, we need to go on the road, show Elementals everywhere that Vela's gifts have emerged, and that she is the Chosen One."

Adele bounces her leg and asks in an excited voice, "We get to leave here? When? And where are we going first?"

Glancing at Linc, I give him a small smile and say, "We'll find out which state will allow me to get married at seventeen and travel to the closest one. After that, I don't know, yet. Texas, maybe, to get the Festans' full support. Now," I say, standing up. "How about we girls start dinner, and the boys can do what boys do while the womenfolk cook?"

James blusters, "How do you know I'm not the one who cooks around here?"

When Sandy and Adele both laugh out loud, I smile and say, "It was just a guess, but it sounds like I was right." He reminds me so much of my adopted dad, I swallow hard.

He smiles good-naturedly. "Okay, my secret is out. I can hardly boil water. But I can chop wood. Can you, young man?" he asks Linc.

Linc nods, kisses the side of my head and stands up, untangling our fingers.

I let him go reluctantly, even though it was my idea for us to split up. It will be a good thing for Linc and James to spend time together. He will soon see the type of guy Linc is and won't be so inclined to object to our marriage.

Adele jumps up and waves me toward the kitchen. "Come on, sis. I'll show you where everything is."

I sigh and follow Adele and Sandy, where they promptly start taking things out of the cupboards. I'm soon impressed with everything they pull out to prepare a meal.

"How did you get your hands on so much cookware?" I ask, fingering a ceramic bowl I know they didn't make out here.

"We inherited most of it when we moved in. The previous owners left most of what they had accumulated, so we got lucky," Sandy says, her head deep in an upper cabinet, emerging with a large bowl. She turns to Adele. "Could you go get what we need for a salad?"

She nods and leaves while I turn my surprised look to Sandy. "You grow lettuce here?"

"The one thing about being a Gyan is I can grow just about whatever I want out here, even if it's not a natural environment for it. I got my hands on seeds, so it was easy."

I smile and feel almost giddy. I haven't had a salad in a while and my stomach grumbles, agreeing it's excited to have a great meal, too. No one at the Polar Bear had access to lettuce seeds, so this is a treat.

"Okay," I say, rubbing my hands together. "What can I do? Do you have the ingredients for bread on a stick?"

She looks at me curiously. "What is that? Is it just what the name describes?"

I look at her with surprise. "You don't eat that out here? It's a staple at the Polar Bear."

She huffs and leans down to pull out a bag of flour from an under cupboard. "If we want bread, we cook it on griddles. They're kind of like pancakes."

"That's good, too," I say, not wanting her to go to too much trouble.

Adele pops back in the kitchen with her arms full of vegetables. "Did I hear you say bread on a stick?" she asks, her face bright with curiosity.

"Uh, huh. You've never had it either?"

She shakes her head, but then she looks around and asks, "Do you have everything you would need to make it? I totally have to try this."

"Do you have oil, salt, sugar, and yeast?"

They both nod.

"Okay, so I'll only need those and some water in addition to the flour."

"Great," Adele chirps and she jumps to attention, spinning around to get the sugar and yeast.

She hands me them, and I ask, "What about the water? Do you guys have a plumbing situation out here, or is there a well?"

Adele smiles prettily and leans over to turn the faucet on and off quickly. Water gushes out and then turns off just as promptly.

"Perfect," I say. "Okay, so let's mix two tablespoons of oil, two teaspoons of salt, sugar, and yeast in with four cups of flour. Then, we'll need two cups of warm water to add to the flour mixture slowly." I'm happy I thought to memorize this recipe and can't wait to have this delicious bread again. Sharing this experience with my new family will be priceless, even though a part of me pinches at how much I miss Greta and Hannah right now.

After we've added all the ingredients and mixed them well, I cover the bowl with a cloth and set it aside. "While the dough rises, we need to collect and prepare the roasting sticks. Green ones, so they won't burn," I instruct. "And we need to either peel or cut the bark off before we wrap the strips of dough around them. The fire is going well?"

Sandy jumps and says, "Oh, yes, that reminds me. Let me prepare the road chickens. They won't take long to cook, but I can get them out of the way now, so we can each cook our own bread on a stick when it's ready."

I laugh. "You call them road chickens, too? I thought that was just a name Hannah gave the pheasants around here."

"Who's Hannah?"

"Oh," I say wistfully. "She's a very dear friend of mine from the Polar Bear. She has a daughter, Greta, and they've become like family to me."

Sandy looks at me with the side of her eye as she reaches in a cooler and pulls out some raw meat. "Hmm, it's nice you've connected with others since you left your adopted family. And you know, there is no other name for those dumb birds. They practically beg you to pick them up and cook them up for dinner. They have no sense of self preservation. It's a good thing they're so prolific because they are on the absolute bottom of the food chain."

I laugh and fondly remember the meal Linc provided me when I first got all my powers. He must have heard my thoughts because he enters the house, his arms full of firewood. My heart jumps at how handsome he is as he gives me a heart-stopping smile and asks, "How's dinner coming along?"

"We're going to have *salad*, Linc. Isn't that amazing?" I ask with a smile.

He laughs. "Can't say that I've ever missed lettuce before, but now that I haven't had it for so long, I would love some."

Adele peeks a look at Linc as he leaves again, and I say, "Are you checking out my Intended? He's mine and only mine." I bump her shoulder.

She laughs and shoves me, nearly knocking me over. "I am *not* looking at him like that. Gross! It's like he's automatically my brother, so ew, don't ever say that again."

Laughing, I straighten, getting my feet under me again. "Just making sure. I can't have him confusing you for me. With how much we look like each other, he just might do that."

She cries and holds her mouth like she's trying not to throw up. "Oh, my gosh, I hope that never happens. I have a boyfriend, anyway," she adds so flippantly, I turn to her in surprise.

"You do? What's his name?"

"Oh, no, she doesn't," Sandy calls from her spot by the fire. "She's not allowed to have a boyfriend yet."

"Mama," Adele whines. "You've always said when I turn sixteen, I could have a boyfriend, and I turned sixteen two weeks ago."

Sandy blows hair out of her eyes as she glares at Adele. "I didn't mean for you to get a boyfriend the *day* of your birthday!"

Adele smiles secretly at me, saying under her breath, "I was already dating him. They just didn't know." Adele says more loudly, "I was just following your orders. How could I help it if Steele asked me out the first day I could accept?"

I give Adele a wide-eyed glance and shake my head. She is a handful. Mama and Papa are going to need my help in corralling her, I can already tell. I might only be a year older, but it's clear I've matured more quickly than her. I've been forced to. My protective instincts are also raring to go.

"Look, young lady, your father has not given his approval, so you do not have a boyfriend. As much as you'd like to say you do," Sandy says in a tired voice, like this is an old argument.

Adele pouts. "Papa's never going to say yes, Mama. You know that. Look how he was with Vela and Linc and they're Intend-eds!"

Sandy looks up from what she's doing, saying, "You cannot compare an Intended relationship with a crush, young lady, and you know it."

"He's the one who has a crush on me! How can I tell him no when he's so cute?"

"Easily," she says dryly.

I laugh and say, "Adele, you have your whole life to find your Intended. You don't need to date just any boy who comes along and likes you."

She leans in and whispers, "What if he's a really good kisser?"

I lean back. "Stop that, right now! You're not already doing that," I whisper furiously at her.

She gives me an amused glance this time. "I'm sixteen. What do you think?"

I snort. "I think you're too young to be talking like this."

She frowns at me. "I'm only one year younger than you, and you're about to be married. I thought sisters were there for each other," she says in a low voice.

"I am," I blush and insist in just as low a voice. "I just want to protect you from boys who are too eager to do things you shouldn't be doing yet."

She looks scandalized and leans in to whisper, "I'm not doing anything but a little kissing. Jeez, who do you think I am?"

Mollified, I whisper back, "Good, as long as that's all you're doing."

"It is, I swear," she promises, her eyes wide and innocent looking.

I groan. "You're going to be the death of me."

"You and me both, Vela," Sandy says as she comes into the kitchen, surprising us.

Adele jumps and looks a little guilty, but I just bump her shoulder and ask, "Do you want to get the green sticks so we can start wrapping this dough?"

She nods, seeming to be happy to escape our frowning mom.

When she goes, Sandy sighs heavily. "She's kept our hands full, that's for sure. I don't know how I'm going to manage both of your hormones."

I blush. She's definitely noticed the looks Linc and I exchanged in front of her. "Linc and I won't do anything we shouldn't be doing."

She gives me a look, asking, "Do I have your promise on that?"

"Yes, that's a promise. It's very important to both Linc and me."

We prepare the salad with ingredients Adele collected. I happily cut the cucumbers and tomatoes while Sandy shreds the lettuce. Once the salad is done, I bring the dough out of the bowl and sprinkle more flour on it. I set it down and knead it before pulling off small balls of dough that I set aside as I wait for Adele to bring the sticks.

Sandy leans her hip against the counter and folds her arms. She studies me, and I'm suddenly self-conscious, so I ask, "What? Is there flour on my face?"

"No," she says softly and reaches up to tuck a stray piece of hair from my braid behind my ear. "I'm just so happy you're here."

"I am, too," I say and wrap my arms around her.

Adele walks in and before I know it, we're wrapped in an emotional group hug.

I hear Linc's voice say, "Uh oh, what happened?"

7

Linc

Brushing my arms of any left-over dirt as I peer in the back door, I see what's happening in the kitchen. Vela, Adele, and Sandy are all crying and hugging. I worry about what I may have missed.

Vela pops her head up first, wiping her eyes, and laughs. "Oh, it's nothing. Girls just being girls."

"Uh huh," I say uncertainly. Without warning, just watching them hugging sends a rush of longing for my little sister through me, overwhelming me for a moment. I put my hand on my chest and look down, trying to control my emotions. Olympia would have loved having Vela for a sister. And she and Adele would be close in age, too, so she would have fit right in to that little scene I just walked in on.

Turning, I go to find a chair so I can compose myself. Vela must have noticed the expression on my face. She untangles herself from the arms of her mother and sister and joins me at the chair, kneeling in front of me. Jack approaches to lend his comfort.

I pet Jack's head and appreciate his loving nature, Vela's too. "Hey, you, okay?" she asks in a low voice, putting her hand on my arm.

Clearing my throat, I say in an undertone, "I just miss my sister sometimes."

Sympathy crowds her eyes. "Oh, Linc, I'm so sorry. I've just gained a sister while you've lost yours."

Sadness fills my chest at her words, and I turn my head to hide a rush of emotions. When I can, I say, "I'll always have her. Here," I say in a choked voice, putting my fist on my heart.

Vela leans in and hugs me tightly. "I'm so sorry, baby. My joy isn't fair to you."

"No," I say fiercely, leaning back, putting both my hands on her shoulders. "Don't ever say that. You deserve this reunion. Please don't let me stop you from enjoying it." I reach up and softly brush her cheek with my knuckle. "I just wish she could meet you. That we didn't have to wait for heaven to have our own reunion."

Vela throws her arms back around my neck. We just hold each other, missing someone Vela's never even met. After a moment, I notice the room has gotten very quiet. I look up from my hug with Vela and try to wipe my eyes inconspicuously.

James, Sandy, and Adele are all standing in the living room, looking uncomfortable.

"I'm sorry," I say hoarsely and know that I owe them some kind of explanation for my emotions. I study the floor and try to keep the grief from taking over again. "I lost my little sister to a terrible accident. I just miss her sometimes." Fisting my hand on my knee, I struggle, embarrassed to have a breakdown in front of virtual strangers like this.

"Son, this display of emotion just makes me like you more. You wouldn't be much of a man if you didn't miss your sister. It's all right. We understand grief, believe me," James says, giving me a sympathetic look.

Sandy wraps her arm around his waist. Adele joins her, and they look at Vela tenderly. Knowing they've just found their long-lost daughter dries up my tears better than anything could, and I straighten. This isn't the time for me to give into grief. But I appreciate their understanding.

Clearing my throat, I say in a surprisingly strong voice, "How's supper coming? I'm starving."

That seems to set everyone in motion, and before I know it, I have a dough-wrapped stick in my hand, and I'm next to Adele by the fire. She's crouched down and watching her dough rise into a puffy shape with an awed look.

"You've never had bread on a stick before?" I ask, surprised.

She shakes her head. "No, my mom usually cooks it over the fire on a griddle."

"Huh," I say. "Hannah back at the Polar Bear must not have a griddle because she always cooks it like this."

"Who's Hannah?" she asks with a puzzled look.

"Oh, she's mine and Vela's very good friend. Vela lived with her when we stayed at the Polar Bear."

Adele turns a dazzling smile at me. "Well, I like Hannah's way so much better. I can't wait to taste it."

"You'll love it. It's delicious."

We resume cooking in a companionable silence until she says in a quiet voice, "My boyfriend will love this. I can't wait to show him."

An uncomfortable pinch hits my chest, and a surge of protectiveness rears its head. "You have a boyfriend?"

I must have asked too loudly, because she whispers at me furiously, "Shhh, Mama and Papa won't let us date, even though I'm at the age they said I could."

Looking at her warily, I turn my bread, careful not to let it burn. I motion for her to do the same and then ask, "What's wrong with this guy that they won't let you date him?"

She looks at me with an innocent expression. "It's not my fault that he's gorgeous. I just get to enjoy it."

"How much do you enjoy it?" I growl.

She giggles and bumps my shoulder. "Don't worry, Vela's already given me the seventh degree that I shouldn't do certain things with him."

"It's the nth degree," I mumble as violence for this unnamed guy roars through me. If James and Sandy won't give their permission for her to date this guy, they must have very good reasons for it. "Please, don't tell me anymore. This conversation has already gone on way too long for my comfort."

She looks at me in outrage. "Do you really think that badly of me?"

"It's not you I'm thinking badly of," I grumble, very uncomfortable with this conversation. I suddenly want this guy's name so I can find and threaten him within an inch of his life. Adele is my sister now, and I won't tolerate any boy asking to do things he shouldn't. And, as far as I'm concerned, they shouldn't be doing *anything* more than talking.

"Whatcha' guys whispering about over here?" Vela asks, crouching down next to us.

Uncaring whether my bread is fully cooked, I stand up and escape. "Nothing," I say firmly. I'll eat this bread raw if it means I can leave this horror. Unwanted images of Adele with some boy flash through my mind, and I give Vela a significant look, "Watch her."

Adele giggles, and Vela gives her a curious look, then looks at me knowingly. "Ah." When I'm positive she understands my implication, I leave to find a better, or rather any other conversation.

James is standing in the kitchen talking to Sandy when I approach. I try to keep a grimace off my face.

I must be unsuccessful because James laughs. "What did Adele say this time? She has a way of making anyone squirm."

I laugh nervously, not wanting to get Adele in any kind of trouble. "Oh, she's just trying to get under my skin."

"Is it working?" Sandy asks with a glimmer in her eye.

"Yes," I say in a firm voice.

They laugh, and I look over at what Sandy's working on. She's cutting up cooked meat, poultry, from the looks of it.

"Looks delicious," I say, rubbing my hungry stomach.

"It's ready. We just need to cook our bread, and we're ready for a five-star meal," Sandy says.

James groans. "Oh honey, remember that restaurant we loved in Charleston?"

Sandy looks wistful as she says, "I do. That was before I got pregnant. It seems our life has been full of ups and downs. We haven't been to a restaurant in a really long time." She takes two wrapped sticks and walks to the fire, then stoops to cook the bread.

"How did you end up way out here, anyway?" I ask James.

He sighs heavily. "Oh, that's a simple enough story. The E.E. kept getting too close for comfort. We had to find somewhere safe and so remote that they would never find us. So, we ended up here."

Vela joins me, a cooked piece of bread on her stick ready to eat. "Did I hear you say the E.E. kept getting too close to you? Where did you last live?"

Sandy calls from her spot by the fire, "Chicago. We thought if we lived in a busy city, we'd shake them off. But they have their tentacles everywhere."

Adele joins us. "We had to leave a great townhouse. I had some good friends, too." Her dejected look makes me feel sorry for her necessarily nomadic life.

"What I want to know is how did you lose me?" Vela asks, twisting the bottom of her shirt.

A look of pain comes over James's eyes, but it's Sandy who answers, "We'll tell our story over dinner. Let's all sit down."

James adjusts his footing and stuffs his hands in his pockets. He does not look like he's looking forward to this conversation.

"I understand," I say. "How can I help put dinner on the table?"

James reaches for wooden plates and hands them to me. "I think there's enough there."

Accepting them, I walk over to the small table and see there are benches instead of chairs, so there's enough room for all of us. I set the table and then turn and almost run into James, who is standing right behind me.

He leans in and says in a low voice, "Please don't judge me too harshly when you hear our story. I did what I thought I had to do." He frowns and says, "It just didn't work out like I thought it would."

Now I'm desperately curious to hear their story. But I can only nod. "I'm sure you did what you had to. I won't judge you," I promise.

He sighs and puts his hand on my shoulder. "I appreciate that. I really do."

The girls come over with the rest of the meal's fixings and start setting food out. I find a spot on one of the benches and am more than a little disconcerted when Adele sits across from me. Vela is to my right, but with me facing Adele, it's like Vela's right in front of me, too.

Adele points at me and laughs, covering her mouth with her hand. "You should see your face right now. Is it really that weird for you to look at me?"

Her reasoning is spot on, but not wanting to make anyone uncomfortable, I hedge. "It's a little strange, but I think I'll get used to it." I look at Vela. "Eventually."

"I know," Vela says, putting her hand on mine. "I feel like I'm looking straight in a mirror when I look at Adele, but then," she says, chuckling, "she opens her mouth."

"Hey," Adele cries, "am I weird or something?"

"Or something," Vela answers, smiling. "No, you just have a much different personality than me. We're alike, but there're enough differences. I think Linc will get used to it."

"Speak for yourself," I say with a laugh. "She's more of a spitfire, granted, but you two are pretty similar."

Vela bumps her shoulder into mine. "Well, maybe I'll dye my hair blue so then you'll have no problem telling us apart."

I raise my eyebrows. "Don't you dare! I love your natural hair. I'll be fine." I shrug. "I just have to get used to it, that's all."

We all hold hands, bend our heads and James prays, "Dear Lord, we can't tell you how grateful we are in this moment to be together." His voice cracks at those words, and he pauses. "But, Lord, You knew this day would happen and for that we give You thanks. We ask for Your protection over our daughters, especially Vela since she will be heavily targeted, and for Your blessing on our meal and each of our futures. Bless this time, Lord."

When I raise my head, I see that James's head is still bowed, but he's let go of my hand. I realize he's still praying. So, I sit and wait for him to finish. We all have the same feeling, and it's not until he raises his head that we start eating.

Adele moans, and I look to see she's taken a bite of her bread on a stick and is chewing with her eyes closed.

I chuckle. "I told you that you'd like it."

She pops open her eyes and exclaims, "This is fantastic. I love the crusty burned side the best."

She overcooked one part of her bread, but she seems to like it that way, so I shrug and take a bite of my own slightly undercooked one. When I remember why it's not fully cooked, I cringe. I never want to have a conversation like I did with Adele again.

When Vela feels me shudder, she looks over at me with her eyebrow raised. I shake my head at her, which she seems to accept.

Sandy wipes her mouth with a cloth napkin and, looking between Adele and Vela, says, "So, James and I want to tell you both the full story of why we had to give up such a precious gift as Vela." Her eyes beseech the sisters to give them mercy and grace, which I hope they do. This was clearly a hard decision.

Vela puts her hand on Sandy's and says, "I can't speak for Adele, but I'll be fine with whatever you tell me. Please go ahead."

Adele pinches her lips together and doesn't give her own version of a promise, so I pray she has an open and understanding heart.

James says, "Well, since it's my fault we lost Vela for so many years, I'll tell the story." His voice shakes, and he clenches his fist and rests it on the table. "So, to start with, just know that most of what I did was done out of fear. Fear for our child, for her life. We made desperate decisions to try to protect our daughter."

"What were those decisions, Papa?" Adele asks.

He looks at her with guilt written all over his face. "Well, we were chased and almost caught by the Extremists when your mom was in labor with Vela."

Vela reaches for my hand, and I fold hers into mine, holding it tightly.

"There was a car chase that nearly ended with us being captured behind a barn. I managed to get us out of there, and we finally lost them when I sent a tornado after them. By that time, Sandy was close to giving birth, so I stopped at the first house I found with the lights on."

Sandy's pained smile is testament enough to what those memories evoked, and I direct my attention back to James.

"Thankfully, an Elemental couple lived there and had experienced home births with their own children. Vela was born in that old farmhouse on September 23rd in 2007." James takes a moment to put his fist on his mouth, like he doesn't want to tell the rest of the story.

With a resigned look, he continues. "The Extremists caught up to us, and we had to make a quick decision. The farm couple gave us the name and last known address of a traveling group of Elemental families."

Sadness fills his eyes. "These people agreed to care for and hide Vela from the Extremists. They told us where they would be next and promised to wait for us. It was supposed to be temporary," he says in a hoarse voice.

Sandy gives James a loving look when it seems he is unable to finish and picks up the story. "Except when we couldn't shake the Extremists off our trail, we arrived much later to the meeting place. And," she says with a soft voice, "they were gone. We lost her. We've been looking for her ever since."

A moment of silence fills the room.

James speaks up. "We realized the nomadic Elementals traveled all over the country. But we were looking in the wrong places. We tracked them throughout the U.S. and Canada, thinking they raised you."

Sandy, with tears in her eyes, reaches for Vela's hand and asks, "Where were you? Who adopted you? How did they find you?"

Vela looks down and composes herself before she says in a trembling voice, "The traveling group must have dropped me off at the Gyan Elder community building in California. My parents had been wanting a daughter and with two sons, gave up having their own and took me in. I was left in a basket with nothing but a note that had my birthday and said I'm the child of the prophecy."

Sandy nods. "That was our note. We left that so any Elemental would know how special of a baby you were. But, California," she breathes. "So close."

"What do you mean, that was so close?" Vela asks.

Sandy, too overcome to speak, bends her head. James picks up the story. "Vela, you were born in Arizona. They must have traveled with you before they dropped you off in the Gyan-controlled part of California."

I sit back in awe. I wonder how she's going to take this news. Not only did Sandy and James give her up, but the traveling Elemental family did, too.

One look at Vela shows she's feeling lost.

8

Vela

I sit in stunned silence. I'd been given up not once, but twice. What was wrong with me that another family didn't want me?

And the travelers didn't even give me to another family, but left me abandoned on the doorstep of an Elder Community Center.

What's wrong with me?

Sandy looks at me with such love-filled eyes, my breath stutters. Now that I've heard their story, I can see why they didn't raise me. It wasn't for lack of wanting me, they just missed a meeting place.

Squeezing my knee, I ask in a shaky voice, "Why did they give me up like that? If my adopted parents had known you were looking for me, they would have given me back to you."

James shakes his head. "We don't know. We've never been able to find that group again." He hangs his head and then looks up. "If I had been able to get rid of the Extremists sooner, we would have made the meeting point. It's my fault we lost you."

Adele looks between Sandy and James and says with gritted teeth. "You're telling me I haven't had a sister my whole life because you couldn't make an appointment?" She lifts her leg over the bench and stands back from the table. "I was meant to have a sister. You both robbed me of that."

Indignation roars through me at how unfair she's being to our parents. I stand up, too. "Wait a minute. First, you don't want me to intrude on the little family you've had your whole life, and now, you're mad at them for being an only child? You can't have it both ways, Adele."

Adele lifts flashing eyes to mine. "You have no room to talk. You've lived a cush life with a family in one house, maybe two. Do you want to know how many houses I've lived in? At least fifteen. I actually don't know because I've lost count. We're constantly on the move because of *you*. If I had had a normal sister, I could have had a normal life. The kind you had. Instead..." she chokes off the rest in a sob and turns, running from the room.

I move to follow her, but Sandy holds her hand out. "No, let me. She's right, she's been through a lot. She's never heard this story, and it's been a lot to take in. Let me talk to her." She rises from her seat and follows Adele's path out the front door.

I sit back, completely deflated now that my anger has had an outlet.

Linc leans in and presses a soft kiss on my temple. He whispers, "Hey, you, okay?"

Feeling kind of empty, I say, "I don't know. Adele's being completely unreasonable, but other than that, I don't know. She's kind of right, though, you know." I look deep into Linc's eyes and try to help him understand because he's looking at me, confused. I shift in my seat to face him. "I have had a great life. I thought I was my adopted mom and dad's only daughter and besides the childhood fire I had, nothing traumatic has happened to me. Well, nothing until recently."

Linc's look turns guilty, and I reach for his hand.

"No, it's not your fault. It's just the direction my life turned. Ever since we met, my path has been set in motion."

James interjects, "No, your path has been set since you were born. God changed your life to what it is today."

My heart warms. Wanting to assure him, because he looks a little lost, too, I hold his hand and say, "Which I'm totally fine with. I have the qualities I have because of you and Mama." Turning loving eyes to Linc, I say, "Linc, too, and my family in Breckenridge, are all parts of my story." I turn my eyes to the front door. "I just want Adele to be okay with all of this."

"Are you really?" Linc asks in a gentle voice. "Okay with all of this? You've just been given a lot of information today."

I sit and think. "I'm torn, because on one hand, I'm thrilled I found Mama, Papa, and Adele. It's clear that how they lost me was completely out of their hands. But I was never out of God's hands, though which gives me so much encouragement. But, for some reason a family gave me up and left me with a note on a doorstep. I was delivered to the family I grew up with. And I can't be upset about that. I've had a great life. I really am good."

Linc smiles and puts his arm around my shoulders. I lean into him and look at Papa. "Hey," I say softly when it's clear his admission took a lot out of him. "I'm good, I promise. You did the best you could. You shouldn't feel guilty for something that was out of your control."

He turns pained eyes to the door, where I know he's waiting for Adele and Sandy to return. "I'm glad you forgive me. I don't know if your sister will."

Anger rushes through me. "If she can't understand your explanation, then she has a lot of growing up to do."

He softly snorts. "She *is* only sixteen."

I sit back, unmollified, and cross my arms. "We all have to grow up sometime."

He smiles sadly at me.

An urge to talk some sense to my sister comes, and I stand up. "Let me see how Mama's doing. I'll hopefully be right back."

Getting off the bench, I stride to the front door, calling Jack to me. I open and close the door once I emerge out into the chilly air. Standing on the doorstep, I look around to see if they're walking back toward the house.

Relief courses through me when I spot Sandy and Adele walking back from the woods, hand in hand.

"Jack!" Adele calls out, and he tugs on his collar to run to her.

I let him go and smile as he bounds over to her, his little tail nub wiggling in happiness when he reaches her. It's clear how much he loves his new family. I've never even seen him get that excited to see even Drew and Kane.

I catch up to Jack and loop my arm in Sandy's as she chuckles with me over Adele's exuberance over Jack. She's cooing in his face and rubbing his dark red coat. Jack licks her face every chance he gets to reach it.

Leaning in, I ask in Mama's ear, "Is she okay?"

She glances at me with a grateful look and says, "I think so. Will you talk to her, though? With all the danger and near misses from the E.E., she's lacked strong girl relationships in her life."

I nod. "Of course. I've dreamed of having a sister my whole life." Smiling down at Adele, I say, "And now my dream has come true."

Sandy squeezes my arm with hers. "So have ours. You're here."

Adele stands up finally and Jack, to my chagrin, stays right next to her. *Wait, what's happening here?* But Adele looks so happy, I don't call him back to me.

"Ready, sis?" I ask.

She smiles and nods.

"Can we talk when we get home? Just the two of us?" I ask her as we walk back to the cozy house.

She glances at me uncertainly. "Can I be honest about how I feel?"

Looking her in the eye, I say, "I wouldn't want it any other way."

She nods. "Then I'd like that."

At that, we make it back rather quickly to the house, letting ourselves in. Adele leads me to a bedroom on the right after I notice that Linc and Papa have cleaned the table off and are sitting in the living room talking lowly. Papa searches Adele's eyes and when he sees a smile, gives us a wink before resuming talking to Linc. I wave at Linc, who watches me with a look of understanding as we walk into Adele's room.

Love swells in my chest for this man who loves me so much. He only wants things to be great between Adele and me and whoever I want in my life. He would do anything for me and for that, I'm incredibly thankful. Grief hits me at the way I allowed Rayne into my life and heart, even if it was for a moment.

I wonder where Rayne is and am sure he will reappear at some point. I resolve to be ready when I do see him. He's such a wild card, it's hard to tell what he will do. Will he try to kill me to get his gifts back? Is he that desperate?

Yes, he is.

Adele plops down on her double-sized bed and looks at me expectantly.

"Sorry," I apologize, realizing I should have prepared what I want to say to my sister, not wasted time worrying about Rayne.

"No, it's fine. It looks like you've got a lot on your mind."

I laugh, rubbing my forehead. "Yeah, you can say that."

"Spill. What is it?"

Taking a seat next to her, I tuck my leg under me and sigh. "I'm sorry, my mind wandered. It's not important. Let's talk about what Papa said at dinner."

"Oh, no," Adele says, "you're not getting out of this. I want to know what that expression of guilt on your face was about."

I cringe. I really don't want to admit how I briefly fell for another guy's charms.

She leans in, squeezing my shoulders. "Don't forget, I can read emotions. And you have guilt spilling out of you. So spill, sister. I need to know. It's a matter of honor, of sister honor, to be completely honest with me."

I wince. "It is a matter of honor. You can't be closer to the truth. But it's hard to admit when you've done something really wrong, okay?"

She gives me a sympathetic smile. "No one is perfect. So, what'd you do?"

I look down, studiously memorizing the pattern of the cover on the bed. "I may have fallen for this guy while I was with Linc." At Adele's raised eyebrow, I reluctantly continue. "And he may have used that to get close to me, which made him think I'd want him over Linc." A flash of anger so hot strikes inside my chest, and I pause for a moment to keep my fire gift contained. Taking a deep breath in my nose, I say with gritted teeth, "Then he accused Linc of something ridiculous and tried to kill him."

"Whoa, what do you mean he tried to kill him? Like it wasn't an accident?"

I look at her with hard eyes. "If you think slicing open Linc's throat with a wind knife was an accident."

Adele leans back, her eyes wide and disbelieving. "Are you serious?"

"I almost lost him," I whisper, holding my hand to my chest. My heart beats painfully against my ribcage just thinking of that devastating moment. My gifts swirl through me at dangerous levels. I'm close to releasing them. My hair floats up around my head in the unbidden breeze emanating from my very soul. Smoke rises from my fingers.

She eyes my elements. "How did Linc survive that?"

Fighting to control my emotions, I say, "He nearly didn't. If it wasn't for my dear friend, Hannah, Linc would be dead. She was able to close his wound in time, but he still almost didn't make it."

"What do you mean?" Adele leans in, completely captivated.

My breath stutters at my memory of Linc's ashen face and motionless form when he was unconscious. Despite my best efforts, wind, again, lifts my hair at my painful memories. "God spared him. He brought him out of a coma. Linc says he heard God's voice tell him he needed to live. To help me in my quest."

Adele sits silent for a beat then says fiercely, "I'm going to find my Intended. If it's the last thing I do, I will find him. I don't care if it takes my entire life to do it."

Now that I've shared the most painful part of my story, my hair falls back down, and I look at her fondly. "Yes, Linc is very special because of our bond, but Adele, it's up to God who He brings in your life." I think fondly of Kane and Elia, who I am sure are together by now. She's officially eighteen, so she's entirely dateable for Kane. I'm full of regret that I missed her birthday.

"Now who are you thinking about?" Adele asks, her eyes bright.

I smile. "You've gotten very good at reading my face in a very short time."

She scoffs and waves her hand. "Remember, I sense emotions. But I don't have to. You're an open book."

I ruffle her hair. "I don't need to hide my expressions from you. We're sisters, remember?"

She smiles widely. "Yes, we are. We have a lot of catching up to do."

"Talking of catching up, do you want to tell me what all that at dinner was about? You're furious one minute and fine the next."

She blows out a breath, bringing her knees to her chest. "I know. I just get so mad sometimes thinking about my life. I've only ever wanted normalcy, you know? The kind of life you've had. I guess I just got really jealous."

I reach and take her hand, holding it carefully. "You don't need to be jealous of me, ever. I understand that you'd like a life like mine, but I'm sure you've had a lot of wonderful moments with people all over."

She looks at me sadly. "Do you know how many best friends I've had?"

I can imagine the list is high. "No idea. How many?"

"None." She says it with such finality I wince.

"Surely, you've made friends…"

"Yeah," she says with a hard laugh. "I've made lots of friends, but how much can you get to know someone when you have to move in a month, or even two?"

Squeezing her fingers, I say with my heart torn for my little sister. "I'm sorry." I don't try to tell her I was sure she had to move for her own protection, because I know she's heard that reason more times than I could imagine.

She squeezes my hand back and says after a shrug, "It's okay, I guess. Mama and Papa were just doing their best to keep us alive."

So, she does know all the moving was for her protection.

"This place is the longest we've been in one place in my whole life."

"Really? How long have you lived here?"

"Three years. But we're leaving soon, right?" She looks at me with such lost eyes I rush to reassure her, "Yes, we are, but I will always be a relationship you can count on. Now that I've found you, I won't give you up. Ever."

Turning her head, she says in a resigned voice, "It's not that I want to leave here, but I would like to have a cell phone again. I would just miss the two friends I've made here. And," she says, turning to look at me with a focused gaze, "you say that now, but your responsibilities are going to take you everywhere. You really can't promise you'll always be with me."

"I certainly can. If you want to, you can travel with me wherever I go. I know you don't like to travel, but we can at least stay together."

When she gives me a look filled with such heart-breaking pain, my breath catches. "It's not the travel that bothers me; it's all the people I'll leave behind. Like here, I'll probably never talk to my friends again."

"Now, how do you know that? Cell phones are a powerful thing."

"Vela, how many cell phones do you think are around here?"

That's true. I fumble with a way she could stay in touch with her new friends. Coming up with one, I say quickly, "Hey, so I've invited anyone in the community to travel with me to help with my protection. What if your friends and their families came with us, too?"

Hope brightens her eyes. "Really? You did that?"

I nod happily. "I did. You weren't there for that conversation. You were off hiding from me."

She snorts, looking a little guilty.

"Hey, it's okay. So, we're good?"

Jumping up, she says, "Yep, let's see what that hot fiancé of yours is doing."

Knowing now she's just trying to get under my skin, I ask, "Hey, when am I going to meet your hot boyfriend?"

She smiles at me so wide I get nervous. "How does tonight sound?"

"Okay," I say slowly. "Is he going to come over?"

"No, silly," she says, smacking my arm. "Remember, Mama and Papa won't let me have a boyfriend. We'll sneak out."

Okay, this wild behavior has to stop. "Um, no. I'm going to meet him properly. Not after sneaking out. Get that out of your head right now. Why are you dating him when you're not allowed?"

A stubborn look comes over her. "You're not going to let me sneak out, are you?" she says without answering my question.

This makes me nervous.

"Adele, Mama and Papa probably have very good reasons for not allowing you to date this guy. What's wrong with him?"

Indignation flashes from her eyes. "Nothing. He's a little bit of a bad boy, I guess, but I've tamed him."

I cross my arms. "You've tamed him?" I ask doubtfully. "Bad boys are notoriously hard to tame. What makes him a bad boy, anyway?"

She angles her body away from me and fingers her bedding, saying, "Nothing, except he may have dated all the girls here at some point."

I narrow my eyes at her. "Is he playing all of them?"

She spins to face me. "What do you mean, playing?"

"Ah, there are many explanations. But the main one is when he tells the same love story to multiple girls, stringing them all along."

"He only dated the other girls because he was trying to get me jealous. He's not like that now. He's only dating me."

I snort. "That you know. Adele, if he was willing to break hearts to get yours, do you think he's trustworthy with it?"

An uncertain look comes in her eyes, then resolve. "I'm sure he cares about only me."

"Are you sure he's still not whispering in the ears of the other girls? I'm only asking, because I know all about guys like him. And what kind of guy plays with girls' affections only to get your attention?"

Her eyes flashing, she asks, "The kind of guy who really wants me. And what are you talking about, the guy who tried to take you from Linc? What was his name, anyway?"

I reluctantly say the name that's plaguing me. "His name is Rayne, and yes, he's one of the guys who's taught me not to trust pretty words or faces."

Resolve to teach my wayward sister the right way to go about this boyfriend business fills me. "Look, I don't want to fight with you. If you really want to be this guy's girlfriend, then you need Mama and Papa's permission. So, let's get them to agree to letting you have a boyfriend, so you don't need to sneak anywhere."

A thoughtful look comes into her eyes.

This way, Linc and I can help keep an eye out for Adele. "What is this heartbreaker's name?"

"Steele."

"Please, just trust Mama and Papa's decision. Don't go against them. Remember, God sees all. Nothing you do is hidden." I put my arm around her shoulders. "Come on, let's go talk to Mama and Papa, and maybe you can go get this Casanova of yours and bring him here. I'd like to meet him."

She lets me lead her out of the room.

I'm worried for Adele and her heart, but I'm happy about the state of my relationship with my precious sister.

9

Rayne

I watch Vela's little sister leave her cabin and follow her as she walks toward another house. I'm confused when she goes to the back of it and knocks on the window.

That strange pull toward her fills my chest, and I fight back the feeling to approach her.

Why wouldn't she just go to the front door?

I soon see why when a face peeks at her and disappears. Since I'm so far away, I don't know if it's a guy or girl, but my suspicions tell me it's a guy.

They're proven correct when a tall, lean, dark-haired guy steps from the back door and approaches Vela's sister.

My throat tightens when I see him draw her in for a hug and then a long kiss. Anger rushes through me, and I hate myself for feeling such a thing for a perfect stranger. Is it because she looks just like Vela?

And why do I care if this girl kisses another guy? I don't even know her.

Trying to ignore the piercing tug of jealousy in my stomach, I turn my eyes away to give them a little privacy. I'm not a voyeur, after all.

When they finish what they're doing, they turn to head back to her house, though the guy seems to follow rather reluctantly. I'm puzzled as she tugs on his hand until he stops. They have a heated conversation, and finally she gets him to agree to go with her.

I can see from here that she's not happy about his hesitation. I wonder what that's all about.

When they return to her house and go inside, I turn away to look out into the forest again. Tucking my hands in my pockets for warmth, I wish I had thought to pack *something* when I left. I don't have a change of clothes or anything. Thankfully, I had my knife strapped to my leg, so I've been able to hunt and keep myself fed. But what I'd really like is to change into a fresh shirt. It's not too cold to wash my shirt, though. I'd just have to sit in this October weather without a shirt on until it dries. I can't go too much longer, though, without a jacket.

I'd give anything for my homemade pine soap, too. My grand plan of running off after nearly killing Linc was pretty stupid. I should have at least snuck in and gotten my pack I left with Vela.

Thinking about her makes my frustration rise. I just need to talk to her alone. Get her to agree to give me my powers back. I highly doubt Linc would allow her to return the powers that nearly took his life.

Turning back around, I watch the house and keep my eyes peeled for Vela to leave. When she emerged earlier, I very nearly ran out into the street to convince her to come into the woods with me, but then she joined her sister and mom and returned to the house.

I won't make the mistake of missing another chance to talk to her.

My life depends on it. I cannot survive without my powers. I need them back and refuse to contemplate a life without them.

10

Linc

I fist my hands at my side and fight the urge to take the guy Adele brought home out back to have a little chat with him. Basically, he gives me the major creeps.

I see what Adele sees in him; he has the good looks that would attract any girl. But what's got my hackles up is how uncomfortable he looks at being here, and I have to wonder why. If he had good intentions toward my soon-to-be sister-in-law, he shouldn't be unhappy standing here among her family. But it's clear he is.

James seems to have the same mindset as me, because he's glaring at the kid with his arms crossed.

What am I missing about this guy? It can't be anything good.

"So, Steele, come sit and tell us about you," Vela says, leading him and Adele to the sitting area.

It's clear it was Vela's idea to have this guy over. It's painfully obvious James doesn't want him here, and even Sandy looks uncertain. Steele can tell he's not that welcome. He barely glances at me, and I wonder what is it that's made him so wary?

Could it be that he liked his hidden relationship with their daughter? Why, though? That's the question. And one I don't like at all.

I walk over to the living room but remain standing with my arms crossed as I watch this kid, Steele.

He sits with his back bowed and keeps his hands stuffed in his pockets. Adele sits next to him but only glances at him, like she's uncomfortable, too.

Vela asks him, "So, Steele, it's nice to meet you. How are you?"

He shrugs. "I'm fine, I guess."

"Have you had a good day?" she asks.

"It's been whatever."

Whatever? Does he have a vocabulary?

"Okay, so can I ask you, what are your plans for the future?"

"My future?" he asks, with an annoyed expression.

"Yes, what kind of job would you like to have?"

He pauses, then huffs. "What kind of job could I have out here? We basically survive and that's it."

Vela tries again. "Yeah, but now that I'm here, you and your family could leave with my group and see the world. You wouldn't have to hide here."

He straightens a little at that and says, "That would be something, I guess."

He guesses? Okay, this attitude is getting old.

I take two steps to stand over him. When he looks up at me, I say, "Look, kid, Vela has just offered you an amazing opportunity. Don't you think you owe her a thank you?"

I watch as he swallows, his throat moving up and down convulsively. "Uh, yeah, sure. I mean, yeah, thank you. I guess." He glances at me than away.

I glare at him.

He shoots up and says to the room, "I think I have to go." With four long strides, he quits the house, leaving Adele spluttering in his wake.

She turns to the room and shrieks, "Why did you guys have to treat him like that?"

Vela stands. "Adele, we tried to be very welcoming."

Adele's face screws up in anger. "What? You call grilling him like that welcoming?"

Vela's face looks lost, and I step in. "Adele, it was very clear to all of us he did not want to be here. If he took offense, it was his own fault."

"How?" she fires at me.

"Because anyone can see he does not have good intentions toward you. He likes having your attention in the dark, but when you bring him into the light, he shrinks from it."

She trembles in fury, her fists at her side. I notice there's a breeze in the room that wasn't there before.

Sandy must notice it, too, because she says, "Adele, honey, let's sit and talk about this. You asked to have him over and we agreed. What happened wasn't our fault. He did not want to be here. We can guess why, but can you?"

"The only thing I could see was him being grilled, then attacked." She turns furious eyes to me. "Why did you run him off like that?"

Crossing my arms, I say, "Because he needs to know you are not a trinket to be played with. He needs to respect you and to do that, he needs some manners. I tried to teach him some."

Adele glares at all of us. "You wonder why I didn't tell you about my relationship. This is why." She stomps to her room and slams the door.

I remain where I am but watch Vela as she slumps back in her seat.

James looks wearily at Adele's door and says, "This is why we didn't give her our permission to date Steele. He's not trustworthy."

Sandy nods her head in agreement. "We've watched over the past three years while he's strung along every single teen girl here and any other ones who've traveled through. He's got only one thing on his mind."

It is very clear to me what that thing is. I fight back the urge to go outside and find the kid. Beat a little fear into him about ever trying anything like that with Adele.

James seems to be struggling with the same urge I have. Annoyance crosses his face, and he spits out, "If he even thinks he can treat Adele like that, he's got another thing coming."

Vela looks unhappy with this conversation, so I put my anger on the back burner and go to her. I sit next to her and reach for her hand. "Hey, you did great. It wasn't your fault he's such a jerk."

"Is he, though? Did we treat him badly? Maybe he was just on the defensive. No one is at their best when they feel they're being attacked." She gives me a look, and I shrug.

"That kid deserved what I said. He should have been grateful for your offer. He wasn't."

She sighs. "He seemed a little unhappy. Oh, who am I kidding? He is a jerk. You're right, as usual." She leans her head on my shoulder, and I kiss the side of her head.

"The bad ones are usually pretty easy to spot. Once you have them cornered, anyway." I smile at the thought that we made him squirm. Maybe now he'll think twice about dating Adele. She's too much work and guys like him never like that.

Vela picks her head up. "You know, this was all my idea. I should go and talk to Adele."

Before I can, Sandy discourages her. "No. Let her really think through that whole conversation. Maybe she'll realize we're right."

Vela nearly jumps up. "Does her window open?"

"No, it's just glass set in a frame. It can't open," James says, like he's already thought of that.

Vela slumps next to me again. "Oh, good. I wouldn't want her to sneak off to find him."

"Is that what she's been doing?" James growls.

"Uh, I'm not sure. I think, maybe. But," Vela says quickly, "I'll help you keep an eye on her. I'll try to talk to her, too. What does she see in him?"

Sandy sighs. "Besides that he's one of the only eligible boys in this place? His looks, maybe?"

"Yeah, she said something about that," Vela says, tapping her knee with her fingers. "I didn't think she was that serious about him. I don't know why she flew off the handle like that."

"She's sixteen, that's why," I say, pressing my lips together because memories of my poor sister in a very similar situation flood my mind. A guy was interested in her but acted much like Steele had. I soon gave him good reason to find his prey elsewhere. My sister didn't forgive me for a while after that. I'd do it again, however. I wish I could fight these battles for her. I wish more than anything she was here with us. I wish she had a chance to live.

Turning my head, so Vela won't catch my pained expression. I do my best to smooth out my furrowed brow. Moments like this happen, but I try to keep them to myself. This is my grief to bear. According to my parents, I'm the reason for her death. I hired the trainer to show my sister how to rock climb, and one of her practice sessions led to her death. For that, I deserve these moments of pain.

Peace, my son.

A wave of warmth fills me, and I almost look up to the heavens to acknowledge God's presence in the room. It's like He's sitting here with us; I feel His presence so strongly. I bow my head and thank Him for His gift of peace.

I'm not responsible for my sister's death, as much as my parents blame me. Thank you, God, for not blaming me. That's enough for me.

Lost in my introspection, I've missed most of the conversation between Vela and her parents.

"So, when do you want to leave?" James asks Vela.

She looks at me, and I raise my eyebrows. "This is your show, sweetheart. I'm just along for the ride."

She smiles at me. "You know you have more say than anyone. What do you think? Do we have a couple of days for Mama, Papa, and Adele to get ready to go with us?"

I chafe at the thought of waiting longer to leave. That's just longer for me to get Vela in front of a preacher. I need to wed her and soon.

Shoving back my first thought, I know she needs to be ready in the mission God gave her. I need to help her prepare well. In order to accomplish that, I'll have to wait a little longer. Not too long, though. Even I have my limits.

"We can give them time to get ready to leave with us," I say grudgingly. "That way whoever from the community who wants to join can travel with us, too."

"We'll be our own band of traveling Elementals," Vela says, smiling. Then her smile drops when she sees her parents' faces. "Sorry, bad joke. You guys do want to go with us, right?"

Sandy's pained look disappears, and she leans in and says, "Of course we do. We've been waiting for you. We'll help you with whatever you need. We just..." she trails off and looks helplessly at James.

With a chagrined face, he picks up where she left off. "We worry about Adele. She's done nothing but hide her whole life. We came out here to free her from a life of danger. We don't want to hide anymore, but we need to talk over whether traveling with you will be good for her."

A sad look passes over Vela's face, but she smooths her expression and straightens. "I understand. Please do what you feel is best for your family."

Now a pained look comes on James's face, and he says, "Vela, you are our family, too. We are finally complete. And we want to be there for you, but..."

His speech is interrupted when Adele opens the door, striding into the room. "Don't think that I'm too tender to handle traveling. We are a family. I will not be separated from my sister. Now that I've found her, I'm not giving her up. So, stop babying me."

James stands up. "Now, look. We've put up with your outbursts long enough. We've done it because we're sensitive to your feelings, but this needs to stop. Stop treating your mother and I disrespectfully. We will discuss whether this is a good course of action for you and that's final."

Adele backs down, and she says, chagrined, "Just keep in mind how I feel about it, okay? I'm a big girl. I can handle it, Papa. Please let Vela and I stay together."

He walks over to her and puts an arm around her shoulder. "Your mother and I will do everything we can to keep you two together. But let us discuss it, okay?"

She nods, then walks over to sit by Vela. With all three of us on the couch, it's a tight fit, but I don't mind when Vela scoots closer to me. Any contact with her is pure heaven for me. I've missed having her to myself. I wrap an arm over her shoulder, tugging her closer to me.

Our trip here was everything I wanted when I lost her in the woods with Rayne. I wanted nothing other than to have her all to myself. And besides the barely there presence of our guide, I had that. I want it back. But it looks like I'm going to have to share my time with her for the foreseeable future.

"So, let Sandy and I talk in the bedroom. We will pray over a decision," James says, leading Sandy away to their room.

I glance at Adele, who's biting her lip. I wonder what she's thinking.

She doesn't keep me waiting long to find out. She turns to Vela. "You really don't like him, do you?"

"Who?" Vela asks, looking genuinely confused.

"Steele," Adele says in an exasperated voice.

"Oh," Vela says, and looks down like she's found her sweater to be particularly fascinating.

I jump in to help her. "Adele, you know what we think of him. We've already told you. Do you see what we mean? Do you think he has your best interests at heart, like I do Vela's?"

She frowns. "He's not my Intended, so he won't feel for me what you feel for Vela."

"No," I say with frustration. "That's not what I mean. He doesn't want our good opinion at all. He didn't even try to win it. What do you think that says about him?"

She shrugs. "He's shy?"

I snort. "I doubt he was very shy when he got you to agree to date him behind your parents' backs."

At that comment, she bends her head and runs her hands through her hair. "I don't know what to think," she moans.

Vela puts her arm over Adele's shoulder. "You shouldn't hide a guy like that from Mama and Papa. He'll only take advantage of it."

"How?" Adele asks, looking up with a confused look.

Is she really that naïve, or is it just pure innocence?

I try to say as gently as I can, "Adele, when guys don't want anything to do with parents, or a protective brother or sister, it's usually because they just want one thing from the girl."

Her wide-eyed look turns to one of horror. "He wouldn't! He's not that kind of guy."

Vela says, "Yet. He's not that kind of guy, yet. The signs are all there, Adele. Sadly, Linc's very likely right."

Adele crosses her arms and turns a defiant chin to the wall. "I don't believe it. Steele had to work so hard to get me. He wouldn't ruin it by being that way."

"Have you thought that maybe he did that with those other girls, too?" Vela asks gently.

This time Adele half rises. "That's not true. You don't know that about him. He was just trying to get me jealous. And it worked. I finally caved."

"What kind of guy does that?" I ask in a hard voice. I am definitely going to find this kid after this. "He *dated* all the girls here to get to you? He must be a world-class jerk to use them like that."

She sets her chin in a stubborn tilt. "I don't think so. I think it's romantic."

"What planet are you on?" I burst, not able to keep my frustration in anymore.

Vela puts her hand on my leg and gives me a warning glance. "Adele, what he means is, you need to realize that it wasn't very nice for him to use those girls. Aren't they your friends? Don't you care that he broke their hearts?"

This time Adele's face fills with an expression of realization. "I don't know if Cara and Jenny's feeling are hurt or not. They won't talk to me."

"I wonder why," I mumble under my breath.

Adele hears me easily though and turns to face me. "I've been so caught up with Steele that I haven't tried talking to them. I figured I did something they would eventually forgive me for."

"It doesn't sound like you're the one who needs forgiveness," I say definitively. I stand up, because I can't stand this anymore. I'm going to find Steele right now. "I'm going for a walk. You guys talk things over. I won't be long."

Vela looks at me with a raised eyebrow, then gives me a warning glance that's loaded with the message for me to take it easy on the guy.

I return her look, saying I'll do what I need to do and then walk to the door. Opening it, I inhale a few cool, calming breaths. It won't do to go into this next conversation too angry. Asking God for patience, I stride over to Petra's house.

After knocking, I sit back and wait. Petra answers and when she sees it's me, her face turns contemplative. "Have you guys decided when you're leaving?"

"Uh, no. Not yet. James and Sandy are discussing it now. I'm actually here to ask where I can find Steele."

Her face registers confusion at my question, then she mechanically points at a cabin three houses down.

"Thanks. We'll contact you when we've decided something." She nods, still a little confused, and I walk away.

Knowing I'm going to have a talk with this little punk sends heat swarming through my muscles. I crack my knuckles and silently promise myself I won't use them if I don't have to.

They're itching to deliver some punishment for what this kid's already done to the poor innocent hearts in this community. And I'm sure he has that same intention with young Adele, too. Well, that thought is going to be shut down tonight. In about five minutes.

I make it to the right door, knocking firmly on it.

A tall woman with dark pepper colored hair opens the door and looks at me quizzically before a light dawns at who I am. "Can I help you?"

"Yes. I'm here to talk to your son, Steele."

Her irritation surprises me. "Son?" she spits. "You mean my nephew. I'll get him. Hold on."

She turns to call Steele, and I suddenly understand a little bit of why Steele feels like he can walk over every teenage heart here. He's being walked on. This is typical bully behavior.

Compassion filters through my rage, cooling it better than anything else could.

Steele comes to the door, looking annoyed. "What is it?" he asks, looking at me with a healthy dose of uncertainty.

He should be wary of me. He's not stupid, this one.

"I'd like to talk to you. Can we take a walk?" I ask, tempering my voice.

A moment or two passes before he says, "I guess."

There's the 'I guess' remark again. Does he have anything else in his vocabulary?

Without telling his aunt where he's going, he steps outside, his shoulders hunched and fists shoved in his pockets.

We start walking, and I decide to give him the benefit of the doubt. "So, I would just like to talk with you about Adele. How long have you been dating?"

He looks at me with warranted concern; I know all about their secret relationship.

"About a few months, I guess," he finally admits.

"You didn't think to get the permission from her parents first?" I ask, because I have to know the full extent of his guilt.

He shrugs. "They didn't seem to like me much, so I didn't see the point."

He didn't see the point? Was I ever this dense?

"I think that's a sad excuse for hiding your relationship with their daughter. Just because you've dated every girl here, doesn't give you the permission to date the last one you haven't touched."

At that, his face goes pale. "I, I haven't..." he mutters, looking at me with panic.

And this is where I really get his attention.

I stop and grab his shirt, pulling him to me so I'm talking directly to his face. We're the same height, so it's not too hard. He stiffens.

"I am going to make myself very clear here. You will not be touching Adele. Now or ever. She is off limits in that way. If you finally have the nerve to get permission to date her from her parents, you may hold her hand and *that's it.* Am I understood?"

His throat moves up and down before he croaks out, "Yes, I understand."

Giving him a moment to see my deadly serious eyes, I let him go. He stumbles and starts to walk back toward his house, before he spins around, pointing at me with a shaking hand.

"You're not God, you know."

"Oh, but to you, I am God's personal servant. I am Adele's protector, as is her father. You will face both of us if you break your agreement."

Anger flashes across his face and he looks like he wants to say something but seeing my fierce expression, he changes his mind. He turns and walks quickly back to his house.

I watch him go and for a moment, I feel sorry for him. It's obvious he has no love in his own home. He's just looking for love in the arms of my pretty little sister. I squash the feeling because he can feel as sorry for himself as he wants.

He's not touching Adele.

11

Vela

Linc is strangely happy when he returns from his walk. I will get his story from him when we're alone. He did something, and I want to know what it is. He has such a satisfied look, my guess is he went to see Steele.

I'll get Linc's story from him later. Then, Rayne pops into my mind. Has he followed us here? Is he somewhere around?

Adele sits next to me, and she jumps in her seat at my expression. "Hey, what's that look? You're thinking of someone and it isn't Linc," she accuses, her knowing eyes razing my face.

I blink. "How can you possibly know that?"

She smiles. "Because you have a special look on your face whenever Linc is on your mind. This one is different. And you're feeling guilty."

I slap her arm. "Stop reading my emotions! That's so rude."

She shrugs. "I can't help it. And I can tell you because we're sisters."

"Well, it was nothing."

"It wasn't nothing. Tell me."

I debate whether to talk to her about Rayne. He needs to stay in my past. And he's definitely not someone I want to talk about in front of Linc. He's dealt with enough when it comes to that guy.

But then Linc tells us he's going to go chop some firewood, saying he noticed the pile was low.

It's like fate opened up her arms for me to share these painful memories with my sister. Once Linc shuts the door after him, I give Adele a long look. "What we say now stays between us and only us. Promise me. Pinkie swear."

She gives me a happy look and hooks her pinkie with mine, shaking vigorously. "This has to do with Rayne, doesn't it?"

I nod miserably.

She puts her hand to stop me from talking and says, "I like his name, whoever this guy is. It's got such a romantic sound to it."

I huff. "You should meet the guy. He's Adonis himself."

Her brow scrunches up. "Is that a Greek god?"

"Only the god of beauty. He's the most handsome guy I've ever seen, besides Linc. He's light to Linc's dark."

A twinkle enters Adele's eye, and she fidgets. "Oh, this is getting good. Continue."

I inhale a deep breath and run my hands over my legs. "So, Rayne had a way of looking right inside me and saying the most honest and real things. He really made me think through things." My face crumples when I think of our kiss and that I took his elements.

It's not permanent. Even now I can feel his gifts inside, waiting for me to give back to him.

"That," Adele says, pointing at me, "What's that look? What happened?"

I blow out my breath. "Well, we kissed, but it was only once," I finish in a rush.

Adele looks shocked. "Wait, you kissed someone else when you have an Intended?"

I cringe and slump my shoulders. "I know. It was horrible. Especially because Linc saw the whole thing."

Adele puts her face in her hands. "That is horrible."

"Linc forgave me though, amazingly enough. He had a huge moment with God that prepared him for what he saw. If I could take it all back, I would."

Adele picks her head up and then asks, "Didn't you say you took Rayne's elements?"

"Yes, I took them after he tried to kill Linc. He ran off, and I just want to see him so I can give them back."

Adele's face clouds over. "Did he use his gifts to try to kill Linc?" She already feels protective of Linc, and I love that.

"He did. But, Adele, I really feel like he needs them back. For whatever reason, he hurt Linc the way he did, and I can't give his gifts to anyone else. I just can't. But I have no idea where he is."

Adele's lips press together as she thinks. "If I had to guess, I think he wouldn't go too far from you. I'm sure he'll turn up soon to convince you to return his elements."

"Just because I want to give him back what's his, doesn't mean I want to be alone with him. I hope he doesn't try to take me anywhere. I'm really powerful, Adele. I'm afraid what my knee-jerk reaction would be."

She cocks her head. "What is it like having all four elements? Do you feel like you're going to explode at any moment?"

I think over her question for a minute. "No, I mean, yes, it is a lot of power to contain, but I've kind of gotten used to the feeling, honestly. It's when I get really emotional that it's hard to control."

She nods knowingly. "I can imagine. It's hard for me to contain my wind gift sometimes, too. I don't really have to out here, so it'll be hard to keep my emotions controlled once we go back out into the real world." She looks out the window like she can see our new path.

"I hope Mama and Papa let you come with me. I don't want to leave you behind." I hold my hand out to her.

She takes it and squeezes. "I think they'll come to their senses and see that I'm a big girl. I'm sure they will."

We look up when our parents emerge from their bedroom. "You must have heard us talking," I say to them with a smile.

James smiles tiredly at me before he says, "No, we didn't. But we have come to a decision." Taking Sandy's hand, he looks fondly at Adele and says, "We're ready to leave when you are. With one condition." He looks directly at me and waits for me to nod.

"If at any point our travels with you become too hard for Adele, we're going to have to leave your group. We need to keep her welfare in mind."

I laugh happily and wrap my arms around Adele's neck. Her wide smile shows how pleased she is with the news. We both look up at Papa and say at the same time, "Thank you."

He looks at our embrace with fondness and says, "Of course. We're a family. We're going to do everything we can to stay together."

Linc had re-entered the house while James was talking. He asks, "So, does that mean we can leave soon?"

"What about the rest of the community? That doesn't give them much time to leave their homes." Sandy says.

"How about we go see Petra," Linc suggests. "See if she's found anyone who wants to join us."

"We'll go with you," James says, reaching for his coat.

That seems to get all of us in motion. Adele jumps up from the couch and runs to her room to get her jacket. I put mine on and Linc does the same.

I pat Jack's head and call him to my side, then march to the door once we're all ready. I say a prayer on our way to Petra's that she'll have some answers.

We walk briskly to Petra's door and knock. It opens quickly. She peers out at all of us and asks, "Where's the fire?"

James says hurriedly, "No, Petra, we just want to talk to you about who might want to join with us. Do you think whoever wants to go will be willing to leave soon?"

She grimaces and gives us a long-suffering look. "Come in," she says gruffly. "Let's talk over the details."

As we walk inside, I notice Petra give Adele a long hug. She whispers something to her, and I smile. I'm glad Adele has someone like Hannah in her life. It takes a tribe to raise a child, and Adele is no exception.

Once we're all inside, Linc stands awkwardly by the door and moves from one foot to another. Probably because he wants to leave as soon as possible to get us married sooner. I hide a smile. He's so adorable in his quest to make me his wife. I secretly love it.

Okay, who am I kidding? I openly love it. Who wouldn't?

Once Petra's finished greeting Adele, she turns to all of us, motioning us to the chairs like before. Once we're all seated, she asks, in a business-like way, "What's the plan? Where will we go first? Give me the details of your traveling agenda."

I try to hide my cringe because Linc and I haven't gotten that far yet in planning. He seems as uncomfortable as I am because he says, "We don't have the pertinent details yet, Petra. We need to get back to the leaders at Polar Bear to answer those questions. While we've been here, they've been making our travel plans."

"Who is that?" Petra fires at him. "Rick and Gary?" Her disbelieving tone seems to question our choice for leaders.

"Yes," I say. "They are well traveled, and we trust their judgment."

"You need more than those two guiding you," she says, sniffing. "If you leave it to them, you'll end up in Timbuktu."

Hope rises in me. "Would you like to join our leadership team, Petra? We could use a few more good minds to help us figure out how to spread the news that I'm here and ready to start my mission."

"Which is?" she asks, her piercing eyes studying me intently.

"To unite our world," I say simply. "That's it. I know it's a big job, well, impossible really, but I'm ready to try."

She thinks for a moment before she looks around the room and says, "And all of you are ready to follow her anywhere?"

A resounding chorus of yes fills the air.

"Well, it's clear you won't be able to do this thing without a few good minds guiding you. I'll join you."

I take a look around and ask hesitantly, "And are you married? Are you bringing a husband?"

She shakes her head. "I'm not the marrying kind. Maybe if I found my Intended, I would be, but it hasn't happened yet. But I still have hope." Her face has such a wistful look I can't help but wish the same for her. To find her soulmate.

I smile widely at her. I've always wondered about Elementals who won't settle for any partner but their Intended and I've just found one. And in Petra of all people. I try to hide my surprise at the romantic in her. I suddenly hope she finds him during our travels.

That's one of the reasons I'm taking on this impossible mission. So that Elementals can live together in peace and have a better chance to find their other halves.

But, when I think of Kane and Elia who clearly aren't each other's Intended, I worry what will happen if they commit to one another and then find their soulmates. What would happen then?

"So," Petra says, back to her business-like tone. "We need to find out who wants to leave here and join your little posse. Let me take care of that. I'll have an answer for you in a couple of hours. Will that work?"

We all nod, impressed with her promise.

Adele is bouncing in her seat and looks like she wants to leave. I'm guessing she wants to talk to Steele to see if he's coming with us.

James and Sandy look determined, as if they're ready for anything. Petra is calm, unbothered in the way only a leader could be, as she sizes up her troops.

Linc stands and says, "Well, we'll let you get to it then. You know where to find us when you've learned who's willing to leave tomorrow."

Petra nods serenely, and we all stand to leave. But before we go, she says, "If you all have a mind to allow me one more person, I'd like to be responsible for young Steele." She looks at Adele, who brightens at the news. "I don't think his aunt will be too keen on traveling all over the world. She's wanted her freedom for a while. I don't mind taking over his guardianship."

Adele puts her hands on her mouth, her eyes dancing in excitement. I hold back a groan. I was hoping to separate them, and by the looks of it, so were our parents.

Petra guesses their thoughts. She holds up her hand. "Now, before you get your hackles up, just listen. That boy has had nothing but hardships his whole life. He's been abandoned by both parents, and his aunt hasn't exactly been a loving mother figure. I'd like to give him a different future. And I think the start of it will be with all of you."

At her words, we all capitulate, but Linc says, "He just needs to keep his hands to himself."

Adele blushes darkly and opens her mouth in embarrassment. But Petra answers before Adele can say anything, "I'm perfectly aware of young Steele's proclivities. I will be responsible for him."

We have no choice but to accept. I need her on my leadership team. I'll just have to get used to Steele being a part of her package. If I can take on a job like Chosen Child, I can be Adele's protector.

And by the looks of James and Linc, I won't be the only one.

12

Linc

As we leave Petra's house, my head is reeling. I can't believe her one condition means we're stuck with that kid, Steele. He's such a wild card, I don't like that I'm going to have to keep one eye on him during our travels.

Petra's explanation of his past makes his surly attitude somewhat more understandable. It doesn't change the fact, however, that he's targeting my new little sister. And if I have anything to say about it, he won't be doing that for very long.

Even the cynical side of me knows that there's hope for him, though. If he's willing to be taught and led into a different kind of future, I think he has a shot at being a good guy.

I'm guessing his sordid romantic history is due to boredom, and possibly he hopes to replace his sorely lacking familial relationships with romantic ones. There's literally nothing to do out here but survive. Not exactly an environment conducive for a teen guy to grow up.

Adele tries to invent an excuse to leave our group, one I don't hear. We all know she's not going to do whatever she's asking but going straight to Steele's. I'm not surprised when James and Sandy give her a resounding no.

Her shoulders slump, and she grumbles while she walks next to Vela. I pick up my pace to find out what they're talking about.

"I only wanted to go talk to Helen and Debra," Adele is saying. Her hands are stuffed in her pockets, and her mouth is set in a pout. She looks so much like Vela, I can't help but smile. I make sure to hide it behind my hand, though. Adele doesn't seem like she's in any mood to be teased.

"We're not stupid, Adele," Vela says lowly. "Mama and Papa know you were just trying to go see Steele."

"I was going to stop by there, but I really was going to go see my friends," Adele argues. "I can't tell my friends I'm leaving? And ask them if they're coming?"

I interject, "Why don't you let Petra break the news to Steele that he's joining our group?"

She scrunches up her eyebrows. "I really wanted to see his expression. He's going to be so excited to leave here."

I think of Steel's life. Hardships can either embitter and harden you or make you flexible and ready for a change in any environment. I just don't know which way Steele will choose. I wonder if he has any faith at all. I'll make sure to share mine with him.

"How about if I offer to go with you to your friends? I'd like to meet them," Vela offers.

I lift my eyebrow at her. She gives me a questioning look. I want to spend time with her, too. I'm feeling a little abandoned.

She must guess my train of thoughts because she smiles and leans in close where I get a whiff of her delicious rose and honey-butter roll fragrance. How those two scents can smell so good together, I'll never know, but Vela wears them beautifully.

"Don't worry, we'll take a walk later," she promises me.

My heart warms. She's been so good about giving me her undivided attention, and I've lapped it up like a starving man. I can't get enough time with my beautiful girl.

When my distracting thoughts of being alone with Vela make me unaware of the girls' new plans, I pay closer attention to what they're saying.

They're asking James and Sandy again if Adele can go visit her friends, but this time with Vela in tow. They seem to trust Vela to not allow Adele to be alone with the untrustworthy secret boyfriend, because they agree.

Adele squeals and tugs at Vela's hand to lead her off in a different direction. Vela gives me a promising wink and leaves with Adele.

A face flashes in the group of trees just off to the side of the community. Someone's out there, and my heart pounds at the thought that it could be Rayne following Vela.

Not questioning my instincts, I take off into the trees. I catch a flash of a shirt and then it's gone. I wish I had Jack with me to track whoever it is, but Vela's trusty dog is with her.

Picking up my pace, I race around a bend of trees and find...nothing. Looking in every direction, I expand my other senses and search for traces of body heat. Again, nothing. Where did the person go?

I didn't catch a face or any features, so I'm not even sure if it was a guy or a girl. And why would they run from me? Walking the tree line, I search the ground for tracks. Again, nothing.

Thinking, I look up in the trees, wondering if they scaled a tree to get away from me. That, too, returns zero results. Abandoning my search, I go to find Vela to ask if I can borrow Jack. I could use his animal senses to help me.

Jogging back to the community, I keep an ear out for any branches breaking or any sound at all that would alert me to where the person went. Frustrated at my fruitless search, I hunt down Vela and Adele.

I finally spot them down at the end of the community. Jack is receiving all kinds of warm greetings from two unknown girls. They must be Helen and Debra.

The sun is low in the sky, so I know I have to use what light I have left. Catching up to Vela, I lean in and ask in her ear if I can borrow Jack.

She nods, giving me a questioning look, but I shake my head at her. I don't want her to worry about the possibility of Rayne following her.

Jack comes with me easily. I decide to stick close to where Vela is, knowing that if it is Rayne, he'd stay near to try to get her alone. I growl at that thought.

Over my dead body.

With Jack beside me, I give him the command, "Seek, boy." I know from traveling with Vela the past couple of days that he will go ahead of me and track anything he can. If Rayne is out here, I'm sure Jack will find him.

Jack immediately sets out in the woods, his nose first in the air, then on the ground. He finds something close to where I lost my quarry and sets off in a run, stopping to sniff every few yards or so. He goes further in the woods and then, with his sights set on something I can't see, he's off.

I race after Jack. He's barking now, and I hear crashing ahead of me. I hope whoever Jack is chasing isn't an innocent member of this community. If so, he's terrorizing them.

I lose sight of Jack, but when I hear a shout of pain and a familiar male voice begging Jack to leave him alone, I break through the brush, two fireballs in my hands ready to take my enemy down.

Jack has his teeth on Rayne's pant leg as he lies on the ground, trying to get away from Vela's vicious guard dog. A twinge of regret pierces me because I know why Rayne is so afraid of Jack. He has firsthand knowledge what a true bite from Jack can do after I sicced the dog on him over a month ago.

I soon banish that thought and growl, "Rayne, don't move."

He turns terrified eyes to me and then he's back to watching Jack.

"Jack, release him," I command, and Jack immediately lets go of Rayne.

Rayne scoots back, his hands sliding in the dirt. "What are you going to do?" he asks, a fierce light entering his eyes now that Jack has backed off.

What's strange though is not sensing the water and wind gift in him. He's pretty brave without his elements. Then I remember he's got a knife strapped to his leg. I recall seeing it on him.

He's inching his hand toward his leg, but I warn him, "Hold your hands up, Rayne. I'm not going to fall for your tricks again. I know you'll just slice my neck open again with a metal knife this time." Anger and memory of pain from the last time he did that fill me to the brim, making my vision narrow.

Frustration fills his face, but he obeys and holds up his hands.

Wanting his weapon away from him, I approach slowly and look to see which leg he's got that wicked knife strapped to. I soon see it's his right, which means I'll have to reach across him to get it.

"Don't. Move," I order Rayne.

Dousing the fire in my hands, I lean over and just when I go to grab the knife, Rayne lunges and wraps my neck in his strong arm, pulling me down to the ground. I use the momentum to roll to the side, pulling Rayne's knife from the sheath. We roll on the ground, both of us trying to get the advantage. I use everything I have to end up on top. Jack, growling, gets a hold on Rayne's shirt, making him absolutely immobile.

Bringing Rayne's knife up, I place it at his neck and say quietly, "Don't move."

He's breathing hard, but obeys, looking at Jack with fear. I'm a little winded, too, but I hold the knife steady and ask, "What are you doing out here? Trying to get Vela alone, maybe?"

He presses his lips together, refusing to speak as his eyes flash in anger.

"No answers for me? That's fine, I've got you figured out. You want your powers back, and you were going to do whatever you could to get them from Vela. Am I right?"

He shakes his head in tiny movements so his knife won't nick his neck. "I wouldn't hurt Vela," he wheezes.

"Oh, only me, right? It wasn't enough to practically chop my head off. You had to try to finish the job."

Again, he shakes his head. "I shouldn't have tried to kill you. I'm sorry, Linc. I really am."

"Big words," I growl. "for someone who has a knife at his neck."

"I mean it. I shouldn't have used my wind knives. Believe me, I regret it."

"I guess you would regret it since Vela punished you by taking your gifts away."

He slumps, his body limp. All fight leaves him. "I need them back, Linc. You don't know what it's like to lose your powers. It's like I have nothing left to live for."

"Sure, you do. You have your whole life to live. Just not as an Elemental," I say easily. I figure I have to make him squirm as much as possible, considering I know full well Vela wants to return his gifts. But he deserves my punishment, too. He did try to kill me, after all.

I give him a little room for movement when I call Jack off.

A groan comes from Rayne's throat. "Please, Linc. Accept my apology and let me talk to Vela. I won't try to take her from you. That's over. I promise."

It's strange. It doesn't make me feel good to hear Rayne beg. I just feel sorry for him.

"Oh, I know you won't try to take Vela from me. She's made her decision very clear." I can't help but rub a little more salt in his wounds. If he has any.

He does. He winces. "Hey, man, I'm sorry. I really didn't understand the Intended bond thing."

"And now you do? What, did you find your Intended out here all the sudden?"

He seems to be considering his words before answering.

Wait. Did he find his Intended? That's literally impossible, since he hasn't met anyone out here hiding all by himself.

I shake him, pressing the knife into his neck just a little as a horrible feeling snakes through my veins. "Answer me. Did you find her?"

"No! I mean I don't know."

Not liking his response, I wait for him to say more.

Visibly swallowing, he says in a rush, "Look, I just caught a glimpse of Vela's younger sister, and the strangest feeling came over me. I can't explain it. But I haven't even talked to her, so I don't know if it's anything. I've just been thinking...maybe she could be my Intended." He says it with such a sense of awe, but it only makes me want to punch his face.

I resist, barely, gritting my teeth as I digest his words.

Starting to panic, he says, "I'm not even sure. It could explain why I was so drawn to Vela. I just had the wrong sister. I don't know, man; it just feels right."

"You won't have either sister," I promise, pressing the knife harder. My vision is turning red. First, he tries to take Vela from me, not caring about my Intended bond with her. Now, he's trying to say he has that same bond with Adele.

Quickly moving the knife away, I bring my forearm up into his throat and press down and say slowly, "You will not have anything to do with Adele. She's too young for anyone right now." I'm really getting tired of guys targeting Vela's little sister.

He hesitates, then nods. "Okay, I won't have anything to do with her. Just please, let me talk to Vela. Beg her for my powers back. I know she hasn't given them away yet."

"You've been watching her this entire time?" I ask in a dark voice.

How have I not sensed his presence?

I curse his tracking abilities. He must be exceptional at them for me to not know he's been around.

He nods. "Yeah, you would have too, if she took your fire away from you. You'd do whatever you needed to get it back."

I inhale, praying for patience. "So, what was your plan? To get her alone and then what?"

"Beg," he says simply. "I was going to beg her for forgiveness and promise her whatever she wanted if she returned my powers."

I hold him down and think. Vela wants to give him his elements back. But how do I manage to get her out here without Adele? She's Vela's shadow now that they've found each other.

The way I see it, I have little choice. Vela's made her decision. I just have to keep her safe while she talks to Rayne. And now, Adele, too. I pray that he's wrong, and he doesn't have a bond with my future little sister.

If Rayne does have an Intended bond with my future sister-in-law...well, I can only imagine how awkward those family dinners will be.

13

Rayne

L inc allows me to get up, and I watch him warily since he's still holding my knife. I wasn't going to do anything but threaten him with it, I tell myself. Though my temper has always been vicious when provoked and our fight was definitely provoking.

He points my knife at me and motions for me to walk.

"Where are we going?" I ask. If he's leading me to the community who would gladly mob me for stalking their precious Chosen Child, I'm going to have some words with Linc over that plan.

"I'm taking you exactly where you want to go, to Vela," he says. Then speaking under his breath, I hear him say, "I just hope Adele isn't with her."

Adele? I don't know how I feel about that name. I roll it around in my mind and find I like it. It's different for a girl. I've always known I would fall for a girl who would surprise me at every turn. For a while, I thought that girl was Vela, but life turned out very differently than even I could imagine.

Her little sister does things to my insides that I never felt for Vela. I have a longing, a pull from my gut to talk to this Adele and find out if she really is my other half. I start walking in the direction Linc points with *my* knife and think. By the look on Linc's face, he is very unhappy I could have a connection to Adele. Or is it Vela he's still worried about?

I dismiss that thought just as easily. I tried my best to get her to think of me as a love interest, but I don't think she ever really fell for it. Well, I think back to our kiss, maybe for a moment she did. I'm pretty sure she deeply regrets that impulse, however.

I know I do. And now that I might have an Intended bond with her sister, I don't think Adele would appreciate what I did. Then I scoff at myself. I don't even know what, if anything, I have with Vela's little sister.

And I never should have tried to pull Vela from Linc. Their bond is sacred. I know that now, because if they feel half of what I'm feeling for someone I haven't even met yet, then I was a first-class jerk for trying to tear them apart.

"Keep your hands away from your body," Linc orders, and I comply, holding my arms up.

If he's taking me to Vela, I will offer nothing but complete submission. I'll do anything to get my gifts back. I vowed to follow her to the ends of the earth, and I stand by that promise. If she lets me, I'll be on the first line of her defense as a thank you for saving my gifts for me.

She punished the invading Extremists by taking their elements and giving them to volunteering Elementals in the Polar Bear. I still wonder why she didn't give my gifts away. When I realized she could, I kept my eyes peeled for the recipient. But, to my surprise, she held on to my gifts.

Even now, I reach for my powers and my hands come up empty. Looking ahead, I fist them well away from my body. Linc leads me to the back of the house that appears to belong to her birth parents. A big part of me hopes Adele happens to come back here. But I doubt I'll get to meet her. Not if Linc has anything to say about it.

"Put your back to the wall," Linc says gruffly, looking all around.

"She's not here," I tell him tersely, irritated he's keeping me from meeting my possible Intended.

He whips his head to me. "Who?"

I lift my eyebrows. "Adele. She's not around."

"How do you know?" He gives me a dark look.

"Because I can feel when she's close." I shrug. "I told you; it doesn't make sense. Except when it does."

He glares at me and knocks on the back door. He keeps me way off to the side so there's no chance for me to look inside the house.

The door opens and Vela's father pokes his head out. "Linc? What are you doing out here?"

Linc motions for him to come out and he starts in surprise when he sees me. Then he notices the knife in Linc's hand.

"What's going on?" he asks, instantly on guard.

"This is Rayne," Linc says, keeping a close eye on me. Even though it isn't necessary. There's nowhere else in the world I'd rather be but right here.

"Who's Rayne?" Vela's father asks as he closes the door.

"Rayne is from the Polar Bear. He's the guy who tried to kill me."

Vela's father scowls and turns to me. "This is him? What's a human doing living at the Polar Bear?"

"I'm not human, I'm an Elemental," I grit out. "Or I was until Vela took my gifts."

Understanding falls on his face, and he stiffens when he realizes what I want. "You want your gifts back."

"I do."

He crosses his arms and looks at Linc, who hasn't stopped watching me. "What are you thinking, Linc?"

Linc scowls. "This isn't the only issue we're dealing with, James."

And here comes the part where an overprotective father tries to kill me. No, Linc, don't tell him.

"He thinks he has an Intended bond with Adele."

And he tells him. Great.

A cloud of anger comes over James's face, and he turns to me with a quick turn. "Is this true?"

I reluctantly nod. "I'm not sure. I just have a very strong feeling every time I see her that she's more than just a pretty girl."

Fury enters his eyes at my words, and it looks like he's physically restraining himself from attacking me. He turns to Linc. "I don't want him anywhere near my daughter."

"I agree," Linc says easily, but with a little pity. His eyes flick my way. He must know that I'm dying to meet her. Just to see if it could be true.

"Okay," James says after a moment of thought. "I'll bring Vela out here, but we have to keep Adele from him at all costs."

"Wait a minute," I argue. "Doesn't she have a right to see if I'm her Intended? She'll always wonder who it is if you don't let us at least meet each other."

"I don't care," James whips at me. "You tried to murder another Elemental. That means you lose any right to finding your Intended."

I slump against the wall, feeling defeated. He's right. I am a foul excuse for a person. I'll forever regret trying to kill Linc. I was a hot-headed fool. I let my poisonous thoughts override my reason. I truly believed Linc was responsible for the Extremists attacking our community, and I wanted him to hurt for it. Except, I went way, way too far. Also, I was enraged that Linc was the guy Vela chose. I have never been on the losing end before and for the first bitter time; I found myself as the loser. It was humiliating. Something my pride could not stand. Many things culminated in that terrible moment, and I allowed rage to fuel my decisions. It seems I'm to be further punished by keeping me from my Intended.

"James, would you go get Vela? She's been wanting to give Rayne's gifts back to him. She's saved them for him," Linc asks.

I look up in surprise at hearing that. So, Linc just made me sweat as I wondered if Vela would return my gifts.

James looks at me suspiciously, then moves to go back inside. Before he does, he points his finger at me. "You will not meet Adele. Not under any conditions will I allow it."

At that, he leaves to find Vela and my spirits plummet. I've never thought I wanted to meet my Intended, but all that changed when I got a glimpse of Adele. Now, I have to know.

Linc takes one look at the anguish on my face and says, "You did it to yourself, you know. What do you expect him to do? Welcome a potential murderer with open arms?"

"I know that, Linc. But to never meet her? That's harsh," I say, looking out in the distance, wondering where she is. Just then, I get a pull on my middle, and I know she's close. She must be approaching the house and coming in the front door.

I turn my head in that direction and Linc knowingly says, "Don't even think about it. I'm an excellent knife thrower. I'll just stop you in your tracks if you try to run for it."

Adrenaline races through my body as I sense Adele's nearness, but I force myself to be still. I have to be compliant to get my gifts back. That's the only thing stopping me from trying a valiant, but stupid, attempt to meet Adele. But there's a big part of me that's willing to sacrifice even the return of my gifts just to meet her.

"Hey, let's get you your gifts back and then we'll cross any other bridge after that, okay?" Linc says, accurately reading my intent.

Vela emerges from the back door, her face open in surprise at seeing me. "Rayne?"

"Hi, Vela," I say gently, not wanting to scare her. The last time she saw me, I was a mess of pure rage, first at Linc, then at her.

She stands next to Linc, noting his hold on my knife. James is right behind her, and it looks like he's guarding the door.

I can see why. I'm big enough to look like a potential threat.

"Vela, I'd like to ask your forgiveness. I never should have tried to kill Linc. I'm just glad he's not dead. I know I'm a failure at being a good Elemental, but I'd like to have that gift back. To be an Elemental again. Vela," I plead. "I'm nothing without my gifts. Please, give them back to me?"

Vela doesn't hesitate, and she turns a beaming smile at Linc. "See, I told you he regrets what he did. I knew he would come to his senses."

I nod hard and say, "I really have. Please don't give my elements to anyone else."

She turns kind eyes to me I don't deserve and says, "Rayne, I wouldn't do that. I've been saving them for when I'd see you again." Her look hardens, however, and my gut clenches with anticipation. "Do you promise to never harm an innocent ever again? To only use your gifts against the Extremists, and even then, to show kindness?"

I nod and say in a deep voice, "I'll make that promise. And I'll make you another one. I vow to protect you from this day forward. Whether you accept me in your group or not, I'll always be close keeping an eye on you."

She looks at me warily. "Rayne, I don't know if that's a good idea. I'll have plenty of protectors when we travel. You don't need to make that promise."

"But I do, Vela. If you give me my life back, I'll dedicate it to your mission, to your protection. I won't fail in my responsibility to protect and not harm."

She hesitates and then looks at James and Linc, deciding my fate.

James speaks up, "Vela, you can't allow this man into your circle. He's proved that he's capable of violent tendencies."

"I know," she says, biting her lip. She looks out into the forest deep in thought.

Linc, surprisingly, stays quiet, ever her supporter.

Just then, someone from inside pushes on the door. I hear Adele calling out, "Hello? Why is the door not opening?"

Everything screams at me to pull the door open, no matter who's standing in the way. I fist my hands to keep myself from doing anything rash.

Vela looks at her father with a question in her eyes.

He looks resolutely at her and obstinately keeps the door closed, despite Adele calling out for him to open it. After a moment, Adele stops because there's no more knocking and calling.

We all realize at the same time she's going out the front door and coming around the house. I brace myself to meet this girl who's thrown my life out of orbit.

James, not knowing which side to intercept her, hesitates, then chooses the left. Vela looks on in confusion at the stony faces of James and Linc. "What's going on?" she asks. "Why can't he meet Adele?"

Linc just shakes his head at her.

James chose wrong, because Adele comes running around the right side of the house, directly where I'm standing. I spin to face her, and my eyes drink her in, all while the wind blows her scent to me. It envelops me. The tantalizing fragrance of jasmine and berries makes my head spin with its meaning.

She stands in shock, looking at me wide eyed. She's out of breath from running, and it takes every atom in my body to keep myself from embracing her.

Adele is my Intended. It's true, I was right.

"Who are you?" she asks me directly.

Even her voice is a delight to my senses, and I answer quickly, "Rayne. I'm your..."

"Stop!" James bellows from the left side of the house. He runs up to Adele and quickly drapes his arm around her shoulders, pulling her away from me.

"*You're* Rayne?" she asks, her face full of disbelief. She looks at Vela over her dad's shoulder and then she's back to looking at me. "You're here for your gifts, aren't you?"

She resists her dad's efforts to drag her away. "Vela, what are you going to do?" Just then, the wind changes. She inhales deeply and with a gasp, she throws her dad's arms away and runs to me.

She slams against my chest, and I rock back, keeping my balance by holding onto Adele's arms. "*You?* You're my Intended?" she asks, hungrily gazing over my features, just like I'm doing with hers. It's uncanny how much she looks like Vela, but I can easily tell them apart. Adele's eyes are more direct and intense. I find I like it a lot. I drink her presence in like warm milk. I can only nod.

She fists her hands in my shirt and asks, "My dad wasn't going to let you meet me, was he?" She turns furious eyes to her father, who's standing like he doesn't know what to do with his reaching arms.

"I have a right to meet him!" she yells.

She turns to Vela. "Did you know?"

Vela shakes her head and goes into Linc's arms as he watches all of this with hard eyes.

Suddenly Adele spins back to Vela. "Wait. You *kissed* my *Intended*?"

Vela splutters helplessly. I don't even know what to say to that. Vela must have told her about our terrible mistake.

Adele turns back to me, and I open and close my mouth, completely speechless. I say the only thing I can, "I'm sorry, Adele. It was a total mistake for both of us."

She steps away from me, her chest heaving. "I don't even know what to say."

"Okay, this has gone on long enough," James growls, and steps between us. He puts his hand on Adele's shoulder. "You, young lady, stay right there."

"He's my Intended. I have every right to speak to him," she says, trying to move around him.

"You realize he tried to kill your sister's fiancé?" he asks.

Pain crosses her face, and she looks over at Linc, then at me.

Grief pierces my stomach when she asks, "Why did you do that? Linc is amazing. Why would you try to kill him?"

Regret pushes me to say, "I should never have done it. Believe me, I deeply regret what I did, and I'm very thankful he's alive." I run my hand over my face, remembering the stress of when I committed the heinous act. "I've asked for his forgiveness, but believe me when I say, I don't deserve it."

James gives me a frustrated look but says to Vela, "Are you giving him back his elements?"

I notice Adele listens as intently as I do.

To my great relief, Vela nods and then steps away from Linc. "I can do it right here."

Adele struggles against her father's hold on her. "Vela, you are not touching him again. And you," she seethes at me. "You need to promise you will never use your gifts for harm again."

My chest warms at not only her jealousy but her insistence I become someone good. That must mean she wants to care for me but can't if I don't make this promise.

"I've already told Vela I won't," I say firmly. "I stand by that oath."

Vela says to Adele, "Don't worry. I don't need to touch Rayne to give him back his powers." Then she turns to Linc. "Are you okay with me returning the powers of someone who tried to use them to kill you?"

He stares at me hard for a long moment before he nods. "I forgive him for what he did. He seems to regret it, so I think you can trust him with his powers."

At his words, Vela moves toward me, holding her hands up. Linc follows, keeping close behind her. I know from before that he should stay close, because she'll fall backward from using this gift.

I brace myself and hold my breath. This is what I've been waiting, hoping, and praying for since my gifts were torn from my body. Emotion overwhelms me, but it's nothing compared to when Vela's power shoots into me.

Unadulterated heat bursts into my chest, then spreads. I reel backwards, landing on my back. Tears trickle down my face as I feel the blessed and miraculous presence of my gifts once again. A chill speeds through my veins, icing them as it travels throughout my extremities. That's my Borean wind gift returning.

Then my blood rushes like a tidal wave from my head to my toes. The greatest of relief fills me as I understand my Neronian gifts are back, too. I feel around for the secondary powers and realize even those have returned.

I can sense emotions with my Borean element, and if I wanted to, I could temporarily take someone's gift, incapacitating them, using my Neronian gift. As good as it feels to have all my powers back, I accept the tremendous duty of using them responsibly. I will never use my gifts to harm again, unless my life, or someone else's, is on the line.

My chest heaves as all these feelings rush from my head down to my toes. It takes me several minutes to readjust. Once I do, I get to my feet and use a surge of power to jump into the air. I push wind under my feet and soar upwards.

With a whoop, I flip in the air, glad I remembered how to command the air. Relishing the cool rush of wind on my face, in my hair, I laugh outright and hold my arms up, soaring into the sky. When I start to feel my strength wane, I command the wind to lessen. I hover in place, and I take a moment to look around. I love being this high. I feel indomitable, unreachable. I see Adele way below me and even from up here, I long to be near her. My muscles are stretched to their limit anyway, so I pull the air away from under my feet and come down slowly. No need to break a leg just when I've gotten my elemental powers back.

When my foot touches the ground, I fall down to the earth, laughing. Almost as if my body is attuned to her, I look and see Adele tear herself away from her dad and run toward me. She falls to the ground on her knees next to me. She puts her hand on my chest, and I cover her hand with mine.

"Are you okay?" Adele asks, her eyes worried as she looks me over.

I nod happily, sniffing, my eyes and nose watering from the change in height I just experienced. "I'm great. Better than great. I'm back to myself."

She huffs out a breath of relief. "That's good. You're sure you're okay?" she asks, searching my eyes and running her gaze all over me.

I give her a warm smile. "Yes."

"Then why aren't you sitting up? Why did you fall down like that?"

"I don't know. Just enjoying the feelings, I guess."

She frowns. "Can you sit up for me? Just to prove you're as good as you say you are?"

To please her, because I realize I really do want to make my Intended happy, I sit up in one fluid motion. That puts our faces close, and she sits back, stunned. Her nostrils flare in an adorable way.

"What do I smell like?" I ask, powerful emotions overwhelming me. I've found my Intended. My other half. I will forever cherish her if she lets me.

Her faces scrunches up in thought. "I can't explain it. I smell a homemade soap on you, but what I'm really noticing is... peppermint and chocolate?"

She says it like she's asking me, and I point to my chest. "It's not what I think. I can't smell what you do. I notice something completely different."

Her eyes light up. "You mean my scent?"

I nod.

A curious look comes over her, then she blushes. "Are you going to tell me?"

Just to tease her because I don't know how much time we have left to talk, I ask, "You really want to know?"

"It's bad, isn't it? I smell like something horrible."

"What would be horrible?"

"Oh, like onions or grass or something."

She pouts, and it takes everything in me not to reach for her. Instead, I smile. "I happen to like the smell of fresh cut grass. But no. You have a jasmine and berry fragrance that I find utterly captivating." Even saying that surprises me. I don't usually talk like this. She's bringing out a whole new side to me.

She smiles widely. "I like that."

Before I can respond, Adele is pulled up by her father. Her mother joins them, and they lead her away for a furiously whispered conversation. I don't want to tear my eyes away from Adele, but I want to be sure Vela is all right after using her powers on me. She's leaning against Linc, looking tired, but other than that, seems fine.

I breathe a sigh of relief. There was no harm done, and for that, I'm eternally grateful. I give Vela a smile and say with complete sincerity, "Thank you, Vela. You've given me two great gifts: forgiveness and my returned elements. I will be forever in your debt."

I stand up slowly to not alarm anyone with sudden movements. Before, I took the power of my gifts for granted, but I hold them like treasures now.

Vela says tiredly, "You're welcome. Just remember your promises."

Holding my hand to my chest, I say, "I won't forget."

Life cannot get any better for me. I vow to never make such catastrophic mistakes again.

14

Vela

After watching Rayne fly around, I wonder if I can do the same. I'm sure I can, but don't relish the idea of practicing that particular talent. I lean on Linc's solid chest and enjoy the feeling of him. With his arm around my waist, I watch looks of longing pass between Adele and Rayne.

I lift my head to look at Linc, and he's watching them, too. "Do you remember our first meeting?" I whisper.

He smiles down at me fondly. "I sure do, but it's not their experience. I didn't get to enjoy our connection for a long while. I distinctly remember one little Intended running away like a scared rabbit, or was it a fierce kitten?"

I snuggle my face into his chest. "You're never going to let me live that comment down."

"You've got that right. A kitten is only snuggly. I've never met a fierce kitten in my life."

"They exist," I mumble. Then I'm sure to say, "I'm sorry for running from you. I wish I was as brave as my little sister."

He snorts. "I wouldn't say she's feeling brave. More like desperate to get to her other half."

"What are the odds we're going to be able to keep them apart?"

He huffs a laugh. "Next to nothing. I've never seen anyone more determined to fall in love than your sister."

I smack his arm. "Hey, don't talk badly of her. She's sixteen. That explains everything."

He cocks his eyebrow at me. "Were you like that at sixteen?"

"Why?" I ask, grinning, looking up at him. "Jealous?"

"Insanely," he says, squeezing his arm around me. Then he sighs. "What do you think Steele is going to do when he finds out about this?"

I roll my eyes. "I say that Rayne is going to get his just deserts for trying to take me from you. Because Steele is going to do the exact same thing Rayne did. I foresee drama with a capital D in our future."

"*Our* future? Why am I involved in this?" He gives me an amused look.

Looking up at him lovingly, I say, "Because you're in my life, and that makes my life yours."

He nuzzles my hair. "I can't argue with that."

"Good." Then I sigh deeply. "They have a long road ahead of them. And I don't envy Mama and Papa one bit."

"Well, it seems pretty positive that they are each other's Intendeds, so hopefully your parents will understand their need to be around each other."

"They won't care about that. I think they need to know who Rayne is as a person. He really isn't a bad guy, except for the almost killing you thing."

Linc runs a distracting finger down my arm. "So, you don't mind Adele bonding with him?"

He says it lightly, but I turn to look at him and force his chin down to look back at me. He's purposely avoiding my eyes. I wait until I have his attention. "Lincoln Stevenson, I made a mistake in allowing Rayne into my life as anything other than a friend. That alone proves that he is a good guy. But I don't have a smidgeon of romantic feelings for him, so get that out of your head right now."

He wraps his other arm around me and hugs me from behind. "Just making sure," he says into my neck, pressing soft kisses there.

I lean away from him, giggling. "Hey, enough of that. We're in public."

He reaches for me again and when he captures me, he growls into my ear, "I know, and I'm dying to get you alone. Can't you tell?"

I laugh. "Yes, but we're not alone yet, so no kisses. Just hold me."

"Gladly," he says and squeezes my middle.

When I return my attention back to what's happening, I see that Rayne is trying to approach Mama, Papa, and Adele. He's holding his hands up like he's approaching a dangerous creature, which he might as well be with my angry father.

"May I have a word with all of you?" he asks respectfully.

Sandy puts a restraining arm on James and nods warily.

He clears his throat. "I know that Adele is young, and that is one of your main concerns. It's one of mine, too. If I promise to all of you that I will not do or say anything to her romantically until she's of age, will you allow me to be her friend?"

James spits out, "You don't know what you're saying. Intendeds can't be friends, they're lifelong mates. Don't you think we know that?"

Rayne acknowledges his comment by putting his hands down and holding them in a supplication. "I just want to be around her. I won't do anything you won't want me to. How old are you, Adele?"

Adele looks at our parents, then says with a frown, "Sixteen."

"Okay, so if I wait until she's eighteen or close to it to start dating, will that be all right? Please don't separate us completely, that's all I'm asking."

Adele looks hopefully at our parents, and they look at each other, having a silent conversation with their eyes.

Sandy turns back to Rayne and says, "Look, we don't know anything about you. All we know is that you tried to kill our future son-in-law. That's not a good recommendation, even you can understand that."

"I do, and I will do everything in my power to prove to you I'm no longer that guy. I will never do anything like that ever again. And I can tell you anything you want to know about me."

James stands tall and with his arm over Adele's shoulders, says, "We will need to talk about this as a family, which you are not a part of. So, you'll have to wait for our decision."

Rayne's shoulders slump, but he concedes, "I understand. Where would you like me to wait while you talk?"

I turn my attention to James because I'm curious about what we're supposed to do with Rayne now that he's here and not hiding.

"You are Petra's problem, as far as I'm concerned. She's the leader of this community," he says.

Rayne nods and with one last look at Adele, he walks in the direction of Petra's house.

I look up at Linc. "How does he know where she lives?'

He frowns as his gaze follows Rayne walking away. "He's been watching us this entire time. It also looks like he's been to this community before."

"Okay, everyone inside. We need to have a family discussion," James announces.

Adele's eyes never leave Rayne's back as he makes his way to Petra's house. When she loses sight of him, she turns a tortured gaze to me.

Linc squeezes my middle. "It looks like you're up. Sister duties coming in."

I nod and follow Papa into the house, beckoning Adele to follow me. I'll be here for her, however she needs me, and I have a feeling she'll need all the support she can get. I just hope she forgives me for kissing Rayne.

And despite that I took Rayne's powers, I really don't have any hard feelings. He's been properly punished for what he did, and Linc forgives him, too. I hope Rayne gets his happily ever after, even if it is with my newfound sister.

James leads us to the living room, and I make sure Jack is inside before the door is closed. I don't want him to be tempted to explore around the community. The need for him to be close to me is as strong as ever.

He lays by my feet when I sit on the couch. Linc settles next to me, and we look at James expectantly.

He gives Adele a firm look and says, "We're going to discuss the issue with Rayne later, understand? I'm not in a good head space right now. You're going to need to be patient while you wait."

Pressing her lips into a thin line, she gives me an angry look, like this is my fault, or is she still angry about that ill-advised kiss? Either way, this is out of my hands.

James turns to Linc. "What is the goal when we get our group assembled? Are we just traveling from state to state announcing Vela as we go along?"

Linc speaks up once I nod. "After we get married, I think we should start in Texas where my mom reigns as the Festan Grand Elder. Then we'll need to decide which way we go from there. East, west, or north."

Petting Jack's head, I say, "I think we should go west. My family used to live in Southern California before we moved to Colorado." I huff. "I mean, my other family. We still have contacts there and they'll help us spread the word."

Linc nods. "We won't hit every state, but we'll make sure to get to all the Grand Elders' bases. Once we've traveled throughout the United States, then we'll go on a world tour."

Once he mentions going out into the world announcing my new status, I start sweating. Just when I think I'm settled in thinking about my role, I hear something that practically gives me hives.

I know I should be okay with all of this, but really, who am I to be this esteemed person? I'm just me, little old Vela whose grandest aspiration was to own a flower shop. Now, we're talking about world tours on a mission from God. I swallow nervously, trying to get moisture back in my throat and look like I'm keeping it all together. But I'm sure I'm failing spectacularly.

Luckily, Linc's gaze is trained on Papa, so he doesn't notice my mini freakout. I don't want him to worry about me.

He continues, "I say we start in Central Europe, go south to Africa, then east to Australia. From there we'll go north to Asia and Russia. After that, we'll hit Alaska and make our way down to Mexico and South America."

I'm shaking by the time he finishes, and he notices right away. Looking over at me, he starts when he sees the blood drain from my face. "Vela, are you okay?"

I choke out, "I'll be fine."

Sandy rises from her seat and kneels next to me. "Honey, it's going to be all right. I know it sounds like a lot, but you'll have so much support around you that it will seem manageable."

I nod, twisting my fingers into my sweatshirt. Jack whines and sits up, putting his sleek head in my lap. I pet his head and lean over, kissing him. He's been with me since I was nothing, and he loves me. Maybe others will, too?

"Vela, what's wrong?" Linc asks softly. "Is it all the traveling you're worried about?"

I shake my head and look up. Unable to look anyone in the eye, I say, "I feel like I'm letting everyone in this room down, but I'm not sure I'll be likeable or believable. What if no one listens to me? What if I can't unite the clans?" I flush at admitting my imposter syndrome.

Sandy squeezes my knees. "Your gifts will prove to everyone you are the Chosen Child. And you'll make fans out of everyone who meets you. Just be yourself, honey, that's all."

"Vela, you are sorely misjudging your qualifications," James says. "You are the Chosen Child, of that there's no doubt, and you have more confidence than you think."

I raise my gaze to his. "How will I get everyone to set aside their prejudices and live united?"

That's the million-dollar question, because the room falls silent. Finally, it's Linc who says, "I think that you're going to have to rely on God's guidance. He clearly chose you for this role, so He won't leave you stranded when the time comes to convince the world to change."

The pressure on my chest lightens at his words, and I smile softly at him. I force myself to nod, trying to believe their assurances. "You're right. Thank you." Then I look at everyone. "Thank you for supporting me in this crazy business of being the Chosen One. I can't do any of it without you."

"Sure, you could," James says with confidence. "You can knock this out of the park with the gifts God gave you now and when you were born. Don't forget you were born for this role, honey. Don't doubt yourself. But it's okay that you do. It only shows how suited for this you are."

When I look at him quizzically, he explains. "If you walked in here saying you could do this in your sleep, I'd have my doubts. It's your humble attitude that makes you perfect for this. Your willingness to admit you need God's help."

Flushing, I look down and meet Sandy's gaze. She smiles at me warmly and I return it with one of my own.

"Okay, I believe you. Just remind me occasionally. Well," I say chuckling, "Maybe more frequently. I'm sure I'll need this pep talk again soon."

"And we're happy to give it," James says.

Looking around the room, Adele asks, "Now can I bring up my Intended? Can we talk about whether I'll be able to spend any time with him?"

Sandy rises from in front of me and returns to her seat. She gives a loaded glance to James, and I know what she's going to say.

"Adele, this is something your father and I will need to discuss alone before we talk about it with the family," she says firmly.

When James nods, Adele's face falls. She slumps in her seat and says, "I don't see how you can keep me away from the one person who's designed to be the other half of me." She raises tear-filled eyes to mine, and I pinch my lips together to stay out of this argument.

James and Sandy need to give their permission before Adele can spend time with Rayne. But I'll be her sounding board all day long on how she can get them to agree. I give her an encouraging nod, and she sniffs.

She looks at them and says, "I know I'm young, but how can you keep us apart?"

"Because he's proved to be unstable and dangerous," James growls. "We are not going to allow anyone like that around you, and certainly not a boy who's probably three or four years older than you. I don't care if he is your Intended."

"Vela, how old is Rayne?" Adele asks.

"Eighteen or nineteen, I'm not sure," I say.

Tears fall down my sister's face, and my heart breaks for her. Every Elemental girl has two dreams: finding her Intended and walking down the aisle to meet him at the altar on their wedding day.

I almost messed up having both of those dreams come true, but thankfully I'll get to see them happen for me. I want that for my sister, too.

"Mama and Papa, if she's not alone with him, but chaperoned, would that work for now? I'm sure Linc will agree that we can fill that role," I ask hopefully.

Linc looks sharply at me, and I breathe a sigh of relief when he stays quiet and doesn't refute my statement.

Adele sits up and looks hopefully at our parents. They look at each other at my offer, but it's James who says, "We need to discuss the possibility of allowing Adele any contact with that young man."

I feel for my newfound parents. Knowing their daughter has an Intended bond with a criminal has to be horrifying for them.

But I know Rayne better than anyone here, and I can say with all certainty he is not one of those rare Elementals who is untrustworthy. His actions, however, contradict my belief in him. Rayne has a lot of work ahead to prove himself as an ideal potential son-in-law.

James and Sandy take the lull in conversation to hide themselves in their bedroom for that much needed discussion. Adele gets up to sit closer to us, and I hold my hand out to her. She takes it and sits down on my other side. I scoot over to give her room to sit, but she's too despondent to get more comfortable.

"Hey," I say softly. "Do you forgive me?"

She looks hard at me. "For kissing my Intended before I have? Yes, honestly."

Very uncomfortable to be having this conversation in front of Linc, I say, "Believe me, I regret it deeply. Even he said it was a huge mistake."

She snorts and crosses her arms.

"You know this will all work out, right?" I tell her gently.,

She huffs. "You say that, but you're not forbidden from even talking to your Intended. He's accepted with open arms," she says, waving her arm at Linc, who sits watching us with level eyes.

"Adele," Linc says, "your parents have a right to be protective of you. Rayne did try to kill me. Doesn't it concern you that he has a wild temper?"

She lifts her eyes and studies him before answering. "Yes," she finally says. "I am concerned. I hate that he did that. But is it right that we be kept apart from each other?"

"If he's dangerous, then yes," I say with all frankness. "He needs to prove to your parents that he's a decent human being and Elemental. And I'm sure he needs to prove that to himself, too. Allow him to make amends."

Linc nods, agreeing with me.

Adele leans against the couch, leaning her chin on her hand. "I can't believe I found my Intended," she says wistfully. "I thought it would never happen. And now that it has…"

"You can't talk to him," I finish for her. "I know. It sucks. But, let things fall into place. Rayne needs to prove himself to everyone and he will, I'm sure of it. Now that he's found you, he won't want to let you go."

At my words, she jumps up. "Oh, my gosh! What is Steele going to say? I didn't even think about him until now." She bites her thumbnail. I hold in a snicker.

"He's going to have to understand that he needs to let you choose," I say, instead of giving into my mirth over her now being in the exact predicament I was…with the same guy.

But I doubt he will. And Steele worked too hard to get her. He's not going to let her go easily either.

Confusion settles over her face.

I say gently. "Adele, do you want to give Steele up?"

Oh no. This might be a very complicated situation in about two seconds.

"I don't know. I thought I only wanted to be with Steele, but the moment I saw Rayne, everything and everyone melted away until Rayne was all I could think about. But then I remembered my feelings for Steele..."

"Are they still there?" I ask gently.

She nods miserably. "What do I do?" she asks.

"Pray," I say simply. "Ask God who He wants in your life, and He will guide you to the right person."

She straightens. "I need to talk to Steele. I don't want him to hear about this from someone else. It needs to come from me."

"Well, here's the difficult part, Adele," Linc says. "Your parents don't want you talking to Steele or Rayne. How are you going to tell him?"

She looks directly at me. "Vela is going with me."

"I am?" I ask with surprise.

"Yes," she says with certainty. "Let's go to Steele's house, so I can tell him what's going on."

"I don't think he's going to take it well," I say plainly.

"We'll see about that. He won't like it, but he deserves to know."

"Does he, though?" I ask. "He wanted to keep your relationship secret."

"That was different. Come on, Vela. While Mama and Papa are in their room."

"You're going to leave me here to tell them where you went?" Linc asks with alarm.

Adele is already pulling me up and toward the door. I command Jack to come with me, and I'm following her out the door when she says, "Yep. Tell them I have Vela with me, and they'll be fine."

"Let's hope so," Linc says adamantly.

I turn and wink at him before I'm pulled out of the house entirely.

We're down the street in seconds and knocking on a door I haven't been to yet. True to her promise, Adele tucks her arm in mine and waits for the door to open. A middle-aged woman peers out and when she sees Adele, she frowns. "Yes?" she asks with annoyance, then looks wary when she sees Jack.

"May I speak with Steele? It's important," Adele says with more confidence than I would have when faced with this intimidating looking woman.

She looks down at Adele for a moment before she nods curtly and disappears inside and shuts the door.

"Friendly woman," I comment.

"She blames Steele for being out in the middle of nowhere," Adele says offhandedly. Like that isn't one of the saddest things I've heard.

Steele appears and shuts the door behind him. He looks at me and Jack warily, then at Adele. "You have something important to tell me?"

"Yes, I do. Steele, I don't know how to say this, but I've met someone very important to me."

He looks at me, then turns back to her. "Yes, I know." He waves a hand at me. "You've met your sister. It's pretty obvious you two are related."

Adele huffs and unloops her arm from mine. She gives me a look, and I translate that correctly. I step back and give them some privacy. I take a few steps back but stay close enough to keep an eye on her and to hear their conversation.

"No, Steele," Adele says with impatience. "I just met my Intended. He's here in Saddleback."

Steele's eyes widen, and he steps back in surprise. "He's *here*? Where?" He looks around with a sharp eye, and I see his body stiffen, like he's ready for a fight.

I've seen enough jealous males to know when one is about to attack. If Rayne shows his face right now, I have no doubt blows will fall. Rayne would never back down, either, so I pray he stays hidden wherever he is.

Looking intently at Adele, Steele asks, "So, is that it? You're dumping me just like that?"

"No!" Adele cries. "It's not like that at all."

Steele looks surprised. "You still want to be my girlfriend?"

"Well, no," Adele says, looking flustered. "I don't mean that, either."

"So, what are you saying, Adele?"

My insides twist at my sister's predicament. I know what she's going through. I step in when it seems Adele is lost for words. "Steele?" He turns furious eyes to me. "If I may say something. Adele has just been given a great shock. Give her a little breathing room. She's not allowed to see either of you right now, and I happen to agree that our parents are right in that decision."

He looks at Adele. "You can't see me?"

"When have I ever been allowed to see you?" she asks with exasperation.

He shrugs. "Still, even though you weren't allowed, you did."

"Which was wrong," I interject sharply. "You should be enough of a man to not hide your relationship. I want my sister to be proud of who she chooses to date. She shouldn't have to hide any relationship." I say that last part with some emphasis, because she hasn't decided who wants in her life and Steele needs to know that.

He frowns deeply but remains silent.

This is going to be a very sticky situation. I can just feel it.

15

Rayne

I'm sweating bullets when I knock on Petra's door. She's not known for being easy to talk to. But she's a fair leader, so I can only hope she'll hear my story out before she rains judgement on me.

I just need a place to crash because I have a feeling Vela, Linc, and her entourage will be leaving in the morning. I don't relish the idea of spending the night outside again.

Petra opens the door and eyes me suspiciously, looking around like someone should be with me.

"Hi, Petra. I'm Rayne Williams."

She gives me a glare. "How do you know my name? I don't know you."

"We've met," I tell her, keeping myself relaxed. "I was a lot younger when I was last here. Do you remember my parents, Elliot and Mary? From the Pola Bear."

Recognition flares in her eyes, and she nods. "I remember you now. It's been a while. How's your family?"

I last came to this community with my parents and other families. "We're all good. But," I say, rubbing my neck, wondering how I'm going to explain all that's transpired, "I have some news to share about myself, Vela, and Linc. I need to know if I'll be welcome in your community after you hear it."

Sharp eyes look me over, and she steps closer to me. "I'll listen to what you have to say. Have you seen Vela yet?"

I nod. "She just gave me my powers back."

After I share my shameful story of how I tried to kill Linc, she leans back, looking surprised. "That's quite a story. I'm intrigued. If Vela feels you're worthy enough to have your powers returned, despite what you did, then I'm sure you'll be all right to stay. So, what else do you have to tell me that has you still acting so nervous?"

Impressed Vela has gotten this formidable woman behind her, I ask, "Can we sit?" I stuff my hands in my pockets.

She agrees, and I proceed to tell her everything that's happening with Adele. When I finish, she sits back and sucks on her teeth, thinking.

"Adele is your Intended, huh?" When I nod, she chuckles. "That poor kid can't catch any breaks."

I wonder if she's talking about Adele or that boy I saw Adele kissing. I stamp down the surge of jealousy that roars through me.

She eyes me knowingly. "Yep, this will be a sticky situation, all right. You're determined to stick close to Vela?"

"Yes. I've promised to protect her."

"And it doesn't hurt that where Vela goes, her baby sister goes, too." She laughs at my sheepish expression. "Yes, sir, this is a pickle."

When I stay silent, she claps her hands on her knees. "I've always loved a good drama. You can stay put for now. You've vowed to protect the innocent and not harm them, right?"

When I nod, she does, too. "Okay, for the sake of your family, I'm going to believe you. But," she warns, putting her finger in my face, "one move out of place, and I'll send you packing myself. And don't think I can't do it."

I agree because I can sense water and wind in her, which I know from experience are a formidable combination. I don't doubt her for one second.

"So, let's go find you a place to sleep for the night. I don't have room here, unless you want to sleep on the floor?"

When I give her a frown, she laughs and claps me on the shoulder. "Don't worry, I'll find you a bed. We leave in the morning, well, those of us traveling with Vela. You haven't gotten permission to go with her, yet?"

I shake my head, and she clucks. "I can understand James' concerns. Poor man. You've given him a run for his money going after both of his daughters."

Not knowing what to say to that, I remain silent as she shakes her head and leads me outside.

We step out, and the first thing I see is Adele talking to that guy she kissed earlier today. The light is going down but there's enough that I can memorize his face. The way they're talking, she's telling him something he doesn't like. His body is stiff, and he's towering over her.

I almost run over there to stop his threatening posture, but Petra holds my arm and keeps me from doing just that.

"Easy," she says under her breath.

Vela's dog Jack instantly eyes me and stands, watching me with eagle eyes. He never really warmed up to me, preferring to be around Linc. I guess I can't blame the dog. He senses the connection between his mistress and Linc.

A connection I now have with Adele. Just watching her makes me want to be near her, guarding and protecting her. I promised to protect Vela, but it goes without saying that I'm making that same vow to Adele. I'm trusting Vela right now to keep her little sister safe, with all her powers. Steele better step back soon, if he has any sense.

Vela notices Jack watching me and she looks over at me, her body stiffening. She should be concerned.

"Easy, fella," Petra says. "They're just talking. She can talk to a boy, can't she?"

I almost growl a resounding no, but just then, Adele whips her head at me. Her eyes widen, and she tries to block my presence with her body. She's too short, however, and Steele looks over her head and spots me glaring at him.

Every atom in my body wants to tear him away from *my* Intended. Why is he looking so possessively at her? He has no right.

Just then, I glance at Vela and recognize her expression for what it is. Understanding. I was in just that guy's position with her and Linc. I again curse myself for daring to come between two people joined by such a strong bond. But am I doing something similar by coming in between an established couple? I want my Intended bond to trump all else, but something in me stops myself from doing the same thing I did before. I just can't help that everything roars in me to be with my Intended, despite all costs.

Steele points at me and then asks Adele a question. I'm too far away to hear her answer, but it's obvious she's just pointed me out as her Intended.

She tries to stop him from going toward me, but he's too strong. He shakes her off and strides toward me.

I fist my hands at my sides. I don't like how he just shook her off like that. And I won't take anything from this guy. He doesn't scare me at all. I wait and relish the chance to give him what I've wanted to do since I saw him kiss Jean.

A good punch in the face.

Except, this time I will be the better guy and restrain my violence. This guy has been given a crappy hand when his girlfriend finds her Intended. But even my restraint has limits. If he throws a punch, I won't take that well.

And, by the look on his face, I might just get some violence thrown at me. I loosen my muscles and get ready for anything.

16

Vela

S teele is practically running toward Rayne, who's waiting for him with what looks like fierce anticipation.

This is just what I was afraid of. I take off and race ahead of Steele, putting my body between these two dominant males.

Steele stops, giving me a murderous glare. "Get out of my way."

"No. You need to calm down and play nice. This can be friendly or not, but there will not be violence," I say, holding my hands out.

He moves to go around me, but I step in his way.

Giving me a frustrated look, he goes the other way. Knowing I only have one choice, I pull from my powers and draw up a wall of earth higher than his head.

He spits at me. "Your powers don't scare me. Get. Out. Of. My. Way."

"Not until you've calmed down."

Giving a huff, he throws his hands down and uses wind to lift himself over my dirt obstruction.

Undeterred, I use my wind gift to fight with his, overpowering him easily. I bring him back, drawing my hand down until he's on the ground in front of me.

He yells at me, "Will you stop that? Let me talk to him."

"When I'm sure that all you'll do is talk, then I'll allow it," I say, crossing my arms, watching him carefully. His other gift is water, so I'm prepared for any ice nonsense he might throw at me.

He regards me with a new respect and crosses his arms, too. "Who made you judge and jury?"

"God," I answer simply. "He's made me the unifier of our race. And I don't want to start my job with you fighting with my little sister's Intended."

"How do you know I was going to fight him?" he asks with a sneer.

"Call it intuition," I say dryly.

Putting his hands on his hips, he huffs and says, "Fine. I'll just talk to him, then."

When I'm sure he's sincere, I nod and step back allowing him to approach Rayne. But I follow at a close distance.

Rayne is standing with an amused look, which I'm sure enrages Steele. I hope he can control his temper, because we've already drawn a crowd, and I don't want to embarrass Steele any further.

"Can I help you?" Rayne asks, his brown eyes piercing Steele's.

Adele runs up to me, standing at my side. Her eyes are wide as she watches the interaction of the two guys in her life.

Poor kid.

"Yeah, stay away from Adele," Steele spits out.

"Careful, young Steele," Petra says from Rayne's side. "This is a guest of our town. Like Vela, I won't tolerate any nonsense."

"Is it nonsense to tell him to stay away from my girlfriend?" he asks her angrily.

Petra doesn't answer, but Rayne does. He asks Adele, "Is it true? Are you dating this guy?"

Adele gives him a bold look. "I was. I'm not sure now."

Rayne leans back, seeming satisfied with her answer. Steele, however, is not.

He spins to her. "So, you *are* breaking up with me."

She glares at him. "We were never allowed to date anyway, Steele. Nothing is really any different."

"It is for me," he says, his eyebrows drawn down in two angry lines.

"You don't understand," Adele says, throwing her arms out. "You haven't met your Intended. You'd understand if you did."

This time Steele throws his arm out. "And how do you expect me to do that out here in the middle of nowhere?"

I notice Rayne giving Steele a sympathetic glance. He knows exactly how Steele feels.

"Please," Steele asks in a low voice, stepping closer to Adele. "Don't break up with me over this guy. You don't even know him. He could be dangerous."

I almost laugh because he doesn't know how right he is.

"You don't know anything about me," Rayne says, his lips in a thin line as he steps toward Steele, a dark look coming into his eyes.

I move toward him, this time needing to disarm Rayne. I swear, I'm getting tired of this.

"Rayne," I warn. "Stay calm, he's right. No one knows you here."

"And how do you know he even wants anything to do with you?" Steele fires at Adele, waving his arm in Rayne's direction.

"Now, that's enough. I do want a relationship with her. She is everything to me now, *everything*," Rayne says, inching toward Adele. He looks at Steele with what looks like patience in his eyes. "Look, I get it. You've got a great girl, then she finds her Intended. But," he says, inhaling deeply, "I'm not going anywhere, unless her family forbids me to be near her. You don't understand what this bond feels like. It's like I'm tethered to her with a steel line. This feeling just doesn't go away."

Adele seems to melt next to me, and even I can appreciate the sincerity in Rayne's voice.

"Rayne," I say, "You were in a very similar situation not too long ago. Since you understand Steele's position, be as accommodating as you can be. Don't do anything you'll regret. Remember what you promised me?"

Rayne gives me a look like he deeply regrets making that promise, but then his face clears even though his eyes narrow. "Okay, I'll give him some credit. Look," he directs at Steele. "I know you don't want to hear this, but I understand where you're coming from. Take it from me, you don't want to do this. You don't want to get in the middle of an Intended bond."

"How do you know what I want? You can go back to whatever hole you crawled out of if you think I'm just going to just hand her over to you," Steele spits out. With one move, he sends a blast of air at Rayne, throwing Rayne's head back.

He's quick, I give him that. I couldn't even stop that punch of air.

Rayne blinks the cheap shot away and he's moving toward Steele with dangerous intent.

I'm about to move in his way, when Linc appears, moving me aside. "Rayne, keep a cool head," he cautions, holding out his hand. "Remember, you're trying to show you've changed." He flicks a glance at James and Sandy who are running toward us.

"Is that so?" Steele asks, a wicked look coming into his eyes. "You're not *allowed* to fight?"

Rayne looks like he's seriously warring with himself on whether if he's going to keep up his promise. He clenches and unclenches his hands in frustration. He stares darkly at Steele who's waiting for the fight to happen that he started.

Just as Sandy and James skid to a stop in front of us, Rayne inhales deeply and points at Steele. "I'll give you that one shot. But that's the only one you're ever going to get."

"We'll see about that," Steele sneers. "Especially with your pacifist mentality."

"What's going on?" James asks, putting himself next to Adele and me.

"We're taking care of it," I say.

"How? They look like they're ready to kill each other," he says, looking between the two angry guys.

"I agree, they do, but Rayne is cooling off. Now, it seems Steele is next," I say firmly.

Steele looks like he's ready to blow up with anger, but he presses his lips together, looking between Adele, Rayne and James.

James turns to me. "Vela, you two don't need to try to handle this on your own. Neither one of these young men will have anything to do with my daughter, not if I have breath in my body. So, there should be no argument at all. Is that clear?" His hard voice rings out into the air.

Rayne and Steele exchange looks of disgust before they turn their gazes to my angry Papa.

"Did I make myself clear?" he repeats, staring both of them down.

Rayne relents first and steps back. "Yes, sir," he says respectfully.

Steele isn't as accommodating. He scoffs and spins, saying over his shoulder, "Whatever."

James gives him a withering look that Steele can't see, but I have no hope for him to ever secure permission to date Adele.

I shake my head but look to my sister to see how she's taking all of this.

She looks torn as she watches Steele walk away from her. Her shoulders slump and with a sob, she looks between Steele and Rayne, then runs in the direction of home.

"I'll go stay with her," I offer, and take off after her, gladly leaving that confusing situation behind me. I can sense Jack and Linc following me, and I feel better as I go into Adele's bedroom.

What a mess, I think sadly. I can only hope that things will work out. I don't dislike Steele, but he could have shown some backbone to James or respect at the very least. I blame the lack of a male figure in his life for that.

Adele is sobbing on her bed when I walk in. Giving Linc a loving look, I shut the door on him and go to her, intent on giving her what comfort I can.

She cries for an hour before she exhausts herself, and I just hold her, petting her hair. I keep telling her things will work out. She just needs to give her situation to God, but I don't know if she's listening.

When she's finally quiet, it's completely dark outside.

"Hey, you have a lot to look forward to. You found your Intended, I mean just that alone means things are looking up," I say softly.

She sits up but bleakly looks outside. She doesn't say a word, and I'm suddenly worried about her keeping all of her feelings in instead of out. She's better off railing and shouting. This silence is worrisome.

"Adele, are you okay?"

She moves her gaze from the window to me and just shrugs.

I put my hand on her shoulder. "What are you worried about?"

Her voice is hoarse as she answers with one word that crushes me, "Everything."

"Hey, I've been through almost the same thing you are and look at Linc and I now. We got through it. That's proof you will, too."

Her eyes are so loaded with pain I almost can't breathe with my sadness for her. Tears slip from her eyes, and she lies down, covering her face with her arm.

I leave her, because it seems like the only Person who can help her right now is Jesus, and for that, she needs to be alone.

Making my way into the living room, I shut Adele's bedroom quietly. Jack greets me, and I pet him absentmindedly, my thoughts full of my little sister and her predicament.

James is tending the fire and looks his shoulder at me. "How is she?" His gaze is worried, as it should be.

"She's not doing so well. I think she needs to be alone for a while. There's nothing I can really say to her, but that things will work out."

His eyes harden, and he seems to take great pleasure in breaking sticks to add to the flames. "Not if I have anything to say about it. She can't be with that boy."

"Which one?" I ask.

"Either," he mutters with an exhale. He shakes his head. He looks to Sandy and says bleakly, "I wanted our daughters to find their Intendeds. I thought I wanted that more than anything, but not at this cost."

Sandy nods sadly and pats the seat next to her. He moves to sit by her and since they have the couch, I sit in a chair next to Linc, Jack at my feet.

We all look on moodily as the fire greedily eats away at the wood and its hypnotizing flames relax me for a moment.

"I wish she had an easier time of it, but the fact of the matter, she doesn't. We just need to roll with the punches," I say, leaning my head on my hand.

James sighs, looking resigned to the difficulty of the situation, and says, "We have a big day tomorrow. Petra got a group together already. We leave at first light. Let's all get as much rest as we can. Nothing can be solved tonight concerning Adele."

Sandy makes a bed for Linc by the fire, and I wait for her to leave before I sit next to him on the floor. I look in his eyes and see he looks tired but suddenly energized at the same time.

"What is it?" I ask, smiling.

He gives me a predatory look and leans in, kissing me in answer. I embrace his move by wrapping my arms around his neck and kissing him back.

"Finally," he says as he tears his lips off mine. "I've been waiting to get you alone all day." He grabs my face and presses his warm lips to mine in a searing kiss that I won't forget for some time.

I'm so absorbed in our kiss anyone could walk in, and I wouldn't know it. When he gives me a second to breathe, I say in a breathless voice, "I had no idea you were so desperate for this."

"Are you kidding? Your kiss is all I could think about for most of the day," he says before leaning in again. He tucks me against his side and kisses me so tenderly my breath is almost stolen away.

I lean into him and press soft kisses to his cheeks, eyes, chin, then lips, which seem to drive him crazy because he growls and shifts so he can kiss me better. After a tantalizing while, he slants his head and teases me by pressing the lightest kisses on my neck.

"Kiss me again," I demand, grabbing his hair.

"Isn't that what I'm doing?" he asks in a teasing voice.

"You know what I mean," I warn before I press a harder kiss on his lips.

He responds by kissing me so deeply, I'm lost in his arms for who knows how long. When it becomes so much that we're both breathing heavily, he leans away from me, saying, "You need to go to bed now, you vixen."

"Vixen?" I ask, laughing. "You were the one kissing me."

He pushes me away with one arm and refuses to look at me. He points toward Adele's door. "Go," he commands in a deep, strained voice.

I reach for him, but he scoots away from me. "You said you wanted to keep things pure before marriage. This is me trying to do that. So, please, Vela, I'm asking you to leave. Please."

Hurt pangs through me that he's pushing me away, but I accept his request and pick myself up off the floor. He glances at me, but I leave him behind as I return to Adele's room, feeling all kinds of warm and very well kissed.

I understand, though, it's easy for things to get carried away, and I so appreciate his commitment to keeping ourselves chaste until we get married.

I smile when I think of his insistence on getting married quickly. This must be why. Our chemistry is off the charts, and waiting is hard.

He makes me feel things so new and wonderful I just want to keep exploring until all my questions are answered. Only when we're married, I tell myself firmly when my thoughts turn to things that should be saved for later.

I look for Adele and find her under the covers, her back to me.

I pull my bag to me, find my sleep clothes, and slip them on. Once I'm comfortable, I slide under the covers next to my sister.

For a moment, I have to hold in a sudden rush of tears. I can't count how many times I laid next to Elia and wished she was my actual sister. That I had grown up with her my whole life and could always count on having her in my life.

I can always count on Elia, though. We're good enough friends to say that, but now that I have a sister and she's right next to me, I suddenly want to snuggle with her, as if we'd done it our whole lives.

But I don't. She's hurting, and I need to give her space. I do, however, put my hand on her shoulder and squeeze, telling her

I'm here for her. And I always will be. Now that I know about her, she has my lifelong support.

I fall asleep quickly, my dreams full of the elements and faces flashing over and over. When I wake up, it's pitch dark, and I don't remember a thing of what I dreamt, but instantly I sit up and reach for the space on the bed next to me.

Adele is not there. With my heart pounding in fear, I hurriedly dress and slip on my shoes. Calling Jack to me, I go out into the house, looking for her. I have no idea what time it is, just that it's either the middle of the night or just before dawn.

One thing I do know is that Adele is nowhere to be found in the house. *Please, God, tell me she didn't run away with Rayne or Steele.*

Trying not to worry, I kneel next to Linc and shake his shoulder. He opens his eyes sleepily, but then they narrow at me in concern. "What's wrong?"

"I can't find Adele," I whisper. I don't know why I'm being so quiet. I guess it's because I'm hoping to find her before my parents know she's missing.

He sits up quickly and is ready in moments. He went to sleep in his regular clothes, so he only needs to put on his shoes.

"Where do we go?" he asks, alert and ready for whatever I want to do.

"I think we should check Steele's first," I say quietly. "If she's not there, then we'll find out where Rayne is staying."

"Let's hope we don't have to wake Petra to find that out," he says, and I can't help but agree. "Where do you think she is?"

"I don't know," I say in a worried whisper. "Or, with who."

We quietly leave the house and step out into what I realize is the early morning air. It feels like it's about five in the morning. It's too dark to see very far, but I remember where Steele lives. Linc follows me as I run toward his house, going to the back of it, hoping to find them there.

When we don't find them, I turn to Linc. "Now what?"

He's looking all around and then says, "I found Rayne using Jack. If you think they're in the woods somewhere, he can find them. But he might scare Steele pretty good."

"And Adele," I say, frowning. I don't want to use that tactic unless I have to. "Let's walk around and see if we hear her talking. Maybe she found where Rayne is staying."

"Good idea," he says, and I keep Jack close to me as we walk out into the community.

I keep my ears and eyes peeled for any sight or sound of my little sister. "What does she think she's doing?" I ask with frustration.

"I don't know. But it's clear she isn't going to abide by your father's decision."

I scoff, but my heart pounds in fear. "Yeah, that much is clear. Now, let's be quiet. I just hope she's here somewhere."

"You think she ran away?" he asks in a low, concerned voice.

"I really don't know, Linc. Let's just look."

We walk in silence, and I can only hope we'll find her before I have to tell our father about her absence. He won't take that well, and I'd like to spare Adele that show of fury. *If she's even here.*

I think I hear something to the right at one of the smaller houses, and I hold up my hand putting my finger to my lips.

Knowing I have the Festan gift of sensing heat signatures, I center my thoughts on that gift and focus. There are two people behind the house, and when I look at Linc, he must sense the same thing. He holds his hand on my waist and doesn't allow me to advance. He gives me a look asking to go first, and I agree.

Between Linc and I, I have more power, but he's more practiced at controlling his fire than I am. So, I trust his judgement on what we should do when we find out who is behind that house.

I place my footsteps exactly where he steps, because I realize he knows how to be quiet. Creeping to the side of the house, we hug the wall, and now I hear voices.

Relief crashes through me when I hear Adele's voice.

"...and I won't allow him to dictate my life. We can talk, and there's no reason he should keep us apart."

Rayne answers in a deep voice, sounding tender, "Like I've already said, it's better for us if you obey his wishes. I'll prove to him that I'm a great guy, and then he'll have no reason to separate us."

Linc glances back at me, questioning with his eyes if I want to interrupt them. It doesn't sound like Rayne is convincing her to run away with him, so I shake my head.

Adele's voice raises, "I'm sixteen years old. He can't treat me like a child, Rayne."

Rayne shushes her and says gently, "It's because you're not a child that he's taking these precautions. Please, don't rock the boat, Adele. Trust me and my plan. I'll prove to him I'm the kind of guy he wants for you."

She's quiet for a minute and after I realize they might be doing something they shouldn't, I tap on Linc's shoulder, and he turns the corner with me and Jack in tow.

Rayne steps back from Adele, who is crying on his shoulder. She looks up at us with teary eyes that are full of wariness and accusation.

I hold up my hands. "I was just worried about you. I didn't tell Mama and Papa you weren't home. We decided to try to find you and bring you back before they realize you're gone."

Relief flashes across her face as she turns to Rayne and plants a kiss on his lips, which seems to shock him completely.

Then she spins and walks in determined steps to me and Linc. Without a word, she walks past us, and I share a bewildered glance with Rayne, and then I'm rushing to follow her. I notice

Linc doesn't come with me, and I know he's having a few words with Rayne.

I hope they'll be civil. They don't have a great history of doing that. But a girl can hope. At the moment, my hands are full to the brim with a teen girl who's far too ready to be an adult.

17

Linc

I lean my shoulder on the house we found Rayne and Adele behind and look at him almost lazily. I hope he can sense the tense anger in me and that he's aware my temper is about to show if he makes one wrong move.

"How did she find you?" I ask quietly.

He observes me for a moment and blows out his breath, putting his hands on his hips. "She just knocked on my window. I have no idea how she knew where I was staying. About scared me to death actually," he says with a look of wonder on his face.

I mutter dryly, "Of course. You're completely innocent."

He holds up his hands. "I swear, I am. I came out here because she was knocking on my window so hard I thought she'd wake up the whole house."

I study him and mull over his answers. He seems sincere. But I know him better than that. "You didn't go and get her?" I ask in hard voice. "That seems much more likely than her finding you."

His eyes are wide as he swears, "I'm telling you, man, I have no idea how she found me. She never said. We didn't get a chance to talk about that."

Sighing, I run my hand over my neck, feeling stiffness there. "She is the most stubborn..."

"I know," Rayne says, his eyes dreamy.

I shove him against the wall, putting my forearm in his throat. "Get that look off your face," I say lowly.

He gives me a frank look, not worried in the least that I'm pressing hard into his neck. "You're telling me you wouldn't move heaven and earth to talk to your Intended, to Vela?"

"So, you did go and find her," I growl, shoving my arm up into his throat.

He chokes and taps my arm to lighten up, which I do, slightly. "No," he wheezes. "I swear. She found me, like I said. But I want to talk to her as much as she wants to talk to me. Can't you understand that?"

I look between his earnest eyes and let go, stepping back. I can understand, but I need to get some things straight with him. "You will not seek her out. And if she finds you again, you will convince her to return home. If her father finds out she came to find you, he will not believe anything you say and will think the worst. Got it?"

He slumps and leans against the house, looking away. He turns to me. "What would you do in my situation?"

I'm surprised by the question but try not to show it. I never would have thought Rayne would ask me for advice, yet here we are. I clear my throat. "I would do what you told her you were going to do. Be the kind of guy a father would want for his daughter. Prove that to him and everyone."

He nods, accepting my answer easily. We've come a long way, and I can't help but add, "If you can manage that, I'll be impressed."

He smiles at me half-heartedly. "Thanks." He turns to go back inside the house, then stops. "Hey, did you guys decide if I could join your group?"

Realizing we never discussed that, I shake my head. His head droops as he says, "I guess I'll have to put my tracking skills to use and follow you, then."

I can't believe it when I offer, "I'll try to convince them to let you come with us. Just give me time."

He nods at me in thanks and then slips back into the house.

I walk back to James and Sandy's home in contemplative silence. You never know what life will throw at you. I can only hope I'm a good enough recommendation for Rayne's character, or else he'll be tailing us the entire way.

But once we get to the plane the Extremists left behind, I hope he's done enough to be allowed on. I don't care how good a tracker he is. Once we're in the air, we're as good as gone.

When I walk back inside the house, I find Adele on the couch with Vela. They're whispering, and I walk closer, asking wordlessly if I can join them.

Vela looks up and after glancing at Adele, she says, "Come and sit with us."

I do and sit down slowly. It was kind of a shock to be woken up by my Intended and to race out into the dark morning looking for her missing sister. Now that she's found, I rest my back on the chair and relax until I hear what Adele is saying. I pick my head back up.

"I'll leave, I swear I will. If he won't let me talk to my Intended, I won't stay here," she threatens.

Vela says calmly, "Think rationally, Adele. Don't you understand why Papa feels this way? He needs to trust him with you. And as far as Papa knows, Rayne is dangerous. He needs to prove himself. I don't think that's asking for too much. He deserves that. You deserve that, Adele."

Adele's eyes flash in anger. She pounds her knee with her fist. "He seems very sorry for what he did. What more does he have to do?"

Vela looks up at me, asking for help, and I say, "He needs to show he's changed. Not just say it. Allow him to do that and everything will fall into place."

"What if Papa doesn't allow him to travel with us? What then?"

"Don't assume Papa is going to say no. We have a long walk to get to the plane. Rayne has time to show his mettle and his worth."

Adele listens, then nods and walks to her room.

Vela lets her go but looks unsettled. I move to sit next to her, rubbing her tense neck muscles. "Hey, Adele'll come around. She's gotta' see that Rayne has some work to do. There's nothing we've said that's unfair."

"I know," Vela sighs and rubs her forehead. "She's not thinking straight. I just worry about her doing something extreme. That she will convince Rayne to do something crazy."

"Like running away together? You thought that's what they did this morning?"

She looks up, meeting my eyes and nods, her gaze stressed.

I inhale slowly, thinking. Finally, I say, "I don't think Rayne will do that. He'll talk her out of it, I'm pretty sure."

"Pretty sure isn't what I want to hear, Linc."

"I know," I say, continuing my massage. "But it's the best I've got. Let's hope and pray they don't do anything like that."

"It's going to be hard to do what I need to do on my mission and keep an eye on my little sister," she says.

"I'm sorry, baby. I really am. Family is hard."

"Of course, you would know. You handle the death of your sister so well, I forget that you know all about family dynamics." She looks up at me, her eyes soft.

My throat closes at her words. I lean in and kiss her softly. "It's okay. I don't talk about her much. But I need to. Olympia needs to be a part of our lives, even if she is in heaven."

Sandy comes out of the bedroom, looking sleepy. "What are you two doing up?" she asks, rubbing her eyes.

Vela squeezes my hand, giving me a loving look that spells she was listening to my last request to include Olympia in our conversations. She answers her mom, "We've been up for a while. We figured we'd have some alone time before we travel with a big group."

I lean back and don't refute her words. We did have a few moments alone, but I don't comment on what else we've been doing. I'll follow Vela's lead on what we share about Adele.

"Mama?" Vela asks. When Sandy turns, she says, "We need to keep an eye on Adele. She's making me nervous with her attitude about Rayne."

Personally, I think we should tell Vela's parents about what happened. It's very concerning what Adele is willing to do to get to her Intended. I think they need more of a warning than what Vela is giving them. But I'll follow her lead on this.

Sandy nods grimly, frowning. "I agree with you, Vela. Your father and I have already discussed this. Will you help us with that?"

"I'll do the best I can, Mama, but Adele is a big girl. It's not easy to guess what she's going to do. And I have my mission to think about. But I'll do the best I can."

"I will too," I add. "You have my eyes and ears, and gifts if you need them."

Sandy gives me an appreciative look and then says briskly, "I need to wake up. I have quite a bit of packing to do. Do you two mind waiting for breakfast?"

Vela shakes her head and offers, "I'll get Adele, and we'll start it. Don't you worry about it."

She nods gratefully and moves into her bedroom, shutting the door.

Vela gets up and walks to Adele's room. She sticks her head in, talks quietly, and then Adele comes out and they both head into the kitchen. After about ten minutes, delicious smells waft in and my stomach rumbles in anticipation. Jack, too, stays by Vela's side begging for scraps to be thrown his way, which he receives, often.

James and Sandy eventually emerge from their bedroom, backpacks full to the brim. They deposit their bags by the door and relieve Adele so she can go pack her own bag.

Breakfast is soon under way and as we're eating, I ask what everyone's thinking, "I wonder how many from the community is coming with us."

Vela looks to James, who shakes his head as he takes a big bite of ham and flatbread. "I'd expect the ones who don't have small children are willing to leave, but families with little ones will probably stay until everything is settled."

"By settled, you mean once I've accomplished my mission," Vela says, taking a bite of her own breakfast sandwich.

He nods and Sandy says, "I've gotten to know the members here pretty well and some of them are really happy out here. I can see some of them staying, regardless."

"There is a certain freedom and charm living way out here," I say, chewing thoughtfully. "It's a simple life. I can see how people would like it."

"We're not those people," James says, smiling as he hands a flatbread to Adele. "Are we, young one? We love to travel and see new things, and we enjoy the finer things of life, which include electricity."

Adele shrugs and stays quiet.

Vela adds, "I hope at least a few kids end up going, because I'm pretty sure Hannah and Greta are joining our party, and I'd like Greta to have a friend with her. I hate ripping her from everything she's ever known."

"I'm looking forward to meeting her," Sandy says warmly. "It sounds like Hannah's been quite a support for you, Vela."

"She has," Vela agrees. "She saved Linc's life, too, so I'm forever indebted to her."

"Sounds like she would do that for anyone," Sandy says with a smile.

Vela shakes her head, contradicting her. "Oh no, if you're an Extremist who's attacking her town, she has no mercy. She doesn't hold back. Trust me, you don't want to be on her bad side."

"Well, then we're just glad she's in our corner," James says, wiping his mouth with a cloth napkin.

"Me too," Vela says.

I notice Adele has been very quiet and from my experience, both personally and with friends, I know that a quiet teenager is usually plotting something. What is my little sister up to now?

I try to include Adele in our conversation. "So, do you know if any of your friends will be joining our group?"

She shakes her head, and that's all the response I get.

I look to Vela for help, and she shakes her head slightly to tell me to quit.

There's a brisk knock on the door and James rises quickly. "That must be Petra," he says, leaving the table.

Sure enough, Petra marches in with Steele in tow. She looks around, noticing the bags by the door and our breakfast on the table.

"Did you eat breakfast, Petra? If not, you're welcome to what we have left," Sandy offers.

Petra shakes her head but points back to Steele over her shoulder. "I've already eaten, but young Steele here might be hungry."

Steele looks hungrily at the spread and Sandy waves him over. "Of course, please Steele, eat something."

He lunges toward the food, and I notice Adele giving him a look of longing and confusion. I do not envy her romantic dilemma one bit. Vela, Rayne, and I were so entangled in one that I never want to endure such drama again. And yet, here I am again, reliving it all over with Adele and her two love interests.

I shake my head as I see Steele avoid Adele's gaze and focus on his food. Ignoring them, I go to Petra. "How many have decided to travel with us?"

"There are fifteen of us total. Families with young ones are all staying, as I expected. Well, we have one family with a nine-year-old. So, that's not necessarily true."

James joins our conversation, overhearing what Petra says. "Fifteen is a good number. Glad to have them."

"I told them to meet in the center of the community," Petra says. She looks over at Steele and Adele, who are studiously ignoring each other. "You two work things out?"

Adele stifles a sob and runs out the front door. Steele looks stonily at the door but refuses to chase after her.

I shake my head and Petra sighs heavily. "Can't say I blame them. They're in a pickle, that's for sure. It's why I never ended up in a relationship. I didn't want this very thing to happen to me."

Stepping back in surprise that she would throw around information about her love life, I can only stare at her with my mouth open.

She chuckles at my expression then waves me away. "Never mind me. Now, let's get a move on."

With the tense scene just now between Steele and Adele, I don't think it's a good time to ask for Rayne to join our group, so I make myself aware of where he could be hiding since I know he'll be trailing us.

And just like that, we all shoulder our packs and follow Petra to the center of the complex. Vela and I walk together, and I enjoy the feel of her hand in mine. I love any contact with my Intended, but I let go once we arrive to the group waiting for us. I see Gene and Jerry are at the front, and I'm happy they're coming with us. I lean into Vela's ear, "You're up. Knock 'em dead."

She eyes me nervously and then inhales before she strides to the head of the group. Every eye is on her, so there's no problem with her commanding attention.

"Thank you all for joining me. My goal, our goal, is simple. To unite the clans. We will travel across the U.S. before we hit Europe and the rest of the world. You are welcome to stay for the whole of this great journey. You're also welcome to leave if at any point you feel you have reached the end of your personal mission." She looks each of them in the eye as she speaks, and my chest swells with pride at her speech. "Now," she shouts, holding up her fists, "who's ready to change the world?!"

The crowd cheers and my ears ring. My applause joins with theirs and we all laugh and clap each other on the back.

Vela turns to Petra and asks, "Who will be our illustrious guides back to the Polar Bear?"

Petra nods over at Gene and Jerry and they both smile at Vela effusively.

Vela returns their smiles and asks, "Well, are you ready to take us to the Polar Bear to join the rest of our group?"

They nod and off we go. I could have led us back, but it's nice having others do it. I catch Rayne in the trees going to the back of the group, and I'm strangely happy he's with us. I have a lot of conflicting feelings about that guy. But I'm kind of rooting for him to prove his worth.

Everyone makes mistakes. Some are just worse than others. But nothing's unforgivable, not in God's eyes, so I can only hope Rayne will get what he wants.

But then I see Steele slouched and trudging along as he tries to avoid Adele's gaze. This is going to be a tricky trip.

18

Vela

We've been marching for an hour when the enormity of what I'm doing hits me again. I'm leading a group of people I don't even know to a future Elementals have only dreamed about for thousands of years.

I've been taking one step at a time, but I need to look at the big picture, too. I must keep a good eye on all fronts of this massive undertaking. Because I'm not alone in this. I have a team of people behind me who support me a hundred percent. They're proving it by following a perfect stranger out of their refuge to face a harsh world that has proved nothing but dangerous.

They've lived off the grid to protect their families from the Extremists who've hunted any couple with two different elements. It makes me so angry what this band of volunteers, and those waiting to join us at the Polar Bear, have had to sacrifice family, friends, their whole lives, because of that horrible, violent group. If it takes everything in me, I will put an end to the Extremists.

I think of little Greta and all that she's missed out on because she's had to hide in the Polar Bear for the sake of her young life.

Looking ahead, I see Adele walking with her friends, Debra and Helen. I don't know their stories, but Adele's is familiar to me now. She's had to run for her life multiple times, and I will make the Extremists pay for that burden.

I think of poor Steele, too. He's not only been brought into a world unwanted, but has had to hide for the sake of his life. He's walking in a dejected way, off to the side of Adele, keeping an eye on her, but staying out of her sight.

I wonder why he's not pressing his luck with Rayne out of the picture for the moment. Linc told me that Rayne is tracking us, so I know he's close and watching everything. I wonder if that's why Adele is also staying away from her former boyfriend. Rayne probably told her he wouldn't be far, so she's keeping her distance.

I'm also really looking forward to seeing my friends at the Polar Bear. I look back at the young guys who've joined my mission, and I think of Tonya, Jennifer, Claudette, and Alice and think they are going to absolutely love meeting new guys. Who knows, maybe they'll meet their Intendeds? Maybe Steele will stop fixating on Adele if he meets other girls.

As we walk, I've been talking with and getting to know some of the Saddleback members. They are full of optimism and hope for a better future. I've had to stay out of my comfort zone and make promises I only hope I can keep. Sometimes I still feel like the girl from California who's afraid of fires and hates Festans. But I'm proud to say I've grown so much since then.

I have a lot more to learn. And one of those things is diplomacy. So, I talk to my new friends and learn from their wisdom. I always loved sitting at my late grandparents' feet, listening to their stories and gleaning from their life experiences. So, today I do the same.

Deciding to get to know Adele's friends, I jog to catch up to the three girls, the three amigas, I'm calling them.

"Hey," I say breathlessly, embarrassed at how out of shape I am from that pathetic little jog. Linc smirks at me, so I stick my tongue at him and turn to Helen and Debra. "So, I wanted to get to know you girls."

They both give me friendly smiles. Helen has honey-brown hair, the cutest freckles all over her face, and big brown eyes. Debra's bright blonde hair is in a bob cut and her sunny smile can be seen from thirty feet away.

"Were you two born in Saddleback?" I ask, while watching where I'm stepping. Hearing Linc's tale of twisting his ankle in a hole made a lasting impression on me.

Helen nods while Debra shakes her head.

"Saddleback is all I've ever known, so I'm so excited to see other places," Helen gushes, gripping her backpack straps.

"I was born in the States," Debra says, "but we had to come out here about eight years ago when the Extremists finally found us." She frowns, but then she brightens. "I've met the best people out here, though. I can't complain. My little sister has only known Saddleback as a home."

That must be the nine-year-old traveling with us who I'm hoping will become friends with Greta. "What's her name?"

"Linda," she says easily, with a fond smile. "She's way up at the front. She wants to be one of the first to see the Polar Bear. She's a firecracker, that's for sure."

I study Adele for a bit because she looks withdrawn. When she catches me watching her, she turns her head to study the trail to the side of her.

I stifle a sigh because I see so much of myself in her. We're a lot different, but still so similar. It's strange, I want to comfort her, but I know from experience she needs her space. I know because that's how I am.

"What are you two most looking forward to?" I ask the both of her friends.

"Meeting new Elementals," Debra says first.

163

Helen nods enthusiastically and adds, "I'm hoping to find my Intended on these travels."

Deciding to have a little fun at Petra's expense, I lower my voice and say, "You're not the only one. Petra has never given up hope of finding hers."

We all giggle, but then sober, because it's really a sad story. She's chosen to live alone her whole life because she's never found her other half.

I count myself extremely fortunate to have found Linc when we were both young. And to think I was going to throw away our bond. I shudder at the thought. I would have ruined my chance at happiness, all because of a prejudice I had against Festans.

"Well, I hope you two find him, wherever they are. We're going to be traveling to so many places, chances are pretty good you'll cross paths. Well, much better than they were in Saddleback."

They smile at each other happily while Adele's face becomes more withdrawn. She looks behind us, trying to catch a glimpse of Rayne, I'm sure. I move to walk by her side, and I bump her hip with mine. "Hey," I say softly. "You holding up, okay?"

She shrugs and gives me such a pained look, my heart pinches for her. She wipes all emotion off her face when James and Sandy walk past us. They have their eyes on Gene and Jerry and are making a beeline for our guides.

"They're not the enemy, sister," I tell her gently. "They only want what's best for you."

"What's best for me is to be at my Intended's side, not hiding my feelings for him," she hisses at me through pursed lips.

As she glares at their backs, I try again. "It's not to punish you, it's to protect you."

She opens her mouth to say something, when we hear the scream of a child in the front of our traveling group. I, along with everyone else, break into a run to see what happened.

My eyes widen when I come to the scene. A little girl, Linda, by the looks of it, is laying on the ground, shielding her head with her arm. She's sobbing and holding her bleeding leg with her other arm.

Rayne is guarding her, looking out into the woods. He's holding his knife out in a defensive crouch.

"What happened?" I ask.

Debra lets out a cry and rushes to her little sister. Adele follows her and stands at Rayne's side, talking to him quietly. He's answering questions, I gather, but his eyes are trained on the foliage surrounding us.

Sandy kneels next to Linda and carefully holds Linda's leg, passing her hand over a gash or is it a bite mark?

Linc and I jog up to Rayne's other side, and Linc asks, "What are you looking for? Did you chase something off?"

"A lone wolf," Rayne says grimly. "He was looking for easy pickings and tried to drag this little girl into the woods."

My heart stutters. If Rayne hadn't been guarding our group, this girl would have been eaten alive. I turn to James, who's joined us. "He saved her life," I say gravely.

James nods his head as he watches Linda and her family sobbing together. "She was very lucky," he says.

"Papa, if it wasn't for Rayne watching over us, Linda would be dead," Adele says.

Gratitude fills his expression as he looks at Rayne, who's satisfied enough that the wolf has been run off, so he faces us instead of the forest. James nods at Rayne and says, "Thank you for saving her life. That family is indebted to you."

"As much as I appreciate that, it's your approval I'm trying to gain. I want to prove I'm decent enough to travel with your group," Rayne says soberly.

James analyzes him for a moment before he finally nods. "If you can promise to keep your hands to yourself, you're welcome to travel with us. Will you help keep our group safe?"

Adele's and Rayne's faces break out into wide smiles. "I'd be happy to, sir," Rayne says before he turns to beam at Adele. They become lost in each other's gazes, so I go back to Sandy, who is crouched next to Linda, healing her.

"Do you need any help?"

She studies the skin she healed, passing her hand over the area again. "No," she says, closing her eyes to better sense the wound. "I think I got everything. I just want to be sure I got all the nerves and to minimize the scar."

I know from experience the faster you perform a healing, the cruder the scar. If you go slow, the effects are less noticeable. Sometimes you can make it so there's barely a scar at all.

"May I?" I ask, reaching my hand out.

"Of course, I'd like your opinion."

Running my fingers gently over the bite mark, I close my eyes and search for any residual injury. Not finding anything abnormal, I look up proudly at my birth mother. "You healed her perfectly. And the scar looks great."

She nods and rubs her neck.

"Do you need to take a break?" I ask, laying my hand on her arm.

She shakes her head. "No, I'll be fine. I think I have another hour or two of hiking in me."

Studying her to be sure she's able to travel, I nod and stride to Petra, who's joined James, Rayne, and Linc.

She's praising Rayne's quick actions, "Good thing you were watching over us, youngun. We'd have lost her for sure."

"Mama is able to travel for a little while, but can we take a break when she needs it?" I ask Petra.

She nods easily.

With Linda firmly situated in the middle of our group, we place the hunters on the edges to keep an eye out for any more hungry wolves looking for an easy dinner.

I stick close to my parents and keep an eye out for any sign Sandy's too tired to continue. She makes it about two hours before James calls a halt to our progress. The temperature has dropped, and we huddle in our coats and work together to build several fires to warm ourselves.

The trip has been a gorgeous one. The leaves have ranged from sunny yellow to deep red, and every color in between. As I sit by one of the fires, I breathe in the crisp autumn air enjoying the moment and the stunning seasonal display. I feel like I'm in a dream, walking toward my destiny with a glorious fall scene to bless my trip.

I relax until an argument breaks out between Steele and Petra. I instantly look to Rayne to see if he's involved somehow, but he's off to the side, watching Petra stand up under Steele's glower.

"Now, look here. I took you in to give you a decent chance at the life you've been dealt. But you will respect me. I won't tolerate anything less. Is that understood?"

I don't know what started the problem, but Steele looks at her first with defiance, then submission. He ducks his head, stoops his shoulders and with a muttered, "Whatever," he stalks to the edge of the group, seeking out any other company but hers.

Petra looks drained as she slumps beside me at the fire, sighing deeply. "That boy is going to send me to an early grave," she mutters.

I pat her shoulder. "I think it's great that you took him in."

She looks tiredly in his direction and shakes her head. "I only hope I'm not too late coming into his life. He's known nothing but hardships. And now his sweetheart finds her Intended; I worry that might be the last straw."

I don't know what to say, so I stay quiet to give her a listening ear if that's what she needs. She doesn't, and she stares into the fire lost in her own thoughts. I'm suddenly so grateful she's come with me on this crazy journey that I tell her, "I don't know if I've thanked you yet."

"For what?" She slides her green eyes to me.

"For leaving your community and coming with me. You've already been invaluable."

I, more than anything, want her to find her own happiness after all of her sacrifices. Not just with me, but with Steele, too. "Oh, it's fine. Don't bother about me. I'm happy just about anywhere," she says gruffly.

"Well, I'm grateful."

"Me, too," Linc adds, who joins us at the fire. "Vela needs as much leadership support as she can get. We are blessed to have you on our team."

She waves us off. "Off with you two now. You're going to give me a bigger head than I need on my shoulders."

We laugh and do as she says, finding Adele staring into another fire, looking contemplative. I sit next to her. "I thought I'd see you dancing circles around the fire since Rayne has joined our group."

She smiles at that and says, "I would, but I don't want to look like an immature teenager. I'm trying to keep his attention, not drive it away."

I laugh. "You could do handstands next to him, and he would only look at you adoringly."

We look over at Rayne, who's talking to some of the younger guys, and she catches his eye. They smile at each other, and Adele blushes. She ducks her head in a failed attempt to hide the proof that Rayne has taken over her world.

Thinking through whether I want to involve Adele in my next request, I decide to ask her, "Who else is Steele friends with in our group?"

She looks everyone over and shakes her head. "He's somewhat friendly with a few of the guys, but with how he's treated the girls in the community, he's made enemies out of most."

I shake my head, disappointed. There are three other teen guys in the group. It's too bad Steele's on the outs with them.

"Why?" she asks, studying the side of my face.

"I just feel bad for him. Petra is trying to provide him a better life, and it doesn't look like he's appreciating it much."

"No, he is," she breathes as she searches until she finds him off to the side by himself. "He does appreciate it. He's just so angry at life, you know?"

I look over at Linc. He reads my unspoken request correctly and with a sigh gets up and walks over to Steele.

"What's he doing?" she asks, looking concerned.

"Don't worry, he's going to just be a friend to the guy. It looks like he could use someone in his corner. He'll just give some friendly advice."

Adele turns her head away from Rayne, who continues to glance over at her to hide her worried expression. "I just worry about him, you know?"

"I do know. If he has an ounce of brains in his head, he'll see this trip as a blessing and take advantage of it. Let Linc try to talk to him." I say a little prayer in my head for Linc to have the words that Steele needs to hear.

We rest for about an hour before Gene calls the group to put out the fires and start walking again. Linc has been hanging out with Steele, and they begin the hike together, but it doesn't look like there's much talking. Sometimes all you need is friendly company, though. I'm hoping Linc has been able to talk some sense into the young guy.

We walk until dark is almost upon us, and at Jerry's command, we set up camp for the night. Some have tents, but most sleep under the stars. James produces a tent, which he gives to me and Adele.

Linc helps to organize several men to sit up and watch over us for the night. It's not unheard of for bears and wolves to descend on sleeping campers. We've already had one attack, we don't need another.

Now that Rayne is officially part of our group, Adele happily settles for the night. She faces me and closes her eyes with a smile on her face. Content to see her happy for once, I smile back at her, even though she can't see me.

Suddenly, her smile disappears and her forehead furrows. With her eyes still closed, she asks, "Do you think I'm being unfair to Steele?"

"In what way?"

"By breaking up with him," she says, biting her lip. Opening her eyes, she gives me a pained look. "What else was I supposed to do?"

"Do you still care for him?" I ask quietly.

She nods miserably. "I do. I thought I'd be able to shut those feelings off as soon as I found my Intended. But it doesn't change everything I liked about him."

"Your first crush holds a lot of power."

She nods and dips her head. "My heart feels torn in two different directions. When I'm with Rayne, I'm so happy I could scream to the tops of the trees. But when I see how miserable Steele is, I feel so guilty, because I know that I caused his unhappiness."

I shake my head. "You aren't the whole reason he's sad, Adele. He's had a lot of hard knocks in life. This is just another one."

She buries her face in the sweater she's using as a pillow. "I don't want to cause anyone pain, Vela. This is so hard."

"I know it is, sweetie. I'm sorry," I say, not knowing what else to say.

Silence descends, and I fall asleep to my prayers for Adele and the rest of our group.

19

Rayne

On our way to the Polar Bear Lodge, I signed up for the first shift that first night. I happily volunteered because my Intended is sleeping in one of these tents, and I will do my part to be sure she's safe. She and her family.

It's still unbelievable that I have an Intended bond with Vela's sister. I would never have guessed it. Never in a million years.

As far as that Steele guy goes, however, I know I need to keep my distance. I don't quite trust myself to not say or do something I'll regret. Even with that cheap shot he gave me, a part of me feels sorry for him. After all, I was in his position, or similar to it, just a week ago. It really is a bad position for him. Because of Jean and I's soulmate connection, I'm ripping his girlfriend away from him. What am I supposed to do, though? Ignore my bond with Jean, so Steele feels better? No. I'm not altruistic enough for that, even if I am compassionate to his situation.

I'd like to give him the advice that it's impossible to fight against a sacred bond like an Intended soulmate. I watch where he's sleeping under the open stars. He's just close enough to Adele's tent, I notice. I'll be watching him to be sure he leaves her alone. If she approaches him, there's nothing I can do about it, but I can be sure to keep him away from her with my warning glares.

The hours pass pretty quickly, and before I know it, another guy shows up to relieve me.

I go to make myself a spot close to Adele's tent to try to catch some shuteye. Someone very generously gave me a blanket, which I've laid out on the ground. I'm about to drift off to sleep when I hear a noise by Adele's tent.

I'm quiet as I get up and follow the sound, being sure to stay in the shadows.

Anger hits me hard as I see Steele holding up a tent spike and speaking to someone in Adele's tent. It comes as no surprise to hear Adele's voice. I only listen because I want to be sure she wants to talk to him, and this isn't an unwanted invasion of privacy.

"Why are you staying away from me?" Steele furiously whispers.

"I'm not...well, I guess I am. I don't know Steele; you've been avoiding me just as much."

"I wouldn't stop talking to you if I knew you wanted to talk to me," Steele says.

"I do! You're still my friend, Steele. I just...can't you understand my position?"

"No, I can't. I don't care if I ever meet my Intended if it means I have to let you go."

I scoff silently because I felt the exact same way. But he has no idea the power his Intended will hold over him. I'm about to leave them to their conversation, when I hear Adele's next request.

"Please, Steele, leave me alone. I need to sleep, and I don't have any answers for you."

"I need to know that I mean something to you. I'm not leaving until you tell me something."

Okay, I've heard enough.

Not bothering to be quiet, I walk up to the couple, and I pull Steele's collar until he's standing next to me. "Did you hear her? She wants you to go. Respect her wishes now, or I'll be sure you do."

"Rayne," Adele cries, crawling out of the tent. "Let him go!"

Keeping a firm grip on Steele's collar, I turn to her. "I heard you tell him to leave you alone, and he didn't."

She looks shocked as she spits out, "You overheard that whole conversation?"

"Not the whole thing, just the last part."

Her face turns red as she commands, "Put him down, Rayne. Now."

"Yeah, Rayne, put me down. You're not supposed to fight, remember?" Steele asks in a sneer.

I force myself to obey and turn to Steele, who has murder in his eyes.

"Now, you're going to pay for that," Steele spits as he raises his hands.

I scoff. "Who's going to make me? You? Give me your best shot. One that you don't have to sneak at me. Fight me like a man."

Steele and I are shoved apart when Adele inserts herself between us. "Stop this, both of you!"

Vela crawls out of the tent looking sleepy but wary. "What's going on?"

I volunteer, "She asked him politely to leave, and he didn't. So, I made him."

She turns to Steele. "Is this true?"

By this time, several people have joined our midnight conversation, including Linc. He goes to stand by Vela protectively.

"I just wanted to talk to her alone," Steele mutters, shoving his hands in his pockets, since it's clear he's changed his mind about attacking me in front of witnesses.

"You had every opportunity during the day, Steele," Vela says with a frown. "Talk to her in the morning. Everyone else go to bed." She looks around the group, and everyone melts back to their beds in the dark night.

Everyone except Linc, of course. "Is there going to be any trouble?" he asks me and Steele.

I shake my head, and Steele does the same before he walks back to his pack.

Striding over to my bed, I ball everything up and bring it back to the entrance of Adele's tent, making myself comfortable.

"What are you doing?" Adele asks with wide eyes.

"Protecting you from unwanted visitors."

She splutters. "I don't need protection."

I eye her. "Obviously you do. Now, if you don't mind, I need to get some sleep tonight." I lie down and hide a smile when she angrily steps over me to go into the tent. She slams the flap in my face, and I can't help but laugh.

"It's not funny," her voice seethes from inside the tent.

"Are you going to be okay?" Linc asks Vela.

She looks over at me with an exasperated look. "I'll be fine. We'll be fine. Don't worry about us."

"Hard not to," he mutters before turning to his bed and pack. As he passes me, he throws over his shoulder, "Better watch yourself. I know an angry woman when I see one. You're going to be in trouble for this."

I fold my arms over my chest.

It's worth it if she's safe.

And I don't find Steele to be part of her safety. He's going to push my buttons too hard one of these days, and he's not going to like what happens.

The rest of the night passes peacefully, and I wake up feeling pretty refreshed if not uncertain what Linc meant by me being in Adele's bad graces.

I brace myself for when she emerges from the tent, but it's not her cold stare that freezes me in my tracks. It's her silent treatment. She walks right by me and doesn't say a word. When Vela follows her outside, she gives me a sympathetic pat. "Good luck," she whispers as she passes.

I decide to make myself useful and hopefully get back on her good side by breaking down her and Vela's tent. But my effort goes unnoticed except for Linc, who takes the tent bundle out of my hands. "I told you," he says, smirking.

Frustrated that I somehow became the bad guy in this when it's clearly Steele who's at fault, I find myself trailing Adele when the camp is ready to resume our trek.

Unlike yesterday, to my utter annoyance, Steele is not avoiding Adele. In fact, they're walking together and talking quietly.

I pay attention to her body language, however, because if I feel in any way she doesn't want Steele as a hiking partner, I'll be sure to drive him off.

But as the day goes on, I don't see any sign she doesn't want him there. She even laughs and smiles up at him. I can't help but hold back my huffs of anger at that sight. But I won't be the guy who won't allow his girlfriend to talk to other guys her age. My next thought almost stops me in my tracks. I'm assuming she's agreed to be my girlfriend since we found each other, but she's made no such promises. The worse part of this is he's gotten in one good hit on me, and my hands are tied. I can't reciprocate, since I'm trying to prove I'm a changed guy.

I find Linc beside me at some point and when I turn to look at him, he says, "It sucks, doesn't it?"

I can only nod, unhappy that my former rival is giving me sympathy. For something I did myself to his Intended.

Oh, how the tables have turned.

In Linc's defense, I can only give him credit when he doesn't say what we're clearly both thinking.

"I'm really sorry, Linc," I say gruffly, trying to ignore the giggles Adele is giving to something Steele just said. "I shouldn't have come between you and Vela. In all fairness, though, I didn't know what it was like. I should never have made Vela choose between us. I put her in a pretty bad position, and for that I'm sorry."

"And now you do," Linc accepts with a glance at me.

"And now I do," I agree. "How did you keep your temper?"

He laughs. "I distinctly remember not keeping my temper, Rayne. Several times."

I rub my shoulder where Jack bit me. "Yeah, I guess you didn't. I can't blame you. I have to be the bigger guy, though, and not bash in his head just for looking at her the way he is."

Linc nods. "Yes, it's not going to be easy. Many times, you won't be able to win for trying."

"Like last night," I say, sighing.

"So, she really did ask him to leave?"

"Yes, and when he didn't listen, I made him listen."

"And now you're the bad guy," Linc says ruefully.

I sigh. "Apparently."

"Can I give you some advice?"

"Sure, if anyone can tell me what to do, it's you."

"Don't force yourself on her. Let her come to you, ask you for protection, things like that. If you force it, it may not go your way."

"Like now," I say, waving my hand in Adele's direction.

"Exactly, my friend," Linc says, clapping his hand on my shoulder.

I turn to look at him with surprise. "You really are the better man, Linc. In more ways than one."

"Thanks, but it took some direction from the Almighty Himself for me to get to this point."

"Noted." I sink into my thoughts then and there and wonder about this God who can change someone like Linc into the guy he is. I'd like to know more about Him.

While I'm silent, Linc asks, "Have you ever wondered if He's real?"

"All the time," I admit.

"He is. My faith has gotten me through some rough times. I'd be a different guy if it wasn't for God's guiding hand. My parents…" he falters as if choosing his words carefully. "As much as I respect them, don't love me like you'd think parents would. They expect me to fall in their footsteps by default."

"By default?" I ask, studying his expression. It's not telling me much.

"My mother became Grand Elder from the graces of her lineage. Her grandfather was Grand Elder before her. And even though the title isn't supposed to be inherited, she earned it with her hard work, determination, and family name. She wants that for me, too. But I don't want that future. Not if it means turning out like her. Don't get me wrong," he says quickly. "I respect her for her position as Grand Elder and as my mother. But," he says, sighing, "I don't want to be blamed for my sister's death anymore and I'm afraid she'll hold that over me for the rest of my life. When it should have been her making decisions at that time and not a seventeen-year-old kid."

I nod, silently wondering what happened with his sister. My situation is much different, but my father holds high expectations also, and I've always chafed under his direction. He doesn't guide; he bulldozes. Where I would teach, he commands. I don't want to be that kind of man.

I'd like a different Guide. And if what Linc says is true, then I can turn my attention to the Lord for that kind of instruction. I suddenly want to be worthy of God's love and trust. By extension, Adele's love, too. Not just because I'm her Intended, but because she respects the man I am or could be.

I haven't exactly been that guy. Everything came crashing down on me when I nearly killed Linc in anger and not in self-defense. My world came into clear focus, and I did not like the guy I saw in myself.

Unable to blame everything on my controlling father, I have to come to terms with my actions and decisions.

"How do you, you know, find out what God wants to teach you?" I ask, a bright curiosity coming over me.

He swings his pack down and fishes inside, pulling out a book. "This," he says, zipping his bag back up and holding out a small Bible. "Everything you need to know is right in these pages. And prayer, of course."

"Of course," I say dumbly, because I have no idea what he means.

"You know, like talk to God in your head? Or out loud. However you want to communicate with him. But the important thing is to share your heart and everything else on your mind."

"Doesn't He already know everything you're thinking?" I've heard that and have always felt uncomfortable with the idea, but if it's true, then I have a lot to be sorry for.

Linc laughs. "He does, but He wants you to give Him not only your thoughts, but your heart. It's a give and take situation."

"How is it a give and take? Doesn't He have all kinds of rules you have to follow or else?"

"Or else what?"

"You know, go to a pit of fire." I shudder. I've definitely heard that, too.

He puts his hand on my shoulder, squeezing. "You don't need to worry about that if you give your heart and mind for Him to keep. He keeps those who love Him close."

"Love God? Is that actually possible? I understand respecting Him, but how do you love someone you can't see?"

His face turns wistful, and he puts the Bible on my chest. Once I hold on to it, he drops his hand. I hold it close, almost reverently. I've never held a Bible before. "Read this. Find out Who you are to worship, and yes, love. He loves you with a fullness you'll never get anywhere else. Not even from your Intended. Read how He died for you, lived life as a man just so He can truly know the thoughts, desires, grief, and emotions we feel. Give Him a chance and see how you come out the other side of it. And any questions you have you come to me, and I'll be happy to talk to you about it."

"How can you forgive me so easily? For what I did to you?" I ask, moved he would give me such a gift.

"Forgiveness." He points to the Bible in my hand. "Read that book and you'll see for yourself how I can do it. I need forgiveness just as much as you do. I'm just as much of a jerk as anyone without Christ in my life. Believe me when I say that when you trust God with your life you will feel such freedom. It's like the world opens up to you in a way that's true and real. Read John 8:32, it says, *Then you will know truth, and the truth will set you free.* Who doesn't want that? Here, I'll show you."

He reaches for the Bible, and when I hand it to him, he flips to a page. He shows the verse he just quoted to me. "Start with this verse. Then, read all the Gospels, starting with Matthew, then Mark, Luke and John."

He hands me back the Bible, and I mull over everything he says and open it up, skimming over words. A sudden desire to understand everything God is offering me comes over, and if I could, I would find a quiet place to spend the rest of the day reading. I'll have to settle for reading what I can as we walk.

For the first time, I don't care who sees me reading a Bible, something I would have scoffed at before this. An insatiable curiosity to know everything about God has taken over, and I fall into it learning about a love like Christ's.

If He loves me, I want to deserve it. But I know more than anything that I never could.

20

Linc

I leave Rayne behind as he reads and walks, and my heart is lighter than it's been since we started this trek. Because I know how he's feeling right now. A desire to know God has come over him, and if Rayne allows it, he'll soon be a changed man.

God will do things in his life and make him into the man God Himself designed him to be. I smile at that. I have a long way to go until I'm that guy, too, but I hope to keep learning until one day I reach the heavenly gates, and God can tell me if I've done the job. I hope to hear the words, "Well done, good and faithful servant."

As I walk beside Grant, Debra's and Linda's father, I can't help but notice that he's keeping a close eye on his adventurous nine-year-old.

"What's it like having daughters?" I ask him.

He laughs, a booming sound that goes into the trees. "Terrifying. I'm always surprised at what comes out of their mouths from one moment to the next. I thought it was hard keeping up with my wife, who keeps me on my toes. But with my daughters? I'm a ballerina. Have sons, that's my advice to you. You won't be outnumbered in that case."

I chuckle, loving the idea of having children with Vela. We're nowhere near ready for that to happen, but when it does, I'll treasure a son or a daughter. I hope to have both one day.

"I don't think I'll have much choice about that, but I can see how having a daughter is an experience." I sober, thinking of my own adventurous sister. "I had a sister who constantly had her head in the clouds. It was hard keeping her grounded."

He gives me a sympathetic glance. "Had?"

"Yes," I say simply. I know I need to talk about her more, but it's so hard to keep the guilt and regret from crashing down on me. So, to keep the pain from drowning me I usually don't talk about her. I decide to change that. I share, "Olympia had a way of looking at things so differently from others, it just blew you away constantly."

He hums. "Tell me about it. I feel that all the time with my three ladies." He looks lovingly in their direction. Then he glances behind him at Rayne. "So, tell me about that young man who saved my daughter's life. Why wasn't he traveling with us?"

Not wanting to give a bad impression of Rayne, I say, "That's his story to tell, but he's a good guy. He's actually Adele's Intended."

His brows raise. "Is that so? Interesting. She's one lucky girl to find him so young." He looks over at his wife and points at her. "I was blessed, too. I found my Mary when I was fifteen years old. My family was traveling through a Neronian town on our way to a beach in Florida when I crossed paths with her. I'm a Festan, so you can imagine my surprise to find my Intended is a Water Elemental. We exchanged addresses and wrote letters until I was old enough to come back for her. You young people don't know what you're missing by not writing letters to each other. It's nothing like text messages. It's more personal, more of an insight into the soul. Anyway," he says with a wistful sigh,

"We got married as soon as we turned eighteen." He eyes me with a twinkle in his eyes. "We've been inseparable ever since then. I hear you and Vela are a matched pair, too. And that you plan to marry, first thing."

When I nod, he says, "I can only tell you life gets better and better with your Intended by your side. Keep her close, but not so close that she can't fly. Give her the wings to come back to you every time. And she will." Nothing but love fills his eyes as he gazes at his wife and daughters. "And if you're lucky, God will gift you another one, or two, who're just like her," he says, laughing. "I'm a blessed man. I pray the same for you."

"Thank you," I say with a full heart. "I am, too. I almost lost Vela, but God brought her back to me. To let me live and experience this crazy world with her. She has a big job, though."

"That she does," he says, sobering quickly. "She'll have my family's support. We've been waiting for her for a long time. Don't know how she's going to do it all."

"We have some ideas. Her powers, for one, will be a testament to who she is. We could use a good speech writer, though."

His eyes light up. "I used to do PR for a firm in Atlanta before we had to go into hiding. I'd be happy to earn my family's way on this trip and try my hand at a few words."

I eye him gratefully. "That would be great. I'll give Vela whatever you write, and we'll go over it. Thank you."

"Happy to be a part of something so life changing."

We hike through the morning and stop for lunch. I've enjoyed getting to know Grant and later Mary, too. We're getting close to the Polar Bear now, and I wonder if my mother is still there.

I hope for Vela's sake, she's gone. They didn't have the best start to a fruitful mother and daughter-in-law relationship.

Sure enough, smoke from fires in the Polar Bear competes with the afternoon sun in my eyes and we walk in that direction. I notice Vela has a pep in her step, and I know she's looking forward to seeing Greta, Hannah, and her friends. I love that she's grown close to them; she misses her other family so.

I offer to run up ahead and warn them a big group is coming in to stay in the community. Rayne asks to go with me so he can explain his actions, and I agree, thinking this is a good time for me to vouch for him. I don't want him tied up as soon as he's spotted.

The first person we see is Gary. As soon as he sees Rayne, he lunges for him. Holding Gary back, I say, "Hey, give me a chance to explain his presence. Rayne's redeemed himself. I wouldn't say that if I didn't mean it." When Gary stops resisting me, I let him go and watch him warily, as does Rayne.

"I've apologized and have been punished appropriately, believe me," Rayne says.

"How?" Gary growls.

"First, as you know, Vela took my powers. But she gave me a great gift by returning those powers. I've also been kept from my Intended because of what I did. Believe me, I was sorry before, but now more than ever," Rayne says with a twist of his lips and pain in his eyes.

Gary looks at me for confirmation. When I give it, he says, "That's harsh, even after what you did, Rayne."

Rayne accepts this and steps back as Gary walks with us. I notice there are more lean-to's temporarily protecting the members from the elements, since most of the buildings were either burned down or are uninhabitable since the Extremists' fires.

Gary notices my attention on their progress, or lack of progress in rebuilding. "We haven't decided how many homes to rebuild. That depends on who's staying out here, and who's going with Vela."

I nod with a serious set of my lips. "That is a big decision."

"Let's go to Rick's. He'll want to hear about Rayne." Gary says as he adjusts his belt around his wide girth.

When we arrive at Rick's lean-to, he's chopping wood. He almost comes at Rayne with the axe when Gary and I stop him. I urge him to forgive Rayne, too. He gives Rayne a skeptical look when he asks me, "Vela feels the same way?"

I nod, and when he hears of Rayne's plight with his Intended, he's less sympathetic than Gary and shoots Rayne angry glares before we start figuring out how to make room for fifteen more people in the camp. It isn't easy, especially since homes haven't been rebuilt in just a few days. We will have to make room for the Saddleback group by cutting a few more trees for a couple more makeshift shelters.

Rayne leaves to find his family and by the time Rick and Gary have made the necessary plans for accommodating the Saddleback members, they arrive. Greetings are shared, old friends welcomed, and new acquaintances made. I smile when I see Vela's happy reunion with the girls from the Polar Bear. She hugs Tonya, Jennifer, Claudette, and Alice fiercely and they have a furious conversation. I notice Vela's friends giving shy glances at the new guys we brought back, and a healthy exchange of interested looks are returned.

I give my attention back to Rick and Gary when Petra joins us. That's when a startling discovery is made.

"What do you mean, the plane is gone?" Petra barks at Rick, who is the unfortunate one to deliver the news.

He steps back and says, "Elizabeth and her husband said they needed it, and they'll bring it back in four days."

"My mother took the plane?" I ask, anger surfacing. "How? Who flew the plane for her?"

Gary answers with chagrin, since he sees how upset I am, "We actually had a former pilot living out here, and he agreed to fly the plane if he could take his family back to the states. The fire really shook him up."

Vela walks up to us, her arms around Tonya and Alice. Jennifer and Claudette follow. "What happened?" Vela asks, noticing my expression.

"Linc's mom happened," Tonya says with a twist of her lips. "She took the plane. The only good news is she took the captured Extremists with her."

Vela looks at me, and I shake my head. "It's just like her to commandeer the plane when we need it. Turning to Vela, I say under my breath, "I know why she did this. Well, her real reason."

"We were going to bring the Extremists to her anyway, so why is it a big deal that she took them?"

"Vela, she doesn't want us to get married. She's trying my patience with this antic of hers."

"What's four more days going to do?" Vela asks, frowning. "We'll just wait her out."

Tonya, Alice, Jennifer, and Claudette all nod eagerly and it looks like we have four more ready attendees for our wedding.

"I know my mother, though," I say lowly. "She'll have some other plan blocking us. When she wants something, or doesn't in this case, she usually gets her way."

"Well, not this time," Vela vows, putting her hands on her hips. "If we have to wait for the plane, fine, that just gives us girls," she nods at her friends, "my sister, and Mama more time to plan the wedding."

"Aren't you forgetting a couple of people? I ask, admiring her angry and determined look. Especially when it comes to us getting married. "I'm pretty sure Hannah and Greta will want to have some input."

"You really think so?"

I snort. "What woman doesn't like to plan a wedding for someone they love? And Hannah and Greta love you just as much as your family."

"You're right." Her face gets all soft. "I'm so lucky, aren't I?"

186

"Ask me that when we're standing in front of the preacher with a ring on your finger."

She smacks me on my arm. "Conceited much?"

"Right?" Tonya joins in, shamelessly eavesdropping on our conversation. "You're a piece of work, Linc." The rest of the girls nod, agreeing with Tonya and Vela.

I hold up my hands to ward off their teasing accusations. "No!" I say, laughing. "That's not what I meant. If we can manage to get married without my mother's interference, I'll be surprised."

Vela's face goes from one of outrage to sympathy. Tonya gives me the same look. "I can't imagine what you've gone through with her as your mother," Vela says.

I shrug, but her words hit me hard. "I dealt with it." I narrow my eyes. "She will not succeed in separating us. I will marry you." Not able to help myself, I grab her and pick her up, spinning her slowly. Holding her around her waist to my chest, I say, "You are one incredible woman, Vela Ashcroft, soon to be Stevenson. You really want to marry me?"

She looks down at me with love shining in her eyes as she moves her hands from my shoulders to cup my face. "I do. I really do. I want to officially make you mine. Are you agreeable to that?"

To answer her, I drop her to the ground and give her such a searing kiss, she leans back with the force of my show of affection. "Does that answer your question?" I ask into her neck, pressing kisses on the softest part of her skin.

While Vela's girlfriends groan at our display of affection, Vela giggles and leans away. At this point, she's practically bending over backward. "Linc, let me up. I'm about to fall."

"I would *never* allow you to fall when you're in my arms," I say and capture her lips again.

"Could have fooled me," she says after I release her lips.

"I would never kid you about kissing you, nor wanting to marry you, for that matter." Feeling the heat rising, I force myself to only kiss her softly, not deeply, like I really want. I pull away from her taking a full step back.

"*Thank you*," Tonya says in a distinct voice. "You guys are gross."

Vela bumps her shoulder with hers. "Hey, if you were in my position, you'd be doing the same thing."

"You're darn straight I would, just please, give us some warning before you guys do that," Tonya grumbles.

Alice laughs and adds, "Yes, we all love watching a real-life romance, but that was a bit much."

Vela blushes, which only makes me want to do a repeat performance, but I restrain myself. A guy can only handle so much.

Vela walks away with her friends, but gives me a parting shot, "Glad to know I have power over the mighty Lincoln Stevenson."

Oh, she doesn't know the half of it. She has more control over me than I do. And that's saying something. So, with a self-deprecating chuckle, I follow my fiancée.

Vela parts ways with her friends and asks around where we can find Hannah. Once she's given directions to one of the many lean-tos that litter this once well-built space, we walk into Hannah's new clinic. When Hannah looks up and sees Vela, shock comes over her face and then, in an almost girlish way, she squeals and jumps into Vela's arms.

"You're a sight for sore eyes," Hannah says, leaning back to look Vela over. "Wait until Greta knows you're back, she'll be ecstatic! She's been talking about the upcoming trip for days."

Almost as if she heard her mom's words, Greta walks in, her eyes brightening when she sees Vela. Like her mother, she squeals and runs into Vela's arms. They laugh and hug each other, and I smile at how good Vela is with children. What will it be like for our own children to hug her like that? Even as young as I am, I can hardly wait to see that.

After the joyful reunion, talk immediately turns to our wedding.

"Well, thanks to Linc's mother, we can't leave until she returns the plane," Vela says with a frown, folding her arms in front of her.

Andy makes his entrance, ducking his large frame into the space. I notice this is a larger structure than the others, and guess it's to accommodate Andy's size. When he sees Vela and me, his eyes grow warm. "Well, hello, you two. How was your trip? Was it successful?" he asks Vela.

I wrap my arm around Vela's shoulder, so happy she finally found her family.

"Yes, it was amazing. Well, at first it got a little dicey, since they didn't really believe I am the Chosen Child, but once I showed off my powers, they came on board soon enough."

"And your family?" Hannah asks, stepping next to Andy.

Vela's eyes grow wet. "I found them," she says hoarsely.

Hannah claps her hands to her chest. "Oh, Vela, that's wonderful." Then her face hardens. "Oh, why did that woman, sorry Linc, take the plane? We could get you and Linc married tomorrow if we had that plane."

Andy laughs. "You know, it's like Hannah didn't get the message that Elizabeth is the *Grand Elder of Festans.* When Elizabeth announced she was taking the plane, Hannah stood up to her like an avenging angel. She defended you two to the hilt. And she wouldn't back down, either, until Linc's mother promised to bring the plane back in no more than four days."

I look at Hannah with surprise, but she just smiles and gives me a shrug. "Who does she think she is, anyway? She's not God, that's for sure, as much as she thinks she is."

When Hannah scoffs, I laugh and let go of Vela to give Hannah a side hug. "I knew there was a reason we loved you so much."

"Who else will stick up for Vela when she has no other family out here? Well, now you do, technically. But I consider us family, so you get the family treatment. I go after anyone who messes with my people."

"Yeah, that Festan lady didn't like that very much," Greta says seriously. "She was real mad."

"I'm not afraid of a little temper," Hannah says airily.

Andy laughs and wraps his big arms around her waist. "You should have seen her. She was glorious. Hannah's beautiful anyway, but you should see her when she's all worked up. She's a goddess."

Hannah blushes and lightly smacks his arm as he grins down at her. "Stop that. I'm no one special."

"You are to me," Andy says, a big beaming smile on his face. He leans in to kiss her softly.

"Please stop!" Greta cries, covering her eyes. "I was hoping all of that stuff would stop now that you're back, Vela."

Vela laughs. "I'm sorry, Greta, I have no control over those kinds of things. I don't think I want to, anyway. I've been hoping these two would get together even before I met you guys."

"Well, now that you're here, I have some questions about your wedding. Like how do you feel about me training one of my babies to walk your ring down the aisle?" Greta asks.

Vela, Andy, Hannah, and I all laugh.

"Well, since our wedding is being all planned out by you conniving females, I'm going to go make us some dinner," I announce.

Vela looks at me with surprise. "Really? You'll fix dinner?"

"How hard can it be? I'll go hunting. It'll be a protein-rich dinner, if that's okay."

Hannah smiles softly. "We've managed to scrounge up some flour that survived the fire. I'll have some flatbreads ready."

I smile at her. I take one last look at Vela, because, really, I can't help myself. Giving her a wink, I leave to hunt.

As I walk away, my heart feels fuller than it's ever been. Even with the impending danger of the Extremists finding us again, my future is sweet indeed.

21

Vela

While Linc is hunting, I catch up on all the news that happened during our trip to Saddleback. I tell Hannah about Petra and how she's joined my leadership team.

"Petra's here?" Hannah gushes, jumping up. "I have to go greet her. I've missed her like crazy. I haven't seen her in like a year. Greta, get the dough ready for flatbreads, I'll be back in a little while."

Greta frowns down at canisters that must be flour, and I laugh. "Don't like to cook, Greta?"

"No," she says with a pout. "I can't believe Momma is trusting me to do this, actually."

"You want some help?" I offer.

She shakes her head. "Nah, I'll be alright. Do you have something to do?"

"Actually, I do. I need to go see where my family set up camp."

She nods, and I leave the lean-to, looking around for my family.

I spot Adele walking ahead of me, and I run to catch up to her.

"Hey," I say, a little out of breath.

"Hey, yourself," she says with a small smile.

"Have you met the girls, yet?" I ask, looking around so I can introduce my friends to my little sister.

"Should I know who the girls are?"

"Sorry, I meant my friends from here."

When she shakes her head, I spot Grace and realize I haven't said hello to her yet.

"Grace," I call and when she turns to look at me, she smiles shyly and walks over. I go to meet her and give her a warm hug. "How are you?"

"I'm good," she says quietly. "We've missed you."

"I've missed you all, too. Let me introduce you to my little sister. Adele, this is Grace. She's a painter, so you two have the arts in common."

Grace shakes Adele's hand and gives her an interested look. "You're an artist, too?"

Adele grimaces. "I wish I could paint. I'm more of a graphic artist. I like to design on the computer, which is in sore demand out here."

Grace gives her a pained look. "Oh, I'm sorry. It must be hard not to have an outlet for your creativity. When I don't have any paint, I'm lost." She looks around with soulful eyes at the burned out shells left by the devastating fires of the E.E. An angry look comes over her. "I had so many pieces destroyed."

Adele looks around. "You had canvases way out here?"

"No," I jump in because I have to praise Grace's work. "She used the houses as her canvases. I wish you could have seen her work. It was stunning."

Grace blushes and looks down. "Thank you, Vela," she says quietly.

Adele asks, "So all your paint was destroyed, too?"

"Yes," Grace says quietly.

"Grace," I ask, "are you coming with me to the States?"

"I don't know," she says, a faraway look coming in her eyes. "I'm not sure I'm really cut out to travel like that."

"Well, you'd be welcome," I assure her.

"Thank you, Vela," she says again and then, with a wave, turns to leave.

I bump Adele's shoulder once Grace leaves. "No smitten guys trailing you right now?"

When she gives me a pained look, I rush to say, "I'm sorry. I know it's complicated."

She blows out a breath. "Yeah, it's complicated. You know, I'm not talking to Rayne right now. But I feel like he's hardly noticed. He's devouring his new Bible as fast as he can read it."

I look at her curiously. "Is that a problem for you?" I'm suddenly nervous that my sister doesn't know Christ.

"I guess it's fine, it's just I don't know if I believe in all of that stuff."

My heart clamps tight. "And when you say stuff, you mean Christianity."

"Yeah, I think that it's kind of important for my Intended and I to see eye to eye on things like that."

"What exactly do you believe, Adele?"

She throws her arms out wide. "I'm sure there's some big explanation with why everything was created the way it is, but I just want to live my life not having to answer to some big God."

Sorrow for my sister leaves me breathless. "What have Mama and Papa said about it?"

"Oh, they believe in God and everything. I've heard all the stories. I just don't know if I believe it."

I stop her from walking and say with all earnestness, "Will you be open minded and let me tell you about who Jesus is to me?"

"What, right now?" she looks around.

"What else do you have to do?"

"I was going to help Mama and Papa build their shelter."

"Okay, I'll help. And while we build, I'll tell you my story."

She looks at me and then nods. I follow her while she walks to where Mama and Papa are putting together a lean-to, like all the other ones.

We're in the tree line of the former Polar Bear since trees are needed to structure the temporary housing. Mama and Papa are standing in between two trees that are about five feet apart. They have a stack of large branches and they're methodically placing them next to each other in between two six-foot logs that hold up the lean-to.

Adele and I join them and while we work, I start my story. "So, I was about six years old, and I had just left Sunday School. I couldn't shake what the teacher said, and I finally asked my mom about it."

"What did you hear?" Sandy asks, joining our conversation. James, too, listens in.

"My teacher said Jesus could be my best friend. And that just blew my mind. I mean, I had heard all these stories about Jesus and the miracles He did, and I was like I could have *Him* as my best friend? I couldn't believe it. I mean, He healed the blind, the lame, every sickness He came across. He even raised people from the dead."

"Yeah, that is kind of hard to wrap your mind around," Adele says as she heaves a large stick up and drags it over to me.

I accept it from her and pull it over to the one I had just situated. "So, when I got home, I asked my mom if it was true."

"And what did she say?" Sandy asks with a soft look in her eyes.

"She told me it was true. But I said, 'I can't even see Jesus, so how is that possible?'"

Adele looks at me curiously, and I pray my words sink into her heart and take root.

"She said His physical body isn't here for me to see, but His Holy Spirit would be with me always if I asked Him into my heart. I would be a vessel, with Jesus and the Holy Spirit living inside me."

"Yeah, that's always confused me. How can He be two different things?" Adele asks as she pauses in her work.

"He's not two different things, He's three. He's the Triune. The Trinity. He's God, the Holy Spirit, and Jesus all at the same time. He has been for all time."

Adele's face looks contemplative, so I continue. "So, that's what makes what He did all the more important. Jesus, as a man, chose to take on all the sins of humanity and die on the cross for *you,* for *me.* When he sacrificed Himself, he took yours and my sins and wiped them clean. But by doing that, He separated Himself from God, the Father, and that was more painful for Him than anything the soldiers did to Him."

"It is hard to believe He endured so much pain for us," James says, wiping his forehead off.

I nod, agreeing. "It hurts my heart every time I read it in the Gospels. My mom told me Jesus died on the cross so that I could be free of my sin. That way, the Holy Spirit could live in my heart. Hearing that, I prayed the Sinner's Prayer with my mom right there and then."

Adele picks up a big stick with a grunt and pulls it over to me. "It feels like I'm being forced to accept this as truth."

"You have a choice, Adele. We all do," I say softly, hoping against all hope she hears me. "Jesus would never force this down our throats, but He is truth. All the stories are true. It's just a matter of believing in Him and asking Him to come into your life."

She thrusts the branch at me, and I barely catch it. "I don't know what to believe."

My heart sinks. "Well, will you just think about it? Try praying. He'll listen. He's waiting for you, Adele. He can even help you with your situation with Rayne and Steele."

Adele's face looks troubled, and James and Sandy give me heavy looks, while casting worried glances at Adele. We work in silence until the lean-to is finished.

When Adele walks away from our group, I walk over to my parents.

Sandy says, "We've always worried about Adele and what she believes, truly believes to the bottom of her heart. But it's pretty clear now she's unsure." She shakes her head sadly.

James wraps his arm around her shoulder and kisses the side of her head. "We've laid the groundwork, but Vela here has planted some seeds. Let's pray they take root."

Knowing I can do nothing more than pray and be an example of Christ to my little sister, I excuse myself to find my Intended.

He's with Andy, who's doing the backbreaking work of hacking at the shells of burned out homes, clearing them away to make room for new logs. I stand and admire my fiancé for a moment.

He catches me watching him. He stops for a moment and calls out, "You coming to help?"

"No, I'm good where I am," I reply, knowing a twinkle is in my eye.

He laughs, wiping off his hands. "I got us a few fat road chickens and dropped them off with Greta."

"Thanks! I'm going to get Mama and go find Hannah. We need to get dinner finished and make some wedding plans."

I head back to our makeshift shelter and invite my mom, but when I don't include Papa, he cries foul. "I'd like some say in this wedding, too."

I laugh and include him in the invitation and we're off to find Hannah, who I'm sure is still with Petra. I only know because she was so excited to hear that Petra is here, I could tell that would be a long visit.

Turns out, I'm right because when Mama, Papa, and I hunt down Hannah, she's tucked away in a tent with Petra, who's regaling her with my grand entrance into Saddleback.

"Vela," Hannah cries when she spots me through the tent flaps. "You left out so much when you told me about going to see Petra's community. Why didn't you go into detail?"

I blush and shrug.

Petra gives me a calculated look. "Humility does our girl good," she says with a proud smile.

I blush harder, but my chest lifts, knowing Petra is proud of me.

"I was just going to see if we could all go over some wedding plans while we work on dinner," I say, nerves suddenly coming hard and fast. I mean, *I'm getting married soon.*

Petra scowls. "This really isn't my expertise."

Wanting to hear her input, despite her never been married, I ask, "Please join us." I fight back my growing nerves, blaming it on how tired I am. Is this what cold feet means? If so, I don't like it.

She looks skeptical but climbs out of the tent and joins us.

Hannah makes her way out of the tent, too, and rubs her hands together vigorously. "Okay, wedding plans. Let's get started. Then we need to head back and help Greta finish dinner."

Knowing our wedding needs to be planned in days and not months is daunting to say the least. Maybe this is where my anxiety is coming from.

Mama and Papa both agree with me when I insist on having a preacher. "It will make the day perfect knowing the officiant can marry us with God's permission," I say to Hannah's soft smile.

"Okay, well, we're going to have to figure out where you can get married. Since we don't have computers out here, anyone know anything?" Hannah asks the group.

Sandy wrinkles her nose in thought. James taps his lip, but to my surprise it's Petra who raises her hand. "I can't believe I can contribute, but I know of a few states where you can get married at seventeen with only parental permission."

I lift my eyebrows and wait.

"Arkansas, Alabama, and Arizona," she says and then clamps her lips shut like even knowing that pains her.

I laugh and squeeze her shoulder. "Thank you, Petra! That really helps!"

"I only know that because I remember it was the three A's," she grumbles.

"Well, let's pick one of those states." I say, excitement replacing the nervousness I felt at the start of this conversation.

"Wait," James says, holding out his hand. "Let's be strategic about this. I assume we need to get the Grand Elders' support to back Vela's claim as Chosen Child, right?"

"Yes," I say, biting my lip at the remote possibility of gaining the support of each, including Linc's mother, who hates me.

"Okay, well, doesn't the Gyan Grand Elder live in Wyoming? What's the closest possible early marriage state to him?"

"Arizona," we all say in unison.

"Then I think we have a winner," he says, his eyes gleaming.

I blow out a breath. "Okay, so Linc and I get married in Arizona. I need to get my parents, er, my other parents on board with that. To meet me out there."

"Does the satellite phone you folks have still work?" Petra asks, her eyes hard on Hannah.

"It does, amazingly enough," she responds.

"Well, then get your pretty little self over to it and call your mother," Petra orders me.

"Where is it right now, Hannah?" I ask.

She points. "It's always with Gary. He had the mind to save it from the fire once the battle was over. He almost lost his arm rescuing that thing. He's pretty attached to it."

I salute everyone with two fingers and leave to go make a call to my parents, who I suddenly need to talk to.

22

Vela

I jog over to Gary because he's currently alone and looking down at something, which, to my joy, is the satellite phone.

"Hey Gary, may I use that?" I ask once I reach him.

He glances up at me. "Sure, I just made a call on it, so I know it works."

"I heard you saved its life," I say with a smile.

He cracks a smile, too, and hands over the phone. "Well, I knew how important it was that we have it. Please be sure to keep the minutes down on your call. We've had to use it quite a bit."

I agree and walk away with it. I quickly dial mom's number and am overjoyed when I hear her voice. "Mom," I gush. "How are you?"

"Vela? Oh my gosh, I'm good! How are *you,* sweetie?"

"I'm good, well okay. Mom, Linc and I are finalizing our wedding plans, and I'm suddenly nervous. Like really nervous."

"Oh, honey, that's perfectly normal. You should be nervous. You're talking about tying yourself with someone for the rest of your life."

I blow out a breath and glance over at Gary who's looking at me, his eyebrows drawn down. "I have to keep this really short since I'm on the Polar Bear satellite phone. I called to ask you if you and dad can meet Linc and me with our group in Arizona so we can get your permission to marry?"

"You're sure you're ready to get married, honey?"

"Yes," I say after a beat. "Because I really can't imagine my life without Linc."

"Well then, I'll speak to your father."

"No, don't do that. I'll have Linc call. He technically hasn't asked for permission, yet, has he?"

"No."

"Okay, then Linc will call tonight."

"Once that's done, which town are we meeting you in?" she asks.

"Phoenix. And Mom, thank you. I can't wait for you to meet my other family."

She's silent for a beat. "You found them?"

"Yes! And I have a little sister; can you believe it?"

"Honey, that's wonderful. When should we meet you?"

"We can't get our ride back for four days. Does that give you enough time?"

"It should. Honey, I'm so happy for you."

"Thank you, Mom. I love you and miss you so much." I look over at Gary, who taps the top of his wrist with his finger. "I'm sorry, but I have to go. I can't wait to see you, let's shoot to meet in the early afternoon."

"Okay, honey."

When she clicks off the phone, my heart feels bereft for a moment. In the excitement of finding Mama, Papa and Adele, I forgot how much I need my adopted family. I suddenly miss them fiercely. I frown down at the phone because I forgot to ask her if Kane and Drew could come. Also, I'm feeling a little guilty for my nerves about marrying Linc.

Linc's delicious scent washes over me before he whispers in my ear, "Why is my fiancée frowning?"

I spin to face him. My mind goes blank for a second before I say, "I forgot to ask my mom if Drew and Kane will come to our wedding."

"And do we know where it will be yet?"

I nod. "Yep, we're getting married in Arizona."

He wraps his sweaty arms around my waist and rubs his whiskered cheek against my smooth one. "I don't care if I have to marry you on the moon. I can't wait."

"Neither can I," I breathe, all my senses going haywire with his proximity. I spin in his arms. "Have I mentioned that I like the scruffy look on you?"

"Do you now?" he asks, his eyes twinkling, because he knows full well his effect on me.

"Mm, hmmm. It's a very good look on you." I rub my hand over his soft beard, enjoying just touching him.

"I'm glad you enjoy my rustic look. I'll be sure to wear a beard just for you," he murmurs. "Any more plans for the wedding made?"

"Actually, yes." I say. "Can your mom take us to Phoenix? If not, we can always fly there after she takes us wherever she was planning to go."

"I don't see why she can't. I'll ask her."

Then, I take a deep breath. "Also, there's something else." I finger his shirt and look up at him through my eyelashes. "It's customary for the guy to ask the girl's father for permission to marry."

He leans back. "Ah. Yes, that is my responsibility."

"I kind of told my mom you'd call tonight."

His eyes glint at me. "You're trying to make me an honest man, aren't you?"

I rub his nose with mine. "Always."

"Okay, should I ask James, too?"

"Probably a good idea, just to cover all your bases."

He leans in after his gaze drops to my lips. "Anything else?" His husky voice sends a shiver down my spine.

I shake my head and tug away from his arms. "I have plans to make, and they won't be made if you keep distracting me."

He reaches for me again, but I dodge his grasp, holding out my finger to him. "I mean it, Lincoln. Keep your distance."

A hungry look comes in his eyes. "You know, when you say no, it only makes me want to change your mind."

I squeal and run to Petra's tent, knowing Linc is hunting me. I make it, but Linc is right there, scooping me up and spinning me around. I laugh while he spins, finally slowing down. Once he drops me, I turn and tuck my face into his neck, breathing in his scent deeply and trying to stop my dizziness.

"Linc Stevenson. Were you chasing your Intended?" Hannah scolds.

I peek out at her, and she's somehow got a scowl and a smile while she faces off with Linc.

"I was. I'm not anymore," he says smoothly, still holding me up.

"Well, put her down. We have work to do," Petra chides. I'm surprised to see her still here planning my wedding.

"I don't think so," Linc says.

"Linc," James growls.

Linc sighs heavily and sets me down gently. "We will finish this discussion later," he promises before he kisses me lightly on the lips. "Sir," he asks James. "I have something I should have asked you yesterday. Can we talk privately?"

They both stride away, and my heart is full as I watch him go. My lips tingle from Linc's soft kiss until Hannah complains, "Seriously, you're marrying the guy in four days. Care to cool it for us?"

I sigh and drag my eyes away, only to see Sandy frowning at me. I blush. "Sorry, I'll do better. But I did try to escape the PDA."

"Look where that got you," Hannah grumbles under her breath, but it's loud enough for everyone to hear.

"Okay, so what's next to plan?" I ask.

"Everything," Hannah says with exasperation.

"Are you guys planning Vela's wedding?" Adele asks, poking her face in the tent.

I nod. "Wanna join?"

"Umm, yes!" she gushes, and we all sit down to plan one of the biggest days of my life.

Greta grumbles when we spend about two hours going over wedding plans. She had made the flatbreads, but we got so busy talking, food literally went on the back burner.

I had so much fun, though. We talked about what can be bought quickly and what we don't have time for, like personalized wedding favors. I'm okay with all of it because if that means I marry my best friend in four days, I'm happy to skip over the wedding details I could get caught up in. Honestly, I'd probably stress out over half of them, so I'm fine with a rushed wedding.

It's dinner time when we call it quits, and my stomach is ready for a meal. Hannah comes through with Linc's road chickens and some potatoes. Since they're in season and not affected by the fire, Hannah dug them up, peeled, cut them into small pieces and set them to boil in a pot. They're ready quickly before I know it.

Linc and James rejoin us after they set up the tent for Linc.

James pulls me aside. "I'm appreciative of the young man you've chosen. He asked for your hand in marriage, like a well brought up man should."

I blush. "I'm glad. He's got to do it twice. That's not easy."

"No, it isn't. But I appreciate that he did it nonetheless, even though I wasn't blessed enough to raise you."

I look at his misty eyes and hug his neck. "I'm sorry for that Papa, I really am. I'm just glad we've found each other now."

"I am, too," he says in a hoarse voice as he squeezes me back. He pulls away and goes to speak to Sandy, and after they talk quietly, she turns shining eyes to me.

I smile at her, and then we all sit down to eat our meal.

I squeeze Linc's hand, whispering, "Thank you."

He squeezes my hand back and James prays, "Father, for this day, we are grateful that we are together and healthy. Thank you for happy reunions and blessed relationships. Bless this food and allow it to nourish our bodies. Thank you for Your provision. Amen."

We all say amen and dig in. There's plenty of laughter going around, and if it wasn't for us sitting on the ground eating our meal, I'd say everything is normal.

The burned out shells of the Polar Bear are a stark reminder of all that was lost. Two lives were taken that night and for that we mourn. As we eat, I remember their sacrifice to keep us safe in this place. I look around at all the meals being shared and quiet conversations as well as laughter in the air and know this group is too tough to be stamped out by a power hungry organization. "So, everyone is going to rebuild?" I ask, popping some chicken in my mouth.

Andy answers, "No. The ones who've received extra elements from you and some others are leaving with us. I don't know if they'll come back to rebuild. Hopefully, they won't have to."

A lot rests on my shoulders with that statement. Basically, he means if I succeed in convincing the world that I'm the Chosen Child, mixed Elementals will finally be able to rejoin society.

"And the ones who aren't coming with us?" I ask in a tight voice.

"Will rebuild," he answers, looking guilty. "I wish I could help them, but since I'm joining your party, I won't be able to."

"I'm sorry," I say quietly.

He shrugs and smiles at me. "I can't be in two places at once and this lady," he says, holding Hannah's knee, "insists on having me close." He smiles sweetly at her.

"I would say I'm sorry, but I'm not. I need you with me. I don't want to be apart when we just settled things." She looks down at her lap.

"For the record, I'm not complaining," he says and kisses her on the cheek.

She blushes, and her comment makes me want to ask her what she means by settling things. *Are they thinking of getting married?* I vow to get that answer tonight. She couldn't possibly sit on that if it's true.

We all help clean up our dinner, which isn't much, since most of the wooden plates were lost in the fire. We ate communal style almost straight from the fire, and as much as I hate that's the reason, I enjoyed eating with everyone that way.

Hannah offers to let me use her bucket of water to wash off my hands, but I don't want to dirty the water if I don't have to. It's clean drinking water. "It's fine," I assure her and head down with Linc to the lake, calling Jack to come with us. Linc grabs a big bowl and offers to get her more water, which she gratefully accepts.

We walk to the lake, loosely holding hands, and I appreciate the sunset coming in brilliant colors against the fall backdrop of the trees. The air is cool and crisp, and I enjoy the fall chill.

"How are you feeling about everything?" he asks.

I jump because I'm lost in my thoughts. "Hmm? Oh, umm, I'm feeling really good. Well," I admit. "I got a little nervous. I won't lie. But it lasted only for a few minutes before I got warm feet again."

He looks off in the distance, his expression pensive. "You sure you want to do this?"

He turns so we're facing each other. My heart rate picks up at his nearness and his intense look. My eyes widen. "Do what? Marry you?"

"Yes," he says softly. "You can back out if you want."

"I do not want," I say flatly.

"Tell me what you want, then. How can I make this better or easier for you?"

"I want you with me every step of the way. Please don't feel that I don't want this. I do, more than anything. Is there anything you want?"

He gives me an intense look. "I'll tell you what I've wanted since I met you. And that's to give you my last name. Are you sure you're not getting cold feet?" His eyes flicker with an uncertainty I want to erase immediately.

I reach for him and press my lips to his. I say against the soft heaven of his kiss, "Nothing could tear me away from you. I want to make you all mine."

A heated look comes over him, and he angles his head to attack my lips with such a fierce, yet tender kiss. He drops the bowl and kisses me as if he's never kissed me before, and as much as that's not true, I can't help but enjoy the sensation of being thoroughly kissed by Lincoln Stevenson. This man knows how to sweep me off my feet, I think as I run my hands through his hair, pulling him even tighter against me. I return his kiss with one of my own and when hands clutch my hips, I tear myself away.

Panting, I say, "Okay, we've come this far. We can wait a few more days for more of *that*."

Inhaling deeply through his nose, he says in a thick voice, "Yes, we have. I agree." He says it almost reluctantly, like it takes great effort.

I almost kiss him again in thanks but think better of it.

He takes three steps away from me, breathing deeply.

I mourn how we have to keep our distance, but if we're to honor God, we need to. I love that it's just as important to Linc as it is to me.

Linc retrieves the bowl and scoops up water in it. I call Jack to me from his explorations. Linc follows as I head to my parent's lean-to and after a long loving look to Linc, I crawl into bed fully clothed, too tired to get my pajamas on. I know the sun has just fallen, but I'm asleep in the next breath.

Four days pass in a blur as we help the residents of Polar Bear rebuild their homes. There's just enough of them left to finish building, but I still feel guilty that we're taking so many builders away. Linc called my dad and asked for his permission to marry me, which I'm thankful he gave. It makes our wedding feel official.

We know Elizabeth is coming today because Linc called from the satellite phone to confirm. So, while we wait, we work. This group is anything but idle. I join them because I want to give as much as I can before I take thirty working people away.

The plane is due to arrive around two in the afternoon. When I see it in the distance, much to my relief, I can't help but be surprised. I'd doubted Linc's mother would bring the plane at all. When we make our way to where it lands, I see it's the same plane that we took from the Extremists. Apparently, Elizabeth used her many connections to get the papers switched over, making it legitimately ours, or rather, hers.

When she steps from the plane, she looks directly at me, and I shiver from the iciness of her gaze. *So, she's still not happy I'm marrying her son. Great.*

She greets Linc, who approaches her by asking, "Is this everyone?"

He nods and reaches his hand back for me to take it. I step up to him and grab his hand, holding it tightly.

Elizabeth finally acknowledges me with a cool, "Hello, Vela."

I return her greeting with a warm hello. *Kill a enemy with kindness, right?*

"My plane is ready after everything has been unloaded," she says.

"Wait," Linc asks in a hard voice. "Why are you taking ownership of the plane this group commandeered when they defeated the Extremists?"

She sneers. "I paid for all the necessary paperwork to have this plane legally. To compensate this community, I decided to bring back all the necessary supplies and materials to rebuild this place."

When the group hears that, a cheer goes up. She looks out at them and says, "You can all unload so we can leave as soon as possible."

She turns to Linc. "I'm assuming you're ready to leave?"

He nods stiffly.

"I'd like to have a word with Rick and Gary before we leave."

Linc nods and steps back so Elizabeth can pass him to walk up to the two men. They're in our group, so as soon as she begins to speak to them, I ask Linc quietly, "Did you find out where she's taking us?"

"On the phone, she said back to Texas," he replies lowly.

"Can you ask her to take us to Phoenix instead?" I look up at him coyly. "It would make our wedding plans that much easier to go straight there."

He pulls me to him, holding me at the waist. "Look at me like that, and I'll ask anything you want."

23

Linc

I will my body to cool off after Vela's come-hither look and irresistible smile. I barely restrain myself when she does that. And I don't think she's even aware of the effect she has on me. Shaking my head, I turn to speak to my mother. If anything is going to cool me off, that will do the job.

When I step up to her, Rick, and Gary, she includes me in the conversation. "Linc can bring back more supplies when you let me know what you need."

"No, I can't," I say, gritting my teeth. It's just like my mother to plan my next steps. "I'm getting married. First and foremost, that is happening. And then I'll be traveling with Vela while she garners support as the Chosen Child."

Her eyes narrow. "You're still on the foolish path, I see."

I bite back a harsh retort. "What you see as foolish, I view as a blessing."

She twists her lips. "I see we have two very different views on the definition of what is a blessing."

"Yes, we sure do, Mother." My blood is pounding with anger, and I force my emotions down, so I don't reveal to my indomitable mother just how much she affects me. She's like a shark with blood in the water if the first wisp of my smoke comes out.

She sniffs and walks over to the plane, directing how they unload it.

Gary and Rick both give me sympathetic nods and leave. I seethe but cool a little when Vela slides her smooth hand in mine. "You, okay?"

"I will be. As soon as I'm away from my mother. She's not a fan of us, and I can't be around her negativity much longer."

"We won't be. Did you ask her to take us to Phoenix?"

I curse silently when I shake my head. "No, I forgot. But I'll talk to my dad about it." I walk over to where my dad is helping unload the plane, not letting go of Vela's hand. She stabilizes me and even speaking to my dad makes me need her.

I approach him once he sets down a big box. "Hi Dad. Welcome back."

"Oh, hi, Lincoln. How are you, son?"

"I'll be better if you and Mom would agree to take our group to Phoenix, Arizona."

He looks at me with a question in his eyes. You can almost see his mind churning with one reason after another.

I help him by adding, "It's where Vela and I want to get married."

He reels back, like he did not expect that. "So soon?"

I exhale slowly. "I told you both I was marrying Vela."

"A month before your nineteenth birthday?"

"Yes," I say, trying to be patient. I turn my body so Vela is blocked from my dad's view. I say in a low tone, "Dad, it's not easy being in such close proximity to a girl I'm in love with and honor God with our actions."

Understanding fills my dad's eyes. "I see. Well, let me work my magic with your mother." He slaps his hand on my shoulder, then leans to look at Vela. "You're marrying a beautiful girl and the Chosen Child. Your mother won't be able to argue against that."

I smile. "Thanks Dad. We're very happy together."

"I know."

I lift my eyebrows at him.

"Son, I've noticed quite the change in you since you've met your Intended. It's like you have purpose now, whereas before you were floundering."

I grimace. I was struggling with the death of my sister on my conscience, put there by my mother. "Yeah, well. God blessed me tremendously."

"Me, too," Vela adds, her sweet voice soothing me.

I shift so she's in full view of my dad again, tugging her next to my side. I breathe deeply, her unique scent wrapping around me.

My dad's eyes twinkle at my calmed expression. "Why don't you get on the plane, while we finish getting all these boxes off?"

I nod and call Rick, Gary, and Petra to assemble everyone to start loading up.

I note with amusement that Vela's friends have gotten quite cozy with some of the new guys from Saddleback and are each paired up with a different guy, which includes Steele, interestingly enough. I look to see what Adele thinks of that, but she seems to now be ignoring both Steele and Rayne. *Oh, my poor sister-in-law. She can't catch a break.*

Vela looks back. Once she's sure her parents and Adele are right behind her, she follows me up the steps.

When everything is to my mom's satisfaction, she joins us on the plane, giving me a hard look and then gesturing me to come and speak with her. After the plane takes off and we're in the air, I get up and make my way down the aisle to her. She takes me into the cockpit. It's tight, but we fit barely.

She hisses at me, "What is this? I hear that you're getting *married*?"

"Mother, I told you I was marrying Vela. Why is this coming as such a surprise to you?"

Her eyes flash with anger. "Were you going to invite me to this wedding of yours?"

My heart pounds, but clinches at her words. "I'm sorry, of course we will invite you. I just," I look down, "didn't think you'd want to be involved."

"I have one child to my name. I would like to be a part of his wedding." She looks away as emotion crowds her eyes.

Horror washes through me that she won't even acknowledge my sister's memory. "Mom," I say in a hoarse voice. "She might be gone, but she'll always be with us."

She glares at me so darkly, I flinch. "Considering it's your fault I only have you left, I'd think you'd understand I want her memory to be put to rest." She bares her teeth at me. "If you hadn't..."

I feel my face drain of color. "If *I* hadn't *what*?" I ask, unable to escape this train wreck.

"Hadn't sent her to that place, she'd be here today," she hisses, then smooths her stomach in an effort to control herself.

I glance at the pilot, who is clearly trying not to listen to our disastrous conversation. Humiliation mixed with unending pain tears through me. She couldn't hit me hard enough to wound me as much as her words just did. I blink back tears and turn away from her. Taking deep breaths, I pray for forgiveness for the woman who has no problem spewing hate from her mouth. Finally, I turn back to her, not able to hide the pain from my eyes. "I'm sorry you feel that way, Mother. Vela and I will be married in Phoenix. I will let you know where and when."

At those words, I escape, needing to nurse my deep wounds with my Intended. I trip over Jack where he lies next to Vela's seat. When I stumble into my seat, Vela looks at me with concern.

"Linc, what's wrong?" She puts her hand on my arm.

I lean over and put my elbows on my knees. I feel like I'm being torn apart from the inside out. I squeeze my eyes shut, but tears leak out, despite my best efforts not to cry. While I can't believe my mother would be so hateful, it doesn't surprise me since I've heard her damaging words before. That's what my dad referred to when he called me lost. I was lost in my grief, feeling responsible for my sister's death and shouldering the blame of it from my mother.

"Linc? What happened?" Vela's voice cracks. She knows I'm hurting deeply.

I shake my head, not trusting my words yet.

Vela, thankfully, gives me time to myself.

God, I need You. I don't know why my mom would blame me for losing Olympia. I can't bear this pain. Please help me, Father. Help me to forgive my mother. Help me, God.

I struggle with my emotions and when smoke rises from my hands, Vela gives up waiting and turns my head to her. She's right there, close to my face, and when she sees my tears, she grimaces. "Baby, what happened? What did your mom say to you?"

I manage to get one word out, "Olympia."

Vela's face scrunches in horror. "She blamed you *again*?"

I nod and bury my face in my hands again. Vela growls. I feel her hand turn into a fist.

"Linc," Vela says in my ear. "You cannot take responsibility for your sister's death. You are free from that burden. Don't for one moment feel guilty for it. It was an accident. A horrible accident that ripped Olympia from your lives. Your mother," she sighs heavily, "absolves herself of guilt by putting it on your shoulders. Which she should *never* do. I'm going to go speak to her."

I move so quickly, I half fall out of my seat. "No," I say firmly, wiping my eyes. "Please, Vela, stay out of it. Let me just get myself together. Please," I ask. "Stay with me."

Her eyes reflect a world of pain and anger, but she banks the latter and agrees with a nod, tucking her hand into my arm. "Of course. You have me. I'm here."

I sit back and tuck Vela under my arm. I hold her like that for the whole of the trip.

We're left alone for the journey to wherever we're going. I never did get a confirmation that we would be flown to Phoenix.

It's not until the captain announces we'll be landing in Phoenix, Arizona in fifteen minutes that I relax. I breathe a sigh of relief and Vela, does too.

"Linc," Vela says hesitantly. "I don't think I can have that woman at our wedding."

I understand why she would say that. "Believe me, I've thought of that, but she's my mother, despite what she accuses me of. I think I'll regret it later if I ban her from our wedding."

Vela nods slowly. "Okay," she finally says. "If that's what you want. Of course it's your decision. But, for the record, I think you are the most forgiving," her voice cracks, "most amazing man I've *ever* met. And I love you."

"I love you, too," I say softly and put my forehead to hers, soaking in her love and comfort. I thank God silently for her support and presence in my life.

Everyone starts to file out of the plane, and I realize we've landed. I was so caught up in my pain, I didn't notice. Numbly, I get up and retrieve our bags from the overhead compartment. We file out behind Hannah and Greta. The little sprite turns around and gives me a sympathetic smile.

I guess my tears were noticed, after all.

I return her smile and ruffle her hair, which only makes her giggle. She spins around and chats with Linda, Grant's daughter. Vela seems pleased they've hit it off. I smile at that, too and nod at Hannah, who's also wearing an understanding look. I guess they were seated right in front of Vela and me. Apparently, I was oblivious to anything but my pain.

We walk down the steps and onto the runway. Vela holds my hand securely when I spot my mother leading the parade of passengers to the airport.

Once inside, we walk to find the rental cars, our group chattering excitedly at what's coming ahead. I'm reminded that I'm marrying Vela in the next couple of days. Energy surges through me at the thought, which helps chase the residual feelings of pain away.

Mother and Dad approach me, and I stiffen involuntarily. Her look is cool as she appraises me. "Are you staying with us?" she asks stiffly.

"No," I answer quickly. "I'll get my own place."

Dad looks on blandly. He must not know about our conversation on the plane. Even if he did, he wouldn't get involved. He's always stayed out of her fury for me, instead mourning my sister in his own way.

"Fine," Mother says, sniffing. "If that's what you want."

"Definitely," I say under my breath.

She gives me a sharp look. I must not have been as quiet as I thought. Turning, she marches away, and Dad holds his hand out. "You'll let us know when the wedding is?" he asks as he shakes my hand.

"Yes," I answer, then fall silent. I've never had a close relationship with my dad, and I wish now more than ever that I did. I wish a lot of things. That he would stand up to my mother. Be more present in my life. But I can't wish for things that just aren't possible. He's my mother's right-hand man. He would never go against her in anything. I stopped expecting him to a long time ago.

He nods, then catches up to his wife, who waits impatiently for him by the rental car counter.

As I watch him receive sharp words from my mother, Vela asks me quietly, "I think our group is getting a couple of vans instead of a bunch of cars, to save on money. Do you want to get our own car?"

"Yes," I say, but when I look at the long line of people waiting to rent their own vehicles, I look over at Vela. "Hungry? I can get us some food, if you can get in line for me."

She gives me a grateful look and asks, "Will you find something for Jack, too?"

I nod then leave and wish I could heal my hurting heart as easily as I can order fast food.

I'm glad to be back in civilization and to have access to my own funds as I fish out my card to give the lady at the burger counter. Thankfully, I didn't lose my wallet in the wilderness of Canada. I'm also thankful I made my own money working odd jobs here and there for my mother, and that I opened up my own account. My uncle helped me put my saved money into investments, which the last time I checked were doing really well.

But I also hung on to my old credit cards Mother gave me. I'll use them until they get shut down. If I know her, and I do, I'd bet my bottom dollar she'll close them soon just to be spiteful that I'm marrying against her wishes.

I'm sure if it came down to it and Vela and I needed money, her family would give us the funds we'd need to get started. But that would be our last resort. Supremely satisfied I can provide for Vela, at least for now, I almost don't want to use my mother's cards.

Vela will be mine in a few short days, and then I can figure out how to fund her world tour.

As if we don't have enough problems to overcome, I'm suddenly overwhelmed. Then a thought comes to me. *God will provide for all our needs. If this is what He wants Vela to do, He'll provide a way for her to do it.*

And just like that, my load feels lighter.

24

Vela

L inc finds food quickly, saying there's a burger place in the terminal where we landed.

I've moved up in the car rental line, but there are still several people ahead of me. Once Linc is back with our burgers, I feed Jack right away and Linc teases, "Anything wrong with eating first yourself?"

"What kind of mother would I be if I did that?"

He gives me an affectionate look, and my sore heart feels slightly lighter just being with my fiancé. I am so furious at his mother for hurting him the way she did. I wish he had given me permission to give her a piece of my mind.

Linc interrupts my angry thoughts. "You're the best kind of mother. One day, you can do the same for our little ones."

At that thought, I blush. "That won't be for a long time, hopefully." I look down at the delicious burger waiting for me to eat. I frown at it. "I'll wait to eat this. I don't want to eat standing up."

He nods. "It's fun imagining having kids, though, isn't it?"

I laugh. "Uh, I guess. Since I'm technically still a child myself, it's kind of hard to imagine, but okay."

He sends me to go sit down and eat and asks me to charge his phone. I mourn my phone, long lost somewhere in the wilds of Canada. I'll have to get another one as soon as I can.

Tonya, Claudette, Adele, who's become quite good friends with my Polar Bear girls, Jennifer, and Alice all crowd around me when I sit. I wish Grace had decided to come, but she chose to stay back at the Polar Bear, which I understand is more her speed than my whirlwind one. I had noticed that Alice sat with Steele on the plane. Adele is being a little standoffish with her, but maybe she thinks its for the best? I resolve to ask her about it later.

"Oh my gosh, this is so exciting," Tonya gushes, and I laugh at her expression.

"It's not like we're traveling the world or anything," I tease.

Her eyes gleam, and she looks over her shoulder at the guys they've gotten to know. "It makes me think of how much we're going to see and all the new people we're going to meet."

I notice one particular guy repeatedly glancing over in Tonya's direction. "Well, it certainly looks like you've gotten one guy smitten. Are you planning on conquering others?"

She blushes, her warm chocolate skin darkening prettily, while Adele laughs and Claudette bumps her shoulder. Tonya says, "I'm just saying, there's *a lot* of fish in the sea." She looks around and checks out a guy standing in the line behind Linc.

"Well, be careful you don't break too many hearts," I warn.

"Oh, she's well on her way," Jennifer says as she casts a longing look over at the guy watching Tonya.

My chest pinches at that look because it means there's some unrequited love happening among my friends.

"I'm hungry," Adele announces, and as a group, they all decide to go get some food after getting a card from Rick, who's apparently paying for their meals.

Greta bounds over to me. She'd been standing over by Hannah and Andy, who were waiting in a different car rental line. "You guys got lunch?" She looks longingly at my burger.

Laughing, I hand it to her, because she's never had a fast-food burger in her whole life, and I have to watch her face while she eats it.

She accepts it greedily and takes a bite so big I'm afraid her mouth won't close. Her face transforms into one of pure delight, and I laugh again. Amusement at Greta is a great distraction from what happened with Linc's mother, and I appreciate my little friend more than ever. I hand her a napkin, and she looks at it strangely, while she holds it. Chuckling, I explain, "It's a napkin, Greta."

"Oh! It felt like paper, I wasn't sure." She wipes her face of burger juice, then takes her burger back to her mom and offers her some.

I notice Linc has made it to the front counter and does the business of getting a sedan for us. I'm grateful he's getting us our own vehicle as I definitely don't want an entourage on our upcoming wedding night.

At that thought, my blood heats so hot, I have to take a couple of deep breaths to cool myself off.

Linc walks up almost the same time Rick and Cheri do. Rick smiles at us as Linc joins me. I hand him his burger, which he digs into immediately.

Rick says in a jaunty tone, "We made it to the States. That wasn't so hard."

I smile at his wife, Cheri, who's next to him. I say in a low voice, "Yes, it's pretty easy when you commandeer a private plane from the Extremists for your own personal use."

They both laugh, and then I greet Gary as he walks up. I say hello to his Intended, Shireen, who looks as miserable as she did when I first met her. James and Sandy join us as well.

"It is good to be back in the good ole U.S. of A.," James says, his gaze tired but resolute.

"It is," I say, smiling. I turn to Rick. "Have you made all the arrangements for our stay?"

He nods and fishes a piece of paper from his pocket. "We found a campground with cabins to accommodate all of us." He looks back as the rest of the group filters over.

My head turns in interest. "A campground?"

He nods, looking down at the paper. "There's plenty of room for us, so I booked enough cabins for everyone."

My face drops in concern. "How are we paying for all of that?"

Rick's deep voice is soothing as he assures me, "We have a group fund for the Polar Bear everyone has been contributing to. Don't worry about it. We're happy to fund this to get you started in your mission."

I nod and then ask, "Is there a place there where Linc and I can get married?"

Cheri says, "Oh, Vela, that's a wonderful idea, but don't you want to look around at wedding sites?"

I worry my lip. "Don't we want to get started on my mission soon? If so, then I don't have time to go hunting for the perfect spot. Besides," I say, smiling and tucking my arm into Linc's. "I'd marry this guy anywhere. Why don't we make it as simple as possible?"

Adele walks up with a food bag in her hand and, having overheard my comment, says with a light blazing in her eyes. "Oh, no, you don't get to downplay your wedding. You might pick the spot, but you're getting the whole she-bang...flowers, dinner, everything a bride would want."

I feel a little lost at all that work, and Linc says, "Don't be pressured to do anything you don't want to do, Vela."

I nod but cringe when I see the predatory look on Adele's face. I might not get out of my little sister's plans if I don't put my foot down.

"We'll make it lovely, Vela," Sandy says, "we don't have to do the whole treatment if you don't want." She gives Adele a look that clearly conveys she will be talking with her later.

I'm glad because it'll come better from her than me.

Hannah, Andy, and Greta approach us. Andy says, "Rick, you've rented two vans that fit fifteen people each?"

Rick nods, and then I notice Greta's face looking a little wan. Worried my burger made her sick, I ask, "You okay, sweetie?"

She nods but then, holding her stomach, says, "I don't feel so good."

I turn an anguished gaze to Hannah. "I should never have given her that burger. It was probably way too much grease for her stomach. She's not used to fast food."

Hannah looks down with concern at Greta, pushing the hair away from her face. "I'll keep an eye on her. There's medicine I can get her if we need it. Don't worry about her, Vela. It was sweet to give up your lunch so she could try a burger."

Wanting to distract Greta from her stomach, I ask, "How was your first flight?"

Her eyes are dim, but she scrunches up her cute face in thought. "It was fun. My ears popped a bunch, but Momma says that's normal."

Hannah runs her hand down Greta's long hair and looks at her lovingly. "She had so many questions about the plane that I couldn't answer. So, I asked the pilot if she wouldn't mind some curious questions."

"The pilot said she didn't mind at all," Greta says factually. "I wanna be a pilot when I grow up. It's so interesting."

I can't help but smile at the thoughtful look on her face. I ruffle her hair and say, "I'm glad you have such high aspirations."

She looks up at me, her face screwed up. "Did you just make a joke?"

"I did. It wasn't very good, I'm sorry."

She smiles, but she's lacking her normal exuberance. I notice others who look tired and drawn. "You all must be tired. Let's get out of here."

We all head out, thirty of us in total.

"Rick," I call. He turns and I ask, "Do you know how long it will take to get to the campsite?"

"They said about an hour from the airport, but I'm not sure," he answers.

"Let me check on Linc's phone. I can give you a better time frame." I turn and hold my hand out to Linc, who hands me his now partially charged phone.

Rick looks surprised and comes over to me, looking down at what I'm doing. "I've been gone from civilization for so long, I'm not caught up on the new-fangled devices."

I shrug. "It's not hard. You'll get the hang of it. We'll get the leaders a few burner phones. I'll show you guys how to use them." I pull up the maps app and once I type in the campground's name, it pulls up a more accurate ETA. When the directions pop up, Rick exclaims, "That's amazing! It tells you exactly how to get there?"

I nod and scroll down the directions, showing him the roads we'll take, and he looks on in wide-eyed amazement. "How long have you been living off the grid?" I ask him with some amusement at his wonder.

He huffs. "For about ten years. For some of us, it's been longer. This is going to be an adjustment for a lot of us."

"Don't worry, you'll get the hang of it," I assure him.

We all leave to pick up our rentals, and while we walk, I notice Greta lags behind. I ask Hannah quietly. "Is Greta going to be all right?" Guilt slams in me.

She puts her hand on my arm. "It's all right. I could have done the same thing." She looks behind us and gives Greta a worried look.

"I'm really sorry."

"It's really okay. She's young, she'll bounce back fast," she says. Then we wait for Greta to catch up. Hannah pulls off Greta's backpack to lighten the young one's load.

"Greta, you look sad all the sudden," I comment, trying not to worry about the little girl who's thoroughly ensnared my heart.

Her mouth draws down even more. "I had to leave all of my babies. I won't know if my little kit will get better or not. He wasn't nursing when I left."

Oh, her fur babies. Remembering how well she took care of the area's little animal population, I smile down at her. "I'm sure he will be just fine. Animals have a way of surviving the most strenuous circumstances."

"Yeah," she says tiredly. "I know. But I miss them."

Wishing she was small enough to allow me to carry her, I almost do it anyway, to save her the energy of walking. "I'm really sorry, little one."

She smiles up at me, but it's strained. I glance up at Andy, who's been walking next to us through the airport. He shares a concerned look with me.

"That burger was worth it, even if I do feel bad," Greta tells me.

My stomach pinches at my lack of knowledge on how to care for a child. Especially with someone like Greta, who's lived such a sheltered life.

We make it outside and to the rental pickup counter. Soon, we have our three vehicles. I see Linc speaking with his parents and they go their own way to another rental company's car lot.

I realize Hannah, Andy, and Greta can come with us. When I get their attention, I say, "I thought you could come with us, so you're not so crowded in the vans."

"Thank you," Andy says genuinely.

I smile because getting his big frame in the van with fourteen other people would not be fun.

"I'll buy a car for us sometime soon," Andy says in his deep voice, and I remember he has his own truck at his house.

"You don't mind buying a second vehicle?" I ask while we wait for everyone to pile in the vans. When our car pulls up, I give him the front passenger seat, since he would be more comfortable there.

"Thank you, Vela." He pushes his seat way back right away. "And no, if I get my truck back home, I'll just donate the car I buy to your group. I don't mind."

"That's very generous of you," I say with a smile.

Hannah wraps her arms around Andy's seat and hugs him as much as her arms allow. "That's just Andy," she says lovingly.

He shoots her an embarrassed look. "It's what anyone would do."

"No," Linc says with a snort. "It really isn't."

By the time our conversation ends, I see that everyone's loaded in the two vans. Linc motions to Rick, who's driving the first van to follow us. We're off, and I settle in for a little over an hour's drive.

25

Linc

I'm chomping at the bit to get where we're going and finalize plans to make Vela my bride. I smile at that thought, and I notice Andy giving me a knowing look, like he can read my thoughts.

I wipe my face clear of all emotions and settle in for the drive to the campground. When I spoke to my parents last, they made it very clear they were absolutely not staying in a campground and to let them know when and where the wedding will be. I'm glad, because I need distance from them, my mother especially.

Vela, Greta, and Hannah all chat in the backseat, and Andy and I discuss his hobby. Apparently, he enjoys fixing up old cars. I find it interesting, so I pass the time listening to his projects, because he has more than one. Andy does nothing in half measures.

When we arrive at the campground, the vans are way behind us because they stopped to stock up on food for the group. Once they arrive, it's a blur of getting everyone settled and plans for our wedding are under way.

Petra, surprisingly enough, leads the charge. "We need to give people specific jobs to get this show on the road," she commands as she starts writing notes in a notebook she picked up at the store. "The sooner we can get you two married, the quicker we can get this world united."

Vela gives me a surprised look, but I'm just as shocked as her that Petra would lead all of this.

"Petra, I thought you said you didn't know anything about weddings," Vela accuses with a smile.

Petra looks uncomfortable. "I said it wasn't my expertise, not that I don't know nothin' about it. I've been to a few weddings in my time; how hard can it be?"

I snort because weddings are notoriously difficult to plan. Petra doesn't seem to agree because she's shouting off orders to everyone around her.

Soon, plans for the flowers, which Sandy and Hannah are in charge of, photography which Debra volunteers for, food and drinks for the small reception will be contributed by several people, and a hunt for the perfect spot is all well in hand. Vela's entourage of friends all clamor to be bridesmaids, and I raise my eyebrows because I know I won't have nearly that many groomsmen. I don't have that many close friends. I've only needed Vela in my life, but I look around to see who could join my team.

Petra has that same idea, because she asks me, "Who are you picking, Linc? Looks like Vela's group is all assembled."

"How many do I need?"

Voices clamor again, and Petra raises her voice, "Now, cool it, young'uns. Let's let Vela decide who *she* wants by her side, and then Linc can choose his guys."

Vela looks over at all the pleading faces of her friends and her shoulders drop. *She's going to choose all of them. No way can she say no to those girls.* Sure enough, she names Adele, Tonya, Jennifer, Claudette, Alice, and Hannah. I guess her best friend, Elia, won't be here because if she was, she surely would have made that list.

I blow out my breath and look around. That leaves me with six guys to back me up while I happily tie the knot. I rove my eyes around, and Leon and Rayne stand taller when I pass my gaze over them. Andy gives me a small smile and nods, like he'd be happy to be a groomsman. That's three. Anthony from the Polar Bear gives me a hopeful look, and I count him in my mental list, too. He fought by my side at the Polar Bear and even saved my life once. I pass over James, because he'll be busy with David walking Vela down the aisle.

Vela speaks quietly in my ear, "My brothers would love to stand with you, Linc. I spoke to my mom, they're coming."

I smile at her, because that gives me six. I name my choices to Petra, "Leon, Andy, Anthony, Drew, Kane, and Rayne." I realize it's quite ironic that someone who tried to steal my girl and then kill me is a groomsman at my wedding, but hey, that's how forgiveness works.

Petra nods, writing down my choices and my groomsmen all give me wide smiles, which I return.

"Hey, what about me?" Greta barks, her little face scrunched up in anger.

Petra ruffles her hair. "Well, we do need a flower girl and a ring bearer."

Vela asks quickly, "Greta, will you be my flower girl? I would absolutely love that."

Greta beams in answer and wraps her arms around Vela's waist. I notice she still looks a little peaked, and I hope she's gotten that burger out of her system.

Petra frowns, looking down at her notebook. "That leaves the last thing. The ring bearer."

She looks around the group until Vela says, "I have one."

"You do? Who?" Petra barks.

Vela leans down and kisses Jack's nose. "This guy. He'll be perfect, and I want him a part of our special day."

Petra scowls like this will ruin everything. "You can't have a dog as your ring bearer."

"Sure, I can," Vela says, standing up. "I've trained him quite well. He'll do great."

I nod, loving Vela's choice. Petra gives us a resigned look and sighs. "Fine, but don't blame me if he messes up the whole day."

"He won't," Vela says confidently.

"Okay," Petra announces, "that's everything." She then starts shouting orders left and right.

Adele scowls when Petra is done giving her commands and when it quiets down, says in a sarcastic voice, "Okay, Fairy Godmother, Vela is just like Cinderella, who has everything planned except her dress. You didn't mention that."

Petra's eyebrows draw down in thought, but Vela supplies, "Umm, actually, I spoke to my mom, and she's found the perfect dress for me and is bringing it."

Adele isn't deterred. "Well, what about Linc? Is he going to show up in jeans?"

I laugh because that image just sounds absurd. Not with the plans floating around here.

Vela blushes. "Sorry, I should have said, both Linc and I are handled. My dad is bringing a suit for Linc."

I raise my eyebrows. "Really?"

She nods and then bites her lip. "Is that okay? Or do you want to pick out your own suit?"

"No, I'm fine with that. Makes my life way easier."

"Apparently, the two go together well," she says, blushing, and I approach her and cup her face in my hands.

"I would get married in my t-shirt and shorts as long as I get to really call you mine."

"Oh," she says breathlessly. "Can I make a request?" she asks in a low voice just for me.

"Of course," I murmur.

"Keep the beard."

Not able to help myself, I lean down and softly brush my lips on hers, gently rubbing my face against hers, which makes her shiver. "I wouldn't shave it if my life depended on it, now that I know you love it so much. I cannot believe this is all happening. I never once thought my life would turn out this way. That I would be this *lucky*."

"Blessed," she corrects. "And aren't God's plans wonderful? He brought us here, and I couldn't be happier."

"Me, neither." I kiss her again, and we stop when a chorus of whistles fills the air. I smile against Vela's lips. "I think we've been caught."

She giggles.

"Now, now, you two. Save that for your wedding day, why don't ya?" Petra asks with irritation in her tone, but when I look up at her, she's got a fond look in her eyes.

I reluctantly pull away and give myself distance from my fiancée, because she is just that irresistible.

"That raises the question of what the wedding party will wear," Adele says, a serious look on her face.

"It does," Vela agrees, and everyone thinks that problem through.

"Didn't we pass a mall on the way here?" Petra asks. "Vela will pick a color, and the girls will go find a dress to fit them. They don't all have to be matching. And then, the guys can go and pick out shirts in that same color or whatever Vela and Linc choose." She looks at Vela and I for confirmation that we're good with that plan.

Vela announces, "I'd like pink if you can all find it. Pink dresses for the girls and pink shirts for the guys and khaki pants."

"Well, then that's settled," Petra says, snapping her notebook closed.

"When are we getting married, by the way? That hasn't been mentioned," I ask, because seriously, I need a deadline for when my girl will be *my* girl.

Petra fires at me. "Don't you know it all depends on the location when it's available?"

"No, I don't," I say honestly.

"For someone who doesn't have much expertise," Vela teases, "you sure seem to know quite a lot, Petra."

Petra looks decidedly uncomfortable. "It's not too hard to figure out," she grumbles and then asks, "Now, who's comin' with us to scout out a spot for the ceremony?"

I can't help but laugh, because Petra is really enjoying herself if the gleam in her eyes is any indication. She orders Gene and Jerry to go and find a place where we can have the reception. They nod like they have that job well in hand and jog off.

The whole wedding party groups together to come with us, as well as Vela's parents. They talk quietly, holding hands. Hannah jogs to join Sandy.

Vela sidles up next to me. "I'm surprised Mama is letting Petra make all the plans. It's really my mother's job to do all this. Well, I guess hers and my adopted mom's," she says quietly.

I look over at Sandy, who's in deep discussion with Hannah as they talk over the flower arrangements. "I agree. But who wants to tell Petra she can't do it?"

"Not me," Vela says decidedly.

I smile. "I think she's got a soft spot for weddings she doesn't want anyone to know about."

"Well, she's broadcasting it loud and clear now, isn't she?"

"That she is," I say, then we follow Petra as she leads the way to find the perfect spot for our wedding ceremony. It's a beautiful fall day as we walk, and I can't help but thank God for the sunny day. It's much warmer here than it is in Canada, but my hot temperature loves this weather. I notice Vela wiping her brow, though. "Too hot for you?"

"A little," she admits, shading her eyes from the sun. "It used to get pretty warm in California, too, when I was young, but it's been a while since I've been in these temperatures."

"Why don't you cool yourself off?" I look at her in amusement.

"How?"

"You have the Borean power. Just command a little wind to blow on your face, then use your Neronian gift to cool down the wind."

Her face is one of surprise as she thinks over my suggestion. "That's an amazing idea." And she immediately puts it into use. Soon, a cool wind washes over us, which I don't mind because it's helping my Intended. And what she wants, I want. As much as I love the heat, I love pleasing Vela more.

The campground is right on the lake, which Petra directs us to first. Once we're there, there's a short dock that wouldn't hold the whole wedding party but there are plenty of grassy areas.

"This is a possibility," Petra says, looking over the grassy embankment. Then, for the first time, she turns to Vela's parents. "What do you two think?"

They look surprised, like they're shocked she's addressing them with a question concerning their own daughter's wedding.

James is the first to say, "It's lovely. I think it's a good space to fit everyone. What time will the wedding be?"

"Ten," Vela supplies immediately, and I turn my gaze to hers. She shrugs and says, "Seems like a good time."

Knowing my Vela as well as I do, I put my lips to her ear and ask, "Why, really, Vels?"

She shivers, and I grin that I made her do that. She whispers, "I just want to get married as soon as possible. I don't want to wait the whole day to be your bride."

I nuzzle her neck and kiss the soft skin. "You know just what to say, don't you?"

She turns a heated gaze to me. "It's how I feel."

I almost devour her lips right there and then when James walks to us, effectively stopping me.

Petra says, "Now, we need to check with the campground that we can even have the ceremony here." She fires off a command to Tonya and Alice to go to the office and see what their rules are.

"Next on the list," Petra says, looking down at her notebook, "is the license. This state allows you two to get married with parental permission, correct? That's been confirmed?"

We all nod.

"Okay, so it looks like we can figure out the date of the wedding as soon as we have a license. Vela, which set of parents are on your birth certificate?"

Vela turns a pained gaze to James and Sandy and answers quietly, "David and Whitney."

"Okay, then, Linc, you, Vela, and Vela's adopted parents need to go do that as soon as possible."

I look over at James and Sandy and they both have frowns on their faces.

Vela rushes over to them and hugs them both. She kisses them on the cheeks, and they smile gently at her. So much happened to separate them. I just hate they lost so much time with their daughter.

Petra interrupts their touching scene to ask, "When are your other parents going to be here?"

"Today," Vela answers, holding both James and Sandy's hands. "Around 3:00 p.m."

I can feel Vela's tension from here about how all her parents will react to each other. I try to send her an encouraging look because I'm sure they will all get along well. Vela is the one constant in this, so they have to get along for Vela to be happy. She would hate it if there was any tension between them.

Petra looks down at her watch. "Well, that's in an hour. So, get what you need to prove your identity and be waiting for them. If you're good with time, you should be able to run into town to get that license today. Someone want to check when the courthouse closes?"

Since I'm the only one with a working phone, James's plan had expired long ago, I look up the number to the courthouse and call. The woman on the phone informs me we have until 5:00 p.m. to apply for a license.

Dropping my phone in my pocket, I announce, "All set to go. They close at 5:00 p.m. Vela," I ask her, "you're sure your mom and dad will get here by 3?"

"That's what they said. Let me call again to confirm," she answers, holding out her hand for my phone.

She gets on the phone and calls her parents. After speaking quietly to them, she hangs up and nods, saying with a smile, "Yep, not foreseeing any problems on the road from the airport. They've landed and are on their way."

"There's still one very important detail to be worked out," Petra says with serious eyes. "We need to find a pastor pronto who can perform the ceremony."

My chest tightens. "Isn't that kind of hard to do on short notice?"

Petra looks at me like I've given her a challenge she is eager to attack. "I'll use your phone and make some calls. We'll find someone. Give me a little time, and I'll see it done."

Gene and Jerry come back. "We're set to go on a covered picnic space on the other side of the campground for a reception for tomorrow," Gene says with a beaming smile.

Tonya and Alice come running up, saying breathlessly, "There is nothing planned at the campground tomorrow. The ceremony can happen right here."

Petra takes that information in stride with a brisk nod, then claps her hands. "Okay, people, you have your jobs to get this show on the road. Go, go, go!"

Everyone jumps into action and scurries in every direction.

I look at Vela with wide eyes after handing Petra my phone. It's so cool how everyone is so behind Vela and me getting married. We are truly blessed.

Vela wraps her arms around my waist. "Lincoln Stevenson, it looks like we're getting married tomorrow. Are you ready?"

I kiss her on the forehead. "More than you can know."

And just like that, my wedding to Vela Ashcroft is planned and raring to go.

26

Vela

I'm so excited to see my parents, I can hardly stand it. What I did *not* expect to see is my best friend in the whole world, Elia.

"Elia!" I screech, and then I run at her, nearly bowling her over with my hug.

She laughs and hugs me back just as fiercely. "I wanted to surprise you."

When I finally let her go, I take one look at Linc and point at him. "You're going to need another groomsman. Elia makes seven."

Elia nods enthusiastically.

Linc says easily with a shrug. "I'll get Steele to do it."

I can't help but snort in amusement, because Steele is going to hate that. But then I turn to Elia and say, "You're going to have to go find a dress, though, unless you have something pink you can wear? Hopefully, a dress?"

Her eyebrows raise. "Seriously?" I do have a pink dress!"

I hug her again. "That's so perfect, Leelee. You were born to be in my wedding."

I feel a tap on my shoulder. "Excuse me, but do we get hugs, too?"

Drew was the one to interrupt my greeting to Elia, and he smirks at me and holds out his arms. Laughing, I jump into them and then go to my mom, dad, and Kane, one after another.

"I'm so happy you're all here. It wouldn't have been the same without you," I say once I've finished all my hugs. Jack joins our greetings by jumping on each of my brothers.

Kane pets Jack with one hand and with the other, messes up my hair. "We wouldn't have missed this for the world, little sis. Besides, who's going to give your groom the threat that if he ever, and I mean ever, hurts you, he's a dead man?" he asks in a pleasant voice.

He gives Linc a hard glare to punctuate his words, and I slap his arm. "He wouldn't. You don't have to worry about that."

"I better not," he says, and Linc nods seriously.

"I am warned," Linc says and holds his chest. "Vela's right. I wouldn't knowingly hurt her for any reason. We might get into a disagreement or two. I can't promise that it won't happen, but she'll have my protection and heart for the rest of my life."

Dad, Drew, and Kane all nod, and I turn a blinding smile at Mom.

"Ready to go to the courthouse to get our license?" I ask.

She nods, and I wrap an arm around her, then Elia's waist and we walk to mine and Linc's rental car. "Then, let's make this happen." I hand Jack off to Hannah real quick and then we're on our way.

We finish our job at the courthouse quickly and return to the campground to find boxes and boxes of flowers in front of Hannah's cabin. I retrieve Jack and I marvel how everyone's walking around with their arms full of things we'll need for the reception tomorrow.

"That was fast," I comment as I see Cheri walking past us with a box full of plates and napkins practically spilling out of it.

"Would we have been able to have even half of this wedding without Petra?" Linc asks.

"No way," I say, in awe of Petra's excellent planning and leadership skills.

"Who's Petra?" Elia asks, as Kane tugs her next to his side.

I smile widely at the obvious couple. "Before I answer that, when did that happen?" I point at Kane's arm around her waist.

Elia smiles lovingly up at Kane. "Not too long ago. The day I turned eighteen, actually."

I squeal and hug them both. "This is amazing. Congratulations, and it's *about time*."

Kane smirks but turns just when Elia goes to kiss his cheek. Her lips land on his lips instead.

I laugh and give them a moment to themselves.

Linc goes to tug me to his side. "How about we round up some dinner?"

"First, let me make sure my family is settled in their cabin."

"Okay, meet up in an hour? Have your dad text me when you're ready. We really need to get you another phone, too."

"We will. After the wedding," I promise.

After I've parted from Linc, I get my family all set in their cabins. Linc has already reserved our cabin for tomorrow night, and I can't help but feel swamped with a swarm of butterflies at that thought. It's more excitement than nerves, but the bit of nervousness is still there, I'll admit.

My dad leaves with Drew and Kane to get ingredients for dinner and while he's gone, Mom and I meet up with Hannah, Sandy, and Adele, who are putting together all the bouquets for tomorrow.

This is the first time my two moms are meeting, and I introduce them hoping for the best. I pray they like each other. Adele, too.

I have nothing to worry about. Whitney rushes over to Sandy and wraps her in a tight hug. Sandy seems a bit surprised, then my mama hugs my mom back.

They both lean back after a while and look each other in the eyes.

Whitney says, "Thank you for giving us Vela. But David and I know she's just as much yours as ours."

Sandy, with teary eyes, replies, "We didn't want to give her up. In fact, we were torn apart all these years, hoping and praying a loving family took care of her. From what Vela says, you were exactly that. So, we're forever thankful. For you."

Adele smiles at me, tears in her eyes, too.

Mine are overflowing. My heart is fit to burst to see my two moms loving each other.

Sandy first holds out her arm for Adele, who falls into her. Then Whitney and Sandy hold their arms out to me. I run to meet them, and we all group hug. There's plenty of tears to go around, so when Petra walks in, she asks the room, "What's wrong?"

We all turn laughing. I'm the one who says, "Nothing! Everything is perfect."

Petra nods, and that's when I introduce Petra to Elia and Whitney. "It's nice to meet you both, but really, I just wanted to make sure all the flower arrangements are good to go," Petra says, looking over the bouquets.

"Almost," Hannah promises, her smile tender as she watches my two families meeting.

Petra nods before leaving, and we all get busy helping Hannah with her job.

We're all laughing and having fun together when my dad, Drew, and Kane come back saying they've gotten the groceries and are requesting help with dinner.

At Sandy's request, Adele runs to get Papa so the dads can meet.

It's a much more subdued, but still, an emotional scene. James shakes David's hand, then my brothers', while Adele and Sandy give them hugs.

James says, "You've loved my eldest well," he says in a tight voice.

David's voice is just as taught. "It was easy. Vela is...wonderful."

Everyone then turns to me, and I'm just watching all of this, tears betraying my emotions. I can't help myself. With a cry, I throw myself in their arms and with me in the middle, they hug me as tightly as my moms did.

Before I know it, Drew and Kane join us, then Adele and Whitney and Sandy all come, and we're a tangle of arms as we all cry and laugh at the same time.

David pulls away first, wiping his eyes. "How does dinner sound?"

We all agree and with Hannah and Sandy promising they can finish the flowers without us, we leave to go make dinner. I ask David to text Linc where we are and to join us.

Linc joins us at my family's cabin and after a scrumptious dinner, Linc and I leave to go for a walk. I call Jack to come with us, especially since he probably needs to go out before he's in for the night.

"It's turned out to be a beautiful evening," Linc says, as he interlaces our fingers together.

"It has. Did you check the weather for tomorrow?" I ask, praying for no rain.

"I did and there's zero chance for rain."

I nod and appreciate the pretty campground. Mesquite and pine trees dot the campground and without discussing it, our steps turn toward where our reception will be held tomorrow morning. The moonlight reflects on the water, and I take a moment to enjoy the pretty picture.

Linc comes behind me, wrapping his arms around my waist. He leans his chin on my shoulder. "Penny for your thoughts," he says in my ear.

I rub the goosebumps on my arms and turn to look at his profile. "Do you actually have a penny?"

He chuckles. "How about we put it on credit?"

"Okay," I agree, then look back out at the scenic view. "I wish I had my phone to take a picture of this." I sigh.

"I'll buy you another one," he says. "You'll need it, now that we're in range of cell phone towers."

I turn to look at him with a furrowed brow. "You don't have to do that, Linc. I can ask my parents."

He gives me a gentle smile. "Shouldn't a husband provide for his wife?"

I laugh. "Yes, I guess so. I didn't think of that. This is getting very real, very fast." I hold onto his arms around my waist, needing a tether to remind me this is very real.

"Good, get used to it," he says, holding me tighter. "Because it's officially my job to take care of you, and that includes your finances."

I frown and ask, "Didn't you say your mom was going to close your accounts?"

He nods, his chin digging into my shoulder.

"So, what are we going to live on?" I ask as Jack noses all around the water's edge and chuckle when he backs up before he can get his feet wet.

"I have money of my own, some investments my uncle set me up with. I'm grateful, too, because they've done well. With the way my relationship is with my mother, I figured this day was coming. We'll be okay for a while."

I slump in his arms. "She really hates me, doesn't she?"

Turning me around his arms, he holds me with a serious stare. "Vela, don't care, for one second, about what she thinks."

I give him an alarmed look. "Linc, that's your mother. Don't you care that she hates me enough to disinherit you?"

"No," he says with heat. "I don't care. I stopped caring when she blamed me for my sister's death instead of taking responsibility for it or just acknowledging it as a terrible accident. I stopped caring when she forced me to be my sister's guardian when I was fifteen years old. I stopped caring for a woman who's never once said she loves me."

My eyes swim with tears. "Oh, Linc." I cup his whiskered cheek with my hand. He dips his head, but not before I see pain in his eyes. "Hey, talk to me," I whisper.

"I didn't want to admit that my own mother doesn't love me," he says in a tight voice.

"She loves you in her own way, I'm sure. If she didn't care for you, she wouldn't be coming to our wedding, would she?"

"She's coming to our wedding for pride's sake and that's it. Make no mistake, Vela. My mother is not like either of yours."

Pain rips through me at his words, and I hug him tightly. He holds me to him, then with an anguished groan, I feel his tears drop onto my skin.

"I love you, forever and always," I whisper into his ear. Tears continue to flow, mine joining his, and I can't help but think he needs to let them come. It's cathartic. He'll find once they're all gone, he'll feel better. It'll be like a load has been taken off his shoulders.

Linc's voice tears into me. "I need the power to forgive my mother and father. To love them even though they don't love me." His voice ends cracked, and I know his soul is bleeding.

All I can do is pray for him.

"Vela?" he asks, his face still buried in my shoulder.

"Yes?"

"Can we pray together?"

"I'd love nothing more," I say and my insides crumple at my hurting soulmate.

We bow our heads, and Linc prays, "God, we come and thank You for bringing us together as You intended. Father, we ask that You go before us today, tomorrow, and in all our days together. Not only with what You've tasked Vela to do, but in our lives together. May I be the man You've created me to be and lead our union with Your guiding hand. Help me be the man Vela needs me to be and who You designed me to be." He pauses for a moment, seeming to collect himself.

I squeeze him, and he continues, "Father, be our Guiding Light, our Shepherd. Comfort our hearts, comfort my heart and assure me I am loved." His voice cracks again. "Father, we praise You for this day, and ask You to smooth the way before us. Help us to get married tomorrow, Lord. Create a path for us. Thank You for what You've already done for us. We love You, Lord, and ask for Your blessing in our lives. Amen."

I choke out an Amen, and I press a kiss to his shoulder.

We leave soon after, and I bring Linc to David and Whitney's cabin, where I'm staying, so he can try on the suit they brought.

Linc shakes David's hand and receives a hug from him. I'm moved that he's so welcomed by my parents, considering that he just left tears on my shirt about his own parents. My parents genuinely care about him and Linc's look is one of pure grate-fulness. Maybe with Whitney and David, he'll feel truly loved as a son. I think James and Sandy have welcomed him into the family, too.

David returns and hands Linc a suit, his look sheepish. "Uh, I'm sure you'd rather have your own father do this, but I thought this is the one most likely to fit you well. It's Kane's, but he's the biggest out of all of us. And with your proportions, I think it'll do."

Linc accepts the hanger with a shirt, suit, and tie. He looks moved at David's thoughtfulness. "Thank you, sir."

"Call me Dad," David says with emotion. Then, he says, putting his hand on Linc's shoulder. "You've done for my daughter what no other man could do. You've protected and been there for her in such a way, no father could be prouder to call you his son." Clearing his throat, he hesitates before he asks, "Do you have rings?"

My stomach bottoms out as I lean back, stunned we've forgotten that very important detail. Linc looks just as sickened.

My dad chuckles as he sees the obvious answer and reaches into his pocket. "I know this isn't your first choice, but maybe you can use these as a substitute." He opens a small black box, and my eyes widen at the two rings nestled inside. One that would fit Linc and one for me. I know those rings.

Linc looks up, overwhelmed.

David gives me a loving look. "Your mother and I upgraded our rings on our last anniversary but kept our originals. I'm glad we did."

Linc's mouth opens and shuts but doesn't move to accept them. I'm just as surprised at my dad's generosity. David just smiles and leaves the box on the table next to Linc and I. "Isn't it a thing that a bride needs something borrowed? Well, consider this a loan. Or keep them if you'd like. It's up to you and Vela if you'd like to do your own upgrade. They aren't much."

"Dad," I say, my throat dry. I don't know what to say as I stare at the little black box.

"They're everything," Linc whispers hoarsely, picking up the box and looking at the man-sized ring. He picks it up and puts it on and it's a little snug, but it fits.

He reaches for my mom's ring and, with a long look at me, slides it on my ring finger.

"It fits," I say with a shy smile.

He returns my smile. "It does." Then he turns to David. "Sir, this is a priceless gift. If you want these back, we'll get our own and return them."

"It's completely up to the both of you. Consider it a gift, or a loan, whichever one you want to call it."

David clears his throat, and his eyes shine suspiciously of tears. He gives us a smile and turns to leave the room.

"Wait!" Linc grabs him in a tight hug. "Thank you, sir," he croaks, his throat moving up and down as he hugs my dad. I blink back tears at the sight of Linc hugging my dad when he's been so hurt by his own.

Stunned at first by his display of emotion, David's still, until he returns the embrace. When Linc releases him, David shares a warm smile before hugging me, too. He turns back to Linc, "Oh, I've forgotten one thing. He leaves and returns with a pair of shoes. "Will a ten fit?"

"Yes, sir," Linc answers, his voice tight.

"Dad," David corrects and smiles, handing the shoes over.

Linc goes to the bathroom to try on the suit. While we wait for him to come out, I hold my dad's side, like I did when I was a little girl.

"You really are a great guy," I tell him, cuddling my face into his shirt. He smells like he always has, his aftershave and musk cologne.

"I happen to think the same about you," he says softly.

I laugh.

When Linc emerges from the bathroom, my mouth turns dry at the sight of him decked out in a slim fit dark blue suit.

My mouth is open, and David closes it with a snap. "I think that means that she likes it," he teases.

I drink in the sight and laugh half-heartedly. I do like it. I like it a lot.

"Hey," Linc complains. "Is she supposed to see me in this before the wedding?"

At that I laugh. "No, that tradition is for the bride. I hate to break it to you, but people care more about what the bride wears than the groom."

David looks down at me. "Your mom is in the bedroom, altering your dress. She wants you to come in to make sure the length is right.""

"Is that where she is?" I say, still checking out my Intended.

Linc laughs. "Wow, I've made my girl practically speechless." He smiles. "Vela, don't you want to see your dress?"

I wake from the daze caused by my extremely hot fiancé in formal wear and nod enthusiastically. I rush into my parents' room and find my mom's lap covered in white silk. "Can I try it on?"

Whitney nods and stands up, revealing the most gorgeous dress I've ever seen, and when she turns it around, I see that it's backless.

"You're sure it's going to fit?" I squeak.

"Let's get you out of your clothes and yes, I'm sure it will fit. I've sewn you enough clothes to know it will," she says confidently.

I scramble to get out of my clothes, and Whitney helps me into the softest gown I've ever worn. It slides on like a dream, and I turn so she can button up the back.

I hold my breath, but it's clear. She was right. The dress fits perfectly. I smooth my hands down the dress, and I turn to her.

She gasps as she looks me over. Putting her hand over her mouth, tears glisten in her eyes as she whispers, "You're stunning, baby."

I look down at myself and turn to face the mirror. A woman looks back at me, and I close my gaping mouth. Off the shoulder sleeves trail down my arms and the gown hugs my curves.

"Mom, it's like this dress was made for me," I whisper.

"I know," she chokes. "It's why I got it. I knew you'd love it."

I lunge toward her and give her a tight hug. "Oh, Mom, I love it, thank you."

She pulls away and looks me up and down. She sniffs. "I think it's a little long. Let me fix the hem."

I let her work, unable to take my eyes off the woman in the mirror. It's not that I'm thinner since I left for Canada, just that I'm much more toned and in shape. I'm also tanned from all the time I've spent outside, and my eyes widen with shock. I hope I don't have that look tomorrow, so I school my face so I feel more confident. When Whitney pauses in her pinning, I turn to look at the back and I inhale sharply. *Can I pull this dress off?*

One thing I know is that Linc's going to love this dress. I smile at myself in the mirror.

"Okay, I think that's everything," Whitney says, standing up. "It fits great. I just need to fix the hem, so you don't trip on it."

I hug her again. "Thank you, Mom. I'm so happy, I could cry."

"Well, don't do that. I'm just happy you love it."

I reluctantly come out of the dress, draping it lovingly on the bed. Whitney gets right to work, and I leave her in the room, walking back out into the living room, where David and Linc are talking quietly.

"Sorry, I was just..." I drift off at Linc's smile.

"You love it, don't you?" he asks.

"Yeah, how can you tell?"

"Your face says it all. *I'm* going to love it, aren't I?"

"Uh, yes. You will," I say with a blush, because my father is watching our exchange with amusement. "Sorry I was so long."

"I don't mind at all," Linc says easily.

David returns Linc's smile with one big one of his own. He laughs and claps him on the shoulder. "Well, I know one thing. Just wait till Kane sees how good you look in his suit. He's going to be jealous."

27

Vela

I wake up at the morning's dawn, excitement racing through me that I'm *marrying Linc today.*

Adele, Elia, and I shared a room last night, and we talked into the wee hours of the morning. Thankfully, there were two beds, and we all fit, sleeping comfortably. But suffice it to say, they are both bleary-eyed when I shake them awake.

Elia shuts one eye and shields her face with her hand. "You should see yourself. You're like one bright, happy piece of the sun. Stop dazzling me with your smile. Now, go away."

Adele obediently rises, wiping her eyes with her hands. "What time is it, anyway?"

"Time to get ready for a wedding," I chirp.

I pull Elia's blanket off her. "I can't help but shine today, Leelee. I'm so happy." I jump on her. "I literally have to hug someone right now, if not my husband-to-be." So, I do.

She groans. "You're suffocating me." She pulls away from me with a scowl, pointing her finger in my face. "And that is not happening. You are not seeing Linc before the wedding. Got it?"

"Yeah," Adele says, ganging up on me.

How did they know I wanted to see Linc before the wedding?

I pout. "Fine."

"We mean it," Elia warns. "I'll tie you to the chair if I have to."

"Okay, fine! Now, can we get ready?"

She moans but gets out of bed. Then it's a blur from that moment, one makeup brush after another. Elia makes it her mission to beautify me, and I love it. Adele gives her opinions and helps with my hair. They turn my massive mane into an updo so beautiful I keep turning in the mirror to admire the mound of curls Adele keeps adding. She continues to curl, claiming it adds texture.

"This is like when we were kids and played with mom's makeup," I say when Elia attacks my eyes like a professional makeup artist.

"We are far beyond that," she says, squinting her eyes to concentrate on her work. "Well," she says, pulling away to look me over, "I am way beyond that. You, sadly, are at the same level as when we were twelve."

"Hey," I say, laughing, smacking her hand. "I'm just not obsessed with makeup like you are."

"Just because I've watched tutorials on how to contour and achieve different looks well does not make me obsessed," Elia says with a frown.

"It kind of does. I mean, look at me." I wave a hand at the mirror. "I've never looked like this." I study my face in the mirror. She really has brought out my best features. My eyes are framed with smoky gray eyeshadow, making the blue pop dramatically. And my lips look ready to be kissed with a soft pink lipstick. My skin, tanned by the outdoor sun glows somehow.

She looks worriedly in the mirror. "You don't like it?"

When I say, "No," she jumps back. But then I hurriedly say, "I don't like it, I *love* it."

She slumps in relief. Adele laughs at my little joke.

We have some time before I put my dress on. so I ask Adele, "How's everything going between you, Rayne and Steele?"

She huffs. "Nothing with either one. Steele's attached himself to Alice. So, I guess I've officially been replaced."

"Isn't that what you wanted?" I ask, gently.

She considers that question. "Yes, but I thought it would be more my decision, not his. I get it, he's protecting himself."

"And Rayne? What's going on with him?"

"Nothing," she bites out. "I haven't spoken to him since that little incident at the tent on the way to the Polar Bear."

"I'm sorry, sis. I'll be praying for you."

She thanks me quietly then resumes her job on my hair.

Sandy and Whitney come in the room and when they see me in the mirror, Whitney emits a soft cry, putting her hand on her mouth and Sandy says, "Oh, sweetie, you look lovely."

"Do I?" I ask earnestly, turning my head this way and that, at which I get a slight smack on my arm to stop moving.

"I'm still adding curls," Adele says, cracking a small smile. "But they're right, you are gorgeous."

I realize Whitney is carrying a garment bag.

Elia gasps. "Is that…"

"My wedding dress?" I finish for her.

Whitney's eyes are bright with her smile. "Yes, it is. Are you ready to get in it?"

I nod eagerly, but since I can't move, she unzips the bag. It's even more beautiful than my feeble memories from yesterday. I hungrily look at the dress with its perfect length train.

Adele blows out a breath. "Wow, Vela, it's beautiful."

I turn accusing eyes to her. "Why wouldn't it be?"

She laughs and turns to Sandy. "I love you, Mama, but I would never trust you to pick out my wedding dress."

Whitney turns worried eyes to me. "Vela, do you feel you're being cheated by not picking out your own dress?"

I can't take my eyes off my dress as I shake my head. "It's perfect, Mom." And I mean it.

Once Adele gives me permission, I slip off the chair and approach the dress, itching to get it in it. I take it and some underclothes in the bathroom and am thankful Elia thought to tell me to put on a button-down shirt so I can get out of my clothes easily with my hair like this. I slide the dress on, luxuriating in the silky feel of it.

I call for help to button it up. When I emerge from the bathroom, a collective gasp sounds through the room. Sandy covers her eyes and sobs softly. "Oh, Vela," she says. "It looks perfect on you."

Adele nods vigorously, and a tear slips from her eye, too.

We hear a firm knock on the door, and when Sandy opens it, Petra walks in. She looks me over. "You clean up nice, Ashcroft."

I smile widely at her. "That's probably the last time someone will call me that."

Petra half smiles. "Yes, as long as you say I do today, you'll be a Stevenson." Then she looks over with a frown at Jack. "How are you making him carry your ring?"

I triumphantly show what Adele, Elia, and I had figured out during our late night. We have the rings tied to his collar in a pretty little bow.

"Is that double knotted?" she asks suspiciously.

"Yes it is," I say and double check just to be sure. "We didn't put his collar on until a little bit ago, so he won't be walking around with them for long," I promise.

"Hmph," she says.

I approach her. "Petra, I want to thank you. You took charge and planned my entire wedding. I certainly did not expect that. We are all amazed at what you've done. I cannot thank you enough."

She clears her throat gruffly. "It's nothing to fuss about. You needed to get married, and I managed to get a few people to do a few things."

"A *few* things?" Whitney gushes. "I don't think any of us could have done what you've done."

"Well," Petra says, her cheeks turning pink. "The wedding hasn't even happened yet. Don't thank me yet." And at that, she escapes.

I laugh and am joined by Adele and Sandy, while Whitney and Elia still stare at the door with wide eyes.

"I knew she was going to be good for me as soon as I met her," I say.

Hannah approaches the door, knocking softly. She looks me over with soft eyes. "Oh, Vela, you look beautiful."

I wrap her carefully in a hug, so happy she's with me on this special day. "Thank you, Hannah. I turn to the room. "I want both my moms to know this woman took me under her wing when I desperately missed my family. She's as much a part of my family as any of you."

Hannah blushes deeply and smiles at me. "You make loving you easy, Vela. As all of these wonderful people can attest."

"Well," Whitney says, approaching Hannah and me. "David and I are forever thankful for you watching over and guarding our daughter."

I widen my eyes. I realize I hadn't told my adopted mother about the battle at the Polar Bear. "Mom, you don't know how right you are." And then, as we all finish getting ready, I tell her all about the Polar Bear fight and terrible fire afterwards.

The morning blurs by and suddenly David and James are knocking on my door, saying, "Vela, it's time."

There was no room in the room for all my bridesmaids, so I didn't get to see them all getting ready, but they all stopped by asking me to check over their makeup and outfits.

It's hopelessly too late to change anything, but it turns out, they all look great. They're waiting out in the living room of the cabin for me each holding gorgeous bouquets.

I'm handed my own stunning bouquet and I walk out of the room. Tonya says for all of them, because it seems I've struck everyone speechless. "Girl, you look amazing."

I turn shining eyes to both my dads and their eyes are suspiciously wet, too. "You look stunning, darling," David says, and takes one of my arms.

James takes my other one and says, "I've been cheated of my time with you, but I'm thankful more than anything for being able to spend this day with you."

I kiss him on the cheek and because it looks like he needs it, I give one to David, too. I happily snuggle between them both.

"Papa," Adele scolds, running over, "you're crushing her dress. You have to stand a little further over so she can walk." She looks up at David sheepishly. "You too, sir."

David smiles at her, obediently moving over a fraction, asking, "Is this better?"

When James moves over, too, she nods briskly. "That'll do." She comes up to me. "Are you ready, sister?" Her eyes are brimming, and I know that if I tell her one thing about how I've always wished for this moment to happen with my very own sister, I'd be a blubbering mess. So, I say, "Yes, I am."

She nods; air kisses my cheek and then goes to stand in front of me.

That's when I notice Greta. She's dressed in a pink, frilly mess of lace, looking more adorable than I've ever seen her. Hannah put her hair in an updo of curls that looks so cute. "Oh, Greta, you look so beautiful."

She grins her gap-toothed smile at me. "It's you who's beautiful, Vela. But thanks."

I notice her cheeks are tinged a little pink, and I hope that it's blush and not heat or a fever making them like that. She turns before I can study her more, and then I have to concentrate on walking.

I guess they all practiced last night who was walking first because Petra looks on in a satisfied way when they all take their places.

My bridesmaids lead the way out the door.

Even Greta knows to precede me, and she does so with a basket of petals in her hand.

Petra is glaring down at Jack like he's going to mess this whole ceremony up. I've clipped Jack's leash on just so that Petra won't have a heart attack.

I hold my breath. *This is it. I'm marrying my Intended.* He's become my best friend, too. I marvel at how far he and I have come in our relationship.

David and James look down at me when everyone has left the cabin except for us. Petra holds out her hand, not allowing us to leave until the perfect moment. She watches outside with the door cracked open, and I wait impatiently.

I hear music playing and wonder who it is. People who played in the Polar Bear and Saddleback must have brought their instruments because I hear a guitar and a violin.

My heart starts tripping over itself, and suddenly I want to see Linc more than anything in the world. Ignoring Petra, I disentangle myself from my dads' arms and unclip Jack's leash. I command him to walk, and I re-engage my grip on both arms and start walking. Desperate to see Linc's face at the end of the aisle, I hurry my steps. My dads are quick to come with me.

David opens the door and then Petra sighs as I walk by her, apparently giving up on my perfect moment. But what she doesn't understand is that this moment is perfect. We've come a long way since that moment I first realized Linc was my Intended. We've fought battles together. He's saved my life over and over. He's put me first every time, and now if I don't lay my eyes on him soon, I'm going to start running to find him. He's waiting for me, and I know more than anything he's just as desperate to see me, too.

I'm thrilled that my parents' cabin is close to the ceremony, because David and James escort me directly there as I follow Jack who is doing a great job walking.

Suddenly, as if the clouds parted just to allow the sun to shine on him, I see him, my Intended, the other half of my heart. Linc, my soon-to-be husband, is indeed waiting for me, and he's smiling. He's smiling so wide that it looks like he's laughing.

Our eyes lock, and suddenly everyone disappears, and it's just him and me. I stutter in my steps, but my dads are quick to help me regain my stride. I realize we're not walking to the tempo of the slow music but much faster.

All I know is I can't get to Linc fast enough. His eyes beckon me to join him as he stands with a man in a suit, who I'm guessing is the pastor Petra found. I momentarily marvel at Petra's ability to find one at such short notice. Then my mind and attention are back on Linc. He flicks his fingers for Jack to come to him, and I appreciate how *good* he looks. When I saw him last night, I thought he was handsome, but now, with his trimmed beard and perfectly styled wavy hair, he's heart-stopping gorgeous. He's dropped his smile and now his gaze is burning into me like a thousand suns. I can actually feel the weight of his eyes on me, drinking me in.

Jack reaches him and his body wiggles in excitement that he made it to his co-owner. He performed his part brilliantly, just like I said he would. We walked so fast, we almost caught up to Greta, who's dropping petals at every possible step I could take. I love that she's taking her job so seriously. I smile at her as she takes up her spot by my bridesmaids. They're all arranged in a line, looking fabulous in their pink dresses. The groomsmen, too, look great in their different patterned pink shirts. Everyone has different styles on, but that's perfectly fine with me.

Then, I'm there. I've reached my Linc. My eyes feast on him and my dads let go of my arms. I turn to each one and they kiss me softly on the cheek. I feel so loved by them that my heart clenches. I give them each one last look before I turn to Linc.

He reaches for my hands and finally, finally, I'm touching his hot skin. His emotions are high if his hands are so hot, and I find that I *love* that. I caused that. My Festan gift soaks in his heat.

He leans toward me, whispering, "You are stunning. I can't take my eyes off you."

"Me neither," I whisper back.

Then the pastor starts speaking about love and commitment in the face of God, and I cherish the words as much as my view. That's when Linc's fingers start trembling a little, and I wonder if he's nervous about connecting his life to mine. Does he really want to do this? Is he having second thoughts? But when I look over at him, he gifts me with such a loving look, my heart collides with his, and I know. He feels as much love for me as I do for him.

I smile at him, showing my heart in every motion. His eyes glisten, and we both turn when the pastor asks us, "Vela Ashcroft and Lincoln Stevenson?"

We both nod, and I grip Linc's hand harder, feeling so much emotion nearly overwhelming me. I can hardly contain my sob of excitement.

This is it. I'm going to be Linc's wife, forever his bride.

Suddenly it isn't enough to be his Intended, I want it to be official that I'm his and he's mine.

I drown in a sea of words, trying to keep track of what the man's saying. He asks Linc, "Do you, Lincoln Stevenson, vow to guide and to hold Vela Ashcroft as your wife in sickness and in health in the eyes of God for the rest of your life?" I hold my breath to hear his answer.

Linc gives a clear, "Yes, I do," as he looks deep in my eyes.

"Do you, Vela Ashcroft, vow to guide and to hold Lincoln Stevenson to be your lawful husband in sickness and in health in the eyes of God for the rest of your life?"

I nod happily, tears spilling down my cheeks as I say, "Yes, yes, I do. For forever, I do."

Linc gives me such a tender look, my heart melts into a puddle, never to be reformed.

The pastor chuckles and when he asks Linc, "Do you have the ring?"

Linc leans down to Jack's collar and unties both rings, handing me one as he keeps the other.

My eyes are misting as he repeats the words the pastor says in a clear voice, "With this ring, I thee wed."

My heart is full as he slides my mother's ring onto my finger.

The pastor then asks me then to repeat the same vows to Linc.

Collecting myself, I pause before I repeat, "With this ring, I thee wed." I have to push a little but the ring fits Linc's finger. I squeeze my eyes shut, tears dripping down, as I think of my parents' sacrifice giving us these reminders of their own love.

Linc is waiting for me when I open my eyes, and his face beams when the pastor says, "I now pronounce you man and wife."

I throw my arms around Linc's neck, hugging him to me. "I love you, Lincoln Stevenson."

"And I love you, Vela Stevenson," he says, squeezing me. Then he leans back and complains, "Hey. I do get my kiss, don't I?"

The crowd erupts in such a loud cheer that the whistles are almost lost in the raucous. I recognize my brother's piercing whistle easily.

Laughing, I let go of Linc and the pastor laughs, too, and barely has time to say, "You may now kiss your bride."

Linc dips me back and plants such a hot kiss on me, my whole body lights up like a bonfire. When he straightens us, I keep my lips on his, not wanting to end our first kiss as a married couple. I hope it tells him everything I feel. And I feel *everything* in this moment.

Returning my fervor with some of his own, we hardly hear it when the pastor says, "Please welcome the new Mr. and Mrs. Stevenson."

The cheering continues until we finally break apart, and Linc has to turn me because I don't want his face out of my field of vision. That's when I notice there are two sets of benches on both sides of the aisle. All I saw approaching the ceremony was Linc and a clear path to get to him. Sitting in the front row is the Festan Grand Elder and her husband, aka my new in-laws. He gives me a smile but hers is more forced.

Ignoring her, I sweep my eyes over the rest of the crowd. I smile widely at both sets of my parents and at all my new friends from the Polar Bear and Saddleback. Petra winks at me and Gary, Rick, Gene, and Jerry are all whistling and clapping.

Linc clasps my hand, and I turn happy eyes back to him. I've given my life to this man, and my heart is now forever seared into his. No one can tear us apart. Not his mother, not the Extremists, nor anyone else.

Jack jumps on my side, and I hug him, so happy he could be here in this momentous occasion. Linc pets him, too, and then he leads us down the aisle and past the still cheering crowd. Debra is taking picture after picture, and I can't wait to see how they will turn out. I turn back and see the groomsmen escorting my bridesmaids down the aisle after us, and I catch the eye of Elia, who's walking with Kane. She's got such a happy look on her face after giving Kane a smile that I know she'll be the next one walking down the aisle in a wedding dress. I beam at her.

Linc and I wait for everyone to join us then we're all laughing and hugging. It's a little awkward because I don't want to let go of Linc. I keep hold of his arm or hand, I don't care. I only care about keeping us connected.

Forever, I vow. I will be with this man for the rest of my life. And we'll be supported by this great, wonderful family.

I look around and relish seeing Elia and Adele laughing together. Drew is talking to Andy, while Whitney smiles down at Greta. David and James are nodding at each other, smiling. All smiles. That's all I see everywhere I look.

Kane breaks my hold on Linc's hand when he picks me up and spins me around. "Sister!" he exclaims, "You're married! I can't believe it." He puts me down and looks deep into my eyes. "You're the youngest and you're married first. Are you happy?"

I laugh. "Are you kidding? I'm ecstatic. Linc is everything to me, Kane."

Linc wraps his arms around my waist from behind and says into my neck. "Do you mean that, wife?"

I turn around and loop my arms around his neck. "Yes, husband, I mean it with all my heart."

"Good," he says, kissing the tip of my nose. "That's what I want to hear. Every day, tell me over and over, okay?"

I cock my head. "What if I forget one day?"

He leans in and kisses me soundly on the lips. "Oh, don't worry. I'll remind you."

We're interrupted when Sandy comes and puts her hand on Linc's shoulder. "Ready to celebrate?"

Linc nods, his eyes not leaving mine. It's like he can't get enough of drinking me in. I absolutely love it. I love that I'm what he wants for the rest of his life.

It's mindboggling, really. I'm only seventeen years old, and I'm married.

What universe is this?

Linc's hand is on the skin of my back, and he leans down to tell me in my ear. "You are killing me with this dress, you realize that right?"

I smile up at him and his eyes look like he's drunk on love.

We're led away, both of us gazing at each other. I'm in a dream state. The ceremony was so fast, it's like I haven't been here more than two minutes. Linc seems to be drifting in the same world I'm in, because he has a dazed look on his face, too.

28

Linc

I lead Vela to the other side of the campground with Jack walking next to me. It's like he knows I've just joined his owner's life with mine, and he's claiming allegiance to us both. I look over at Vela to see if she's noticed, but she's only looking at me. If I wasn't leading her, she would have walked straight into a building, and I freaking *love* that she can't take her eyes off me.

I can barely rip my eyes off of her, either. I could not have imagined her in that dress in my wildest dreams. If I could have my way, I would be her sole focus from here on out. But I know I'll have to share my beautiful bride first with this group today, then with the world while she unites us all. Midstride, because I am multi-talented, I turn, lean down and kiss her delectable lips. Lips that I'd very much love to kiss all the lipstick completely off right now.

But now is not the time for that. I break my kiss as I stop to hold on to her. She stumbles, looking dazed, and I almost sweep her off her feet to carry her to our bridal suite, but think about the reception that has been planned for us. I hang onto the thought that so much preparation has gone into making this day happen. I can't be selfish now. Even if I very much want to be.

I resume leading a very merry party to the pavilion where lunch is planned. I think back to first seeing Vela walking down the aisle.

My heart stopped when I saw her walking with David and James. Was she walking quickly, or was that my wish that she would reach me faster? It seemed like everything had suddenly gone in slow motion. My mouth dropped at seeing her beautiful dress. It hugged her in *every* possible way, highlighting the beauty of the most stunning woman I've ever laid eyes on. It's like she'd dropped straight from heaven itself to walk toward me. All moisture disappeared from my mouth, or I was sure I'd be drooling. Her hair was done up in a style I've never seen her wear before, and it showed off the graceful column of her neck.

I heard laughing from my groomsmen, but all of my attention was zeroed in on this girl who was looking at me with that come-hither look that makes me crumble at her feet. *Every time.*

Torn from my thoughts and back to the present, we reach the pavilion, and I hear Vela gasp next to me. Our friends have transformed a plain wooden structure into a garden wonderland overnight. I'm sure their Elemental gifts went into the construction of this floral explosion. Vines crawl up every possible path, with flowers interwoven in their leaves.

Petra somehow beat us here. She must have slipped past us when we greeted our family after the ceremony. She's directing the placement of the food. She turns and sees us, then waves us to sit at a picnic table set apart from all the rest that's covered with a tablecloth.

"The wedding party will sit at two tables, but you two go ahead and sit at this one," she instructs.

When Vela and I obey, she leans down between us, her hands on both of our shoulders. "Congratulations, lovebirds."

Vela looks up at her and gives her a side hug. "We couldn't have had such a great day without you, Petra."

Petra pulls away. "You would have gotten hitched, but not with such pizzazz, I must admit. Maybe my future career is as a wedding planner."

I say, "Petra, you'd get a five-star rating from your first one."

She stands up, looking affronted. "Who's to say you're my first one?"

I laugh as she walks away. "She'll never stop surprising us, will she?" I ask Vela.

She shakes her head and reaches for a cup decorated with the word, "Bride."

We get visitor after visitor after that, and we have more conversations than I can count. The lunch passes in a blur much like the ceremony did.

David comes by to get another hug. "It's so good to see you and my girl getting married. Thank you for taking such good care of her."

I think back to where she was injured by the Neronians on our way to the Polar Bear for the first time and swallow guiltily. I didn't protect her from that.

Whitney beams, agreeing with David. "Canada was good for the both of you. You're both a little slimmer maybe, but you got a great tan out of it."

Looking back, I remember almost losing her to Rayne. Even if it was momentary, it was too long of a time when she wasn't my girl.

I study my bride as she laughs with Adele. Vela's white off-the-shoulder gown mesmerizes me. Something on the dress is sparkling, or is that her? That is one mystery I don't think I'll ever solve. Maybe tonight, when the dress is off her, I can figure it out.

I reach for my cup, labeled, 'Groom' and take a large swallow because suddenly my throat has gone very dry.

Vela puts her hand on mine and almost as if it's subconscious, she starts drawing patterns on my skin. It lights me on fire, and suddenly I'm very ready to have her alone.

We've socialized, we've eaten, now it's my turn to have her undivided attention. I'm just about to whisk her away when I hear a loud, "No!"

I look up and Kane is standing up looking at his phone with a horrified expression.

"What's wrong?" I demand and stand up.

"They've found you guys," Kane spits out. He runs over to Elia and hands her the phone. She furiously reads it and then looks at me with fear on her face.

"We've gotta' get you both out of here." After a beat, she says, "Now."

"What do you mean?" Vela asks. "What's going on?"

"All I know is we have to hide Vela," Elia says with a frown.

"The Extremists found out she's here, and they're mobilizing a unit to find her," Kane says with gritted teeth.

"How do you know all of that?" I growl.

Kane faces us. "Elia and I have been spying on their organization since you've been gone. We just got a text from one of the other spies."

"What?" Vela screeches. "Elia, are you serious? I told you to stay away from them!"

Elia turns to her. "I'm sorry Vela. But it was the only way to protect you. I wouldn't change it for anything. If Kane and I hadn't done it, we'd never have this information."

I swear and turn to Vela, cupping her face in my hands. I say the hardest thing I've ever had to say, "We only have one choice. You have to hide. I'll go another direction to confuse them. They'll expect us to be together."

"What? Why do we have to separate?" Vela cries, blinking back tears.

My heart pounds in my chest. Adrenaline races through me, and I have to fight to keep myself from setting this whole place on fire.

"It's better we split up," I grit out, hating my words. "It'll confuse them a little, but any bit helps. We'll reconnect in a week."

"A week? Linc, I just married you," Vela whispers, tears tracking her cheeks.

I put my forehead on hers and whisper, "I'm sorry, baby. This is the only way to keep you safe."

"Elia and I will take her to hide," Kane offers. "Don't worry, you two will be reunited, Vela."

Drew joins Kane with a granite look on his face. "I'll go with them. I'll help protect her, Linc."

A crowd gathers around our table and other offers of protection are shouted out. David takes control of the mass confusion. "Vela will leave with her brothers and Elia. They need a small car, not a big van that will draw more attention. They will leave now, and the rest of us will disperse. Linc will go with Whitney and I, while the rest of you find another place to hide out. Do they know about this location?" he asks Kane.

"That's unclear," Kane says with frustration. "I'll know more later, but right now, Vela, we have to go."

Sobbing, Vela kisses me hard. I taste her tears. "Please don't leave me, Linc," she begs. "I can't be separated from you again, not now. I need you."

I inhale shakily. *If I had an Extremist in front of me, they would not survive my rage.* "Baby, you're going to have to be strong. Stay safe with your brothers and Elia. I will find you, and we'll be together. Nothing will drag me away from you once we're together again."

"Linc," Drew orders. "Go with my parents. I'll go grab Vela's things and we'll disappear."

"No," I say in a hard voice. "She can buy things later. You need to disappear *now*. Go. And Drew and Kane," I say, swallowing painfully, "Protect her with your lives."

"We will," they both promise.

Pulling Vela up, Drew and Kane help her off the bench and lead her away. She doesn't take her eyes off me, but wind knocks all the decorations around. Her distress is palpable.

So is mine. Smoke rises off my hands, and I run through my hair and pull the ends as I watch my barely made bride walk away from me. She doesn't take her eyes off me, not once.

David is at my side with James, too, looking ominous. They allow me to watch Vela being pulled away, giving me time to compose myself.

"What is the meaning of this?" my mother's waspish tone cuts through the furious talking happening all around me.

I step away from the bench and barely have it in me to deal with her.

"Lincoln, you and Vela are in danger? Am I hearing that correctly?"

I turn to face her and dad, who's wearing an expression of concern.

"Yes," I grit out. "We're always in danger. I just didn't think they'd find us this soon."

"Well, what did you expect using your own IDs getting your marriage certificate? Of course, the E.E. will find you."

"It was the only way to get married," I spit out.

"Well, you'll leave with us." She turns away.

"I will not."

She half turns, looking over her shoulder. "What?"

"I said, I will not. I'll be leaving with Vela's parents."

She looks them over with a sneer. "They can't protect you like I can."

Barely reining in my anger at being separated from my Intended on our wedding day, I grit out, "Have you thought, Mother, that you're the one I need protecting from right now?"

The whole crowd goes silent at my words, but I don't regret them. Let them think what they want about my perfect mother and her perfect Grand Elder position. She is not who I need right now. The only person I really need is driving away, and I can barely see straight through my rage.

David tries to soothe ruffled feathers. "Elizabeth, we can keep your son safe. We have a place to take him that is untraceable. We used to live close to there."

Mother straightens and spears me with a cold look, sniffing at the smoke rising from my hands. Then, she turns to leave and drags my father with her.

I breathe in relief and James leans in. "Are you sure you don't want your mom's protection? She has resources we don't."

David answers for me, "We really do know a great hiding spot. He'll be fine there. It's Vela who needs to disappear. They're after her first and foremost."

James's face tightens in worry. Sandy and Adele, at his side, look the same.

Petra takes command. "Everyone, we need to get to our belongings and leave pronto. Let's get this mess cleared up as best we can."

David nods at me, and I follow him and Whitney out of this place meant for celebration but turned to one of mourning.

If Vela is found by the Extremists, then I've seen her face alive and healthy for the last time. I shut down those thoughts. Because I will see my bride again. I pray harder than I've ever prayed before for her to be safe and that the week passes like the blink of an eye.

29

Vela

In less than five minutes after Kane got his text, we're gone and speeding away from the person I just promised my life to. I look out the back window and watch the pavilion with my husband in it get smaller and smaller. Then Kane turns the car down another street and Linc's gone from my view.

Resting my head on the headrest, I cry harder than I have in a long time. Elia hugs me to her, allowing me to wet her shoulder with my tears. She pats my head, attempting to console me with empty promises. But the truth is, the Extremists might track Linc first, and he could forever be taken from my life.

What would I do without Linc?

I realize I've come to rely on my Intended for support. I feel bereft without his strong and steady presence beside me. Jack is whining, too, but I don't have the heart to comfort him. I put my hand on his head, but that's all I can give when I'm so heartbroken.

How did this happen? Why is Linc being ripped from me on our wedding day?

We drive the rest of the day and into the night, and I'm in a fog the entire time. I finally pick my head off Elia's lap and look around. It's dark out, so there's not much to see. I'm grateful that I must have fallen asleep.

"Where are we?" I croak, my throat swollen from so much sobbing.

"Utah," Kane answers, looking me over. His eyes are full of sympathy, but there's another emotion there, too, determination. "I'm trying to get us close to Salt Lake City. I figure we'll hide out in an outlying suburb. I want to get you as close to the main airport as we can, so you can connect with Linc and the others once it's safe."

I nod, feeling completely empty. I look down at myself, and when I see the dress I put on so happily this morning, tears flood my eyes all over again.

Elia guides me back to her shoulder, and I dissolve into tears again. I didn't think I had any more in me, but that's proved wrong.

Kane and Drew exchange looks at my tears, but there's nothing to be done but drive.

Kane goes at a measured pace, not speeding, but right at the speed limit. I guess he doesn't want to get pulled over and risk gaining attention. There's no telling if police officers are on the Extremists' payroll. It wouldn't surprise me if they were.

These thoughts and others run through my mind in fractured pieces. The dominant one being that I miss Linc so desperately I would do just about anything to be reunited. We were supposed to be spending the rest of our lives together starting today. Instead, we've been torn apart. It's grossly unfair.

I find myself laying my head back on Elia's lap, and when I rouse from sleep again, she's speaking to Kane. I perk up my ears to hear what they're saying.

"You're sure this is a good place?" she asks with a worried tone.

"It's good," he confirms. "It's small enough to get off the radar, but it's not so small that everyone will notice us in town. You guys can find some regular clothes, too."

After hearing we've made it somewhere safe, I tune them out and do what I should have been doing the entire time. I pray.

God, keep us safe. Keep my husband safe and my parents. Lord, I can't do this without You. I didn't think I could do it without Linc, but You've allowed us to be separated. I don't know if I can bear this Lord, so help me. Help me, God, to see You in all of this.

30

Linc

I yank open the door to David and Whitney's car so hard, I'm half afraid I've ripped it off the hinges. When I see it still works, I get in and slam it shut.

"What's the plan?" I ask, my eyes tracking everyone's frantic running around, trying to leave the campground behind. I have to keep myself talking, because if I examine my feelings too much, I will erupt in flames, which are closer to the surface than they've ever been.

"We will hide in California. I'll have Petra stay with the group and the plane. We can find an airport to meet up wherever they end up," David says.

I turn my eyes to the window, my insides a torrid mess. I've been torn from the one person I never wanted to be separated from again. Just when we tied our lives together, we're torn apart.

The only thing that keeps me from screaming at the top of my lungs in fury is that I'll be with Vela again in one short week. I stop myself from falling into the abyss of worry that something could happen to her. I can't think about that possibility. I've put my trust in Drew, Kane, and Elia to keep her safe.

No, I'm putting her in God's hands. God, please, I'm begging You. Keep my wife safe. Scramble the E.E.'s tracks. Don't let them find her or me. Keep us safe, I pray. Help us, God.

Once I've prayed my short prayer, I feel slightly better, but just as angry.

"Do you think the Extremists know she's the Chosen One?" I ask. My mind spins to figure out how they could. I thought we'd captured all the Extremists who attacked the Polar Bear. But it's possible someone escaped.

"I don't know. I can call Kane to find out," David offers.

"No, it's fine. Let him concentrate on getting Vela to safety. Where is he taking her?"

"He said Salt Lake City. They have a big airport your friends can fly right into. And there are small towns around it where they can hide."

I nod, agreeing with his choice. My heart feels shredded, but I shut down all emotion.

"I'd like to figure out a way to get mine and Vela's bags. When I reconnect with her, I'd like to give her things back."

"We can grab them now," Whitney says, and David turns the car around. We haven't gone far, so it's no trouble.

I settle into my seat, my thoughts tumbling on all the possible outcomes for this tragic day.

No, it's not tragic. Vela is safe. God, keep her safe.

After a harried trip to my unused honeymoon cabin to grab our bags, we head back out. David and Whitney leave me to my tumultuous thoughts, and the day passes quickly as we fly down the highway. Five hours later, I see we've arrived in San Diego. We eventually pull into a driveway of a house in the suburbs.

"This is my friend's house. He won't mind us staying here," David says, giving me a regretful look.

I get out of the car, pent up with all kinds of restless and angry emotions. I need a release, so instead of going in the house, I let myself into the fenced in back yard, thankful for the high fence.

An explanation for my actions isn't necessary, and I couldn't give one if I tried. I'm about to explode with flames, and I need a place to do that quickly. My emotions have never been so volatile. Not since I was young. I'm full of furious anger at leaving my new bride to hide somewhere I can't protect her.

Relieved to have an open place in the backyard, I take off Kane's suit jacket, throwing it to the ground. The shirt is next, since he doesn't wear clothes that are flame resistant. I raise my hands in the air and give off such a blazing hot stream of fire, even I wince.

I only give myself a moment before I drop my hands, panting. I have to admit the action has helped me get my head on straight.

I hold my chest, grasping at the hole that was made when I left Vela in her brothers' care. But, if I'm going to do what I can to keep her safe, I have to pull myself together. I'll call the others and let them know what's going on. We need to set up a rendezvous point, too.

I also need to get Vela a fake ID so she can travel incognito. We don't need a repeat of today. Scooping up the coat and shirt, I walk briskly inside, shaking off the rest of the smoke that lingers behind me. I enter the house, buttoning up my shirt when I find David and Whitney. They're in the living room and look up at me with concern.

"I'm fine," I say, embarrassed I had to let go like I did. "We need to get Vela a fake ID and a burner phone. Something that can't be traced."

David nods and holds his phone to his ear. I would ask my mother for help with this, but I'm not sure she'd be willing now that I've married against her wishes and embarrassed her in front of all the wedding guests. Frustration bubbles up, and I push it down. Irritation will cause me to make mistakes, and I can't afford that.

While David is on the phone, I pull out my phone and dial the Polar Bear's satellite phone, relieved it survived the devastating fire. Gary answers after five rings.

"Gary, how are all of you doing?"

"We're fine," he says, briskly. "We've found another campground a couple hours from where you were married and we're all bunkering down."

"And the plane?"

"In the same place. We're keeping it there since we're so close." He clears his throat. "Your mother has some, uh, conditions for allowing us to use it."

"What are they?" I growl.

He murmurs, with what sounds like regret, "She is demanding an apology."

"For what?" I grit out, rubbing my aching forehead.

"Linc, I think you know."

I heave a big sigh of anger and regret at lashing at my mom, both in equal measure. "Fine, I'll call her."

"Any news on Vela?" he asks.

"Kane and Drew are taking her to Salt Lake City or somewhere close. We'll be able to meet you all there."

"Got it. Where did you end up?"

"San Diego. That's it for now. And Gary?"

"Yeah?"

"Keep everyone safe. You have some of Vela's favorite people with you. She'll want them protected."

"Absolutely."

"Also, we need to give Vela a different name when referring to her in all communications," I make sure to mention.

"Okay, what do you want to call her?"

"Something different than what her fake ID will say," I answer, thinking fast. "How about Eve?"

"Sounds good to us."

"Keep the phone near you. I'll contact you to ensure it's safe for everyone to meet in Salt Lake City... and that Vela's safe. Once we're together, we'll figure out a plan of attack to unite the clans."

"Of course. I will. I'm actually getting a phone so we don't use this expensive one. Give me your number, and I'll call you as soon as I do."

I relay the digits.

"Gary, please ask everyone to pray we can stay under the radar. Especially Vela."

"We will. Stay safe, Linc."

I agree and we hang up, because I know every minute adds up on the satellite phone.

When I end the call, I look immediately to David and see that he's still on his phone.

Whitney gives me what looks like regret in her eyes. "I'm sorry, Linc. We should have thought to hide Vela's name sooner."

"It's my fault, too," I say, sighing. "I was in such a hurry to marry her, I didn't think our actions through. This is more my fault than anyone else's."

I look down, my chest burning again at her words. I take a moment to push down the impulse to set off more fire. I'm so angry at myself for putting Vela in danger like this. I should have known better. I'd like to place blame on someone, like the Extremists, but really this is my responsibility. Now, our wedding day is ruined because of my limited view. All I could see was her, and it shortsighted my protection of her.

I excuse myself to call my mother.

Her phone rings three times before my dad answers. "Linc?"

"Yes, Dad, it's me. Can I please talk to Mother?"

He hesitates. "Yes, she's right here."

I hear her ask who it is and when she answers, it's a full minute before she's on the line. "Yes?"

"Mother," I say, sighing. "I understand you're holding the plane hostage until I apologize?"

"Do you expect me to stand there and be insulted in front of all your guests without some repercussion?"

"Did you think about what I even said to you?"

She's silent for a beat. "It was ridiculous. Why would you need protecting from me?"

I decide to bare my soul. It's dangerous to do that with my mother, but I take the risk. "Because you can hurt me more than you realize."

She huffs. "How is that possible?"

"Are you serious?"

"Look, is this an apology or not?"

I blow up. "What should I apologize for more, Mother? Killing my sister or embarrassing you at my wedding?"

She's silent for so long I look down at my phone to see if she's still there. "You didn't kill your sister, your actions did," she says quietly.

"What's the difference?" I ask in a tired voice, worn out from all my strung-out emotions.

"Which one are you apologizing for?" she finally asks.

My mouth is open like a dying fish. I kind of feel like one. Like she just ripped me from the water, and I can't breathe. I ask hoarsely, "You want me to apologize for Olympia's death? The day of my wedding when my wife got torn from me? Are you really asking me that, Mother?"

"Yes."

Knowing that my friends need her plane is the only reason I choke out, "I apologize for both, then."

I hang up, hanging my head when sobs tear from me. I kneel on the ground, holding my head in my hands and miss Vela more now than I can possibly describe. I wish for her soothing hands, her sweet embrace. I raise my head and ask out loud, "Why, God? Why do You make me suffer like this?"

Tears sting my throat and stream down my face. I feel more helpless now than I ever have before. I failed in protecting my sister. I failed in protecting my wife. I can't help but think, *I'm worthless.*

In my anguish, I feel a cool wind caress my wet face. I turn my head to the side and hear a whisper, "You are loved."

I pop my eyes open, but no one's there. I close them again and wait in expectant silence to hear, *You are valued.*

I hang my head and let those words wash over me, soothing and comforting the ragged edges of my soul. I kneel there for some time thanking God for His words, for His healing presence.

Taking deep breaths through my nose for a moment, I collect myself. Wiping my eyes, I raise my head and rise from the ground feeling washed clean. I know that God has just healed the long gaping wound of my sister's death because of my mother's hateful words. He used Vela's absence and my mother's anger to bring me to the moment of release. *Thank you, God.* I can't change my mom, but I can do something about my thoughts. I no longer feel responsible for Olympia's death. While tragic, it wasn't my fault. God healed that deep wound.

I walk back into the house, knowing my eyes are red-rimmed. Whitney looks at me startled but doesn't say anything.

"Well," David says, hanging up his phone. "I've got someone working on fake IDs for you and Vela. We should get our hands on them in a day. And burner phones are easy enough. I'll go out and get four tonight. What did you find out?" He notices the look on my face. "Son, are you all right?"

I nod tiredly. "I really am. My mother and I just had a hard conversation. One that's been due for a long time."

"Now, she decides to hash out something with you?" His face transforms in anger.

"Well, let's just say it's been on the surface of our feelings for a long time. It just became glaringly obvious now."

David gusts a sigh. "Well, I'm sorry. You look like...well, like you've been through a lot."

"I have. But you know how God is. He turned a truly horrendous conversation into one of healing. Well," I modify. "After I hung up, I mean. My mother hasn't changed." I sigh.

Whitney stands up and puts her hand on my arm. "I'm sorry, Linc. Your mom seems...well, hard to be around." Sympathy swims in her eyes.

"She is. Always has been. God is bigger than even her hurtful words, though."

David stands and walks up to me. He puts his hand on my shoulder. "God is good. I'm sorry you had to deal with that, but I'm happy you seem to be okay."

"I really am. She wouldn't allow us to use the plane until I apologized, and let's just say my apology covered all the bases for things she's held against me."

Whitney puts her arm around me. "We're thankful for you, Linc."

I turn into her and enfold her in a hug, fighting back more tears. David pats my back, and I appreciate marrying into this family more and more. I finally pull away.

"Gary, by the way, says they're all safe. They're only a couple hours from the first campsite. We're giving Vela a code name for when we refer to her in communications. We're calling her Eve. What name did you give her for the fake ID?" I ask with a shaky breath.

He looks sheepish. "I don't know what my guy is going to come up with. I told him to choose."

"Make sure it isn't Eve," I request.

He nods. "Would you like to go and rest?"

I nod wearily. I'm suddenly exhausted.

Whitney points to the other side of the house, where I'm guessing there are bedrooms. I make my way to one.

Hobbling to the first bedroom I find, I stumble inside and blearily undo two buttons on my shirt before giving up any hope of removing it. I'm too tired. Dropping on the bed, I kick off my shoes and then fall back onto the comforter.

My last thought before I succumb to sleep is that Vela should have been lying next to me, her hair all over my pillow. We should have been enjoying our wedding night. I fight back a growing feeling of frustration before everything goes black.

I wake up with a start, dreaming I had married Vela and then we'd been forced apart. It takes a minute before I realize that's exactly what happened yesterday. I moan and rub my eyes.

Getting up, I check my phone before I realize Vela doesn't have a phone yet. I'll call Kane and ask him to get her one, wherever they're holed up.

I go to the bathroom and brush my teeth, wondering if Vela is awake yet. I look at myself in the mirror and study the man reflected back at me. My eyes have dark circles, despite the hours of sleep I got, and I look....sad.

Well, I am. I miss Vela more than my breath.

Walking out to the living room, I find David and Whitney talking quietly. They look up and give me small smiles.

"Good morning," I say and go over to the kitchen to find a pot of brewed coffee waiting for me. I hurry and make myself a cup, needing caffeine immediately. It's been weeks since I've had coffee, and I burn my mouth on my first sip.

I bring the mug back to the living room and set it down on the coffee table to let it cool.

"Want to go over some logistics of Vela's mission?" David asks.

Wishing more than anything Vela was here to go over these details, I push the pain of being separated down and focus on the conversation.

"Sure. Before Vela and I left the Polar Bar to find her...other parents," I say with some hesitation. They don't seem to mind me mentioning that Vela has other parents, so I continue, "Gary, Rick, Hannah, Andy, and I discussed that if Vela starts with the Grand Elders, they can direct her to places within their territories to give her message."

"Okay, who are you starting with?" Whitney asks.

I contain a sigh. "I hoped to begin with my mother, but she's proving...difficult to work with."

David gives a snort of incredulity. "She doesn't want to support her own son's Intended?"

"She's had plans for me to marry someone of her choosing for as long as I can remember. And," I say, rubbing my neck, "she doesn't believe Vela is the Chosen Child."

"What?" Whitney's eyes are hard as she leans in to ask, "Can you please repeat that?"

I fist my hand. "I don't know why. She's going to need some convincing. We might need to make the Festans the last stop."

"That's ridiculous," Whitney spits out and turns her head, staring off into the distance. "Wait," she says, turning her head to me slowly. "What if we start with the Festans? Just not in her area?"

"It would be a waste of time," I disagree, shaking my head. "She would counteract anything we do. No, we'll have to save the Festans for last."

That last sentence burns as I say it. The fact that my own clan will be against Vela is more than I can stand. I try not to allow resentment cloud my thoughts. I ask God for clarity and say, "I say we begin with Vela's own clan."

Whitney's face brightens. "She's in Borean territory, but a short car ride will bring her back into Gyan land. And it's not far from the Gyan Grand Elder. That could work."

"What then? Where should she go after that?" David asks.

"I think we should make that first step our priority and focus on that. Let the rest happen organically." I say with certainty.

"That's ridiculous. We need a plan," David argues.

"Maybe he's right, David," Whitney says. "Once we convince one of the four clans that Vela is the Chosen Child, news will spread like wildfire. We'll know what our next step is after that. The Gyan Grand Elder can give us his opinion on which clan to target next."

"We might not need his help," I say, after taking a sip of my now cooled coffee. "If I know how word spreads, that one clan might be all we need. We can unite the entire Elemental race with her starting with the Gyans. With social media, our job could be finished by the time Vela is through touring through one Gyan state."

David fidgets in his seat, his excitement building. "Do you really think so? She won't have to show her powers to the other clans?"

"She can, but the internet will do that for us. Every clan in America and beyond will have already seen what she can do. This is our plan. Vela's notoriety. Let her legend spread by what she does first."

Whitney sits back, looking awed. "You really think it will be that easy?"

"It won't be easy, no," I say, shaking my head. "Vela has her work cut out for her. We need to get her to the Gyan Grand Elder. Once she shows him her powers and convinces him of her heritage and how she fulfills the prophecies, the next plan will be enacted."

"What's that?" David asks, his face skeptical.

"We'll get a place where a large group of Elementals can gather. She'll show off what she can do and from there, it will go viral."

David rubs his day-old beard. "That part won't be easy. We're going to have a large gathering of only Elementals? How will we prevent humans from entering?"

"It will have to be a private event. We can even ticket it and make some money to help cover our travel costs. Give them a show."

"How will we get them in there?" Whitney asks.

"That's the difficult part. But, once we have the Gyan Grand Elder on our side, he'll help. One word from him and other Gyan Elders across the country will learn about the Chosen Child. Hundreds of Elementals will come to us."

David sits back, folding his arms, a contemplative look on his face. "That could work."

"It *will* work," I promise as I lean forward. "One show from Vela in a contained space and every Gyan will do our job for us. We'll have to hide her to prevent a mob from coming to get her."

"You're a genius," Whitney breathes.

I give a short laugh. "It wasn't all me. Like I said, others at the Polar Bear gave their input. But we all agree. It's the best way."

"And Vela is on board with all of this?" David asks.

I nod. "Of course. She knows the power of a whispered rumor. This will be a wildfire. It will be hard to contain. That's what we need to be planning. How to hide her from overzealous Elementals and Extremists."

David grabs his head. "This is more than my head can hold. I'm still in shock that Vela is the Chosen Child."

"That's what will happen across the country and the world. But once the fire starts, we need to be prepared to move her and get her safely to places that need further proof."

"Do you really think just by showing her powers, she'll convince Elementals to put aside centuries of prejudices and hate for other clans?" David asks.

Rubbing my chin I say, "We're going to need some good speeches for Vela, which she'll help write, so it'll come naturally for her. We have someone in our group who's already offered to write some material for her, so that's a start. We could use a PR team."

David nods. "I can get you some help with that. I know a guy who runs a great firm in Denver. I think we can get his crew on board."

"That will be perfect. The sooner you can get them writing, the better."

Now that the plan has been explained, it's just a waiting game for me to see my bride.

31

Vela

I wake up with crusty eyes on Elia's lap. The car has stopped, and Elia is gently shaking me with a worried look on her face. I snap awake.

"What's wrong?"

She smiles sadly. "Nothing other than this is your wedding night, and we're in the middle of nowhere with no groom."

My chest crushes in at her words, and I moan.

She rushes to apologize. "I'm sorry Vels. I didn't mean to remind you, but I didn't want you thinking Extremists were on our tail or anything."

"I think I would have preferred that," I mumble, swatting my hair out of my face. Jack sits up and when he moves to sit over my lap, whining softly, I allow him.

"I know, boy. Daddy should be here, too," I say with anguish coursing through me. I bury my head into his neck and breathe in his scent. It's always calmed me down before, but even his scent does nothing for my fractured heart.

"He's been crying since you fell asleep," Elia says, rubbing Jack's head.

"He always knows when I'm upset. Where are we? And where are Drew and Kane?" I finally realize they're not in the vehicle, but I can't see anything. With no outside lights, darkness permeates the area. In the moonlight, I can see outlines of trees and a house in front of us, but that's it.

"We're at a rental home," Elia says. "We didn't want to go to a hotel, so I found us this place on my phone."

"And no one can find us with our names?" I ask, worried. I hold Jack to my chest, wishing I could see where we are.

"We found this cabin outside of Salt Lake City and used a fake ID to rent it. We're safe." Elia promises, her voice determined.

Ever since I got torn from my husband on our wedding day, I struggle to believe her.

The driver's side door opens, and Kane sticks his head in. "We should be safe here. Come on in," he says, his voice breathless. He sounds like he just finished with a run. I'm proved right when he says, "Drew and I just ran the perimeter of the house and its yard. There's no one in sight of the cabin."

"We could be tracked here, and there's no one around to even see if something happens to us," I say, my voice rising.

"Vela, don't worry," Elia rushes to say, her hand on my arm. "I'm a computer genius remember? I made Kane and myself fake IDs ages ago that we used to book this house. No one knows we're here. And they won't find us, either."

Why does Elia need a fake ID? I wonder. *Oh right, because she's a spy.* Worry for her comes over me, and I struggle with what to say. My emotions feel so scattered, I can only blink around. Elia takes my hand. "Come on, let's get you settled inside. You need rest."

"That's all I've had," I protest weakly, but allow her to lead me out of the car. Commanding Jack to stay by me is my only thought as we walk into the small cabin in the middle of nowhere. Jack immediately goes to investigate all the rooms.

The cabin is nothing to write home about, but it's cozy. It would have been perfect if it was just me and Linc. I somehow hold back tears, glad to spare my already swollen eyes.

Looking helplessly around, I walk to the couch and sit down, clenching my hands to keep from tearing my hair out.

How did I get here? Why am I the Chosen Child that everyone is hunting? Why can't I just be normal?

"Come on, let's get your hair down so you're more comfortable," Elia suggests.

I follow her numbly into a bedroom. I sit down on the bed, and Elia sits next to me and starts picking out bobby pins one at a time. "What are you thinking about right now?" she asks.

"I'm thinking, why am I the Chosen Child? Why couldn't it be someone else?"

"Now that's just the thing I don't want you thinking about. Come on, Vels. Don't go down that road. This is one hiccup that you can get over." She pulls more bobby pins from my updo, making slow but steady progress.

I narrow my eyes at her. "I'm married, Elia. This is my *wedding night, and I'm alone.*"

"Well, that's only partly true. You're not really alone."

I sigh deeply. "I know that, Elia, but I just wanted my first night with Linc, the most romantic night of my life, to be tonight. But that was taken from me. Now I'm spending my wedding night with my brothers and my best friend. I just didn't expect it to happen like this." A tear slips down my cheek and I let it. I can't hold back anymore.

"Hey," Elia says, putting her hand on mine. "Don't fall into a pity party. Nothing good can come from it. But," she says, looking into my eyes, "I understand. You were robbed of a beautiful night with your husband. It's horrible. It really is. For what it's worth, I'm sorry this happened."

I slump as she pulls the last of the pins from my hair. She runs her hands through my hair, shaking out my curls. I get up slowly and make my way out to the living room where Kane is kneeling at the fireplace.

I sit down on the couch and lean my head back. "I've always wondered about my wedding night, what it would be like, you know?"

"Yeah," Elia says, sitting next to me, eyeing Kane, who's trying to pretend he's not hearing our conversation as he lights a fire. She says, "I've thought about mine a lot, too." And Kane stiffens.

I can't help but snort.

Kane turns and gives me a scathing look, like he knows what I'm laughing about, but Elia only laughs at his expression.

"Oh, don't give her that look," Elia scolds. "At least she laughed. If it was at your expense, so what?"

He mumbles something and turns back to his work.

Drew leans down and pets Jack's face saying, "Vela, we would never have wanted this for you. It makes me sick with rage that we had to pull you away from Linc, but you're safe right now. We all promise that we will make it our life's mission to get you reunited with your husband. I'm sorry, sis." He cups my cheek, and I dissolve in tears again. How can I possibly have any moisture left in my body?

"Thank you, Drew," I say in a broken voice.

"Hey, look. Tell me things you loved about today," Elia says gently.

The edges of my fractured heart soften a little as I think back to all that I will never forget. "The look in Linc's eyes when I walked down the aisle. At first, I thought he was laughing, but he wasn't. Just really smiling. That will forever be imprinted in my mind. Like I was his north star. That one look held our future, our life together, a promise of our story."

"Okay," Elia says with a smile. "That's a good start. What else?"

I smile painfully. "Saying I do. I think I said it like five times."

Elia laughs. "That's awesome, Vels."

"Yeah," I say and look down, remembering more. "When he said his vows, his hands got really hot, like he was holding in his fire. It showed me he was really feeling it."

"Go on," Elia urges.

"I love that Jack and all of you were there. I was willing to marry Linc anywhere, anytime, but the fact that all of you were with me made it so special."

"Keep going," she softly urges.

I smile sadly. "Let's see. Linc gave me the best kiss when we were announced as man and wife."

Kane groans as he gets up and goes into the kitchen. Drew turns away, holding his hands over his ears. I laugh, feeling slightly better. "Well, it was good."

"Hey, give her that, guys. Let her relive her happiest moments," Elia calls after them.

"It really was happy. I just wish..." I trail off, sighing, falling into the pity party Elia warned me against.

"Let's go to bed. It's really late," Elia says with a yawn.

"What time is it, anyway?" I ask.

"Almost midnight," Kane says in a tired voice.

For the sake of my brothers and my best friend, I nod and get up to find a bedroom. It looks like there are three, and I'm glad. I need to be alone tonight.

Jack follows me to the bedroom where Elia took my hair down, and I shut the door, leaning on it with my forehead, suddenly completely exhausted. Jack whines softly and nudges my hand with his wet nose.

That does it.

With a sob, I drop to my knees and bury my face in his neck. I cry for Linc, for our lost night, just him. I miss him so much, my chest aches down to the deepest parts of me.

Linc texted Kane and said for us not to call him, in case his phone is being tracked somehow. He planned to call with a burner phone but hasn't yet.

I wish more than anything that I could hear his voice right now. I'd do just about anything for that. All energy seeps out with my tears, and I fall to the floor, curling in on myself.

Oh, God, help me get through this night.

Jack, who's crying now, lies down next to me, and nudges my face with his nose. Unable to acknowledge even him in my grief, I sob uncontrollably.

God, please. I want Linc to hold me. I can't get through this night alone.

All I can do in this moment is hold my aching chest and cry. I don't think I've experienced this much pain before, except when I thought I'd lost Linc. That was a different kind of pain, horrible, yet still all-consuming. And this is like that, nearly as painful. Our souls were just joined in marriage and now we're apart. It's gut wrenching because I know he's somewhere, just not here. And for all I know, he's in as much danger as I am.

Protect him, Lord. Why do we have to be separated?

My sobs continue, and the pain is so real and deep, I think I'm going to faint. Then an impossible thought enters my mind.

Jesus, hold me. Linc can't be here, I know that. But, Lord, I ask You to hold me since he can't. Give me the comfort and peace only You can give. Please Lord, hold me.

I repeat my prayer over and over until it becomes a mantra in my mind.

As I lie curled up on the cold floor, wetting the carpet with my tears, I feel a warmth at the base of my spine. I still, holding in my sobs, and open my eyes in the dark, trying to find the source of the heat.

Am I imagining it? No, I can feel it.

My eyes widen as the warmth travels. It slowly works its way up my spine until it's covered. Then, the most inviting, loving heat moves again. This time, it spreads across my back, enveloping me on both sides. I'm so entranced, I have no idea what's happening. I'm surrounded by the heavenly warmth, like a warm cocoon. Then I realize the Source. I lie in complete, stunned silence. I forget to breathe.

Jesus answered my prayer. He is hugging me.

I take a sudden breath and relish the healing comfort God is providing. I've never felt so loved and cared for. New tears come, but this time in joy.

Thank you, Father. Thank you for holding me when I need You. You are a Divine Father, and I thank you.

I fall asleep to the sound of my voice thanking Jesus.

I open my eyes to a bright morning. My mind's muddled with sleep, but then I remember yesterday and what happened. Expecting crushing grief to immobilize me again, I wait for it. When only a lingering pain follows, I frown.

Then, I remember what the Lord did for me to heal me of my debilitating pain.

I gasp and squeeze my eyes shut.

Of Father, thank you for healing and comforting me last night. Thank you, Lord.

Opening my eyes, I realize I'm on the bed. Looking around in confusion, I wonder how I got from the floor to the bed?

Kane or Drew must have put me here last night. My heart warms with thanks to my brothers. I push off the covers and put my feet on the floor.

Thanking God again for His miracle, I straighten my sleep-wrinkled dress and go to find a bathroom to freshen up before I settle in for a long, boring wait to see my husband.

32

Rayne

33

Linc

I've waited long enough to see my bride, and I'm over the moon that I finally get to see her this afternoon, if everything goes well. After hiding out in San Diego for what felt like an interminably long time, we finally accomplished all the essential tasks to keep Vela safe. David got us burner phones, and mine and Vela's fake IDs are safely in my pocket. Both sets of Vela's parents and Adele now have fake IDs too, since the Extremists have, or will be tracking them also.

We landed in Utah and met up with the Canadian group at another campground closer to Vela in Salt Lake City. It's funny, they've lived so long off the grid, it's like they need a little bit of home, which is why they keep choosing campgrounds. The fact that they're cheaper to stay at is also another reason.

And one thing is for sure, they're all just as ready to see Vela as I am. Adele, Tonya, and the rest of the Girls, I'm calling them, Vela's friends from the Polar Bear, are asking constantly for updates.

It seems everyone is ready for Vela to be safe in their midst and to start her mission.

I've barely resisted the impulse to go find Vela myself and make sure she's safe. Sometimes it's taken hourly reports from David and Vela to keep me in check. Anger has been ever present inside me, fuming, blistering my chest until all I can think about is how I've been robbed of time with Vela. This last week has been one of the most painful of my life, to say the least.

I was able to speak with Vela on the phone once we got burner phones, but it's not the same. I can tell she's struggling and missing me, too. She told me, though, of a miraculous moment with the Lord who helped soothe her pain. I shared with her how God healed me of my pain over Olympia, too. I also told her about my painful conversation with my mother, which prompted that healing.

It's pretty incredible how God will use any situation to heal you of long-held pain. Prayer has helped me get through the week, too, but I'm fighting feelings of frustration that God could have prevented this whole thing. Only Psalm 102:13 has cooled my rage. *You will arise and have compassion on Zion, for it is time to show favor to her; the appointed time has come.* I just know that it's our time for favor. Today is the appointed time for Vela and me to be reunited, never to be separated again. I pray not, anyway.

Vela and I agreed that I would wait at the campground, since my flight came in so much earlier than I thought it would. Her crew is racing to get here, but they're driving. She wanted me to be comfortable while I waited. But I can't keep still. I'm pacing in the parking lot, keeping an eye on every car that passes.

I stop when Rayne walks up to me, reaching out to shake my hand. I return his greeting easily.

"How are you?" he asks, a sympathetic look in his eyes.

"I'm hanging in there," I say with a frown.

"Hey, for what it's worth, congratulations, man." He says it with such sincerity; I look at him with surprise.

"I appreciate that."

"Honestly, I don't know how you've managed being apart from your Intended, especially now that she's also your wife."

I run my hands over my beard. "It hasn't been easy."

"Yeah, Adele ignored me for a whole week, and I thought I was going to lose it. And that was being near her."

I huff a laugh, surprised I can. "She did? Because of you sleeping in front of her tent? She's still mad about that?"

"Not anymore. I may have been a little overprotective. She was also, uh, jealous about what happened with Vela." He looks very uncomfortable bringing that topic up.

A car approaches, and I stiffen, looking to see if it's Kane's car. When it's not his, I slump.

I give Rayne back my attention. He says, "If I've learned anything from the Bible you gave me, is that God is with you, no matter where you are. Or where Vela is. He's with you both."

I crack a smile. "You're right. I'm happy to hear you've been reading my Bible."

"I have. Do you want it back?"

"No, keep it. I can get another one."

Rayne gives me a searching look. "I'm sure you want to know why God allowed this."

I squint my eye to look at him, because the sun is bright. "I did ask God that."

"And what did He say?"

I hold his gaze and say, "To trust Him. No matter what. Trust His way and no one else's."

He huffs a laugh. "That's not easy to do."

"No, it wasn't." I look out at the street leading to the campground. "But I do trust Him. God knows our ways better than anyone."

Rayne is silent for a beat. "I want to thank you for introducing me to God. And for sharing what you have today. It means a lot."

I put my hand on his shoulder. "It's not real unless we're authentic. And, you need to know, your life has value. Don't waste it."

"I won't."

Andy approaches us, his voice breaking up the conversation. "I can't imagine what you're going through. We all feel for you and are rooting for your reunion to happen soon. If I was separated from Hannah on our wedding day, I don't think I would have handled it as admirably as you have."

"I appreciate that." My phone dings with a message, and I look down to see that Vela texted me.

Wife: Twenty minutes away, my love.

Linc: I cannot wait that long. Make it five. I might be able to handle that.

Wife: Where are you?

Linc: Waiting in the parking lot.

Wife: Perfect.

Linc: No, that's you.

Wife: Impossible.

Linc: Why?

Wife: Because that's how I feel about you. It's impossible to have two perfect people.

Linc: ETA?

Wife: Nineteen minutes.

Linc: Too long.

"Linc?"

I start when I realize Hannah has tried getting my attention a couple of times, by the expectant look in her eye.

"I'm sorry, yes?" I ask, my eyes re-scanning the road leading into the campground, hoping Vela's time is wrong.

"Is she almost here?" Hannah asks. There's a tightness in her eyes that wasn't there before.

"Nineteen minutes. Hannah, is everything all right?"

"Well, a few other people have fallen sick. And Greta is still not bouncing back. She's laid up with a fever."

Alarm pounds through me. "Greta is still sick?" Vela will not like that at all.

"It seems like she's picked up a virus, and the others, too. I can't seem to cure it. It's going to have to run its course."

I frown. "Is that common for Gyans to not be able to heal a virus?"

Her forehead scrunches in thought. "No, it's not common. But some viruses are so widespread throughout the body that it's impossible to get it all. This one is particularly vicious."

"What are the symptoms?"

"Fever, mostly. But it's making her too weak to take in much liquid, which is concerning. She is drinking and eating a little, though. Hopefully, she'll turn a corner soon."

"Thank you for letting me know. I'll tell Vela."

She puts her hand on my arm. "Don't tell her until tomorrow. Give her a day to be happy and reunited with you. I don't want to spoil this day for her."

I nod, reluctantly. Only because it seems like Greta is in no immediate life-threatening danger. Vela will be furious with me for not telling her, but I'll respect Hannah's wishes.

She pats my arm and walks toward her cabin.

I lean against the side of the lease office and pray for little Greta. I pray for instant healing. Then I think back over what Rayne shared. I thank God for transforming my relationship with my would-be killer and for his new faith.

I send Vela another text, and when I don't get a reply; I start pacing again.

Longing fills me when I realize that I'm going to finally get my night with my bride. I'm happy we have a cabin to ourselves.

I get a text from Vela and my heart stops.

Bride: I'm here.

Looking around wildly, I see her beautiful blonde hair peeking through the window of a car just pulling in. Nearly wild with excitement, I bounce on my toes and run to where I expect Kane will park. Vela sees me through the window and her stunning face glows with excitement and happiness at seeing me. My heart jumps into my throat.

She opens the door before the car stops, and I'm there waiting. In a rush, I pick her up and swing her around, burying my head in her neck, breathing in her scent that's just for me, sweet honey-butter and roses. I inhale deeply.

"Baby," I say over and over. I squeeze her so hard, I'm surprised she doesn't complain, but her grip is just as tight. I relish the feeling of having her in my arms.

"Oh, Linc," she breathes. "I've missed you so much."

I hold her for one more second before I set her gently on her feet. Cradling her face, I look over her features. Two tears are trailing down her cheeks, and I gently wipe them away with my thumbs. "I never want to be parted from you again," I breathe. I drink in her cute nose, her baby blue eyes, rubbing my thumb over her chin.

She shakes her head, loosing another tear. "Neither do I."

Not able to wait another second, I crash my lips to her and kiss her so soundly, I don't even think of breathing. Neither does she, apparently, because she returns my kiss. I enjoy the flavor of her lips as much as I enjoy her scent.

I barely notice laughing and clapping, but I ignore it, as I'd much rather continue greeting my gorgeous wife. It's Vela who breaks away, breathlessly laughing, tucking her head into my chest. I kiss her head and hug her again, holding her as close to me as I can.

Jack jumps up on my leg, and I pet his head distractedly.

I finally look up and see our entire group is celebrating. Rayne is in the front with Adele, clapping and cheering. Vela's Girls are all whistling and clapping loudly. James and Sandy are beaming huge smiles. Petra nods at me, which I return. We're surrounded by happy faces.

"Are you real?" Vela asks into my shirt.

"I am. I'm here, baby." I lay my cheek on her head and enjoy this moment.

Vela leans back, looking around. "My parents, are they here?"

"Which ones?"

"Any, all?"

I point them out grudgingly, knowing she'll leave my arms to greet them. I'm proved right when she spots James, Sandy, and Adele first. I allow her out of my arms so she can go to them. Once they've each hugged her, Vela's Girls have had enough of waiting. Tonya jumps into Vela's arms as soon as they're free. The rest follow. David and Whitney get their hugs, too and I hope Vela doesn't worry about not seeing Hannah, Andy, and Greta. She really is going to kill me for not telling her that her favorite little girl is sick.

I've had enough of her out of my arms, so I walk up to her and tuck her into my side. She happily settles there, her shining eyes adoring me.

I lean in and kiss her softly. She kisses me back, and I suddenly need to be alone with her.

Breaking away from our gentle kiss, I look up at our audience.

"I think we're going to head to our cabin now," I say with such a feeling of satisfaction, nothing could dampen it.

Vela tucks her face back into my shirt, and I kiss her head. "They'll forgive us for wanting time alone. You do want to be alone, right?" I ask, holding my breath.

She nods vigorously.

That does it.

"Kane, take care of Jack for us?" I ask not wanting to worry about any other needs but Vela's and mine.

"Of course," he says and comes and takes Jack by the collar.

I take a moment to say to him, Drew, and Elia, "Thank you for keeping her safe."

They nod, and without another word, I escort Vela to the car. Our cabin is a fair walk away, and I want to get there as soon as possible. I'm not wasting any more time on travel or goodbyes. They'll forgive us for wanting to leave quickly.

Vela leaves my arms to get into the car, and I miss her touch already. I drive as quickly as possible without running anyone over and find our cabin easily.

"Linc, I don't have my bag," Vela suddenly exclaims, getting out of the car.

"You can use mine," I answer and take her by the hand, pulling her to the door. She comes with me easily once she laughs and agrees.

"I'll get it for you tomorrow. Tonight, it's just us, no one else." I unlock the door and turn to swing her up in my arms. She squeals a laugh, then her lips are on my neck and all thought abandons me. I step in and don't even look around. My lips are on hers immediately.

I somehow remember to shut the door as I carry my bride inside to have our belated wedding night. Finally, in each other's arms.

34

Vela

I wake up wrapped up in two strong arms and smile as I snuggle into Linc, happier than I've been in a long time.

Linc's phone blares a ringtone that I vow to change immediately. If he wants it to wake the dead, then he successfully picked the right one. One of his arms that I'd prefer remained around me reaches, fumbling until he grabs the phone.

"Hello?" he asks groggily, tightening his remaining arm around me.

I hear a voice mumbling into the phone but can't catch the conversation.

"Okay. We'll be right there," Linc says in an annoyed voice and ends the call.

My stomach drops because I was in a glow just thinking about spending the whole day alone with my new husband. "We have to go, really?" I ask, and I know he can hear the pout in my voice.

He drops the phone on the bed, and reaches for me, tucking me even more tightly against his chest. Kissing my neck, he mumbles, "Unfortunately."

His kisses tickle the sensitive skin of my neck, and I giggle.

"We really do have to go," he says, groaning and then pulls away, leaving the bed and going into the bathroom.

I lie there, feeling abandoned for a moment.

"Please Vela, I know this isn't what either of us wanted, but we have to get ready," he says through the door.

Remembering my mission, I swallow my complaints and decide not to be difficult, so I swing my legs out of the bed. I rummage through his bag attempting to find something of Linc's that could possibly fit me when Linc calls, "Elia dropped your bag off. It's at the door."

Happy to have my stuff returned to me, I go retrieve it.

"We need to get going, so try to hurry if you can."

I obey, a little perturbed to be so rushed this morning. I'm dressed and brushing my hair by the time Linc leaves the bathroom, looking freshly showered.

"I'm sorry we have to rush out so soon," he says as he rummages through his bag.

"I'm not happy about it, but I guess it's important?"

"Yes, unfortunately, it is," he says gruffly, sitting on the bed to put on his shoes.

I take my morning bag into the bathroom and finish getting ready in there. "Are you going to tell me why?"

He looks up at me, and his eyes tighten. "I need to leave this bedroom, so I'll have a clear head to explain anything," he says in a gruff voice and leaves to go into the living room.

I smile, glad I'm not the only one frustrated that our morning has been cut short.

Once I'm satisfied with my hair, I grab my jacket and join Linc. The air is getting cooler, the later it gets in October, so I'm happy to have my winter gear.

Linc looks up when I enter the living area, and he rubs his beard, looking away. "Sorry about earlier," he says with a crooked grin. "You're just too tempting. I needed some distance between us to even attempt to form a coherent thought."

I finger the couch, wanting at least a kiss before we go. "So, where are we going?" I look up at him underneath my lashes and see something in him snap.

In two strides, he's in front of me, capturing my lips with his. I smile against his mouth and wrap my arms around his neck. I kiss him blissfully for a solid minute when he switches his attention from my mouth to my neck. "Finally, this is what I've wanted since I woke up," I say breathlessly. I run my fingers through his soft beard that is one of my favorite features of his.

"We really do need to leave," he says between kisses.

"Can't we have a few minutes?" And with those words, Linc wrenches himself away, and he's on the other side of the room, breathing heavily, hanging his head.

I stand, all my nerve endings firing fire and ice, panting, too.

"If this wasn't so important, I wouldn't care what they have to tell us. But we really need to meet with leadership."

"Wait. Have we decided who's on our leadership team?" I ask, effectively cooling off thinking that over.

He grabs the keys off a side table and waits at the door for me to join him. Reluctantly, I trudge over, wishing more than anything that we could have this day to ourselves.

"They've elected themselves, and when you see, you'll understand. There are no surprises."

When he opens the door, he looks longingly at me, and I'm tempted to drag him inside so we can have some time alone before all this important business starts. When he looks away quickly, I change my mind. If he thinks we need to leave this urgently, it must be really serious.

He drives us toward another cabin, and I notice it's ten in the morning. I didn't realize we'd slept quite that late.

That's what a blissful night with Linc will do.

"Last night was..." I say in an awed tone.

"Perfect?" Linc finishes with a small smile. He raises his eyebrow at me, and I blush.

"Yes. I loved every minute of it," I tell him and look his face over, memorizing this moment. He looks as satisfied as I do, and I don't want to forget his expression.

"Oh, believe me when I say I loved it, too. I just wish we could have had more time together this morning," he says, pressing his lips together.

I reach for his hand. "We'll have every morning to wake up together for the rest of our lives. And we'll be sure not to sleep in."

He blows out a breath, saying, "Yeah, absolutely."

We park at the meeting cabin, but before we get out of the car, I say, "I didn't get to see Greta or Hannah yesterday. They are here, right?"

A shadow comes over Linc's face, which he masks immediately.

My hackles go up, and I ask, "Where are they?"

"They're here," he's quick to say. "Greta's just a little under the weather."

"Greta's sick? What's wrong?" My heart lurches.

"She's just running a low-grade fever. It's nothing to be worried about."

"Hannah isn't worried, is she?"

"Well, a little, but she's getting fluids in her."

"What? She couldn't drink fluids before?" My heart races.

"She is able to drink, she's just a little tired."

I get out of the car slowly, unable to keep from worrying. There are going to be so many germs her body has never experienced living off the grid. I hope she fights off whatever has her sick. Did my airport burger make her system work harder than it should have?

"Why didn't you tell me yesterday?" I ask in a hurt voice.

"I'm sorry, baby. Hannah asked me not to tell you so you could enjoy our time together."

Somewhat appeased, but wildly worried, Linc takes my hand, and we walk to the front door. I try to get my thoughts in order to meet with the team.

He must be able to sense I feel uneasy about this meeting, because he assures me, "Don't worry, you'll do fine."

"I just don't want it to look like I value one person's opinion over another's."

"You won't. Don't worry." He squeezes my hand, then knocks on the door.

It doesn't surprise me when Petra opens it. When she sees me, she huffs and reaches for my hand, pulling me in.

"It's about time you two got here." Her grip is like iron as she leads me to the living room.

I take a moment to look around and immediately find my parents, all four of them, sitting together. Gary and Rick sit next to their wives. Gene and Jerry are talking quietly together. Grant and Mary give me kind smiles. Rayne and Adele are holding hands, which I'm glad to see since she was mad at him last I heard. Kane and Elia sit together, and she winks at me then wiggles her eyebrows at Linc. I laugh, not able to help it. But when I don't see Hannah or Andy, I turn to Linc with a worried look.

"She's okay," he whispers. "Don't worry."

I give him an incredulous look. How could I not worry? I send up a prayer for my sweet little friend.

"Greet everyone, girl. You have an image to establish," Petra growls under her breath.

I straighten my spine, determined to give a good impression to my leaders. I make sure to look everyone in the eye and nod at each of them, greeting them all.

My acknowledgement of everyone seems to satisfy Petra, and she lets go of me, gesturing to a seat in the middle of a circle of chairs. Linc follows and sits next to me.

I take a deep breath once I'm seated. "Thank you, everyone, for being here. This is a big commitment, and it means a lot to me that you've stepped into the role of my leadership team."

Linc gives me a small smile and says to the room, "Sorry we were late. Now, what news do you have?"

David clears his throat. "We've gotten in touch with Alex Colbourn, the Gyan Grand Elder. He's ready to meet you in two days."

I snap my head to Linc. "I thought we were starting our tour with your mother." As the Festan Grand Elder and his own mother, it makes the most sense.

He gives me a short, hard shake of his head. "She's not being cooperative. We're going to have to start with the Gyans. You'll get more support in that corner."

I stifle my disappointment. I knew Elizabeth didn't want me as a daughter-in-law, but is she really fighting that I'm the Chosen Child? I shake my head. "Okay, so where does he live?"

"We don't have far to go, thankfully," David says. "Alex lives just east of here."

Petra nods. "Good. It's not going to be easy to find lodging for all thirty of us as we travel. Let's stay here as long as possible."

"We need to finish the schedule for Vela's security team before she goes anywhere," Gary says with a significant look around the room. "We need her safe."

Elia speaks up, "Her cyber identity is ironclad. The E.E. won't find her again."

"We definitely don't need another repeat of their wedding night," Petra says with a hard look around.

Everyone nods, and I sit back in my seat, unease worming around my stomach.

"We have some changes to make to her protection detail," Petra says. "Unfortunately, a few more of us have come down with whatever virus is going around. I'll have the new list ready by this afternoon."

I sit up. "More people are sick?" I look at Linc. "Why didn't you tell me?"

He grimaces. "I didn't want you to worry too much."

"Worry *too* much? What's the matter with everyone?"

"It's only about ten of us," Petra says, giving me a look like I need to calm down. "They are minor symptoms for now, but we expect it's the flu."

I settle a little. The flu is not fun, but it's usually treatable.

Whitney assures me, "It's just a low-grade fever and fatigue right now. We'll keep a close eye on everyone. Don't worry, please, Vela."

I nod, hating that poor little Greta's introduction to the U.S. is a nasty virus.

"So," Linc says, re-capturing my attention. "Once you meet with the Gyan Grand Elder, we'll eventually set up a large gathering of Elementals so they can see you for themselves."

"You mean see my powers?" I ask. I try to shake off the uncomfortable pinch in my stomach. I'm suddenly swarmed with unanswerable questions.

Will they believe me? Can I actually convince millions to give up their ingrained prejudices and choose peace?

"Yes. Don't worry. Grant is a former public relations manager and is happy to help you write your speeches."

I look over at Grant and give him a tight smile.

My stomach drops as I think of speaking to a large group of potentially hostile people. Sweat breaks out on my forehead.

Linc reaches over and puts his hand on my knee. "You can do this, Vela. It's important that a lot of Elementals see and hear you, so they can spread the word."

"Right," I say with a shuddering breath. I need to make a *stadium-full* of people believe what I have to say. "We need word of mouth to get this all going."

Everyone nods, and Whitney gives me a smile of encouragement. She knows I'm not crazy about public speaking, especially in front of a large group. I've done all right so far, but this is far out of my comfort zone. I give Whitney a panicked look, and she suggests, "We should let her practice first, several times, with just about ten or twenty people."

I breathe in shallow breaths, trying to control my racing heartbeat. I nod vigorously.

It's Petra who agrees with Whitney first. "She can practice her speeches on us, of course. There's thirty of us. Will that do, Vela?"

I clench my hand to control the shaking.

Linc, sensing my turmoil, answers, "I think that'll be good. Vela, we won't throw you in front of a large group unprepared."

I nod and say, "I appreciate that. I would...like some practice, first. It's not going to be easy selling what I have to say to millions of people who feel very strongly about their neighboring clans. We've been warring for centuries."

"I think the world is ready for what you have to say, Vela," Linc says firmly. "It's time for a change. It's time for you to deliver God's message."

Grant speaks up. "I have a speech written up already. After our meeting, I can go over it with you and we can modify it to your preference."

I blow out my breath and keep my eyes down. I'm spiraling into pure panic mode. I need to calm down and somehow hide that I am sorely out of my depth. "That would be great, Grant."

Linc squeezes my knee, and I look over at him. His eyes ask me if I'm okay and my expression must answer that question because he announces. "Okay, that's enough for now. Let's meet again tomorrow. We'll discuss our plan for the meeting with the Grand Elder."

There's some grumbling around the room, but I'm out of my chair and, with as measured steps as I can manage, I'm out the door in the next few moments. I take deep gulps of the cool air, trying to stop my head from spinning. Linc follows and mercifully closes the door so no one can see my breakdown.

Whitney steps out next, and I fall into her arms. "Mom, I can't do this," I whisper into her hair, squeezing her tightly. The door opens again, and I soon find myself surrounded by my adopted and biological family, all around me in a group hug.

Whitney runs her hand down my hair. "You're going to find strength you didn't know you had, Vela. Don't worry. Ask God to give you everything you need."

"And we're here with you, every step of the way," David says next to Whitney.

"So are we," James says behind me. "You have our support and prayers."

Linc says somewhere on my left. "We'll be sure you're ready before we throw you on a stage. And ask God for the words He wants you to say. Remember, you're doing His will."

This is what I needed. My family, Linc, my support system, backing me up. I soak in their encouragement and break away from Whitney. Everyone steps back, and I look around, smiling in relief at all the beloved faces. I look with wide eyes at Elia and Adele standing side by side.

My worlds are colliding, and I couldn't be happier they have.

35

Linc

O n the day of our meeting with the Grand Elder, I say a prayer of favor for my nervous bride as we ride in the back of David and Whitney's car.

We waited to practice using all her powers until late last night. We had to be sure no human in the campground was watching. She wows me every time she commands all the elements. She's mastered using them all together, and I couldn't be prouder of my amazing, powerful wife.

She's noticeably antsy, squeezing her fingers in her lap until I reach over to grab them.

"All you need to do is show your powers," I promise her. "That comes so naturally to you now. You'll do great."

"Well, you are a little biased," she says with a small, nervous smile.

"I'm saying that because I believe it wholeheartedly."

David speaks up from the driver's seat. "Be confident because God chose you for this, Vela. How could anyone argue with that?"

She bites her lip, and I resist the urge to kiss her.

Now is not the time. I'll get my share of kisses later. Tonight.

We've only started our married life, and I can't wait to have a hundred thousand more days and nights with my wife. I focus back on the conversation to pep Vela up.

"Believe in your mission, baby girl," Whitney suggests. "Keep your mind on that."

Vela nods, and we travel the rest of the hour-long drive in relative silence, allowing Vela to think.

We arrive at a non-descript building that houses this area's clan meetings. It's large, to fit the area's Elementals, but it masks as a learning center, like Vela's Breckenridge group. It doesn't surprise me that it's not ostentatious. Elemental gatherings need to stay under the radar.

Vela grips my hand tightly once we get out of the car. She waits for her parents to get out, and I notice her hand is clammy. I lean in to whisper in her ear, "Breathe, Vels. You can do this. You've got the power. Now it's time to show off God's gifts. That's all you're doing."

She gives me a grateful look, her pulse noticeably slowing. I rub my thumb over her wrist, and she straightens her shoulders and walks toward the entrance.

We've decided only some of the leadership will attend this meeting. A van pulls into the parking lot, and I wait with Vela for them to join us.

Petra, Rick, Gary, and Grant leave the van first. Kane and Elia are next, then James, Sandy, Adele, and Rayne are last to leave the van.

I nod at each of them, giving Rayne a smile when he walks up holding Adele's hand.

Vela turns toward the door and rings the doorbell. They seem to have a similar system as other Elemental buildings. It's locked, and the entrance is closely monitored. They need to avoid wayward humans entering. Especially today.

A woman opens the door and looks at Vela. She reels back slightly when she senses all of Vela's gifts. I've grown used to feeling them around my Intended and smirk at the woman's reaction.

"You must be Vela Ashcroft," she says.

"It's Vela Stevenson now," Vela says in a clear voice.

I raise my eyebrow at the woman when she looks at me. My arm is at Vela's back, so it's clear who gave her a new last name.

"Oh...okay. Come this way, please."

The entire group follows her inside, and she leads us to a meeting room that is full of chairs. We walk down the aisle to where a small group of Elementals sits at the front of the room waiting for us, or rather for Vela. It seems we've interrupted a meeting. Or were they waiting for us?

A slender man with gray at his temples stands in front of the group at a podium. He looks over at Vela, who leads the way.

I stand behind her and see her right hand slightly tremble, which she clenches immediately. A surge of pride for my wife fills me. I have no doubt she will easily convince this man she is the Chosen One.

The woman who led us into the room whispers into the man's ear.

His eyebrows shoot up, and I'm guessing he's learning of Vela's new marital status and her powers. I can't help but smile when he looks over at me. I'm standing apart from the rest of the group, just behind Vela. It's clear who I'm claiming.

His eyes flick to the back of the room where Whitney and David stand. He acknowledges them with a nod. It must be because they're Gyan Elders. His eyes narrow at the rest of us, I'm sure because we're all different elements. Vela hasn't united us yet, and it's clear from his reaction and others in the room, they aren't thrilled with us being here.

Finally, he regards Vela with a studied air. "Vela Stevenson," he says in a deep voice. He steps off the stage and approaches her. He reaches out his hand, and when he's close enough to her, his nostrils flair like he, too, is sensing more than one gift in her.

Vela shakes his hand and nods at him. "It's true," she says clearly.

"It's not possible," he says with wide eyes as he looks down at her.

"It is when you're the Chosen Child. You've sensed them correctly. I have all the gifts. I was born with one, a second one was emerging with my age, then God gifted me with the other two at the same time," Vela says, her eyes never leaving his.

He studies her for a full minute. "The Chosen Child is just that, a child. You're a married woman from what I hear."

Vela stiffens. "I'm seventeen, so I'm not considered an adult just yet. As far as my marital state, I had to receive my parents' permission to make that happen."

"Why would you marry so young?" He cocks his head, his face questioning.

"Wouldn't you marry your Intended, too?" Vela asks with a raised eyebrow.

He glances over at me, nods, then turns and gestures to the French doors that lead outside. "Hmmm, since you seem to possess all the elements, I wonder, would you mind providing a demonstration?"

Vela nods regally. She walks over to the doors, opening them. She enters the facility's training grounds, a grass covered expanse, which is much larger than the one of Vela's hometown clan. A large red-brick wall surrounds the area, enclosing us, ensuring our privacy. Trees run along the wall every thirty feet or so. Brightly colored flowers surround the bases of the trees.

I follow Vela until I reach the edge of the field. She continues to the middle and then turns to wait for the group to assemble around me. When they do and all eyes are on her, she raises her arms.

Just like we practiced last night, fire shoots from one hand and water from the other simultaneously. She brings her creations together and when they converge, a great cloud of steam hisses and billows. She sweeps both hands in a circle and wind blows away all the smoke.

Then, as if that wasn't proof enough, she lifts her arms again and four pillars of earth rise in front of her, ripping up the grass. She uses the grass to cover one of the pillars, causing it to sprout up the sides and onto the top, showing off her original Gyan gift. One by one, she moves her hands in a circular motion and creates a demonstration of every element. Like a torch, fire sits burning on the second pillar, then a globe of water spins on the next. Finally, Vela easily creates a mini wind funnel atop the fourth. She looks over her work and then steps to the side, resting her arms, maintaining control of the display with her mind.

That alone shows her strength. Most Elementals have to keep their arms up to maintain the flow of their gifts, but not Vela.

I barely resist cheering her efforts as I watch the Grand Elder and see he's visibly moved by the display.

The group of Gyans with Alex are talking animatedly to each other. Almost all of them have their phones out and are recording Vela's demonstration. Alex, however, is not participating in the conversations, but clearly listening to them. He watches Vela's four pillars and seems to be waiting for something.

I realize he's watching to see how long she can keep up her display of power.

Isn't it enough that she can control all the elements? What does it matter how long she can keep them going? I clench my hands. He's going to make her burn herself out by maintaining her show. Even now, I see her jaw clenching. She stubbornly keeps all the elements going. I step forward to put a stop to this when Alex waves his hand, signaling Vela that she can release her hold.

With one swipe of her hand, the four pillars crash onto the ground and are absorbed immediately into the earth. With a flick of her fingers, grass covers the disturbed area.

I could watch her do this all day long, and she knows it. She looks over at me with a twinkle in her eye. *She'll get all my praise later.* I raise my eyebrows at her and return her smile with a wink.

The rest aren't so quiet. Clapping and cheering erupt in the Gyan Elementals and our group joins them, all smiling and beaming at Vela. It seems they haven't tired of witnessing Vela's abilities either.

"Please, let's go inside. We have much to discuss," Alex says with an air of authority befitting his status as Grand Elder. He easily commands a room, or in this case, an outdoor space.

Vela is the first to follow him, and I'm right behind her, touching her hand as she passes me. She smiles grimly at me, and I know that a lot rides on the following discussion with Alex. I impart as much confidence as I can. She now needs to give her real message, solidifying what the Chosen Child is meant to do: unite the clans.

I try not to be anxious for her. It all starts here. But like I told her, if Alex doesn't want to believe her, we'll go to the other Grand Elders. I don't think we'll need to, though.

At Alex's direction, we all sit down. I note that Vela's team sits on the right side of the room, and Alex's on the left. Vela elects not to sit but stands beside the Grand Elder.

He appraises her choice and then stands aside, gesturing for her to take the podium. "It seems you have a story to tell."

Vela steps toward the podium, closing her eyes for a moment. Opening them, she straightens her shoulders and says in a loud voice, "I am traveling with others who have what I have, more than one gift. Their reason is because they were born to two different Elementals. I am a mixed Elemental too, but there's more to my story. I've been gifted with all the elements, as you've seen. But I've also been given a message. We need to put aside our differences and unite as God wills it. He wants us to live as one clan, not four, any longer."

Alex's side of the room erupts in a roar of exclamations and cries.

Alex holds up his arms and orders his side to quiet down. Once they've complied, he turns to Vela and asks, "You really think you're the Chosen Child?"

"I know I am," she says, her blue eyes piercing his.

"What makes you think that?"

"My age, parentage, birthdate, the prophecies, and the fact that God Himself gave me the message that it's time to stop separating our clans."

Unable to contain themselves, Alex's Gyans furiously talk to each other.

"Quiet!" Alex roars.

This time, it's harder to get his people to accept his order.

Once they finally do, under his steely glare, he turns to Vela. "Explain."

Vela goes into detail about how she fulfills the prophecies of her and her parents' births.

"And the fact that I've been granted all the elements is the final proof," she finishes. "Don't you think our world has been split apart long enough? Can you imagine what we could do, what we could achieve as Guardians of the Earth if we're together? It's time, Alex. It's time to listen to this call because it's not mine, it's God's."

Some of the Gyans yell out expletives, and even Alex can't contain their anger. A few storm out of the room, but others stay put, looking hungry to hear more.

It's to those Vela continues to speak, "We have disasters on our borders daily because of hateful prejudices and revenge." She gestures at the departing Elementals. "We need to stop living with hate and begin our new generation with a message of peace."

I can't remember if those are Grant's words or Vela's, but they couldn't be more perfect.

But just when I think Vela has conquered the room, Alex opens his mouth.

36

Rayne

I'm disgusted when Alex booms out his command, "You will stop this talk of uniting the clans. It's never going to happen. It's impossible. Too much damage has been done."

Before Vela can refute his hateful speech, I stand up, unable to listen to one more of his poisonous words.

"Listen to me, *Gyan Grand Elder*," I spit, as I start walking up the aisle. "I was born with two gifts and for that and that alone, I was born in a wild, remote location, so off the grid, you'd never even find it on any map."

I eye Alex down and clench my hands while keeping a tight grip on my gifts. Then I decide maybe I should demonstrate what I'm saying. I bring up my hands and produce a water cyclone, using wind to contain it. I continue to walk toward the front and say, "Because I was born with two elements, my parents were terrified of the Extremists finding out about me. That I would be murdered on the off chance that I was the Chosen Child."

Alex's mouth opens, but before he can speak, I drop my hands, the water splashing onto the ground. I step into the puddle and continue. "I am, for the first time, living a truly free life, because of her." I point at Vela. "Despite the E.E.'s best efforts, she survived her birth, but only because of the bravery and sacrifice of her biological parents."

I point at Sandy and James, whose faces are flushed with anger at Alex's pronouncement.

"They lost her because they had to hide her birth. Through no fault of their own, Vela was taken to a Gyan family to hide, and they protected her with their lives. If you won't believe Vela's message, then listen to mine."

By this time, I've made it up to the front. I stand directly in front of Alex, whose face is mottled with anger. "There are hundreds, no, thousands of us hiding because of that disgusting group. Why? Why do we hide?"

When he stubbornly doesn't answer, I do. "Because we're terrified of being slaughtered. The Extremists have tried, believe me. We just survived a mass attack on our community. But the they won't stop until *she*," I point again at Vela, "is dead. She *is the Chosen Child*. She's proven it with her birth, the message she received from God Himself and with a show of her truly miraculous gifts. Are you really going to argue with that?"

Alex looks around at his group who are watching for his response with rapt attention.

"And who are you?" he growls.

"My name is Rayne Williams, and I'm done hiding. You need to listen to what she has to say."

With that, I turn to stalk down the aisle to retake my seat, my blood roaring with adrenaline.

If he doesn't start listening to Vela's plan, I don't trust myself to not attack the man.

Linc gives me a nod as I pass, and he folds his arms, waiting to hear Alex's response to my outburst.

After I sit, Adele grabs my hand, her fingers pressing her pleasure at my words.

Alex looks over the remaining members of his group and says to Vela, "While it's true our way of life has not been what you would call ideal…" At that, I snort derisively. Without so much as looking in my direction, he continues, "We have established our world because borders are the safest way to keep us alive."

"Do you know why the E.E. try so hard to eliminate the threat they see in me?" Vela asks.

Alex inclines his head and waits for her answer.

"Because those borders are making them millions of dollars. I'm sure, as the Grand Elder, you know what is happening in your own clan."

She waits for him to answer her question, and when he presses his lips in a thin line, she continues, "Gyans who need fire, wind, and water to help their crops or animals are *paying* the E.E. to find Elementals who are willing to sell their services for the right price. This is what we're doing with our God-given gifts. By forcing us to pay for these abilities, they have, in a sick sort of way, already united to meet these demands. Are we going to allow this to continue? Or can we stand up and stop this abuse of power by uniting worldwide?"

All of her team, including Adele and I, stand up in a show of support, clapping at her impassioned speech. A few on the other side of the room join us.

Once we've settled and taken our seats again, Alex wipes his brow. He bows his head and stands silent for several moments. He looks up and asks, "And you think you're able to convince the world of this?"

Vela's chin rises. I fully believe her when she says, "Yes."

I look over at Adele, who smiles like Vela's already won this battle. Her bright eyes beam at me, and then she turns to watch the front again.

Alex thinks over Vela's declaration. "I need to meet with the other Grand Elders and talk this over. If they decide to meet you, we will be in contact."

Vela's eyes narrow, and I pray she finds the right words.

"I don't think I'll have any problem arranging meetings for myself with the other Grand Elders. But thank you for your offer," she says serenely.

"You know how many times we get false accounts of the Chosen Child?"

"And how many of those were in possession of all four elements?" she counters.

When he has no answer to that, she steps away from the podium and, with a flick of her hand, opens the door we came in.

I almost stay sitting, astonished by her little trick. But, with a shake of my head, I jump up when Linc does and follow him when he motions for the rest of us to head out.

We leave the room that sits in stunned silence, not only at her final words but at her simple gesture that proves her strength as a Wind Elemental. With her other gifts, it's undeniable. And, with her rhetoric, she's unstoppable. She has proven she is who she claims to be.

I can't help it. I laugh as we walk out. And I'm not the only one. Our whole group is talking excitedly about the show Vela just put on.

Adele slips her hand in mine and says, "She's amazing, right? She's doing it, she's really doing it."

I nod. "There's no question about it. But now, we need to get her in front of more Elementals."

Adele looks over her shoulder as we walk outside. "Did you see all the cell phones out recording her when we were outside? That will go viral, just you watch."

Knowing little of cell phones, I can only nod.

Adele laughs and shakes our joined hands. "You don't know what I'm talking about, do you?"

I rub my neck. "Something about it going everywhere?"

"Right! You catch on quick to our techy ways."

"I just need more experience."

"Here," she says, producing her phone from her pocket. "Play around with mine. It's an old model, but you can learn from it."

I guess we're not going to meet as a group until we return to our cabins because Vela, Linc, and her adopted parents are already driving away.

"I really need to learn to drive a car." I sigh.

Adele squeezes my hand before we all load up and drive away. I look around, trying not to let my jaw drop at all the signs and wonders I'm seeing.

I've heard stories of cell phones and computers, but no one mentioned all the things there are to *see*.

My head spins to track a girl on the sidewalk who's dressed in all black, because even the girl's eyes are black, almost like a raccoon.

Adele laughs at my expression. "It's called makeup," she explains and then giggles. "It's cute how much you don't know."

"Why would she want to put all that stuff on her face like that?" I crane my neck to see her again, but we've passed her.

"Well, when a girl uses makeup in a different way, you might like it. It can enhance someone's natural beauty."

I look over her pretty face and shake my head. "You don't need any of that. You're perfect the way you are."

She blushes. "That's because you're used to seeing me like this. But, as soon as we can get to the store, I'm picking up a few things. The last time I was in the States, I was too young for makeup, but I'm not now."

I give her an appreciative look. *No, she's not too young.* Then, I sober. *She's still too young for me to really pursue her. But she seems to like being around me, so I'll take what I can get.*

"What were you thinking just now?" she asks me, leaning her cheek on her hand that rests on the back of the seat.

Her parents are in the front, so I say in a low voice, "Nothing we can do anything about right now. Maybe in a couple of years."

She looks in the front and then back at me like she understands my cause for secrecy. She whispers, "They're being really lenient lately. Maybe they'll allow us to date sooner than you think."

I try to hold back a groan of frustration. *I wish I could fast forward two years right now.* "It can't come soon enough. But," I say, with a twist of my lips, "you might change your mind about dating me in two years."

She cocks her head. "Why would I do that?"

I shrug. "Someone else might interest you."

She narrows her eyes at me. "And who would that be?"

Looking deep in her eyes, I say carefully, "Steele seems pretty interested. You're still friends." I try not to spit out his name and tamp down the surge of jealousy that fills me every time he comes to mind. And to think, I'm bringing this up. But I have to know how much interest she has in him.

She turns and faces the front. "Steele is...I mean, Steele was my boyfriend, but now that I've met you, I don't know," she pauses. Then she looks directly at me, and my chest tightens under her gaze. "It's like anyone else is second best. And I don't want second best."

"Have you told him that?"

"Yes, have you noticed how much he's talking to Alice?"

I sit back, mollified. I lace my fingers in hers, wishing so much that I was allowed to do more. I track her features hungrily, wishing I could kiss her right now. But I rein in the impulse because I've promised her parents I would. And I intend to keep that promise.

I hope that she continues to feel this way for the next two years until I can claim my bond with her and make her mine, like Linc did with Vela. With God's help with my restraint, my dream is to marry Adele, if she'll have me.

Until then, I'll be good. Even if it just might be the death of me to do it.

37

Linc

We celebrated Vela's triumph at the Gyan Grand Elder's with a huge dinner. We had to take both vans to get all the food we needed, but it was worth it. Everyone helped with cooking. Vela's Girls had a heyday with all the choices offered in the grocery stores.

They didn't know what to do with most of the selection, but they were delighted nonetheless. They made do, that's for certain, because I haven't been this full in a long time.

The Girls have joined our leadership team, bullying Vela until they were allowed to join in the meetings. It apparently wasn't enough that they are all on her protection detail. They wanted to know all the ins and outs of what we're doing.

We're in one of these meetings when Petra says, "We need to go over our next steps. We've already heard from Alex Colbourn."

Vela goes to stand in between Adele and Elia, linking her arms with both of them. I like that they're both here to support my girl.

"Also, several more members of our group have fallen ill," Petra continues. "So, if any of you develop symptoms, be sure to quarantine and stay away from Vela."

David speaks up. "I've heard there's some sickness going around all the Elementals in this area. We aren't the only ones affected. We need to be very careful to continually wash our hands and take special care in public right now."

James says, "We might need to leave this place. If it's safer for Vela and the rest of us, we can go somewhere else for Vela to meet with other Elementals."

Several of us nod, and my stomach twists in concern about this mystery virus that's affecting Elementals. "Let me be clear about this. Is this only targeting Elementals? Or are humans affected, too?" I ask, folding my arms across my chest.

"We don't think it's making humans sick. It seems to be an Elemental illness, which makes me strongly suspicious the Extremists have cooked up something," David says with a grim look.

"And Gyans can't heal it?" I ask.

Sandy and Whitney both shake their heads. With Hannah gone, it's clear she's with Greta, who is still sick. Vela has been worried sick about her young friend. She considers the young girl more of her little sister than a friend.

"What did Colbourn have to say?" Vela asks, her face pinched with worry. I like that she doesn't need to put the confident front she had with the Grand Elder. Here she can be more herself.

"He says," Petra finger quotes, "he's intrigued. He'd like to meet with you again."

"He can like to meet with her as much as he wants," I say with no give to my voice, "but if Vela is in danger of getting sick, that's not going to happen. He can travel to wherever we go next to witness her powers again." Because that's what I'm sure he wants.

"Should we really leave because of something going around?" Vela asks.

Sandy says, "Vela, honey, this is something I've never seen. And neither has any other Gyan here."

Whitney nods. "She's right. I've tried treating the sick, and I can't get a handle on what's attacking their immune systems."

Vela leans back as if shocked. I am too, for that matter. That all the Gyans are stumped by some incurable virus is seriously unnerving.

"How many are sick now?" Vela asks.

I look around and notice that Gary and his wife are absent, but everyone else is here from our meeting with Colbourn.

Did Gary get sick just today? This is more serious than I thought.

"Fifteen of us are sick right now," Sandy says. "Hopefully, no more of us will get it."

Vela looks around the room. "Wait, where is Gary? Is he sick, too?"

Sandy nods grimly.

"We should leave, Vela," I say. "I don't want you to get this."

"What are the symptoms of this illness?" she asks.

Whitney answers, "It's presenting much like the flu, but in severe cases, it's knocking them completely out. Several are bedridden."

Vela steps forward. "How bad is Greta?" Her voice is tight with concern.

I go to her side and rub small circles into her back.

Whitney gives her a sympathetic look. "She's one of the ones who's down with it. We're keeping her hydrated, and she's taking in some soup and fluids, but she's struggling."

My chest hurts thinking about that precocious girl being so sick. Vela looks up at me, her eyes tight with fear. "Linc? I want to see her."

I shake my head firmly. "You know that's not wise. She wouldn't want you to get it, too."

Sandy steps to Vela's other side and puts her arm around Vela's shoulders. "The best thing you can do is pray for her, honey. We can't risk you getting sick. It would derail your entire mission."

"So, are we just leaving the sick ones behind when we move on?" Vela asks in a shaking voice.

"That's the wisest thing we can do," David says with a grave look.

Vela turns her head and squeezes her eyes shut at his answer. She looks at me. "If we leave Greta behind, we'll lose Hannah and Andy, too. I want them to stay with us. And I need to keep Greta close to see how she's doing. I don't think I can leave her."

"Baby, I don't think we have a choice," I say. My voice is lost in the din of voices that erupt at Vela's comment. Everyone seems to be of the same mind I am.

I lean in to speak into her ear. "She'll be better off here. She'll be more comfortable staying in one place and not being dragged everywhere."

Vela stiffens and her shoulders slump in defeat.

Rick takes control of the room and quiets everyone down. "We need to discuss what else Alex Colbourn has offered."

Vela picks her head up to listen.

"He's contacted the other Grand Elders and has agreed to host a joint meeting."

"Wait, I thought he just wanted to meet with me again," Vela says.

Petra explains, "He wants to be sure what he saw wasn't some fluke before he makes final preparations for you to meet the other Grand Elders."

"Wait. If we're leaving, how will we meet?" Vela asks.

"We'll tell him we can meet him tomorrow and tomorrow only. If he delays, he'll have to come to wherever we go next," Petra says in an unyielding voice.

"If he's satisfied, he'll still need to travel to us with the rest of the Grand Elders. Where are we going?" Vela asks. "Has that been decided?"

Petra and Rick share a loaded glance, then look right at me. It's Petra who says, "We think we should go to Texas."

"Where my mother is? No. That's not happening," I say, folding my arms over my chest. I do not want Vela to have to face my mother again. "We have two other options. We can meet with the Borean or Neronian Grand Elder instead. There's no reason to go the Festans."

Petra gives me a long look. "You have a tremendous contact with your mother, Linc. We need to take advantage of it."

"My mother is just waiting to turn Vela down. She didn't want us to get married. Do you think she's suddenly going to forgive me?" I hate that my comment makes Vela cringe.

Rick says, "Linc, she attended your wedding, so she can't be too against it. It's clear she's changed her mind. And if she has spoken to Alex by now, she'll be hard pressed to deny the obvious truth in Vela's gifts."

Vela puts her hand on my arm. "Linc, don't think I can't face your mother. Let me do this." She swallows. "I need to face her and prove I am the Chosen Child. Let me surprise you."

I turn to face her fully, unfolding my arms to hold hers. "I *am* surprised by you *every day*. You don't need to prove anything to me or anyone."

Vela grimaces. "Actually, Linc, I do. That's the thing. I need to prove I am who I say I am. You need to let me be in difficult situations." She adds softly, "You can't protect me from everything."

Her beautiful blue eyes beseech me, and I couldn't resist them even if I tried. "If this is what you want to do, of course I'll support you."

Rick adds, "Going to Texas will get us far from the virus in this area. Vela and the rest of us should be safe."

I sigh heavily and run my hand over my beard. "Okay, let's do it. We need to make travel plans."

Vela gives me a grateful look and takes my hand, lacing her fingers in mine.

After much discussion, which I half listen to, our travel plans are set, and I get used to the idea that I'll have to face my mother in two days. We wrap up for the night and everyone returns to their own cabins, leaving Vela and I alone with Jack.

Once we're alone, Vela asks, her eyes swimming with concern, "Do you want to talk about it?"

I huff. "About going home? No, I'm fine," I say, rubbing the back of my neck.

She scoffs. "It doesn't look like it. I know you, you're worried."

I give her a look. "We're talking about my mother. She won't act like she's my mom, Vela. She'll be the indomitable Grand Elder the entire time. Everyone thinks I have some leverage with her, but I don't." I sigh. "Not by a long shot."

She approaches me and wraps her arms around my middle. "That's what I thought you'd want to talk about."

"There's nothing to talk about. I'm pretty sure she's already made her mind up. It would take a miracle to change it."

Vela nuzzles my chest. "Then I'm glad we believe in miracles."

I hold her tightly, appreciating her closeness. I bury my nose in her hair, inhaling her scent deeply. "I just don't want her to hurt you."

"The only way she could do that is by hurting you," she says, her cheek pressed into my shirt.

I lean back and push her gently away to look into her eyes. "Vela, don't think she'll spare my feelings. Like I said, she's the Grand Elder first and foremost and parent in far second. That's if I even make her top ten priorities."

Vela steps forward and squeezes my middle. "That just makes me so angry. It must hurt you, too."

I rest my cheek on top of her head. "I'm used to it. I made my peace with that side of her a long time ago."

Vela looks up at me. "Maybe she'll surprise you."

I laugh. "And the world will turn out to be flat. No, Vela, I don't think so. But I'll let you keep hoping."

"If she has a hint of motherly love in her, there's a chance she'll surprise us both."

I nuzzle her hair. "Okay. You're right. Now, give me a kiss. I think I need one."

Leaning her head way back, she smiles. "Just one?"

Growling, I pick her up and swing her around, backing up into our bedroom. "You know that's not possible."

She giggles, and finally, we call it a night.

38

Vela

The next two days are a blur. After a whirlwind packing session, making travel arrangements, and of course the flight, we've just arrived at our destination in Houston, Texas, where Elizabeth, Linc's mother, and father live.

"Are you ready?" Linc whispers in my ear. He's standing at my back, with his arms around my middle. It's been a busy two days, and I'm thrilled we're finally alone. The only lodging we could find to fit the 15 of us who are healthy enough to travel to Texas is a hotel. Everyone is thrilled, saying we're living "posh."

I ask, leaning back into his chest, "Can we have a code word for that question? You ask me that so often I feel like I have whiplash every time."

I feel his lips move into a smile. "What do you think it should be?"

"I don't know. Something that will make me smile immediately instead of making my heart stop in terror."

He turns me around and studies my eyes. "Is that what that question does, really?"

I shrug. "It just feels like a million things could go wrong when I think of all the possibilities and worst-case scenarios."

He leans back, squeezing my shoulders slightly. "Well, then let's think of a code word or phrase that doesn't do that. What's something I say that makes you perfectly happy?"

I smile, immediately thinking of something. I take a step forward and lean my head on his chest. "Every time you say you love me."

"Vela," he says, sighing, squeezing my shoulders, rubbing my back. "You want that to be the code phrase? What if I just want to say it and not mean I'm asking if you're ready?"

I squeeze his middle. "I'll know the difference."

He pauses. "If you're sure?"

"I am. And for the record, the answer is yes, I'm ready. On the plane, we went over the new speeches from Grant."

"We're meeting with our leadership team in a few minutes."

This time I groan. "Has the security team problem been fixed?"

He nods. "Even though Tonya didn't want to take orders from Rayne, she finally sees Rayne's leadership skills are too good to not put to use."

I huff a laugh. "I guess growing up together has made her resistant to him as a leader."

"Yeah, I'm pretty sure she sees him as a brother and not a boss."

I grin. "Pretty sure she doesn't think of him in a familial way." Remembering how much she commented on his hotness back at the Polar Bear has made me quite sure about that.

"I'm still shocked Rayne has stepped up to the role of leader. What a change I've seen in him. He's been talking to me about what he's been reading in the Bible I gave him. He's a changed man, and for that I'm glad. He's truly sorry for what he did to me."

"He should be. It was horrible." I shudder at the memory, and I can tell Linc knows what I'm remembering by the look on his face. Linc falling to the ground, blood spilling down his neck, soaking the earth.

"Hey," Linc says softly. "Don't go there."

"It's hard not to. I'll take that memory to my grave."

He kisses me softly. "I'm fine," he says firmly.

I finger the thin scar on his neck and place soft kisses over the whole thing. When I'm done, I look up at him. "I know. You can remind me of that any time you want." I press my lips to his, needing to feel and breathe him in to convince myself he really is okay. I still have nightmares about him nearly dying. Those memories don't just go away.

After a good, long kiss, Linc moans and breaks away. "Unfortunately, we don't have time for much more than that, my Intended. We're due downstairs."

As we walk down the hall and into the elevator, poor Jack is given leery looks from a family who go out of their way to avoid him. Because of his Doberman persona, he's feared, and I hate that. He really is the most loveable dog. There's no chance, however, of convincing strangers of that.

We end up in the lobby and most everyone on our leadership team is waiting for us. The security for the day is here, too. The Girls, Leon, Rayne, and another guy named Tex are looking around, checking to be sure we're safe. Tex, like Leon, is huge with muscles as big as the state of Texas, and I wonder if he's from there or just goes by that nickname. He's part of the Saddleback group, and I notice Claudette and Jennifer talking to him with big smiles.

I greet everyone, but after seeing Rick without his wife, I ask him, worry coming in my voice, "Where's Cheri?"

He stuffs his hands in his pockets. "She's not feeling well. She's resting."

I look to Linc. "Another one?"

He gives Rick his attention. "Does she have flu-like symptoms?"

Rick grimaces. "I'm afraid she does. If I start to feel anything like that, I'll quarantine with her."

I turn to Whitney and Sandy. "Do you think it's what everyone else has?"

Whitney answers with a worried crease between her eyes, "I do. I'm trying not to spend too much time in her room, so I don't come down with it, too."

Fearing that this virus is going to claim every one of my team members, I fight down my feelings of overwhelming concern.

"It's just a virus," Sandy says. "I'm sure it's just a week-long illness."

"Except it's been over a week since Greta and the others first showed symptoms. They're not any better, are they?" I ask.

Whitney shakes her head. "No, but sometimes the flu lasts for as long as two weeks. We're keeping a close eye on those who are sick."

Panic strikes me. "Is Greta worse? Are Hannah and Andy sick? Aren't they taking care of everyone?"

Poor, precious Greta! Who will take care of everyone if Hannah and Andy are sick, too? How will Greta get well?

"Hannah and Andy are fine," James says. "They're taking the necessary precautions by wearing masks and gloves. Let's pray they remain healthy."

"Maybe it's time to get Greta to the hospital. Surely, they can do more for her than we can," I say.

"If she starts to need intravenous fluids, we will certainly make sure she gets that care," Sandy assures me.

I try to shake off the unease I feel, but it's difficult. Linc rubs my tense shoulders.

Petra says, "We're meeting with Elizabeth Stevenson in an hour. Are you ready?" Her direct gaze pierces through my worry and forces me to focus my mind on what we're about to do. What I'm about to do.

Linc leans in and whispers in my ear. "I love you."

I smile and reach up, squeezing his hands on my shoulders. I nod at him and tell Petra, "I am," trying to project confidence. I've practically memorized Grant's speeches. I appreciate having him on our team. He's got a talent with words, and I can only hope to do them justice. One of these days, maybe I'll start to feel like I'm worthy of this role.

"Is it really necessary to bring your animal?" Petra asks, waving her hand at Jack.

I bristle. "Jack has been through every step of this journey with me. He stays. He won't be a problem."

She sighs, shaking her head and leads the way outside. I swallow thickly, knowing I'm about to face off with Linc's mother who happens to hate me for marrying her son. In front of three other Grand Elders.

No problem. If I can square off with a seven-foot giant Festan Extremist, one little Festan woman is nothing. Even if she is the Grand Elder.

Linc interprets my look correctly and mouths, "I love you."

I smile at him, take a deep breath, and follow the others outside, Jack close by us.

Our hotel is close to Elizabeth's home base, so we will arrive in under fifteen minutes. I'm happy to be in the van we rented. I'm surrounded by those who are completely supportive, with Jack half on my lap. Being around everyone bolsters my flagging confidence, which I appreciate.

I need all the help I can get.

It's disconcerting that we're down to one van, though, with all those who've fallen ill. Hopefully, they'll recover soon and join us here in Texas. We'll send the private plane back for them when they're back on their feet.

Adele sits behind me and when she starts to massage my shoulders, I lean back and breathe, "Thanks, sis. That feels heavenly."

"Hey, no problem. You just relax for a minute before you face the She-Devil." She glances at Linc, who looks at her with amusement. "Sorry, Linc, but your mother is one scary woman."

He chuckles. "You're not telling me anything I don't already know."

Adele snorts. "That's harsh."

Linc turns halfway around. "If you'd lived under her thumb your whole life, you'd understand."

Adele glances at James and Sandy and smiles at them. "Yeah, I've been pretty lucky."

Linc turns back around. "Yes, you have."

My heart pangs at Linc's tone. He sounds so defeated. I wish he had a loving family like mine to rely on. "Well, now you've married into a family who thinks the world of you." I squeeze his knee. "Both sides of the family," I correct myself.

He gives me half a smile but says nothing.

What kind of damage has Elizabeth done to my husband? Is it repairable?

By the time we get to our destination, my shoulder muscles are relaxed thanks to Adele, but my heart is sore. When I step out of the van, my first look at Elizabeth's base of operations for the Festans has my anxiety spiking. I hand Jack's leash off to Sandy.

One thing is painfully obvious. This is no inconspicuous building. It's a grand red brick structure that looks imposing, with six tall columns on the front porch, giving it an air of superiority. If Elizabeth wants to intimidate people, she's succeeding.

"I feel like I'm at a plantation," Elia says, her hands on her hips as she looks up at the palatial structure.

I nod, my head leaning back to take in the three-story tall building. "Is Scarlett O'Hara going to run around the corner any minute?" I joke.

Linc is at my side, his presence warm and comforting. "Don't think of it as anything but a show. She has to look like she's important." He frowns at the building.

Tonya blows out a breath. "She's doing a good job of it."

Sandy is at my other side, and she flips her hair and says, "It's just a building like Linc says. Don't let this intimidate you. You are the Chosen Child who we've been waiting for hundreds of years. She has nothing on you."

"I'm also just me, Mama."

Leon checks around the left perimeter of the building for any unwanted lurkers. He motions for The Girls to go the other way. He's gone for a few minutes and returns with a troubled look on his face.

"What's the matter?" Linc asks, his body ready for an attack.

"Well," Leon says, looking over his shoulder. "I thought I saw someone running behind that line of trees, but I could be wrong."

"Go check it out," Rayne says, walking up.

Leon nods and he's off in a run. Rayne turns to the rest of us. "It could be nothing, but just in case, get inside. If there's any danger, I'll call David."

Rayne has quickly grown comfortable using a cell phone. David nods, checking to be sure his phone is on and puts it back in his pocket.

Linc takes a deep breath and looks at his mother's building with a mixed expression. "I think you're safer inside, as much as I hate saying that about this place."

"Well, I'm ready," I say after a worried glance around.

Whitney is beside me as we walk closer to the door. She says, "Just remember, you're always going to be you, but you have all of us, too. We are supporting you all the way. Any time you feel like less than, remember that we believe in you."

Elia joins in, holding out her phone. "And I've been tracking all the social media feeds for Elementals, and the posts from the

Gyan Grand Elder's meeting are going viral. There have been thousands of posts already, just from that small group. You're making a splash. Just keep up with our plan of meeting these Grand Elders and soon, the world will know all about you."

"But will they believe in me? Will your mother?" I ask Linc.

"If she doesn't, there are still two other Grand Elders left," Linc says. "She won't be able to ignore your gifts, though. Don't worry, you'll have her attention."

Walking up to the porch, I commit the rest of the meeting to God.

Lord, help me in this meeting. Guide my words and actions. I'm Your vessel. Make my words Yours.

After that short prayer, I feel a measure of peace come over me as I press the button to be allowed in. We wait for a few minutes, and my nerves stretch thin with the wait. I reach for the peace I just felt after my prayer, grasping it desperately.

I want Linc's mother to accept me, Lord. Give Linc and me a little help here?

The door opens and a man who looks like a butler in a gray suit with actual tails says, "May I help you?"

"Pearson, really?" Linc asks, his eyebrow raised.

Pearson's brow rises, and his calm face cracks with surprise. "I'm sorry, Mr. Stevenson. I didn't see you. Please, come in."

We walk into the beautiful entrance, and I can't help but look around in awe. I snap my mouth closed when Linc takes my elbow. "Remember, it's a façade."

Large oil paintings grace the paneled walls on both sides of us. A staircase spirals up to the second and third floors, with wings of hallways on either side. The gleaming cherry wood floor literally sparkles.

Pearson escorts us down the hallway to the right of the staircase and leads us to a double door. With a practiced gesture, he opens up the doors announcing, "Your son, Lincoln, and guests have arrived, Grand Elder."

With one look, I see a large room where three people stand on the far side, waiting for us to approach. It looks to be a small ballroom. Unlike the group who was with the Gyan Grand Elder, the ballroom is empty except for three people and several large potted trees placed by the walls. We're at a distance, but I can plainly see that the other Grand Elders are not here. I look up at Linc and his jaw tightens in frustration.

As we get closer, I nearly stumble in surprise when I see Linc's Uncle Richard standing beside Linc's parents, Elizabeth and Michael.

When we reach them, I glance at Uncle Richard, who gives me a warm smile, but then turns his full attention to Elizabeth. Michael winks at me and then focuses on his wife. He must have much different feelings about me than his clearly unhappy wife.

Elizabeth is giving me a piercing glare. "Welcome to Texas and the Festan holding."

I nod stiffly.

Linc asks in a forced tone. "We were told the other Grand Elders would be here, Mother."

She turns to Linc. "Yes, well. I heard your bride wanted to meet with the Grand Elders with her preposterous claim that she's the Chosen Child. She was an imposter in Canada, and she still is. I put a stop to such a false claim." Her tone is made of steel.

Cries come from my group, who have fanned out around me. Jack pushes his way to stand by my side.

David steps forward, saying in a hard voice, "She's not an imposter. She *is* the Chosen Child."

Her eyebrows rise imperiously. "Is she now?" She looks me over with contempt.

Linc's hand shakes as he grips mine. "Mother, we've come to state our case that Vela is the Chosen One. You will listen to what she has to say. And she will meet with the other Grand Elders without your interference. You can't stop her."

I inhale when Elizabeth spears me with a look full of vitriol. I clasp my fingers tightly to keep from flicking up a wall of elements between us.

"I won't give this girl one second of my time. She's not even a child, she's *married*," she spits. "Now, leave." She points toward the door we came in.

Then I decide, *Why not release my elements?* I'm overwhelmed with such indignant anger at being dismissed, I make my decision.

I'm clearly not going to win her over with my personality, so it's going to have to be with my gifts. I take a large step back, Jack following my lead. I glance behind me and tilt my head for my entourage to give me some room. Linc reads my thoughts and his eyes flash with victory. He nods at me and with his help, everyone steps back.

"What are you doing?" Elizabeth asks.

Ignoring her, I raise my hands and with one motion of my arms, I grab the ten trees along the walls and lift them out of their pots. Using wind, I spin them, shaking off the excess dirt and fly the piles of earth to me.

"Stop that this instance. You're making a mess!" Elizabeth shouts.

Instead of obeying her, I make a point of landing the dirt in one long neat pile in front of her. With one sweep of my hands, I separate the dirt into four round piles, carefully placing the spinning trees back in their pots.

Elizabeth watches all around the room as I use both Earth and Wind to accomplish that.

She steps forward like she's going to stop my demonstration.

Before she can do one thing, I raise both arms and with four flicks, I produce a flame on one pile, a fountain of water on another and a medium-sized cyclone on the third. For my last pile, I cock my eyebrow at her and grow a seedling from one branch of the trees into a small version of its parent.

Elizabeth is sputtering by the time I'm finished, and when I step back from my creations, everyone behind me and even Uncle Richard and Michael, applaud loudly.

"Beautiful!" James shouts.

"Stunning, darling," David joins in.

"Unbelievable," Uncle Richard breathes with wide eyes.

The other exclamations are lost when Elizabeth rages. She sweeps her arm out and tries to destroy all I've created with one huge fire blast.

Linc begins to step forward, but I push him back with wind. The room heats with the force of Elizabeth's fire, but my hands grip the air in front of me, taking control of her flames. When I stop her assault on my creations, she gasps in frustration. I hold back her fiery wall and, with a pinch of my fingers, snuff out her fire as easily as a birthday candle.

My forehead dots with sweat at my show of strength and holding my elements in place. I refuse to let them go to prove to her I'm not an anomaly like she said in Canada.

"I am the Chosen Child, Grand Elder," my voice rings out over the excited murmurs in the room. "I have all four gifts, and my parentage proves I am the one Elementals have been awaiting for thousands of years. Now, can we talk?"

Elizabeth presses her lips into a thin line and her arms tremble at her sides. Michael steps in and says something in her ear. Uncle Richard, too, quietly tells her something. She never takes her eyes off me as she considers what they say.

Finally, she grits out, "It seems we do have some things to discuss. Can you please clean this mess up before we do?" It's only then that she glances at my show of elements and her shoulders tighten. She folds her hands in front of her as she waits for me to do as she asked.

Linc puts his arm on my shoulder, infusing me with strength, and I glance at him in appreciation. I snuff out the fire, wind, and water easily, then, with a sweep of my arms, send the dirt back into the pots and snug the trees back into place. I direct the newly grown tree into Elia's hands, knowing she will find a place to plant it.

With a smile in Elizabeth's direction, I water the trees as an apology for the rudeness I showed them.

Once the room is back to rights, Elizabeth sniffs and then turns, walking away from us. "Follow me," she orders.

And just like that, it seems I've convinced my most formidable opponent to believe me.

I'll leave the rest in God's hands.

39

Linc

I am so freaking proud of my wife as I follow her and Jack out the back door of the ballroom. She rocked, no, slayed it with my mother. I almost laughed when I saw the look in Vela's eyes before she gave that awesome performance. I knew exactly what she was going to do. Well, not exactly; with Vela, it's always a surprise. When my mother attacked her performance with flames, fear for Vela took over and, by instinct, I tried to shield her. But, even then, she pushed me back and easily handled it herself.

She won't stop there, either. She'll continue to rock my world at every turn, I'm sure of it. As we walk to Mother's office, I make a point of thanking God for gifting me with such a wife. I'm convinced only Vela could handle my mother. God knew what He was doing, gifting us with our bond.

There are chuckles and laughs behind me as everyone marvels at Vela's show.

"My best friend is *awesome*," Elia gushes, setting the little tree down to plant later.

"She might be your best friend, but she's my sister," Adele laughs beside her. "I'm related to that amazingness."

"Hey, you two, stop that," Sandy admonishes. "God gifted her with those gifts. You know that."

"Yeah, but Vela put her creative spin on it," Tonya says, completely forgetting to watch for danger as she walks with her girlfriends. They all nod in agreement.

"I just want to say that I knew her before she was famous," Alice gushes, her blonde curls bouncing with every word.

Jennifer adds, "She rocked the house with that genius of hers."

"Did you see the Grand Elder's face? I bet she's never been so shocked in her life," Kane says.

I smile at that last comment because it's true. I've never seen my mom so unsettled. Certainly, she's never *spluttered* before.

I can't help but chuckle quietly. By this time, Mother has led us into her spacious office. If Vela thought the office would be too small to fit us all, she's in for a surprise. Because in Elizabeth's grandiose style, it's an enormous room that easily accommodates us with space to spare.

She walks around her large gleaming desk, sits primly on the hand-stitched leather chair, and folds her hands on the desktop. Father stands next to her, like he always does, but there's a look of anticipation on his face as he waits for everyone to find their places in the room. Uncle Richard shuts the door with a loud click and walks to stand beside me.

I share a smile with him, and he turns curious eyes to Vela. I'm sure he must be wondering how he missed recognizing her as the prophesied Chosen Child.

Vela, as usual, is braced by both of her families behind her. The Girls fan out behind them, finally remembering their guard duties. Rick and Petra stand on the edges of the group, their eyes gleaming with victory.

Mother clears her throat and asks us, "You all believe that Vela fulfills the prophecy?"

James and Sandy step forward. He answers in a compelling voice, "I was born during the Orien Constellation, which is known as the Hunter. During the Winter Solstice in the north, when the Capricorn Constellation, which is known as the Sea Goat, was visible in the northern sky, I met and married my bride, Sandy. My wife's birthday is on the Autumn Equinox.

"The prophecy says, 'When the day and night are of equal length, the Autumn Equinox, a warrior star who will bear the child, will rise. Under the Winter Solstice, the Hunter will emerge. He will capture the Goat under the Northern sky, and they will produce the one who unifies.' We fulfill that part of the prophecy."

Vela steps forward to stand beside them. "And the rest of the prophecy says, 'Though their elements are diverse, through them the Child will command them all.' I'm seventeen, so I'm technically not an adult. My parents have different elements. My father is a Borean, and my mother is a Gyan, making their gifts diverse. And I command all the elements as God granted them to me."

Mother's face freezes as she digests this information, but my father is noticeably excited. He's bouncing on his feet and even my uncle is fidgeting, like he wants to write all this down.

Vela continues, "I understand there's another prophecy that the Chosen One should be born on the Autumn Equinox. I was. I can also take an Elemental's power and gift it to another, which may be a part of that same prophecy."

She falls silent, and Uncle Richard can't contain himself. He steps forward. "Yes." His voice carries in the room. "The second prophecy does say that. It's not well known, but it gives credence to both of those facts."

Vela turns to him with curiosity burning on her lovely face. "Can you tell me this prophecy in full? What does it say?"

Mother looks like she's swallowed a sour lemon, but paying her no heed, Uncle Richard takes a moment to think, rubbing his forehead. "If I'm remembering it correctly, it says, 'The Child, like the mother, will be born when the goat graces the northern skies, in the fall where the day and night are of equal length. Recognize the Child who will take and gift an element. Beware of forces who will snuff out the Child's flame.'"

I stiffen and move to stand beside Vela. I know her life is in danger as the prophesied Child, but to hear it so clearly foretold strikes a cold fear through me, icing my veins. I reach for her hand, and it's as clammy as mine. She squeezes my hand tightly.

The room sobers immediately, and everyone takes a slight step toward Vela, like they hope to protect her with their proximity.

"Well, then," Vela says. "Like my mother, I was born on the Autumn Equinox. And like I said, I can take and gift an element."

Looking like she would rather chew nails, Mother says, "It seems I've been mistaken. You check all the boxes of the Chosen One, Vela. I cannot ignore all the facts and that...display you showed me. Now, the question seems to be of your safety."

"I have a security team," Vela says. "We just need your support in getting the message out to your clan."

Mother nods and pushes her chair back, standing up. "I believe I can help you with that. We can organize an assembly to witness your gifts and message. I take it you want to unify our clans?"

Vela nods. "Yes, I've been given a message from God to stop our clans from fighting and to unite us all to live together as He created us."

Mother's brow furrows. "You'll get the Elementals' attention. There's no mistaking that. But to convince them to abandon their boundaries? You do realize what a massive undertaking that is?"

Vela's face pales slightly. I see her throat swallow. "Yes, I know it won't be easy, but I believe I can get through to them."

"How do you propose to do that?"

Vela stands taller. "God also saw fit to give me the gift of oration. I will use my elements to get their attention, then I will give them a goal of unification that they can't refuse."

"And what would that be?"

"I'm going to paint a picture of what it will look like if we live unified, promising peace for those who maintain it."

Mother cracks a small smile. "You have confidence you can do this?"

"With God, anything is possible. I can do nothing without Him guiding me. These are not my words, but His."

"Hmm, yes. Well, be that is may, you have a big job to do." She turns to Father. "Michael, can you get the clan together for Vela to address? I believe there are some social media posts already showcasing her talents. I don't think it will be too hard to get our clan in front of her."

Of course, Mother knows about the viral posts. She's nothing if not informed.

She then turns to me. "Lincoln, if you would be so kind to dine with us this evening, I would like to spend some time with my son."

I stand shocked at the complete turnaround in her behavior. She tried to throw us out half an hour ago. I lift my eyebrow. "Are you planning on inviting my wife as well?"

Mother clears her throat, delicately. "Yes, of course. Please, Vela, would you join us for dinner?"

Ah, I see. She sees a chance of buttering up the Chosen Child. Now, Vela is valuable to her, possibly even worthy of marrying her only son.

Vela looks uncomfortable as she answers. "Uh, yes, of course."

I put my hand on the small of Vela's back and nudge her toward the door. "Until six then, mother? Dinner is at the usual time?"

She nods regally at me and gives a small smile to Vela. I hold in my growl of annoyance and usher my wife out the door. The rest follows on our heels. And, just like that, we're apparently attending a dinner party with my mother.

40

Vela

As soon as we walk outside, Rayne is there, a concerned look on his face.

"Who was that guy Leon saw?" Linc asks. "Anyone concerning?"

"Actually, he was picked up by a van before we could question him. So that's not ideal. Everything was fine inside?" he asks Tonya and The Girls.

"Everything was safe. You had no reason to worry," Tonya says with a sneer.

Looks like she's still chafing under Rayne's leadership, but she'll need to get over it because he's keeping that position.

Linc, looking decidedly unhappy, rushes me into our van. His face is set in a frown, and his stiff, jerky movements show me he's furious.

Is it the strange guy or his mother he's most upset about? Should I have turned down the invitation to dinner? I thought it was a good sign that his mother extended it.

Once we're settled and on our way back to the hotel, I ask him quietly, "Are you okay?"

He clenches his fist on his knee. "I'm sorry. I don't like that you seem to have a tail and...my mother brings out the worst in me."

"We can't worry about the guy. We have no idea if he was even there because of me. Should I have turned down your mother's invitation?"

He turns to face me. "Vela, we do need to worry about some random guy showing up and then escaping in a van. As for the invitation, usually the host truly wants to get to know the guests. My mother," he pauses, "only wants something from you."

I lean back, a little hurt by his comment. "Okay, well, since we don't know what that guy wanted, let's table that for now. And what? You're saying your mom only wants to be close to me because she finally believes I'm the Chosen Child?"

He gives me a sympathetic look. "Yes. That is the only reason. And I'm sorry."

I push back any kind of naivety that Elizabeth Stevenson in interested in me as her daughter-in-law. "So, she will try to use this to her own advantage."

"Absolutely. I wish I had a mother who would welcome you with open arms because you're my wife. But she's driven by power and for that alone, she's accepting you into her inner circle." He mutters a curse under his breath and looks out the window, holding his forehead in his hand.

I try not to use my Borean gift of sensing emotions; I feel it's intrusive. But I can't ignore the waves of pain emanating from my husband.

"Linc, it's not important to me why she invited us to dinner, but that she did. Let's use this to our advantage and make her get to know us as a couple."

He glances at me but resumes his study of the passing buildings.

I notice we're driving through the same commercial area we did on our way to the meeting. There's nothing interesting for Linc to look at, so I know he's suffering silently.

"You're far too trusting, Vela. I know we're supposed to forgive, but...it's hard."

"Sometimes it's a matter of giving it to God. Give Him your pain of an unloving mother." I thread my fingers through his and lean my head on his shoulder, wishing I had a gift that could take his pain from him.

Before he can respond, the van comes to a screeching halt. Linc throws his arm out to keep me from hitting the seat in front of me, even though I'm buckled in.

I'm alert in a second, wondering why we've stopped. Looking out the front window, I see a lone figure standing right in the middle of the road. James is driving, and he stares with his mouth agape at the man he almost hit. Recovering his wits, James sticks his head out the window and asks if the man is all right. When the man responds, all I see is that he's speaking with a strange smile.

"What is it, Papa?" I ask. "What did he say?"

James pulls his head back in the van, his body stiff. "He says he wants to talk to Vela Stevenson." He turns to look at me. "We should go. This could be an ambush."

"How does he know I'm married?" I ask Linc.

He shakes his head. "We got a license, so it is possible." He glares at the man then turns his furious eyes to mine. "You're not getting out of this van."

I see the man call something out, and James leans out the open window to listen. Once he's heard the message, he turns, his face mottled with anger. "He says he has information about the little girl who's sick."

My heart pounds like an anvil in my chest.

Does he have Greta somewhere? Has she been abducted?

With no idea what I'm doing, just that I'm stricken with fear for Greta, I scramble to get out of the van.

Linc wraps his arms around my waist, locking me in place. "You're not going without me and your security team."

I nod frantically and crawl over Jennifer to get out the sliding door. My entire protection team follows me. Jack barks to join me, and I motion for him to come. He jumps out of the van and is at my side, instantly alert, his dark eyes studying the man in the road.

Jack growls low, and the man in the road tenses. "Hey, call him off, or you're never going to hear what I have to say."

I hold my hand down and Jack stays, but his hackles are up. One sign of danger and the man is in trouble if he tries anything.

Linc steps in front of me, while my guards flank Jack and me. "What do you want?" he asks the man in a hard tone.

I step to look around Linc, calling out, "What do you know about Greta?"

The man slowly smiles again. "I thought that would get your attention."

"Is she safe?"

My heart is in my throat when he shrugs. "I don't know."

"Has she been taken?" Linc asks.

"Not for now. At the moment, she's safe from our special attention. But she's sick, ain't she?"

"How do you know that?" I fire at him, concern for Greta clouding my vision. I hold my arms at my sides, ready to use my gifts to force him to give me answers.

He stuffs his hands in his pockets and grins wolfishly. "Oh, we know all kinds of things. Lots of you are sick, am I right? That's too bad," he says, scuffing his shoe, almost nonchalantly. "Don't be surprised if more of you join 'em. You're kind of like a poison, Vela." He squints at me, like he's studying me.

I stiffen and want nothing more than to hurt this man for what he's insinuating. "I'm not making them sick." I choke out the words.

"No, but if you don't go back to that little hole in Canada, more are going to get sick. And your little friend might not recover. I mean," he says with a maniacal grin, "not without our help."

"Who sent you?" I grit out, fisting my hands, trying to keep my elements in. He should be glad we're in a busy commercial district, or I'd be using my powers to extract more information.

"I think you know who. And," he says, holding my gaze, "if you think you can hurt the messenger, understand that we know where your little Greta is staying, and we could pay her a little visit if something happens to me."

"What do you mean, not without our help?" I ask, ignoring his threat.

He laughs. "You don't think we could heal those affected? We can. We have the antidote. For a price, of course," he answers.

And with that, he turns and whistles, walking leisurely down the street.

I want to scream at the information he just gave us, and knowing my hands are tied makes it so much worse. I want to force the information out of him, but I can't, or Greta will be in even more danger.

Linc turns to me, his eyes raging. Smoke is snaking from his clenched fists, and I put my hand in his to calm him down. "The Extremists are behind the illness," he spits out. "And they're going to try to blame it on you."

"Why aren't we following that guy?" Leon asks, his face twisted in anger.

"Because he's just the messenger," Rayne answers. "He wouldn't be stupid enough to lead us anywhere helpful."

Linc nods, agreeing. My knees are weak as I'm led back to the van while my girlfriends and Tex sweep the area to be sure no more surprises are coming.

I climb back into the van, my gaze unfocused and body limp.

"What happened?" Elia asks, her face worried as she grips my arm.

I say with numb lips, "The E.E. are behind the illnesses like we suspected, and they're going to try to pin it on me somehow. And they're threatening Greta's safety if I, what..." I turn panicked eyes to Linc. "if I don't leave and go back to Canada?"

His face is set in stone as he shakes his head. "You're not running. We'll keep Greta safe."

I grab Linc's arm in a death grip. "How can we be sure?"

He looks to David. "We need to get them out of that place. Get them somewhere safe."

David's look is grim. "It's going to be very hard hiding from the E.E. They have eyes everywhere."

"We're going to go invisible then. I'll get my mother to use her connections. Vela," he says, turning deadly serious eyes to me. "We will keep her safe."

Rayne says, "What about them blaming the illnesses on Vela?"

"I've got that one," Elia says, a fierce look coming over her face. Her head is down, bowed over her phone. "You guys need to get me back to the hotel. I need my computer. Don't worry, Vela, they're not going to do this to you. I'll get in front of it."

"The man claimed they have the antidote. We need to get our hands on it," I say with desperation. Fear suddenly has me holding my head in my hands. "Everyone is in danger because of me."

Linc leans toward me. "Vela, we all knew what we were getting into joining your cause. We knew there would be risks."

I pick my head up and say miserably, "But to blame this illness on me?"

Elia says in a tight voice, "I'm afraid it's not just our group that illness has affected. I'm seeing it all over the country."

"*What*?" I cry. I spin in my seat to face her. "What are you talking about?"

Elia gives me a sobering look. "Vela, this flu-thing is everywhere. Elementals are dropping like flies. They're calling it a pandemic."

"They're *dying*?" Adele asks, her face a picture of terror.

Elia shakes her head. "No one is dying right away, but there are lots of very sick Elementals filling up the hospitals."

Terror climbs my throat at the danger Greta is in. James puts the van into gear and starts driving again.

Linc says, "The Extremists are behind this. They must have made the virus in a lab and are spreading it."

James adds, "And to think that's not enough. They're trying to somehow pin this on Vela. Unbelievable."

"They have the cure! All for a price, the guy said. They're trying to profit from this," I say. "How can they possibly blame this on me? How on earth could I be responsible for something this widespread?"

Petra says hotly, "Vela, this looks bleak, but we'll get ahead of it."

"What about dinner with your mother?" I ask Linc, surprised I could even remember it.

Linc rubs his mouth. "This may be fortuitous timing. She can give us some more insight into what's happening across the country. And we can talk with her about getting our people safely away from Salt Lake City and hidden."

"It is," Elia says grimly as she furiously types on her phone. "I'm seeing more reports here in the U.S., but it's spreading worldwide."

"Linc, we can't possibly have dinner with Elizabeth right now. I'm freaking out here."

He grabs my face and looks directly in my eyes. "Vela, you need to stay on top of this. We expected kickback from the E.E. This is just something we have to handle."

"A *global pandemic*?" I screech. "Linc, this is *insane.*"

"I know it is," he says, trying to sound calm. "But we're going to get ahead of it. Vela, look at me," he orders when my eyes go all over.

I force myself to focus on Linc. "Linc, I can't do this."

He shuts his eyes briefly. Opening them, he says, "Yes, you can. This seems impossible, but it's not. Let's get back to the hotel and regroup. We need to get Greta and the others to safety, and then we can focus on this new threat."

I nod because that's all I'm capable of right now.

God where are You in this? I need Your guidance.

We finish our drive, everyone talking over each other, but I sit in silence, unable to comprehend this entire situation. I suddenly feel every bit of my seventeen years. I'm woefully unprepared for this. Jack whines as he rests his head on my lap.

We make it back to the hotel, and just when I don't think anything else can surprise me, Petra's reaction to a man who passes her on the way to the lobby has me stopping in my tracks. Her face is blank with shock and her body leans, seemingly on its own, toward a tall, lean stranger, who's looking at her with a mirrored expression of shock on his weathered face.

I realize he's an Elemental, but I'm not close enough to tell which element he is. His hands are clenched into fists, and his mouth opens and closes, his face white. His gray hair matches Petra's, and they both are just standing still, dumbly staring at each other.

She approaches him carefully, like one wrong move will make him disappear. Her nose flairs, and I realize that this man is Petra's Intended. My heart, as loaded down with worry about all I've learned from the Extremists, lifts at this miraculous occasion.

"Who are you?" Petra asks.

"My name is Peter," he croaks.

I continue to gape at them, but I'm completely ignored as Petra introduces herself. They're a match made in heaven with their names being so similar. Then an awful thought comes to me. This man might be married.

Petra seems to have that same fear, because she studies Peter's left hand. When she doesn't see a ring, her face breaks out in a great big smile.

"Is it really possible after all these years?" Peter asks, hungrily looking over Petra's face.

She nods happily, and they both turn and walk into the hotel together.

I sigh as Linc walks up to me, his eyes moving everywhere to see what's made me stop like I have. "What is it?" he asks.

Rayne is already on the move, with Tex checking out the area for any more surprises.

"Petra just bumped into her Intended," I say with awe, shaking my head.

He whips his head at me. "Are you serious?"

"Yes. She purposely never married, determined to wait for her Intended, for Peter."

"And he's unattached?" he asks as he takes me by the elbow and pulls me inside.

I allow him to lead me and nod. "It looks like it."

"Unbelievable."

"Definitely." I hold on to this moment of happiness because I know we have a lot to unpack when we get to our room.

Linc instructs everyone, "We have a suite. Let's all meet there in ten minutes. Elia, try to find out what's going on."

Kane guides Elia, who nods distractedly as she's led to her room, since her head is down studying her phone, not watching where she's going.

The Girls take the job of doing a sweep of the perimeter of the hotel. Leon and Tex follow Linc and me to our room to guard the door.

I take Jack's leash from Linc, and we head into the room after Tex checks it's safe. My head is swimming with all that just transpired. When Linc shuts the door to our suite, I go to the couch and drop onto it.

One thing is for sure. I need to get it together. As happy as I am for Petra, Linc is right. This is just one more retaliation from the E.E. It's not the end of the world. But it feels like it.

Linc studies his phone.

I pick my head up. "Everything was going so great. I don't know why I thought the Extremists were just going to let me go viral and unite the country without trying to stop me."

He sets his mouth in a grim line.

"I would never have expected that they would attack their own clans to force me to quit, though."

"They won't stop there. Vela, they want your blood. They want you to disappear, and they just proved they will do everything they can to make that happen. We need to be constantly on the move."

"Linc, this pandemic feels like the end of the world."

He comes to sit next to me. "And they want you to feel defeated when this needs to energize you. Allow the anger to fuel you."

I sit up and take a deep breath. "I'm scared of what they're capable of."

"Then be our protector. Let's think two steps ahead of them, now that we know what they're doing."

I nod and allow the fear to morph to something much more dangerous. Anger.

"We need to find the cure. Didn't Elia and Kane infiltrate the local Extremist unit this year?"

Linc looks up slowly, his eyes tightening.

And then I smile. "I have an idea."

41

Linc

When Vela tells me her idea, I sit back in shock. It's crazy and is also possibly her best idea yet.

She looks at me, her eyes bright with anticipation and anger. I told her to allow her anger to fuel her, but I did not mean this.

"Vela, I don't know. This is..."

"It's brilliant. Linc, we have to take this chance. We need that antidote. Before Elementals start dying. And it's been done before by Elia and Kane."

I blow out my breath. "Vela, what Elia did was crazy, and you're asking her to do it again?" Elia and Kane went undercover with the Extremists while we were in Canada, and as successful as it was, it was dangerous. "They were almost killed!"

"No, not Elia or Kane, obviously, but two other volunteers. I can't do it, for obvious reasons."

Fire dances in my blood. "You are not going undercover. Over my dead body," I say with deadly calm.

She looks exasperated as she drops into a seat next to me. "I just said that I wouldn't go." She fingers the couch cushion. "But I wish I could. I can't just sit here and do nothing."

I run my hands through my hair. "Vela, what you're doing is the most important thing right now. Uniting the clans is God's mission. We'll continue gathering the support of the Grand Elders and putting you in front of Elementals. We're just going to have to be very careful as we move around."

The thought of Vela putting herself out there more than necessary, going undercover, has me wanting to burn a fire so hot it would destroy anything in its path.

A knock sounds, and I get up to let in our first team member. After a quick check through the peephole, I open the door to reveal a group. David and Whitney give me grim looks as they step inside, followed by Elia and Kane. Elia has her computer balanced on one hand while she types with the other. Kane guides her in. I'm surprised to see Petra, who comes in, her face beaming.

"Congratulations, Petra."

She gives me a grateful nod. "This hasn't distracted me from what we came here to do."

I give her a respectful look. "We would all understand if you'd like to go and get to know your Intended."

She gives me a smile. "We have a date later. We have the rest of our lives to get to know each other. Right now, it's important to figure out our next steps."

David raises his voice, so it carries over to us. "We need to make a plan to get out of here. It's clear the E.E. knows where Vela is. We need to do a better job of concealing her travels and location."

"Well, for one thing, our private plane sticks out like a sore thumb," Whitney says, standing next to Vela, who's biting her nail.

"You're right," I say, joining everyone in our small sitting room. "I'll ask my mother if there's an airfield where she can store it."

More arrive, and when I return to the group, Vela starts telling them her idea.

Rayne, Adele, Sandy, and James stand together and when they've gotten caught up on Vela's plan, Rayne gives me an exasperated look. I ignore him and this time, when there's a knock on the door, I let someone else open it.

"I know the perfect candidate, well, one of them," Petra says, her face set in determination.

I have an idea of who she's considering, and I'm not sure I agree with her.

Once I'm sure everyone is here, I call loudly for attention, since everyone's talking. When the room quiets, I say, "Okay, we all know that the E.E. has been busy. They've tracked Vela here, and we need to counter their plan to use Vela as a scapegoat for these illnesses."

"There's a name for it now," Elia says soberly, her eyes finally ungluing from her screen. "They're calling it the Black Fever."

Vela speaks up, "The E.E. has a cure for it, and we need to find it. Who's willing to go undercover and infiltrate the organization?"

James says, "I don't think it should be any of us on the leadership team. We need two healthy volunteers, preferably young adults."

"That leaves just a few options," Vela says. Then her face goes white.

"What is it?" I ask, fearful for what would make the blood drain from her face.

"They also can't have two elements," she says quietly, giving me a meaningful look.

Furrowing my eyebrows. "Well, then we can't send anyone, can we? Everyone who's healthy has two elements."

Vela presses her lips into a thin line. But her eyes are full of an idea. And she doesn't like it. That much I can read.

"What is it, Vela?" I ask.

She breathes out slowly. "We can send two of ours just fine. But I'll have to take one of their gifts and keep it for them."

A gasp sounds around the room.

It's Petra who says, "That sounds like the plan, then. You held Rayne's gifts for a week, didn't ya?"

Vela nods, looking sick. "Who would volunteer for such a thing, though?"

"I think Steele should be one of them. He would be a great candidate," Petra says.

I really hate when I'm right. And Steele would never be altruistic enough to give up an element.

Rayne counters, "He can't be relied on for something like this. I'll go." His voice is strained, probably because he remembers how it felt to have his elements ripped from him. It's pretty courageous of him to offer, really.

Adele was already scowling at him for his comment about Steele, but now she's pushing his shoulder. "You can't go. You're needed here."

"I agree," I say. "You're leading Vela's security team. That's too important a job to abandon."

"What about Debra?" Elia asks. "She has a good head on her shoulders, which you need when going undercover."

Grant objects, "Not my daughter. She's lived too long in Canada. She's still getting used to being back in the States."

"She's adjusting fine," Adele argues. "You just don't want her to be one of the volunteers."

"Well, then, why don't you do it?" Grant fires back.

A contemplative look comes over her face.

"Absolutely not," James and Vela say at the same time. Sandy shakes her head emphatically. Rayne's face is a thundercloud, about to explode.

Rayne argues, "She's not even seventeen! Why can't Tonya or one of the other girls do it?"

"We need them for Vela's protection," Petra says in an un-yielding tone.

"They do like young and impressionable members to join," Elia says with a thoughtful look at Adele.

Kane says, "You had to slather inches of makeup on your face to look older when we went undercover. You can't really expect a sixteen-year-old to do this."

"I was seventeen. If I could do it, she can too," Elia says.

Sandy looks distressed, and James waves his arms. "No way am I letting my daughter go undercover with the Extremists."

"And you want *mine* to volunteer?" Grant asks, his face a mottled red. Mary, too, looks sick at the thought.

"Look," I say, holding out my hands. "We all need to calm down. We need two volunteers. I think that's safer than just one. We don't have a big pool to choose from, and the only ones with no responsibilities right now are the teens. If Steele goes, which I haven't decided is a good fit, he'll need someone with him who's more his age."

"Are there any adults who aren't on the leadership or security team?" Vela asks.

"The last two just came down with the...Black Fever," Whitney says, her face drawn with concern.

"Well, then," Petra says, her hands on her hips. "If we're doing this, sending two undercover, they'll need to be teens."

The room erupts in angry voices, the three loudest, James, Rayne, and Grant as they argue amongst each other.

I'm about to call the room to order, when a piercing whistle fills the air, and all attention is drawn to Adele, who's standing on the table, her fingers in her mouth.

When the room settles, she announces, "I'll do it. I'll go with Steele."

Sandy gasps and James shouts, "No, you won't!" Rayne looks like he's about to pick her up off the table and carry her out the door.

Adele's face hardens. "We need that antidote, don't we? And I can blend in better than Debra when she's not used to the U.S. yet. I work well with Steele, too. They'll never suspect us."

James's jaw clenches in anger. "You are not old enough to make this decision."

"Well, then allow me to go."

"No." He fumes, his jaw working.

"Papa, this is for the benefit of the world. If we get our hands on this antidote, we could use it to cure...how many sick people are there now, Elia?"

"Thousands, and the number is rising," Elia answers.

"See?" Adele flings her arms out. She steps off the table onto a chair, then to the floor. She approaches her dad. "Steele and I will be safe if we keep our heads down, and Elia and Kane tell us everything we need to know to stay undercover."

Rayne explodes into action. In two strides, he's in front of Adele. "If you think I'm going to let you go into the enemy's den with *Steele* to protect you, then you've gone certifiably crazy."

James looks directly at me, and his face hardens. "Whose insane idea was this?"

I cough. Before I can answer, Vela says in a clear voice, "It was mine, Papa."

He gives her a scathing look but remains quiet.

Rayne looks around the room. "You can't all seriously be considering this?"

Vela asks, "Adele looks just like me. What if they confuse her for me?"

"Now, that is a legitimate concern," Petra says.

Elia answers, "Makeup can alter anyone's looks. Add a wig, and I can make her unrecognizable."

James shakes his head and looks down, studying the floor. Rayne clenches his fists at his sides as he glares at Adele, who ignores him.

"If you'll consider allowing Adele to be one of the volunteers, we'll put it to a vote," I say uneasily. I don't know how I feel about Vela's sister doing this crazy mission. Vela looks sick with worry.

James presses his lips together.

Adele moves around the seething Rayne and puts her hand on James's arm. "Papa, I can do this. I want to help."

"At the expense of your life?" he asks in a cracked voice.

"If Elia can do it, I can. I know my limits. Let me do this, Papa."

"Steele hasn't even agreed to this."

"Let's get him in here," I say to Petra, who nods and leaves the room. She returns in a few minutes, with a bewildered Steele in tow.

"We have a job for you, son," Petra says, eyeing him down.

"What is it?" he asks.

Adele walks up to stand next to him when Petra answers, "We need you and Adele to go undercover with the Extremists to find the antidote for this Black Fever that's spread everywhere."

"Is that what it's called now?" he asks.

"It is," Petra says. "Will you do it?"

He shrugs. "Sure. If Adele is going, I'll go."

Vela stands in front of him. "What if I have to take one of your gifts and hold it for you until you find the antidote?"

His face hardens. "You'd give it back?"

"Of course."

"It wouldn't disappear somewhere if it takes a while for us to find the antidote, would it?"

Vela shakes her head. "No, I would hold it for as long as you need me to."

"Why do I have to give up a gift?"

"Are you seriously that dense?" Rayne sneers. "Because the Extremists are extremely prejudiced against mixed races. They'd sniff both your gifts out immediately. The Extremists would kill you on sight if you walked in with two elements."

Vela holds her hand out to calm Rayne down, then turns to Steele. "Rayne is right. But you are not dense. It's a perfectly acceptable question. Are you still willing even if you only have one gift?"

"Can I choose which one I want to keep?" he asks. "My second gift isn't really that well developed yet."

"Absolutely."

Well, okay, maybe he is altruistic enough. Call me surprised.

Adele perks up. "My Gyan gift hasn't even manifested yet. Do you need to take it?"

Vela studies her. "I can still sense it dormant inside you, so yes."

Adele deflates. "Oh, okay, then."

Rayne blows up, looking around the whole room. "Are you all serious about Steele going? Did you see his reaction? He thinks this will be easy. He only cares that he'll get to spend time alone with Adele." He glares at Steele, whose face hardens.

Steele straightens at Rayne's words. "If Adele can do it, so can I," he bites out. "I don't want her to do this alone. Even if I have to go with just one gift."

Rayne leans into Steele's face. "If we asked you to go with anyone else, you'd say no."

Steele lifts a shoulder. "Probably."

The room, again, erupts in angry voices.

"He can't be relied on."

"He's a loose cannon, anyway."

"Steele is the worst person for this job."

I whistle loudly, like Adele did earlier and ask Steele, "Can you tell us one reason why we can rely on you to do this?"

"Sure. Because I would never let anything happen to Adele. She'll be safe with me. And I can pretend to be someone else. That's easy enough."

I move to stand in between Steele and Rayne, who looks like he's ready to put his fist through Steele's face. Steele isn't backing down, either, which makes me respect him more. He'll need nerves of, well steel, to accomplish what we're asking him to do.

"James, Sandy? What do you think? Do you give Adele permission?" I ask.

He studies Steele for a moment and then, after looking at Adele, finally nods. "Only if Steele swears he'll protect our daughter with his life."

"I will," Steele answers promptly, then returns to glaring at Rayne who is the obvious threat.

Adele looks satisfied and then grips Rayne's arm and drags him out the door.

"Rayne, will you ask Leon and Tex to come in and vote on this?" I ask before he leaves the room.

He glares at me and then disappears behind the door with Adele.

One thing is for certain, there's no way we will make it to dinner with my mother, which is the one good thing I can say about this day.

42

Rayne

As soon as we're out the door, Adele spins me around and leans into my face. "What are you doing?" she seethes.

I give a look to Leon and Tex and motion my head for them to give us some room. They back away down the hall, but are still within hearing distance, unfortunately.

I turn to Adele. "Maybe I'm trying to save your life?" I want to shake sense into her stubborn little head but would never do it.

"Did you stop to think for one second that I'm doing this for us?"

I stumble back a step. My face must look as confused as I feel because she leans in again and explains.

"If I can be trusted with something this big, don't you think my father will trust me enough to date you?" She pokes my chest with her finger.

I capture her finger and ask, "You volunteered for an extremely dangerous mission just so you can date me?" I reach and put my hand on her forehead. Nope, no fever.

She smacks my hand away. "Listen, you big oaf. I meant what I said about wanting to save lives. I'd do that in a heartbeat, but it's even better if it means we can enjoy the benefits."

I bark a shocked laugh and turn around, holding my head. "She's crazy. I'm bonded with a crazy person."

With a growl, Adele spins me around again. "No, I'm not," she seethes.

This time, I lean into her face and grab her shoulders. "Adele, you are relying on an *idiot* to protect you. There is no universe where I'll agree to you doing this...especially with that little..."

She clamps her hand over my mouth. "Stop. Stop this alpha male nonsense right now. I am perfectly capable of protecting myself. That you don't agree makes me want to hurt you. So, don't make me."

I shake my head, taking her hand off my mouth. "Adele, I can't let you go into danger with *Steele, of all people.* I wouldn't trust him with my garbage."

Adele's face hardens. "Steele is capable, regardless of whether you believe it. He got a good shot on you, didn't he?"

I throw out my hand. "That was lucky. I was trying to keep that conversation peaceful."

Then she turns to face me fully, crossing her arms over her chest. "Do you want to date me?"

I look at her with wide eyes. "I'm not going to answer that unless you agree to abandon this entirely impossible idea."

She narrows her eyes at me. "Then I guess you'll be waiting a long time. Because I won't abandon it. You don't think I can do this."

I run my hands through my hair. "You're impossible. Adele, I would do anything to date you officially, but not at this cost. The thought of you going into that diabolical group makes me want to kill somebody. I don't think I can handle it."

Her eyes soften. She reaches and holds onto my arms that tremble with the need to protect her, even if it's from herself.

"You can't control me, Rayne. So, please don't try. I can do this. If they vote for me and Steele to go, I'm going."

I look at her, seriously contemplating hauling her over my shoulder and hiding her some place where no one can find her. I shake my head and say, "I think you're capable of great things. Just don't go with Steele. I don't trust him."

Her eyes harden. "You don't trust me to be alone with him."

I exhale. "You're right. I don't trust what he'll do once he gets you alone. He's capable of anything."

"Do you think I can defend myself?" Her eyes pierce through my strongest defenses.

When I don't answer, she laughs in a self-depreciating way. "I didn't think so."

"Look," I rush to say. "I haven't actually seen you fight yet. And I'm sure Steele is useless."

"No, he's not," she fires back. "He's actually a great fighter, and if you had any sense at all, you'd know I am, too."

"*I* want to protect you, not him," I growl.

"Well, you can't! You have to stay here and guard my sister."

I turn my head. "I can't believe Vela is even considering allowing you to go."

"This isn't Vela's decision," she shouts. "It's mine. And mine alone. At least I know what you really think of me." She turns and reaches for the door handle.

Before she can turn it, I grab her hand and pull her back. She steps back but keeps her back to me. I say, "I'm sorry, Adele. I don't want you to be in danger, and this is more dangerous than anything Vela is doing. I can't help but be against it. But, if it matters at all to you, I think you're very qualified and would do an amazing job. I just can't stand the idea of you being in any kind of danger."

She nods at my words and turns the handle, allowing herself back in the room. Leon and Tex walk back, giving me sympathetic looks.

I hold up my hand. "Don't say one word. I don't want to hear it. But you're both wanted inside." Before they can open the door, I hold them both by the shoulders. "If either of you vote for Adele and Steele to go, I will personally make sure you're miserable."

Leon scoffs, but Tex looks appropriately warned.

We walk inside, and I growl when I see Adele standing next to Steele.

Linc is talking, "Anyone who has a reason to think Steele and Adele won't be a good fit, please let us know what those concerns are."

I'm about to speak up when Linc holds his hand up in my direction. "We know your feelings on the subject. Anyone else?"

I lean back, crossing my arms, furious I'm not able to speak my mind.

"No offense, Steele," Grant says, "but you're not known to go out of your way to help others, I mean, at Saddleback, anyway."

Steele scowls but doesn't defend himself. I look on in amusement. He's going to bury himself with his adolescent ways.

"You've never volunteered for a job before," Mary says.

"I didn't volunteer for this one either, but here I am, willing," Steele answers.

The room erupts in mutters, but Linc quiets everyone down.

"You always skimped on the chores around Saddleback, too," James says. "How can we be sure you'll give 110% to this mission?"

Steele opens his mouth, then closes it. He seems to think to himself, then finally answers, "I just will. I wouldn't let Adele get hurt because of something I did."

"Or didn't do," I growl.

He glares at me. "Obviously."

"Actually, no, it's not obvious," I say, ignoring Linc's call for me to stop talking. I go to Steele and lean into his face. "You have proved to just about everyone here that you're completely unreliable."

Even though Steele straightens to his full height, he's still an inch shorter than me, but he looks up at me defiantly. "Just because I wasn't the most helpful guy around Saddleback, doesn't mean I can't do something I actually believe in. And I believe in this. We need that antidote. I'll help get it."

"You mean, you'll help Adele get it," I snarl in his face.

"You've got that right. I'm not afraid of the Extremists. I would never let Adele do this alone."

"Then you're going in blind," Linc says, who's at my side, holding my shoulder back. "You need a healthy fear for an organization that has ended hundreds, no thousands of lives trying to find Vela. And now, they're attempting to murder millions more just to discredit her."

Steele's jaw works. "I understand that more than you know. I've had to hide my whole life because of that group. I'm not hiding anymore, and I'm not afraid to infiltrate them, either."

Linc studies him then turns to the group, keeping a hold of my shoulder. "Let's take this to a vote. Whoever thinks Adele and Steele should go undercover, raise your hands."

Several people seem to have lost their doubts about Steele after his last statement, and I want to scream in frustration. He's fooling them all. I believe his anger at the E.E., but I don't for one second trust him with Adele's life in the balance. I keep my hand down and give Tex and Leon a rather unhinged look that promises punishment if they raise theirs.

Leon smirks at me and, along with half the room, raises his hand. James and Sandy whisper among themselves before they, too, raise their hands.

"That's the majority," Linc announces. "Steele and Adele, you two bunk down with Elia and Kane and find out everything you can about staying under the radar while you go undercover.

When you're done with that, come back here. Vela will take your latent gifts."

I'm still in Vela and Linc's suite with the intention of going over her security, but my mind is far away from our current conversation.

"Let's go over our travel route," Petra says. The others on the leadership team lean over a computer screen and talk over the different routes we could take to throw the E.E. off our trail.

How can any of them be thinking of anything else but the suicide mission they've just agreed for a sixteen-year-old girl and seventeen-year-old kid to undertake?

I realize my name has been spoken several times, and I didn't hear it. "Yes?" I scowl at everyone; furious they all voted for their asinine plan to happen.

Vela says in a gentle tone, "Rayne, if we didn't believe in both Adele's and Steele's capabilities, we wouldn't have voted that they go on this mission."

"It's dangerous," I say between gritted teeth.

"So is this. We're all in danger every day, as long as we oppose the E.E."

"This is different. We're sending them into the lion's den."

"Daniel was protected from three hungry lions," Vela says softly.

I whip my head at her. "The E.E is a significantly larger group than that," I snarl at her.

"Watch your tone, Rayne," Linc warns.

I rub my neck. "I'm sorry Vela. I'm just going crazy with worry."

"We understand that," Vela says, folding her hands together. "This decision was not taken lightly."

"Let me go instead of Steele," I say in a breathless rush. "If Steele is so capable, then put him in my place in charge of security."

Linc says, "It makes more sense for Steele and Adele to go. They're closer in age."

"I'm eighteen. That's not a big age difference."

Vela answers instead of Linc, "You look much older. Steele and Adele just make more sense."

"Not to me, they don't. How are they supposed to do this, exactly? They'll have to stay in one area to earn the E.E.'s trust. You don't expect them to get the answer for the antidote in just one meeting?"

"We'll stay with them," James says. "We'll choose an area and find out where that cell is meeting. They'll keep going until they learn something."

"So now we're going to be separated?" I ask, giving James a look I know he won't appreciate, but I can't hold back my feelings on this subject.

"Yes. I'm sorry, Rayne. You're going to have to trust her mother and me."

I pierce him with a glare. "And Steele."

He nods. "Yes. You have to let her do this, son."

For the first time, I wish my own father was here to lend me his support. Then I dismiss that thought because my father would probably have voted for Adele to go. He's always respected strength and if Adele isn't a display of that, then nothing is.

"Are you going to be able to continue leading my security, Rayne?" Vela asks. "Is this going to distract you too much?"

I think hard about my answer.

What would be better for Adele in the long run? Me staying behind to make sure things run smoothly for Vela, or following Adele wherever she goes to make sure she's safe?

I consider my options. I have no money or way to stay off the beaten path here. If I were in the wilds of Canada, there would be no question; I'd follow Adele in a heartbeat. But, here in the States, I would stick out like a sore thumb. I'd have to live like a homeless person, and Adele would not respect that.

What she would respect is for me to continue keeping her sister safe.

My decision made, I say, "I'll stay and keep you safe. But," I warn James, "if Adele needs me, if she is in any real danger, I want to be notified immediately."

James nods, and we continue with our discussion.

And, just like that, my Intended is going to infiltrate the most lethal group on this planet. With a total buffoon to protect her.

43

Vela

The next couple of weeks are a whirlwind of activity. Linc's mom takes care of squirreling away the sick members of our group, including my precious Greta, out of Salt Lake City. We don't even know where they are; the location is so secret. We don't want to risk any communication between us being intercepted.

It's tricky, but I'm able to extricate Adele's and Steele's second gifts from them. It's not easy to say goodbye to my family. I let Adele, Mama, and Papa go with a sore heart as they leave to find a viable place for Steele and Adele to slip into a meeting without any extra attention.

Elia was instrumental in finding a good place for Steele and Adele. She also taught my sister how to apply makeup well enough to disguise herself from looking too much like me. With a dark brown wig, she truly looks transformed.

I travel to the other two Grand Elders and, just like with the Gyan and Festan Grand Elders, my performances go off without a hitch.

Travel has been tricky, but so far, we've stayed undetected by the Extremists on our journeys to Florida to meet the Neronian Grand Elder and to New York for the Borean Grand Elder.

Elizabeth worked closely with the Borean Grand Elder to get me into the Jones Beach Amphitheater in Wantagh, New York, which seats 15,000. Elizabeth set a date in two days where I'm going in under the guise of an inspirational speaker, which I guess isn't too far from the truth. The four Grand Elders reserved the whole amphitheater, an astronomical feat, so that tickets can only be purchased through them. Elementals will staff the event and guard the entrances to make sure no humans sneak in.

I wonder how successful that will be. We've never met in such large numbers before, so I can only hope our world stays a secret.

Linc says I've clearly made an impression on the four leading members of our clans for them to go these measures to arrange for their clans to hear from me and see my demonstration.

Rayne has had his job tested at every level trying to keep me from being discovered. He worked closely with the leadership team to arrange for us to travel only at night and to take as many back roads as possible.

My team is convinced the main roads are monitored. After that scare with the Extremist stopping us in the street, we've turned in our rentals and purchased two vans with cash so we can travel with no paper trail.

Most of the sick members of our group have recovered and met us in New York to rejoin our efforts. But Elementals continue to get sick, and there have been hundreds of confirmed deaths. The immune-compromised and elderly are most affected.

Some have recovered, but to my great distress, Greta continues to suffer. Hannah calls me to give me updates, but I know she's terrified Greta won't survive this. That makes me want to stop what I'm doing to go to her, but Hannah has been dead set against it. She's convinced me to continue with my mission. That Greta is stable, at the very least, offers me a small amount of comfort and only serves as more motivation.

Hannah thinks that Greta may have an autoimmune disorder that has never been detected because of their remote living in Canada. That could explain why she's been so deeply affected by this illness.

Steele and Adele are working to find the antidote, but they've only attended two meetings. Thanks to me taking their secondary gifts, at least they haven't been discovered, so far.

Right now, I'm in our rental house near Wantagh, a small two-bedroom house, reading over the new speech Grant has just given me. I appreciate the soft pastel colors of this house's style. It reminds me of my mom's décor in our first house in California. I'm on a very comfortable floral couch that makes me want to take a nap. I realize I've gone over the last sentence four times, and it hasn't sunk in yet, so I put the papers down and rub my eyes. Linc rubs my neck.

"If you keep up with that, I'll never learn this," I warn and sigh softly. "I'll fall asleep."

"We can't have that, can we?" he says, and moves his hands to trail kisses down my neck.

"No, not really. I'm supposed to learn this by tonight so I can practice on all of you." I lean away from him and his tempting lips. "My mind is too full, anyway."

He puts his chin on my shoulder and because he knows me so well, asks, "You're worried about Greta, aren't you?"

I nod. "I can't stand that she's so sick."

"I know, but she's going to be okay. She's in the perfect hands."

"Do you think she should go to the hospital?"

"No, they have no cure for her. And if Hannah is right about her having an autoimmune disorder, it would be dangerous for her to go where so many are sick."

"And are the rumors that I've spread a poison among the Elementals still going strong?"

"Elia has been brilliant online, refuting every website that pops up, but she's not catching them all."

"She needs a team of people helping her." I rub my forehead at the headache blooming there.

"Since she's recovered, Helen has been a huge help. She's good with the intricacies of the web and between the two of them, they're chasing down any sites that pop up."

"Can you ask your mom to lend Elia some support? I'm sure she has great connections."

He sighs. "She's still miffed we never had dinner with her. She's insisting we go tonight. They've rented a house near here. Do you want to go? We could ask her then."

I find myself nodding. We've only communicated with his mother through email and phone calls, but she's been surprisingly supportive. "I think we should. Two birds with one stone."

Jack nudges my knee, and I put down my papers and give him proper attention. Dropping to my knees, I bury my face in Jack's neck. "I've sorely neglected you, buddy, I know. When this is all over, I'll get you a friend." I scratch behind his ears where he loves. I look up at Linc. "What do you think about that? Getting your own dog?"

Linc looks thoughtful, but a smile comes out, and I know he likes the idea. "We could get a female," he muses.

"You know," I say mischievously. "Jack isn't neutered. He could make a family if we got a female who hasn't been spayed."

Linc's face lights up. "I would love that. Puppies? Jack, what do you think about that, boy?"

Jack jumps up at the rise in our voices and goes to Linc, wanting to play.

"I think he likes that idea," I say, giggling.

Jack has still accompanied me to my meetings with the Grand Elders, but it's been one meeting after another, and I've barely given him any attention at all.

Linc drops to the ground next to him. He starts to roll around the ground with Jack, who jumps around trying to nip Linc. When Linc can't get a hold of Jack, he comes to me and pushes me to the ground. He's leaning over me, holding my arms over my head and even though I'm laughing, Jack takes exception to this. He pushes himself between us and really does nip Linc, who howls when he gets him in the side.

"Okay, okay, I won't wrestle my own wife," he complains.

Of course, whenever I'm on the ground, Jack knows it's playtime. He barks two short barks and jumps around. I've never been one to rough play with Jack, but Linc has no such compunction. Now that he's not wrestling me, Jack allows Linc to push him around. Jack jumps back onto him, playfully biting Linc's arm. He never bites down, so Linc isn't afraid to continue to toss Jack from one place to another.

I climb back onto the couch and rest the back of my head on the cushion. After a few minutes, Linc tires of his roughhousing with Jack and joins me, flinging his arm over my shoulders.

"It's nice to have a moment of downtime, isn't it?" Linc asks me.

"Mmm, hmmm." I close my eyes for a second, trying to turn off my mind, which started right back on the issues I was worried about before. I open them when Linc presses a soft kiss to my lips.

"Can I distract you from your thoughts?" he asks, a twinkle in his eyes.

I'm about to answer when someone knocks on the door.

Linc yells, "Go away!" He returns to kissing me with delightful intensity.

"Linc," I moan against his lips. "It might be important."

"I don't care," he growls. "We've hardly had any time alone."

I gently push him. "Yes, you do care. Now, go answer the door."

He groans loudly, but with one movement, he's off the couch and strolling toward the door.

"This better be important," he calls and opens the door.

Petra is standing there with a worried look on her face. "We've got a problem."

Linc hangs his head. "Petra, there's always a problem."

She pushes her way inside. "This time it's bad."

I stand up and walk over, shutting the door when Petra forgets to. My heart pounds against my chest, and I whisper the words I don't want to, "Is Greta okay?"

She walks into the small kitchen. "It's not that. The lies the Extremists are spreading about you are starting to push through whatever Elia is doing. There have been some concerns raised about your event."

"Are they canceling her speech?" Linc asks, his hands on his hips.

"Not yet. The email says they want her to go in for some tests. But I think it might be a trap the E.E. are setting for Vela."

"Have you contacted the rest of leadership?" Linc asks.

Petra holds up her phone. "Elia just sent me the email. I came straight over."

Elia set up untraceable email accounts for communications with the Chosen Child, one for overenthusiastic fans and another for contact with area Elders and the Grand Elders.

Linc blows a breath into his hands. "We have dinner with my mother in an hour. I'll pass it to her tech people and see if they can find out if it's legit."

"What do they think?" I ask. "That I'm carrying around a virus that's contaminating everyone?"

Petra nods. "That's exactly what they're spinning. That you're like a poison, infecting Elementals wherever you go."

I look at Linc. "That's what that Extremist said that day on the road. He said I'm a poison. We need Elia here."

"I think this is out of her hands," Petra says with pinched lips.

"Let's gather the team and put our heads together," Linc suggests.

After a few calls, we all assemble. Linc had already sent over the email to his mother, and we wait for a response.

David says, "I don't like this one bit. How do we know that email is from the amphitheater where Vela is scheduled to speak?"

"We need to figure that out," Linc says.

Rick adds, "The Extremists can impersonate anyone."

"So, if I don't submit to these tests, then I can't speak?" I clarify.

Petra nods. "That's what this is saying. But I think it's the E.E."

Elia has been working feverishly on her computer since she arrived, and I ask her, "Elia, what do you think?"

"If this is the E.E.," she answers, "then they're making this email airtight. Everything is saying it's legit. Let me keep looking."

I nod and pace the room. "How close do you think Adele and Steele are to finding out about the antidote?"

Whitney answers, folding her arms as she leans against the kitchen counter. "We have no way of knowing when that information will be revealed in a meeting. We've given them burner phones so nothing can be traced to us, and we've been communicating, but nothing has been said yet."

Linc approaches me. "If we're going to dinner with my mother, we need to leave soon. Do you want to change?"

I look down at my jeans and long-sleeved shirt. "Is this not okay for a private dinner with your parents?"

He looks sheepish. "She usually dresses up for dinner."

"Oh, well, give me a minute then." I rush into our bedroom, Jack following me. I'm glad we've had some time to shop for nicer outfits on our travels. I now have two dresses and a pantsuit I plan to wear when I speak in the amphitheater. *If* I speak in the amphitheater. I debate on whether to wear one of my dresses or the pants to dinner tonight. I choose the suit because it's dressy enough, and I feel like it gives me a measure of confidence with Linc's mother.

I come out dressed, my hair pulled back in a large bun at the base of my neck. While I was in the bathroom putting on my makeup, Linc changed into a shirt and tie.

He gives me an appreciative glance, and I smile.

Why does one look from him turn my knees to jelly?

Linc announces to the room, "Hopefully, my mother's tech team can break through the source of this email. We'll find out tonight if they did."

I say goodbye to my parents and the others, missing James and Sandy, too.

I settle into the car Linc bought not too long ago. We realized we travel faster on our own than in the van, so we wanted our own vehicle. We also appreciate the privacy it affords.

"I'm worried about Adele and Steele. Have they heard anything useful?" I ask, setting my purse on my lap.

Linc puts the address of his parent's rental into the car's navigation system then looks behind him as he backs out of the driveway. "No, not really. I think because they're new members, the organization is careful about what they share in front of them."

"Are we sure it's an actual Extremist meeting?"

"Positive."

"And Greta, any change with her?"

As Linc drives down the road, his face hardens. "No, I'm afraid not."

I fall into silence, my thoughts spinning with worry over my precious little friend and my sister being in the hands of our enemy.

God, I need Your peace right now. Please, Lord, put Your hand over Greta and heal her. And, Lord, I'm begging You, protect my sister and Steele. Help them find the cure for the Black Fever so we can heal Greta and the others. Lord, I can't lose that little girl. If she's dear to me, then I know she's absolutely precious to You. Care for her, Lord. Heal her, I pray.

I look up from my prayer, wiping my damp eyes. Linc gives me a soft smile and covers my hand with his.

We arrive at Linc's parents' rental home, and I'm praying again for answers about this mysterious email. We stop at the front gate, and Linc buzzes for entrance. Our admittance is granted immediately and the gate swings open.

Like her Festan base of operations, this place is enormous. It would easily fit three of my house back in Breckinridge.

I swallow. "This is a mansion, Linc. This is a rental?"

He glances at the building and then smirks as he navigates the circular driveway around a fountain and parks by the double front doors. "It is. I thought you'd expect this of my mother by now?"

I press my back into my seat and ask something that's been lurking in my mind, "Linc, is your father a presence in your life at all? It seems to be your mother that you speak of the most."

Linc frowns and squeezes the steering wheel. "My father is my mother's right-hand man. He has some influence over her, but not much, that I know of anyway. He basically just does whatever she says."

I knit my brow. "He seems more like her secretary than her husband."

He sighs. "Yes, that's how my mother likes it. She keeps him in his place."

"And you're okay with that?"

He cricks his neck. "Vela, it's all I've known. He has strength in him, though."

"Well, yeah," I say, snorting. "He'd have to living with Elizabeth." Linc's expression is pained. "I'm sorry. I don't mean to insult your mom...or your dad."

He shrugs. "You're not saying anything wrong. It's all true. You ready?"

I cock my head. "You mean, I love you?"

He huffs a laugh. "Right. I do love you."

"And, yes, I'm as ready as I'll ever be. I do have a question, though."

"Shoot," he tells me.

"Which version of your mother are we going to get tonight? The nice one or the...other one?"

"With her, it's always hard to guess, but I'm expecting she'll be the nice one tonight."

I blow out my breath. "I don't think I'll ever understand her, Linc. I'm sorry."

"Please. Do not apologize for something I tell myself all the time. Okay, if you're ready, then let's go and get this over with."

I can only hope for a better conversation than my last one with Linc's Grand Elder mother.

44

Linc

I get out of the car and reach for Vela's hand as we walk up to the home. I wish Jack were here, but my mother would never permit him to come inside.

Vela looks shocked when Mother answers the door after I ring the doorbell. I think she expected another butler.

"Welcome, Linc," Mother says, her gleaming smile radiant. "Vela, how are you?"

Vela and I walk in, and she looks more uncertain now than ever. I hope she remembers what I said about my mother cozying up to her for more power. I guess she half believes me.

"I...I'm fine," Vela says. "How are you?"

"I'm excellent, thank you. Follow me, please."

Mother closes the door and leads us out of the immaculate and ornate entrance. When we pass under a giant chandelier dripping with sparkling crystals, I watch Vela snap her mouth shut. I hope my wife knows this is all for show. My parents like to feel bigger than everyone else. Well, my mother does. I don't really know what my father feels. We've never had a substantial or meaningful conversation in my whole life.

When Vela asked me about my dad, it raised old feelings I can only describe as loss. I've always wished I had a dad who would teach me about the world, not just mindlessly follow everything my mother asks of him. But I've been stuck with this puppet instead. He seems satisfied with his life, and I've accepted that long ago. If he's happy, I'll find a way to be happy about it, too.

But when Vela's adopted father treated me more like a son than my father ever has, I felt that difference immensely.

I try to shake off my feelings as we follow my mother further into the house. It grows even more ostentatious as we go. I was correct that Mother would dress elegantly. She's in a dark blue silk dress, so I'm glad I suggested Vela change. She would have been uncomfortable if she had shown up in her casual outfit. And I never want my wife to feel like anything but a queen.

Even as the prophesied Chosen One, though, Vela doesn't feel she's better than anyone else, which makes me love her even more than I thought possible.

We walk by several hallways and Vela looks curious as to where they lead, but my mother offers no explanation and Vela doesn't ask questions. Paintings of figures dressed in old world costumes follow us with their eyes as we pass.

Mother brings us into a dining room that could be a small ballroom it's so large. The dark paneling doesn't detract from the size and not one, but two chandeliers shine a brilliant light over the enormous table. It's laden on one end with gleaming domes of silver, just waiting for us to uncover and consume their contents.

My chest clamps when Father stands, greets Vela and me, then promptly pulls out a chair for Mother, which she grace-fully sits in. I wait for my dad to look at me, but he only looks at Vela.

Sighing, I pull out a chair for Vela, who looks relieved. She was probably uncertain which one to choose. Knowing my mother wants to speak to my prophesied wife, I've apparently chosen Vela's seat correctly. My mother wants my wife directly next to her.

Vela picks up her napkin, smoothing it on her lap, then looks up. Father clears his throat and looks expectantly at Vela. I almost growl because they're testing her social acuity, and I hate that.

"Smells heavenly," Vela says in the awkward silence.

"Roast duck, which I hope you enjoy," Mother says with a warm smile.

"I do," Vela answers. She looks down at the array of silverware and gives me a look so panicked I wink at her and put my hand over the fork that's on the end of the gleaming silver line of tools.

When a server places a small salad in front of her, she follows my example, picking up the correct fork. She looks up first at me, then at my Mother. "Would you mind if I said grace?"

This is one of the few times I've seen my mother surprised, but she soon smooths her face and gestures with her hand. "Please do."

Vela clears her throat and says, "Father, we ask that You bless this food and this time with my new family. Bless our conversation. May all our words honor You, Lord."

I open my eyes and see my mother pinching her lips, then smile her practiced smile at Vela. "Thank you, dear. That was lovely."

Vela just looks at her with wide eyes. Their last conversation was so completely different that I'm sure Vela's head is spinning. Even though Mother has been helpful these past two weeks, her demeanor is so opposite from their last face-to-face meeting, I'm sure Vela is experiencing serious whiplash.

Wanting to alleviate the tension in the air and deciding to get right to the point of us coming tonight, I ask, "Mother, I sent you an email we're concerned about. We're wondering if it's really been sent by the E.E. Would you be amenable to using your contacts to find out if it's a legitimate email from the amphitheater?"

She nods. "I'd be happy to give you the resources at my disposal. I'm happy to help. You do know that don't you?" She looks at both Vela and me.

Vela chokes on a sip of her water, and I rush to check if she's okay. She waves at a hand at me, but her eyes water, and I keep watch over her until I'm sure she's not actually choking.

When Vela's coughing stops, and I'm assured she's fine, I turn to my mother and say, "I do know that. Thank you for your concern." I'm keeping up with this charade at polite conversation because I want Vela to know as little as possible the two sides of my mother she's already shown.

Mother leans toward Vela. "Are you all right? Do you need a doctor?"

Vela shakes her head vehemently and only looks at her with wary eyes.

"Well, as long as you're okay."

Vela sits silently as Father booms. "Well, this is very nice. Isn't it, dear?"

She nods. "Mmm, it is." Then she looks at me. "Is there anything else we can do for Vela?"

I finish chewing a mouthful of salad and say, "Actually, can you call your contacts to look into this email, now? Vela is supposed to speak in two days, and we need to be sure she's set to go."

A line forms between Mother's eyes. "Why wouldn't she be ready to speak?"

I put my fork down. "This email says she won't be allowed to speak until she's checked by a doctor who can say for certain she's not hosting the Black Fever that's going around." I'm a little annoyed she hasn't read my email, yet. But not surprised.

"That's ridiculous. Of course, she's not sick. She's perfectly healthy," Mother says, looking Vela over.

"Mother, you know that the E.E. are spreading lies that Vela is the one who's passing the virus around with her travels."

"And the amphitheater is actually insisting she be checked by a doctor for this illness?"

"Supposedly yes, but we think it's really a trap to get Vela in the E.E.'s hands."

Mother spears me with a look. "Well, you were right to get me involved with this. I'll call my contact right now." She blindly puts her hand out to my dad, who places a phone in it. She dials a number and within seconds, is speaking orders into it.

Within moments, Mother puts her phone down after completing her call. "Well, now that that's settled, can we enjoy our dinner?"

Vela's face is stony as she carefully sets down her fork. She huffs a disbelieving laugh, shakes her head, and looks at me before she directs her flashing eyes at Mother. "I'm sorry, but why are you being so accommodating and pleasant?"

Mother sits back. "Why wouldn't I be accommodating? And pleasant? You're my daughter-in-law."

"The one you didn't want for your son," Vela says with gritted teeth. "Until it was clear that I'm the prophesied One that is."

My chest swells with pride for Vela not mincing words with someone who's not used to being opposed.

Mother wipes her mouth with her napkin delicately and says, "I do understand we got off on the wrong foot..."

"The wrong foot? You have been nothing but angry, spiteful, and rude to me. Until now." Vela looks as if she's planning to leave. I put my napkin on the table, ready to go with her, if that's what she wants.

"Vela, please allow me to rectify my behavior. I'm...not used to surprises and, if I can be frank..."

"Please do. Let's be real and honest for once, please," Vela says loudly, her back ramrod straight.

"I'll admit I'm accustomed to my way of things. I do not handle news that doesn't fit into my plans well. You were something of a shock to carefully constructed plans that I had for my son."

Vela folds her arms on the table. "So, when I became more than an imposter," she quotes with her fingers, "you felt you could finally become a decent person with me and accept me into your family?"

Mother inhales deeply, looking at her salad, at me, and then at Vela. She studies Vela, and I wonder what she could possibly say to explain her past behavior. After a beat of silence, she looks at me. "Do you feel the same way as Vela?"

I laugh. "Mother, I couldn't be prouder of my wife than I am right now. She just called you out on your beyond rude behavior, and I'm dying to know what you have to say for yourself."

Mother straightens in her seat. She asks Vela in a strangled voice, "Will you accept my apology for my past actions? Can we move forward from this in a civilized way?"

I thrum the table with my fingers. I'm enjoying this more than I can say.

"I'm willing to move forward if you are. And I appreciate your apology. It means a lot to me. I've only ever wanted to get along with you. So, if being the Chosen Child means getting your approval, I'm glad that I've filled that role."

"Yes, well, we're just happy you've been found. And I couldn't be prouder that it was my son who found you."

Vela looks at my mother, wondering if she's serious, which I'm sure she is. I can't help but laugh because only my mother could make that sound like a Grand Elder who's found treasure and not a proud mother.

Vela looks at me incredulously, and I can only shrug. "Welcome to my family, Vela." With that, we continue our dinner, and I'm not sure who's happier we got that confounding conversation out of the way, my wife or my mother.

One thing is for certain. Vela now has a good idea of what to expect from my family. And she's not afraid one bit. She's going to need that fearlessness. I'm sure we haven't seen the last of my mother's domineering ways.

45

Vela

Elizabeth's tech team revealed that the email was indeed fake, and I'm spared being abducted by the E.E. It was the one positive thing that came from dinner at the Stevenson palace. Besides the cease-fire between Elizabeth and myself after her late apology.

I'm appreciative of it, but I'm taking it with a grain of salt. If I weren't the Chosen Child, I fully suspect she would have done everything in her considerable power to split Linc and me up.

For that, I'm wary of her nice persona, knowing she could turn on me at any moment.

My protective team has also been a great asset to have, but their exhaustive guardianship is making me feel a little cramped. I keep reminding myself it's for my benefit, but I long for the days when my steps were my own, not guided and directed by my very attentive friends.

It's the morning of the big speech, and I'm pacing the living room at my rental rehearsing in my mind.

I can barely focus because Greta has been moved yet again, for her safety. As happy as I am that I know where she is this time, it's killing me she's taken a turn for the worse. She's only half an hour away, and I've tried going to her several times, but every time, I've been blocked by my prison guards, which I've taken to calling them.

Linc's phone rings, and I glance at him, then return to my speech.

When Linc answers it and then jumps up in one movement, his face is shocked and excited. I go to him. "What is it?"

He listens to the phone, and even I can hear the raised voice on the other end. "They know what the cure is!" Linc yells.

"*What*?" I grip his arms. He hands me the phone, and as soon as my ear hits the earpiece, I hear Adele screech, "Vela, it's you! You're the cure!"

If there wasn't a chair near me, I would have fallen to the ground, but since there is one, I stumble into it. "Explain," I order.

"Vela, we've just found out that you need to use all four elements at the same time to cure someone of the Black Fever. Which only you can do. You're the answer. You're the antidote!"

My face turns red, and it isn't until Linc yells for me to breathe that I do. My hand trembles as I hold on to the phone. "How do I use all four elements to cure someone? What do I do?"

"I don't know, Vela. I only know it takes using all four elements at the same time to cure the illness. We didn't find out the particulars. They ended the meeting after letting that little bit slip. I don't think they meant to share even that with us. We left as quickly as we could to find a secure location and call you. But, Vela, even if they didn't explain how to do it, we thought if anyone could figure it out, it's you." She pauses for a moment, and I hear Steele saying something to her. She comes back to the phone, saying, "If what you say about God is right, then He orchestrated that slip up. We have to go. Vela, figure this out!"

She disconnects the line, and I look at Linc, my mouth hanging open. I shake myself and say urgently, "We have to go to Greta. Linc, she needs me. I'm going."

Linc blinks and nods and then he's up and moving. "We need to leave now, or we'll never be back in time for your speech."

"I don't care about the speech!" I screech. "Greta is most important now."

Linc crosses the room, stopping his frantic readiness to leave and grabs my shoulders. "Vela, if you can heal Greta, you can share it with the world tonight. You can give hope to thousands, possibly millions. We have to try to make it back."

Linc leaves the room to speak to Tonya and Tex, who are my guards right now. I move mechanically, putting on my shoes and grabbing Jack's leash. I can't imagine not having him with us. It's instinctual at this point.

We're out the door in less than three minutes, and as we rush to the car with Tonya and Tex in tow, Linc calls Petra to share what we just found out.

Linc drives the four of us well over the limit and gets to where Greta is staying in just under twenty minutes. I spend the entire drive praying, asking for wisdom on how to accomplish something like healing this illness with four elements, not just my Gyan gift.

When he parks, I fly out of the car, but before I can pound on the door, Tonya is pulling me back.

"Vela, please, let me check the place out first," she asks, putting her body between me and the door.

I grit out, "Tonya, I swear, if you don't get out of my face, I will force you. Do. Not. Get. In. My. Way."

With a hurried look around and a glance at Linc, who's standing back from me, she wisely moves away from the door.

I pound on the door, calling out to Hannah and Andy to let me in. Hannah opens it with a bewildered look, takes in my frantic face, and asks, "What's wrong?"

"It's not what's wrong," I say breathlessly. "It's what's right. I can cure Greta." I look around wildly for my little friend.

As soon as I say that, Hannah stifles a sob in her hand. "What do you mean? How are you going to do that?"

"I have no idea, but apparently only I can."

Hannah looks bewildered as Tonya, Tex, Linc, and I come in. I cross to the bedroom Andy is standing in front of, and when I try to move around him, he puts his big hand on my shoulder and says gravely, "Vela, you can't go in there. You'll get sick."

"You don't understand. Adele and Steele just found out that by using all four elements at once, I can cure this illness. Please Andy, move. I have to try."

He looks at Hannah, whose hands are covering her mouth. She nods at him, tears streaming down her face, and he moves his large frame from the door. I open the door in a rush, but when I see the small still body in the bed, I stop mid-step.

My little Greta, my beautiful little friend who was rosy-cheeked and so full of life last time I saw her, is now a shell of the person she was. She's piled in so many blankets I can barely see her face.

I sob into my arm, not wanting to wake her. But I don't need to worry. She remains asleep. Her skin is so pale, I can see her veins and bones sticking out. Weeks of the Black Fever have taken their toll on her poor little body. Her breathing is shallow, like she's only got a day left of her young life.

Rushing to her bed, I continue to sob as I drop to my knees and put my hand on her head. I instantly reach for my senses to see what's ailing her.

I feel her mid-level fever, but when I send her a wave of healing energy, no change happens. Fever continues to ravage her body. Forcing my tears to stop, I put my hands on my knees and take three deep breaths, thinking furiously about what to do.

Hannah is now in the room and kneels next to me. "You have to use all four elements?"

I nod, scrubbing my cheeks, frustration rising that I have no idea how to do it.

"Okay, let's think about this," Hannah says. "Maybe you're supposed to use heat to sweat the fever out of her."

"And water to cool her when she's finished," Linc's voice rumbles behind me.

"The Gyan gift to infuse her with healing," Andy adds.

"How would I use the wind?" I ask.

Tonya kneels next to us. She turns wide eyes to me. "Boreans can freeze the air with their gift."

"Yes, do you think I should freeze the fever out of her?"

Hannah shakes her head, fisting her hand on the bed. "I don't know. I think we're close, but it's not quite right."

As I'm on my knees, it's not hard to pray.

God, give me wisdom. Show me, Lord, what to do. How do I heal her? Father, show me!

In an instant, an image floods my brain. My body comes alive with the answer, and I sit up, putting both hands on Greta's hot, sticky forehead. "I think I know. It's a combination of all of it," I breathe.

Hannah puts her hand on mine. "Be sure about this, Vela. She can't take much more."

I nod soberly, and inwardly I beg God to give me strength and knowledge.

With a deep breath, and a shocking peace that I have the right answer, I push all four of my gifts into my little friend. While my fire heats up her blood, raising her temperature to a dangerous degree, I infuse her with my Gyan healing and rush the blood through her veins with my water gift. Her blood comes alive under my hands, purifying and cleansing. Then, I add wind to cool everything down as the heat kills the virus. Once I'm sure her whole body has been flushed with this elemental combination, I test her temperature with my hand and her soft skin is miraculously cool.

I remove my hands, feeling exhilarated and drained. I slump to the side and Linc catches me. "I think I did it," I whisper, tears leaking from my eyes, feeling so grateful that God answered my prayer. I could die today and be a happy woman. "Thank you, God."

Hannah utters a cry, and her hands are on Greta, too, checking her forehead, arms and legs. Greta stays asleep, but her breathing is easier and it's plain to see she's healed, just resting from her ordeal.

I lean over and kiss her forehead, feeling the proof with my lips that her temperature has returned to normal. "She needs fluids and food. She'll still need to regain her strength."

Hannah, sobbing now, throws her arms around my neck. "Vela, you did it. You healed my baby." Tonya, Andy, and Linc join in, and we all cry and hold each other.

I pull back first, wiping my eyes. "It was God. He showed me what to do. He gave me the answer. Don't give me the credit."

Andy holds Hannah as she cries softly into his chest. She, too, has lost weight in the three weeks since I last saw her. Andy kisses her on the top of her head, smoothing down her hair. "It's all right. It's all over. She's fine, darling. She's okay."

I lean into Linc, who feeds me some of his energy, which gives the extra benefit of comforting while rehabilitating me at the same time.

Hannah picks her head up off Andy's chest, her eyes anguished. "She had maybe one more day to live, Vela. How did you do it?"

I explain the process to her as best as I can, and then I realize something. "I'm not the only one who can do this," I say with pure awe. Emotions explode inside me, and I jump off the floor, pacing. "This is how we're going to unite the world!"

When everyone gives me perplexed looks, I stop and explain. "Don't you see? I'm not the only one who can cure this illness; I'm just the only one who can do it alone. I can teach the healing method, and it will take four different Elementals or two Elementals with all four gifts between them to heal someone at once, but if they work together, the world can be healed!"

Hannah stands too and says, "One Elemental from each clan must work together," she breathes. "Or two with all four." She turns shining eyes to me. "Vela, that's wonderful!"

I nod, holding my breath, waiting for Tonya, Linc, and Andy to see what I do.

Their faces brighten at the same time, and when Linc turns a beaming smile at me, I turn into his arms and say into his neck, "It doesn't have to be fancy speeches that get the world to unite. It's healing. We'll heal the world with this message."

I laugh, so completely happy in that moment that I could kiss the world. But I settle instead for Linc. I capture his lips, and we celebrate this discovery together.

When I hear a weak voice say, "Vela? Is that you?" I push out of Linc's arms and run to Greta. I drop to the floor by her bed and lean toward an awake, but tired Greta.

"It's me, little one. How are you feeling?" I brush her hair off her forehead and feel it again just to be sure the fever has not returned. She's as cool as a cucumber.

"I've missed you, Vela," she says in a small voice. "But can I ask one thing?"

"Anything, sugar pie. Name it."

Her big gray eyes blink at me. "I'm hungry. Can I have something to eat?"

We all laugh at her wonderful question. Hannah looks at Andy, who immediately gets up from his spot at the foot of the bed, wipes his eyes and goes to the kitchen to find Greta something to eat.

"I'm sorry I woke you up, little one," I say, softly brushing her cheek with my finger.

She leans into my hand and says before closing her eyes. "It's okay. I don't mind. Vela, I'm happy you're here. I dreamed of an angel filling me up with light. Was that you?"

I laugh. "I don't know about being an angel, but I did help heal you. With God's guidance. I'm so happy you're better, baby girl."

After that, I'm ready to fulfill my purpose and share God's message with the world. It's time to unite. The world will be healed, just like Greta.

46

Linc

I stand in Vela's dressing room waiting for Elia to finish applying Vela's makeup. Despite the amphitheater's offers to provide makeup and hair artists, we won't allow anyone else in the room but her leadership and security team.

I fold my arms at the door, guarding it with Rayne and Tex. Two more of our security guards are outside the door, not allowing anyone close to Vela. The rest are combing the amphitheater, looking for any possible threat.

Vela calls from her chair in the corner, "You're sure Adele is on her way? And Mama and Papa?"

"Yes," I answer. "Like the last two times you asked. They're coming."

She nods and then stills to allow Elia to do up her face, which she does not need, in my opinion. She's perfect the way she is. But even I can appreciate the magic Elia is doing to my Intended's eyes.

We got back from Greta's healing in time for Vela to get ready for her speech. The security team and I are on high alert, ready for anything that could happen to stop her from going on stage.

I don't for one minute think the E.E. is going to just allow her to walk up there and proclaim her message.

"This place is full of 15,000 Elementals," Rayne growls next to me. "I'm sure half of them are Extremists."

I stuff down my anxiety, pure focus taking over my mind. "All 15,000 of them can be Extremists, but it won't stop her from giving the world the cure. This event is being live-streamed to Elemental gatherings around the world. Vela will accomplish her mission. We'll make sure she does."

Between my mother's substantial influence and Vela's performances in front of the Grand Elders, she has their full support and access to extra security. Vela has captured the attention of every Elemental across the world in the videos recorded during the Grand Elders' meetings.

Despite the Extremists' best efforts to discredit her, they've only succeeded in making Vela more of a curiosity. This place is sold out because Elementals want to see what she can do.

They might have seen videos, but there's nothing like watching it live and in person.

I lean toward Rayne. "We've vetted everyone who has access to her from here to the stage, right?"

He nods and when someone knocks on the door, I ask before opening it, "Who is it?"

"Five minutes until show time," Tonya calls through.

"Got it," I answer.

Vela waves Elia off and stands up. When she turns to me, I can't help but stumble back at the power of her gaze on me.

My wife is glorious.

"Stop looking at me like that," Vela says, blushing a deep red.

That only makes her more beautiful, and I grin wolfishly at her. She approaches me and pokes my chest. "Focus, Lincoln Stevenson. We need to be on top of our game."

I nod and place a soft kiss on her perfect lips. "Now, I can focus," I say against her mouth. She smiles and pushes me away.

I get into my security mindset and turn to find Rayne and Tex at the door, ready for Vela to make her way to the stage. She turns to the room and everyone beams at her. We filled them in on what happened with Greta and they're as ecstatic as we are that Vela learned the cure and healed Greta.

Vela crosses the room to give Elia and Kane a hug. She approaches Petra, who's holding Peter's hand. He followed us around until Petra allowed him to be a part of our team. Even he had to be thoroughly investigated before she finally allowed it, though. Petra says, "Go get 'em tiger. You did it. It's a cakewalk from here."

David and Whitney approach and embrace Vela. "We're proud of you, honey. Go knock 'em dead. Or, rather, heal 'em all."

Vela softly laughs. "I won't be healing them all. The world is going to do that."

Grant and Mary give her pats on the shoulder as she passes, and Vela smiles beautifully at them. Rick and Gary nod at her and wish her well. Gene and Jerry nod at her, pride shining in their gazes, probably feeling responsible for finding the Chosen Child.

When she makes it back to me, I move to hold her hand. "No," she says, her eyes taking on a worry I wish she didn't have. "I might need to use my hands. Just in case."

I nod soberly and turn to the door. I give Rayne a look, and he cracks the door open, looking out. When he's satisfied, he slips out and Tex follows.

"I love you," I say. "In more ways than the one."

She nods confidently. "I love you too, and yes, I'm ready."

I take a deep breath and hold the door open, ready for anyone and anything to happen. Vela, too, seems wary as she looks around when she steps into the hallway.

Her face brightens when we see Adele running down the hallway, James and Sandy on her heels and Steele walking more slowly behind. Tonya and Alice allow them to get through. "Vela," Adele squeals, and then she's bowling Vela over with her hug.

"You made it! Oh my gosh, I've been so worried about you," Vela says as she embraces her little sister.

I've got half of my attention on their reunion, happy they made it back in time, and the other half looking all around us. We're in a hallway with several doors, so I'm prepared for anyone to emerge from them.

"You cleared these rooms, right Rayne?" I ask.

Rayne nods. "We checked about twenty minutes ago."

As Vela catches Adele and her parents up about Greta's miraculous healing, I nudge Vela to start walking down toward the stage entrance. The closer we get to it, the louder the sound from the amphitheater becomes.

"It sounds like a packed house," Rayne says, looking back at me as he leads the way in front of Vela and her family. He's having a hard time keeping his attention on his surroundings with the arrival of his Intended, who's completely ignoring him.

I feel badly for Rayne, but I need him to be ready for anything with the threat of the E.E. over our heads.

Adele continues to regale Vela with all that happened during her adventure spying on the E.E.

I see Rayne's jaw clench as he overhears her story about Steele, and I'm about to tell him to pay attention to his surroundings when in one horrible moment the hallway explodes in a blinding attack of elements. My next thought, as Extremists shoot elements out of all the now open doorways, is that we should have checked those rooms again.

Wind tears down the hallway, knocking most of us off our feet as vines with six-inch thorns snake in and tear into skin and clothing. Ice shoots by our heads, connecting with some as cries fill the air.

"Vela!" I scream and throw my body over her. She goes down with my body weight but pushes at me to let her up. I shield her and look around as wind knives whiz by, and I desperately search for the attacker so I can attempt to stop this onslaught.

I don't see anyone throwing these elements at us. Only hands appear out of the dozen doorways. I scream at Rayne to find who's doing this.

Rayne jumps up from the ground in front of a door, holding his arms up, a fierce look of concentration on his face. The next moment, he's hauling an Extremist out the door by his shirt, a look of pure rage on the man's face. Rayne must have used his Neronian gifts to take the man's power away from him. But it's only temporary. Rayne makes short work of punching the Extremist in the face to knock him out.

But when another hand comes out of the door behind Rayne, I shout a warning, and Rayne is knocked unconscious with an ice spear to the back of his head.

Everyone is on the ground, covering their heads with their hands. Some of us are trying to fire our powers back at our shielded attackers, but it's completely ineffective because we don't have anyone to shoot at.

"Linc!" Vela screams at me, trying to push me off her. "I need to help. Get off me!"

I ignore her and shoot fire at a vine that's getting too close for comfort.

I hear Vela growl in frustration and then, to my complete shock, she uses her wind to lift me off her. She moves me over to the side, and I flail my arms, but can't get free of her wind grip. When I'm out of the way, she jumps up and holds up her arms, taking command of all the flying elements, stopping them in their tracks.

Squeezing her hands into fists, she pushes and, just like that, blows all the elements safely against the walls. Then, with one sweep of her hands, she closes all the doors with her Borean power. I hear angry cries of frustration when the attackers try to open the doors again, but she holds them shut. When roots sneak out from under a door, she stops them with a thought. She looks back at me, and I force myself to stop marveling at her and command those who are able to guard the doors.

She's breathing heavily as she continues to hold the doors closed and looks around to see how everyone is doing. She kneels down beside Rayne, who's at her feet and shakes his shoulder. It looks like he's been knocked out cold. At least, I hope he's only unconscious.

"He's alive," she tells Adele, who pops up and cries out when she sees Rayne's prone body. She rushes over to him, and Vela watches her to be sure she's okay.

I'm guarding a door, amazed at my wife's abilities, but not surprised. Her power isn't endless, though, and I lay my hands on her and infuse her with energy. After a beat of that, I say in a hurry, "Vela, you need to get on stage where you'll be more visible. They most likely won't attack you in front of everyone."

Vela looks around at the fallen bodies and looks like she can't decide between staying or going.

"Vela, go!"

"Can you hold the E.E. back if I let go?" she asks, her voice strained.

About ten of us are still up, some of us injured but ready to take care of this threat. I nod.

She finally turns and runs to the stage entrance, disappearing from the hallway. I watch her to be sure she's not attacked on the way.

Then I turn my attention to the door I'm in front of. I make sure someone blocks every door. I'm ready for some revenge when Vela finally lets go.

47

Vela

I make it to the stage manager, who seems oblivious to what just happened in the hallway. The E.E. orchestrated their attack well and made sure all eyes were on other places and not on their attack of me and my team.

While I'm being outfitted with a microphone, I pray everyone is all right where I left them. My family is back there, but everyone except for Rayne was up and ready to avenge the attack. I keep my stance ready for more attacks and am surprised to see a dazed-looking Tex, his forehead bleeding, join me.

"How is everything back there?"

He smiles wildly at me. "The problem is being neutralized."

As I stand in the wings of the stage, waiting for my cue to enter, a video the Grand Elders made comes on. It gives the hint that I'm someone we've all been waiting for, but it doesn't come right out and say who I am.

Okay, that's my job then. This is it.

Cracking my neck and trying to shake off that harrowing ordeal in the hallway, I wait for the video to play through. The crowd cheers loudly, and it almost feels like a dream when I walk on stage, waving and smiling.

I smile because I'm going to astound them. And suddenly I can't wait. I'm ready for this moment more than any other I've experienced.

Why tell them who I am when I can show them?

So, without saying a word, I raise my arms then drop them as four columns of earth, wind, water, and fire erupt, all four standing in glory in front of me. We made sure I have access to soil before the event and for that I'm glad because I wouldn't have wanted to hunt for it.

Each column is identical in size and width except for the element itself. Fire blazes, water flows, a cylinder of wind rages, and earth builds until it looks like a pillar covered in vines.

The crowd is stunned silent for a second, then an outburst of wild applause and cheers fill the amphitheater. I watch as everyone jumps up, their eyes full of exultant emotions.

The world has found its Chosen Child.

I let the moment build until I'm sure I have every single person's attention.

Able to hold the elements with my mind, I move to the side of the pillars, lifting my arms again, asking for quiet. Then, I cement my position with one sentence. "I'd like to introduce myself. I'm Vela Stevenson, and I am the Chosen Child."

When the room is still with the shock at my announcement, I say, "I have a message for you. God wants us to unite. It's time to set aside our prejudices, and end territorial disputes and boundary wars, and I know how to do it."

Loud murmurs fill the air, and I say over their voices, "The Black Fever has taken over our world, ravaging the health of Elementals. I know who caused it and it *wasn't* me." I say loudly, "I have the cure that will heal millions. But it will take us working together for the first time in thousands of years."

I walk in front of the pillars of elements I'm still holding with my mind and say, "I've already healed someone who was close to death, someone precious to me from the Black Fever, and she's now resting comfortably, recovering from her ordeal."

I continue as I walk the stage, "The Black Fever was no accident. It was created in a lab by the Elemental Extremists with the express purpose of profiting from the healing. They wanted to make money from our deaths, thinking we'd pay anything for the antidote. One that only they would be able to offer. Until today. This has to end, and I intend to end it right now."

When the crowd starts murmuring again, I say, "I know what the antidote is to this awful illness. And it's not something made in a lab. It's you. You have the power to heal your loved ones." That gets their attention, and the large room quiets. "But only if we work together. It takes one from each Elemental clan, working at the same time, and with all four powers combined, we can kill the Black Fever virus. Or, two mixed elementals who possess all four elements together can cure with just two. Here's how you do it," I say in a clear, commanding voice.

The crowd's questions rise to a fevered pitch, and I hold my arms up again to quiet the room. I then proceed to describe in exact detail how I healed Greta. I explain the temperature the blood has to rise to, the process of purifying the entire bloodstream, healing the body the entire time with the Gyan gift, and finally how to cool the blood.

When I'm finished, the crowd is stunned to silence and then, like before, it erupts in wild cheering and applause.

"It's going to take a coordinated effort from all of us to put aside our long-held hate and fear of other clans and come together to heal our loved ones," I say over the crowd. "But we can do this. We must if we're going to survive the Extremists' pandemic."

I hear some pushback from the crowd and see groups of angry Elementals yelling and gesturing at me. They're dispersed throughout the crowd, and I have a suspicion these are Extremists trying to incite the crowd.

When they're unsuccessful in starting a riot, since most everyone in the crowd is too hopeful that my words are true, I see the individuals push their way to the front.

Once there's a group near the front, they start firing elements at me, which I block easily. I let go of the elemental show I put on, needing my energy for this attack.

When more Extremists arrive, adding to the E.E.'s attack, I move quickly to commandeer and neutralize all the elements being thrown at me. I miss one ice bomb, and it hits me on the forehead, dropping me to my knees in a daze. Blood drips down the side of my face.

I'm dimly aware that the crowd, at first shocked by the flagrant attack, steps up to defend me. Elements fly through the air as more and more join the fight. Screams fill the amphitheater, and I pray this ends quickly and without the loss of life.

Linc rushes on the stage and kneels next to me, holding his shirt sleeve to my head, stemming the flow of blood.

"I'm okay," I say in a rush, leaning on him to stand up.

He faces the crowd and when a flame spear rushes at me, Linc raises a flame wall so tall I can't see any of the crowd at all. The wall swallows the spear easily.

My hair blows back at his show of strength and the rush of heat overheats me quickly. Sweat mixes with the blood on my face. I drag my arm to clear my vision, and when Linc's fire wall drops, I'm ready.

Despite Linc's shout for me to stay behind him, I move to stand at his side and once again, I dodge elements still being thrown at us. More of my team join us on the stage, and I'm now just one of about twenty blocking and throwing our own attacks at the Extremists. I look on with pride as Petra, Peter, both sets of parents, Adele, Rayne, my entire protection and leadership team, including the Girls, Elia and my brothers all fight to defend me. More security the Grand Elders provided join us. I pray no one gets severely hurt.

The Extremists have set themselves apart by joining in a group, making identifying them easy. Yet more join them and by this time, it's a full-fledged war of the elements.

I look at the chaotic air around us and see nothing but wind currents, ice spears, and knives whizzing by. The thorny vines from the hallway are back, and I stop as many as I can from choking off the lives of those trying to defend me.

Adele and Tonya stand next to me. Tonya screams, "We have to get to cover!"

I look around and see partitions off to the side. "Cover me," I order. She obeys and blocks a cyclone coming at me by sending it off in another direction.

Zeroing in on a five-foot-tall partition wall, I raise it up with air and slowly bring it to us, setting it down in front of me and my team. Immediately, we're protected from the rampaging elements. I duck behind the wall to be completely covered.

When I feel a Borean try to move it away from us, I lock on the air currents they're using and bring it back to my control.

A wave of dizziness hits me, and I realize I'm using too much of my power for too long. I'm going to burn out soon.

Linc's face fills my vision, and he searches my eyes. "You might have a concussion," he says with concern.

"I'm fine," I insist. "We have to stop this, Linc."

He huffs. "I don't know how we're going to do that. This is a full-blown war."

An idea takes root, and I look at Linc, knowing he's going to hate this, considering I've almost met my capacity for using my elements. But I don't see any other way around this. "I do. I know how to stop it."

He looks at me warily. "What are you planning, Vela?"

"I need you with me. I need your strength. We're going down there."

Alarm crosses his face. "What? No, are you crazy? That's a dead zone, Vela."

I shake my head. "Linc, I need to take their gifts. That's the only way this fight will stop. I have to literally take their powers from them."

Linc's face turns red. "No, Vela. That's too much. There are hundreds of Extremists down there! No!"

I cup his face and kiss him softly. "I love you." And then, using wind currents, I lift myself up into the air and over the partition before lowering myself down to the floor of the amphitheater.

Linc screams my name, but I know he'll follow me. Bracing myself by putting one foot forward in a lunge, I take aim at an Extremist. He's a Festan, and when I take his fire from him, it hits me, kicking me back, but my back leg stops me from falling. The Festan's face is one of complete horror when he realizes I took his element. He holds his hand out to fire at me, but nothing happens. I grin. He screams in anger.

I turn, searching for a friendly Elemental who isn't a Festan, and I'm blessed enough to be standing right next to one. A Borean girl looks at me with wide eyes, and I tell her only two words, "Get ready." With no other explanation, I point at her and fill her with fire, knocking her completely on her back.

Someone cries, "The Chosen Child is attacking us!" A crowd of about twenty all back up with expressions of fear and worry.

"No," I yell. "I've just gifted her an element. Check her and see for yourself!"

A man rushes over to the girl, and when he senses what I said is true, he points at his chest. "Do me next!"

I turn and rip the power out of a Borean Extremist woman, turning and giving her element to the man who just volunteered for it. The Festan man looks at me with complete rapture from the ground where he falls. He immediately jumps up firing off a wind knife, laughing hysterically.

By this time, Linc is behind me, and he's brought my team to protect me while I do this crazy thing. Linc feeds me his strength while I turn and siphon water from a Neronian Extremist and see a line of volunteers, who have quickly figured out what I'm doing. I give the Neronian gift to one of them before turning and continuing my punishment for this attack.

After I've stolen ten more elements and parceled them away, my head is spinning, and I'm not sure how I'm going to keep this up.

Linc seems to know what I need because he holds my shoulders, feeding me his strength. By this time, the Extremists have zeroed in on my strategy, and they've doubled their attack on me. I'm not paying attention to my defense after countless more reclamations and giftings, and I'm hit with a nasty wind knife that slices into my shaking arm. My team doubles up in front of me, blocking more attacks from coming in.

Despite my injured arm, I can reach over my team and still get to the Extremists who are starting to panic at the possibility of losing their powers. Many of them run off, abandoning the fight.

I should have passed out long ago, but because of Linc's shared energy, I continue taking and dispersing powers. My blood pumps through me, and I use the anger I have at the injustice of the Extremists, and the fact they're destroying our world, to fuel me.

When one Extremist blasts an ice bomb at a teen girl who's defending me with her life, taking her down, I scream in rage and pull the Borean's power out of him so fast, he literally spins, falling to the ground, shaking.

I walk over to the teenager and kneel, feeling for a pulse, and when I find it beating weakly in her, I hold the Borean power in me and heal her injury, which makes spots form in my eyes.

"Vela, you're burning out," Linc warns. He holds my arms back, trying to make me stop.

I shake my head, pushing him off, blinking through the haze of exhaustion that hits me. "I'm not done."

"Vela, you're going to kill yourself. You've done enough!" he yells in my face.

"No," I say with gritted teeth. "I have to do one more thing." My knees drop despite my best efforts at staying upright, and Linc catches me, holding me bridal style.

"Take me to the stage," I ask him weakly. I have an idea that is so perfect, I don't know why I didn't think of it earlier.

He presses his lips together and seems to war with his decision to listen to me or not.

"Please, Linc. Do this for me."

He finally calls to Leon, who's so covered with blood I hardly recognize him. Leon uses his wind and water gifts to cast a net of protection around us as Linc carries me to the stage.

I'm hoping I have enough in me to do this one last thing that I pray will stop this insane fight. I don't want to see anyone else hurt.

Linc runs up to the stage, hiding behind the partition that's somehow still standing. I take every ounce of strength in me and one last prayer to stand and look out over the wall at the fighting crowd.

Up here, I can see half the place has emptied and the rest of the Elementals are fighting. There are more Extremists than I thought. I would say about five hundred are in five different groups fighting the crowd.

I turn to Linc and instruct, "I need you to take the captured Extremists and give them to the Grand Elders. We'll decide their punishments later."

Confusion swims in his eyes. "Vela, they're all still fighting out there."

"Not for long." I should have done this next attack long ago. *Oh well. It's not too late for drastic measures.*

Tonya followed me on the stage, and I look at her. "Follow my lead. Gather more Boreans to help us."

I look over my shoulder at Linc, who has such fear in his eyes that I wink at him and say, "Help me as much as you can with your energy." Filling my lungs with as much air as I can, I use it to fuel me for my last attack. I won't be able to do much after this. I've never experienced burnout before, but I have a feeling I'm going to find out what it feels like. I just pray it doesn't take my life.

We must defeat the Extremists or this world will never be united. So, what I'm going to attempt next will be worth the sacrifice.

And, at that, I stand tall, hold my hands over the partition, and focus on one of the groups of the Extremists. With one squeeze of my fists, I take the air out of their lungs and hold it. They all drop, grabbing their throats, gasping for breath. I wait until one after another, they pass out from lack of air. Letting go of their air, I almost lose consciousness from the effort. I squeeze my eyes shut and shake my head hard.

"Linc, help me!"

He answers by feeding me his strength. Tonya's brought Adele and five other Boreans next to me, and I watch as a combined unit, they take out another group, using my method. Between them and me, one after another, three more groups go down.

By this time, I feel wetness that must be blood trickling out of my nose and ears. I taste the metallic flavor hit my tongue. My head is pounding, but I refuse to stop until this is over. My arms tremble with the effort it takes to hold them up.

I focus on the last group since it looks like my Boreans are flagging. With one last drag of my power, I stop all air from going into the Extremists' lungs and when they drop, so do I.

"Vela!" Linc is at my side on the ground. He couldn't catch me because he was too exhausted himself. He fell, too. He gives me the last of his energy, and I gasp for breath while I worry if he's going to be all right. Gathering me in his arms, he lifts my head to rest it on his chest. "Vela, you did it," he croaks.

The last thing I remember saying is, "No. We did it." Then the world goes black.

48

Linc

It takes Vela a week to recover from the burnout she experienced putting down the Extremists at the amphitheater.

If anyone questioned Vela's identity before, all resistance was put to rest by her astonishing display of power that day. She has the Elemental world hanging onto news about her recovery, and once she's on her feet, she posts daily videos showing herself whole and well.

I have never been more terrified than when she passed out in my arms. I thought she had killed herself with that last maneuver of hers, and I almost fainted in relief when I felt her feeble pulse.

It seems I'm not the only one happy with the news that Vela is well. The whole world has agreed to do as Vela says: unite. Clans have abandoned their borders and territories, and they've agreed to live amongst each other.

The entire reason is because of the Black Fever antidote. Elementals across the country and the world have banded together to heal those with that devastating illness. They've also put their resources together to once and for all hunt down the Extremists.

It seems Vela has succeeded in her mission. Festans are being healed by Gyans. Boreans are powering windmills. Neronians are watering crops in drought-stricken areas. The Elementals of the world have completely embraced helping each other take care of our earth.

And it turns out; Vela didn't even need to go on a world tour. Thanks to social media, cell phones, and the live stream of the amphitheater event, Vela's message was heard loud and clear across the world.

Once everything settled down from her popularity and position, we set up house in Houston, Texas. She says the only thing she hasn't accomplished is a healthy relationship with my mother and father and she thinks living near them will help us do that.

I, of course, defer to her wisdom when it comes to the health of families.

Time passes as time does, and I realize life with Vela is just a series of new adventures.

One I enjoy more than I ever thought possible.

Epilogue

Years pass, and I find I very much enjoy married life with my Intended. In fact, it's not too much longer until Vela gives me the happy news that she's expecting.

And it turns out she's not the only one.

"Linc, are you taking pictures? Look at this one, she's so cute," Vela gushes as she awkwardly bends over to pick up a cute puppy from the nest my dog, Angel, has made for all eight of her puppies.

Three months ago, I found this gorgeous Golden Retriever on the side of the road and happily gave her a home with Vela, Jack, and me. Once we got her completely checked out, we had the option to fix her so she couldn't have puppies. But Vela promised me it would be okay if we had a litter of gorgeous Retriever/Doberman puppies. Which Angel promptly did. Well, Jack and she did.

Vela's belly has swelled to fit our own set of twins. I'm not sure how much more she can grow before she bursts. But she has two months to go. She's told me over and over that the babies will probably be born soon and that thought makes my heart freeze. There's no worse fear for a man than the thought of his wife going into labor.

Even having two Gyan mothers and a dear friend on standby to help with the birth, any number of things can go wrong with a delivery. And Vela has two to do.

"Linc!" Vela says with exasperation when I don't move fast enough to get the shot she wants. Jack nudges her over to nose his little progenies. "Jack," she coos. "And Angel, you both have done so well. These babies are gorgeous."

I take picture after picture, hoping one of them will appease my temperamental wife. Her hormones have just about driven me to exhaustion between the cravings and mood swings. But I don't care about any of that. She is glorious, no matter what.

The puppies are red and golden, a mixture of the bloodlines of Jack and Angel. Instead of the sleek body of Jack, they have soft fur that is so sweet to touch. Vela is certainly enjoying herself and squeals in laughter when a puppy thoroughly washes her face with its tongue.

"Hey, that one's mine," Adele scolds Vela and reaches, taking Vela's bundle out of her hands.

Vela laughs. "You've already decided which one you want?"

Rayne scoffs. "She picked that one out at birth."

It was a family affair when Angel went into labor. David and Whitney as well as Elia and Kane flew down from Colorado. Adele and Rayne, who are officially a couple now that Adele is an adult, drove from one state over where they are both enrolled in Arizona State. It seems Rayne has a thirst for technical knowledge and he's double-majoring in computer science and business. Adele, with her latent Gyan gift now active, is going to nursing school. She's doing graphic design on the side. Steele moved on from his crush with Adele and had a string of girlfriends before he finally found his own Intended. Drew and Jewels came over from New Orleans.

Jack has been a proud father and mate, looking after Angel for her entire pregnancy. Labor was a little too traumatic for him, though, and we had to keep him from the room because he seemed to just worry about Angel.

That's going to be me any day now. I shove the worry down.

"Linc, can you please get me another one? I can't reach any," Vela requests, her eyes feasting on the cuteness of the pack of puppies, all climbing over each other in the pen we made for them.

I put my phone down and reach for one and hand it to Vela. She sighs and buries her nose in its fur as it wiggles in her arms. "It smells so good. Awweee, take a picture, Linc."

Scrambling to get my phone, I hurry and take the requested picture.

"Linc," Elia orders. "Take one of me and my puppy, too."

Every puppy has already been claimed; it's just a matter of everyone fighting over which one they're going to get.

"Hey," Kane argues. "You know that's the one I wanted."

"No," Drew says hotly. "That's mine and Jewels'."

I look over at Jewels, who's a mystery. All I know is that she's human, so how she and Drew have managed to have a relationship is foreign to me.

"I still think we should call them, Dobertrievers," Elia says with a grin.

Kane objects, "No! They very obviously should be called, Retrievermans."

I'm about to put in my two cents when Vela cries out. She holds her distended belly. Her face is one of shock, and she looks down at the puddle of water at her feet.

"It's time!" Adele yells, and the entire place is in motion.

I go to Vela and hold her as she trembles in my arms. A contraction hits her, and she turns pain-filled eyes to me. "Linc, it is, it's time."

My freezing heart pumps wildly despite the fear climbing up my throat. I manage to rasp out, "I love you."

She nods hard and says, "Yes. I'm ready."

She delivers two healthy children, a boy and girl, in a matter of hours. They're small, but perfectly healthy. The girl has dark hair like me, and the boy has blond hair like his mother. I can immediately sense the boy, like his mother has Gyan and Borean gifts, and the girl is a Festan, like me, and a Neronian. I had wondered which gifts they would have, and between the two of them, they have them all. Just like their mama.

When Vela's recovered from labor, I bring them to her, placing one in each arm.

Vela looks up at me with shining eyes. "I guess we're a family now, Lincoln Stevenson."

"You guess? I'd say so, wife. I'm so proud of you, my darling." I kiss her softly and then kiss the soft heads of my two tiny children, breathing contentedly.

I turn warm eyes from hers to my parents with whom, thanks to Vela, I now have a healthy relationship. My dad approaches and puts his hand on my shoulder. "You've done it, son. Congratulations."

The room is full of family and friends and there's nothing but love and laughter. Which is now the story of our lives. We went from a world of animosity and strife to peace and prosperity.

Thanks to God and our Chosen One, my wife, my Vela.

The End

Afterword

Hi my friend!

There were so many God moments in this series. One in particular that happened in this book actually happened to me. When Vela collapses in grief over being separated from Linc on their wedding day, mimics an exact time of grief I experienced. Like Vela, I was healed miraculously in the exact way Vela was. I call that moment, a Heavenly Cocoon, God's Hug. I had lost my mom at fourteen to a senseless murder, and I didn't think I would survive the monstrous grief. In that moment where God held me, I was instantly healed of the devastating pain, and I was able to get out of bed, for the first time, and return to my life.

Friends, I just want to say, moments like that weren't imagined, they actually happen. God is very real, very alive and waiting for you to come to Him as His child. Don't be afraid of calling out to Him when you need Him. I've spent my life following Jesus. In fact, how Vela, at six-years-old, could have her best friend be Jesus? That's my exact story. Except, instead of waiting to talk to my mom about it, I immediately accepted Him into my life. I haven't looked back since.

If you're not sure about whether you want Christ in your life, just think back on this story. I know this is a fantasy, but so many of these moments are real, true events. You can have an awesome, unbelievable relationship with our Creator. You just need to reach out to Him and ask for Him to be in your life. And He will. Email me with any questions, and I would be happy to answer them. My email is sofia@sofiasimpson.com. If anything in this book leaves you with questions, I'm happy to answer them.

Now, if you've made it this far in the book, you've read Vela and Linc's entire journey, with some other awesome characters. I hope you loved it and that it ended the way you hoped it would. If you're wondering about how Elia and Kane became spies, you can read the novella, Operation Kane, to learn their story. If you sign up for my newsletter, you'll get the ebook emailed to you for free. Just go to my website, www.sofiasim pson.com. Sign up is right on my home page.

Most of all, thank you for reading my books!!! I hope to keep you as a life-long reader. You all mean so much to me! Sign up for my newsletter at www.sofiasimpson.com, which will give you updates on any new books!

Love, Sofia

Free Book!

Receive a free novella, Operation Kane, from the Terra, Torch, Tempest and Tidal world if you join my newsletter!

Elia will do anything to get her best friend's older brother to notice she's a woman now, even become a spy.

Dive into this world of Elementals, unrequited love, and the power of hope. Enjoy the best friend's older brother, forbidden love, fake dating, and friends-to-lovers tropes in this powerful story of faith and young love.

Go to: www.sofiasimpson.com to find this charming novella. Connect with me there if you'd like to have me on your podcast.

And if you enjoyed this book, please leave a review on Amazon, Bookbub or Goodreads, or if you're especially generous, all three! It means more to us authors than you know.

ACKNOWLEDGEMENTS

First and foremost, I give all thanks to God for giving me wisdom to finish a 4-book series, which I've never could have done without His inspiration.

I've always felt that a Christian Fantasy should be a fully imaginative book, and if you feel this book did that well, then I give all credit to God, my Savior. I hope I've illustrated Him in these books and in my stories.

Next person I'd like to thank is my husband. If it wasn't for him, I wouldn't be able to write full-time and enable me to put out 2-3 books a year. He is my biggest supporter, and I lean on him the most when the story gets hard.

To my sons for cheering me on, Nicky and Matthew, I love you both more than I can possibly say. Thank you for encouraging and loving your momma.

My dearest friend, Jenny, even though you are not a writer, you hold me accountable and keep me on track. More than that, you love to support my dream, and we share the same vision: point more people to Christ. I love you, sister.

Dana, if I could name my biggest cheerleader, it's you. Whenever I need to hear the words, "You can do it," I call you. Thank you, dear friend, love you!

Darcy, you also are a champion, you are with me every step of the way, and I couldn't thank you enough for your ideas and words of strength.

To my editor, Jessica Gwyn. Your ability to tighten a sentence, making it better is illustrated throughout this entire book. This book took two developmental edits, and I thank you for challenging me to make this the best book it could possibly be.

To my cover designer, Emilie Hendryx, you are genius with covers. I had a basic idea, and you transformed into a stunning visual. Thank you!

To both my writing groups. This series is a great testament to what writing groups can do for you. Word Weavers, you guys are amazing, and Lakeland Writers, thank you from the bottom of my heart.

Join my newsletter, follow my Instagram, Facebook and Tiktok at @sofiasimpsonauthor and keep up to date on all book news!

I have to give a special shout out to my ultra special Super Readers, Charlotte June, Alicia and Sophie.

You guys keep me fueled to continue putting out stories. Thank you for all your support!!